ANIMAL RESCUE FRIENDS

MEIKA HASHIMOTO

GINA LOVELESS

Illustrated by
GENEVIEVE KOTE

Breakdowns by
AXELLE LENOIR

Andrews McMeel
PUBLISHING®

Animal Rescue Friends created by Meika Hashimoto,
Gina Loveless, and Genevieve Kote

Andrews McMeel Publishing
a division of Andrews McMeel Universal
1130 Walnut Street, Kansas City, Missouri 64106

www.andrewsmcmeel.com

Epic! Creations, Inc.
702 Marshall Street, Suite 280
Redwood City, California 94063

www.getepic.com

21 22 23 24 25 SDB 10 9 8 7 6 5 4 3 2 1

Paperback ISBN: 978-1-5248-6734-8
Hardback ISBN: 978-1-5248-6806-2

Library of Congress Control Number: 2020950431

Design by Dan Nordskog

Made by:
King Yip (Dongguan) Printing & Packaging Factory Ltd.
Address and location of manufacturer:
Daning Administrative District, Humen Town
Dongguan Guangdong, China 523930
1st Printing — 3/8/21

ATTENTION: SCHOOLS AND BUSINESSES
Andrews McMeel books are available at quantity discounts
with bulk purchase for educational, business, or sales promotional use.
For information, please e-mail the Andrews McMeel Publishing
Special Sales Department: specialsales@amuniversal.com.

FOR PIPER, BUCKEY, AND MARZIPAN
--M. H.

TO GERDIE--THE BEST RESCUE PUP
IN THE WORLD!
--G. L.

FOR OPAL
--W. M.

TO CLARA AND BORIS, THE BEST
CATS ONE COULD HAVE.
--G. K.

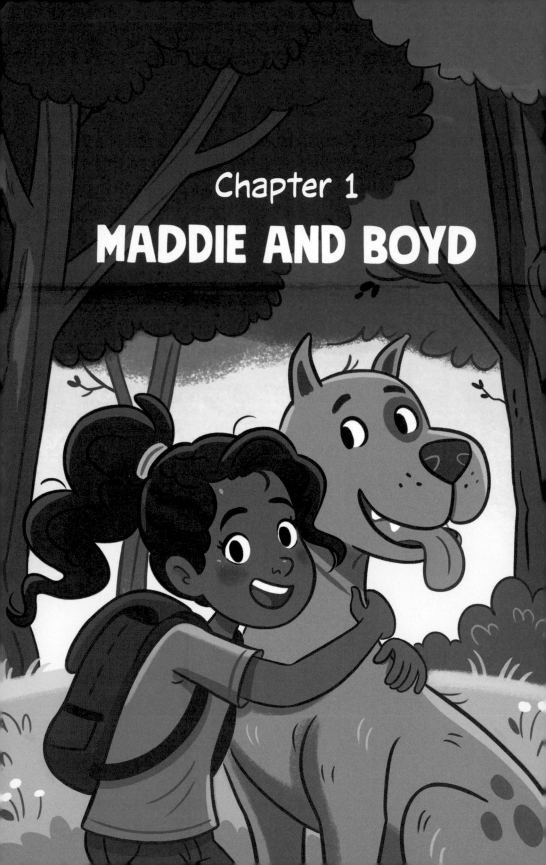

Chapter 1
MADDIE AND BOYD

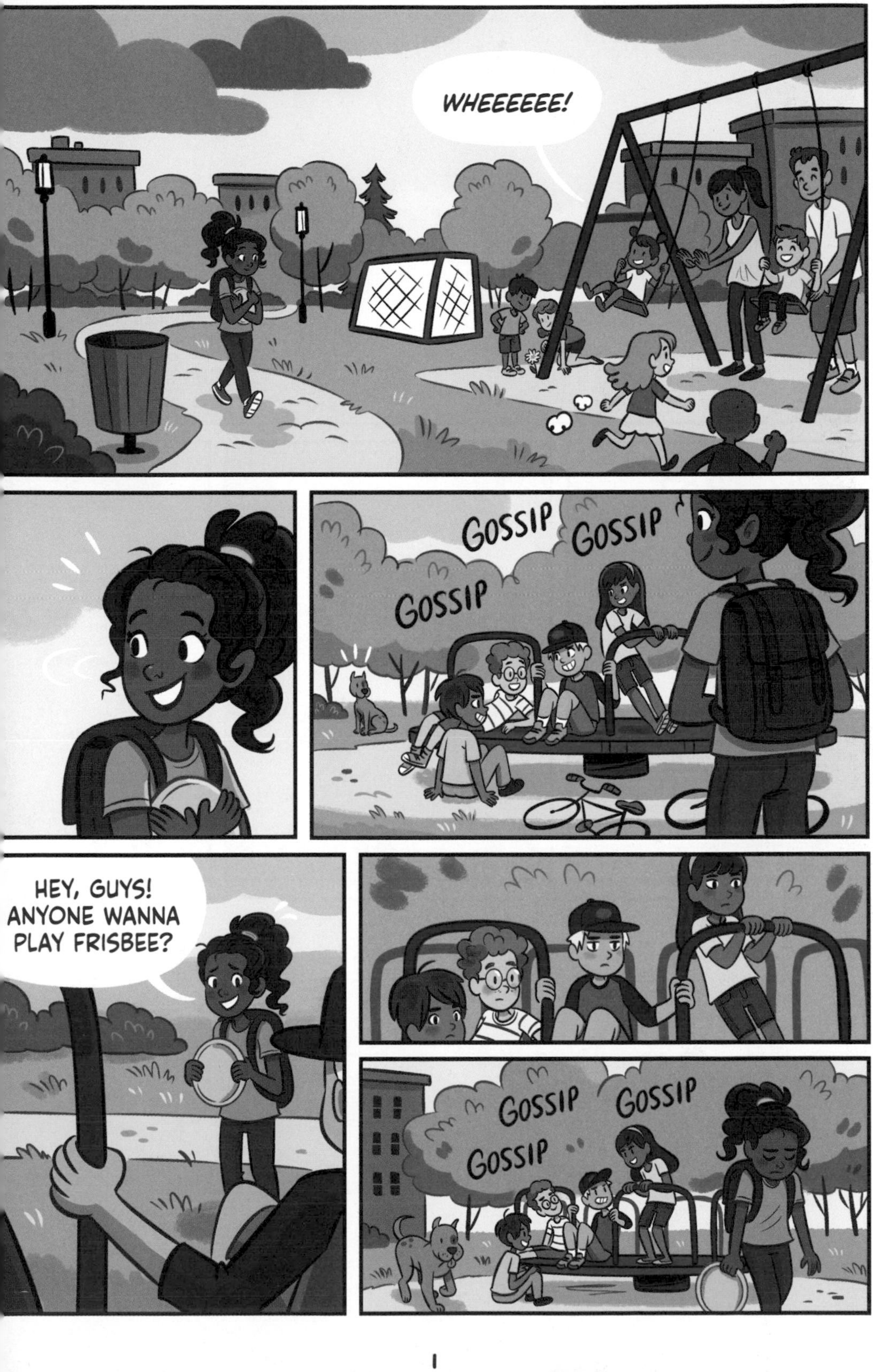
WHEEEEEE!
GOSSIP
GOSSIP
GOSSIP
HEY, GUYS! ANYONE WANNA PLAY FRISBEE?
GOSSIP
GOSSIP
GOSSIP

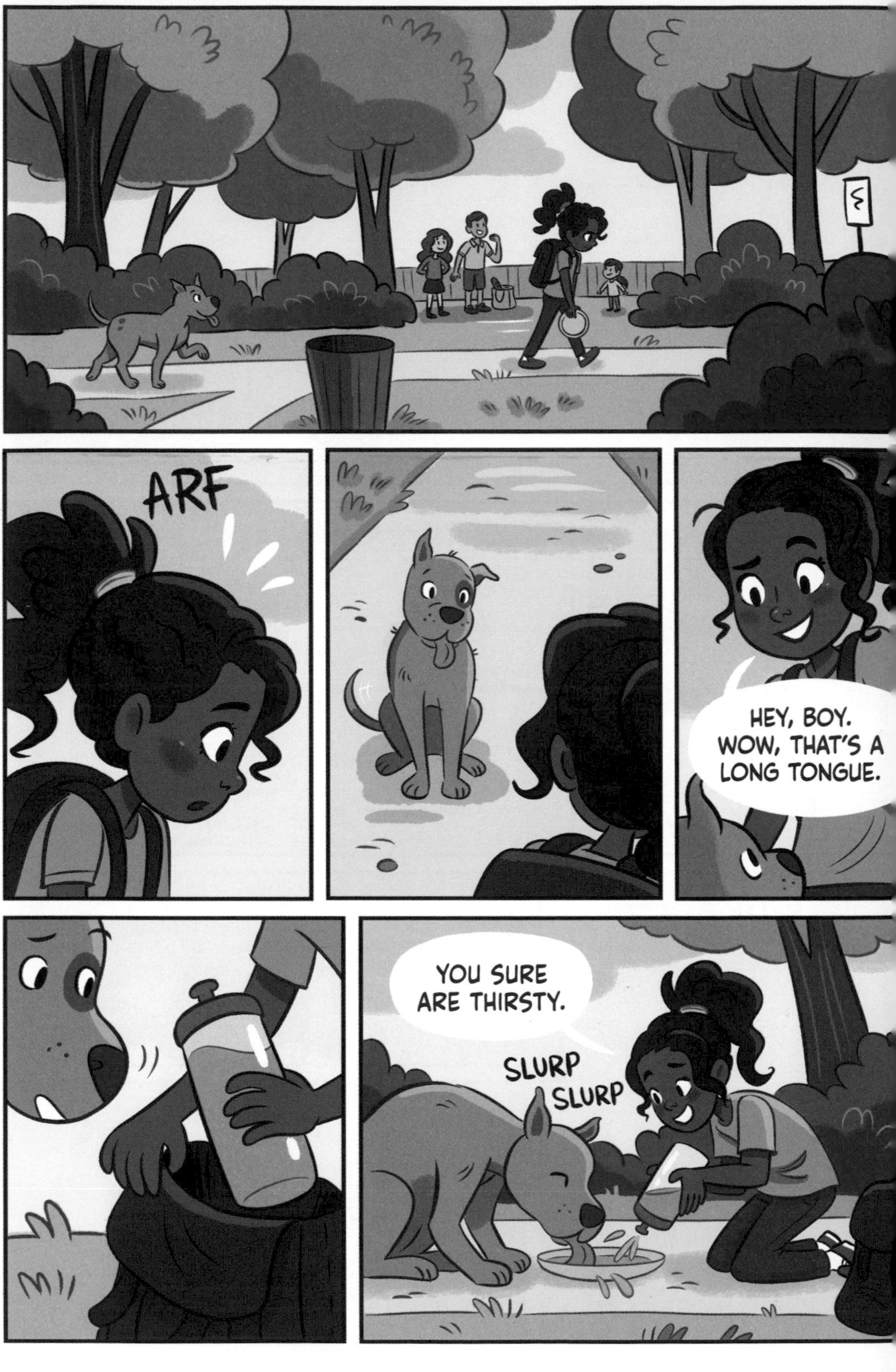
ARF
HEY, BOY. WOW, THAT'S A LONG TONGUE.
YOU SURE ARE THIRSTY.
SLURP
SLURP

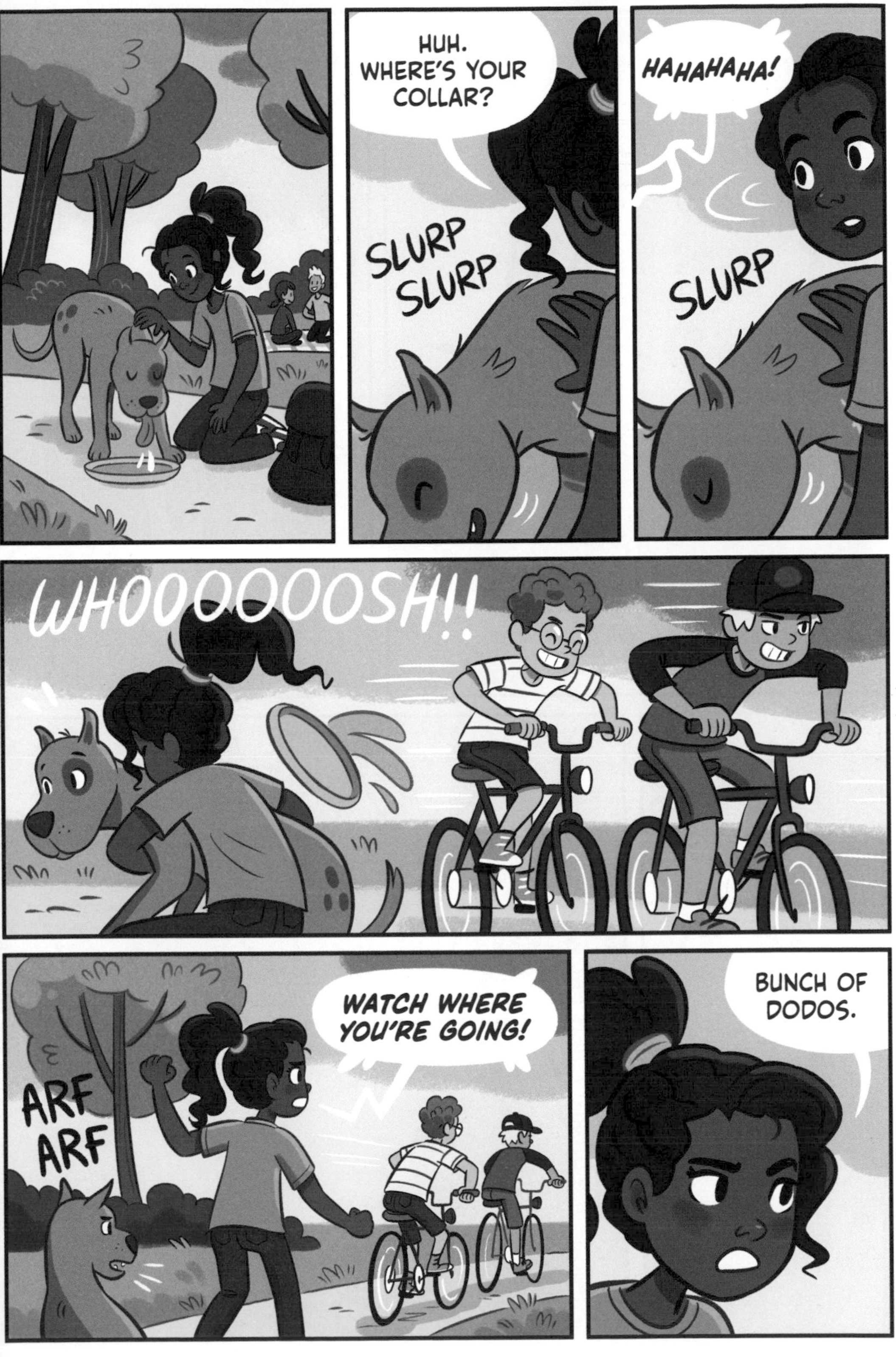
HUH.
WHERE'S YOUR COLLAR?
SLURP
SLURP
HAHAHAHA!
SLURP
WHOOOOOOSH!!
ARF
ARF
WATCH WHERE YOU'RE GOING!
BUNCH OF DODOS.

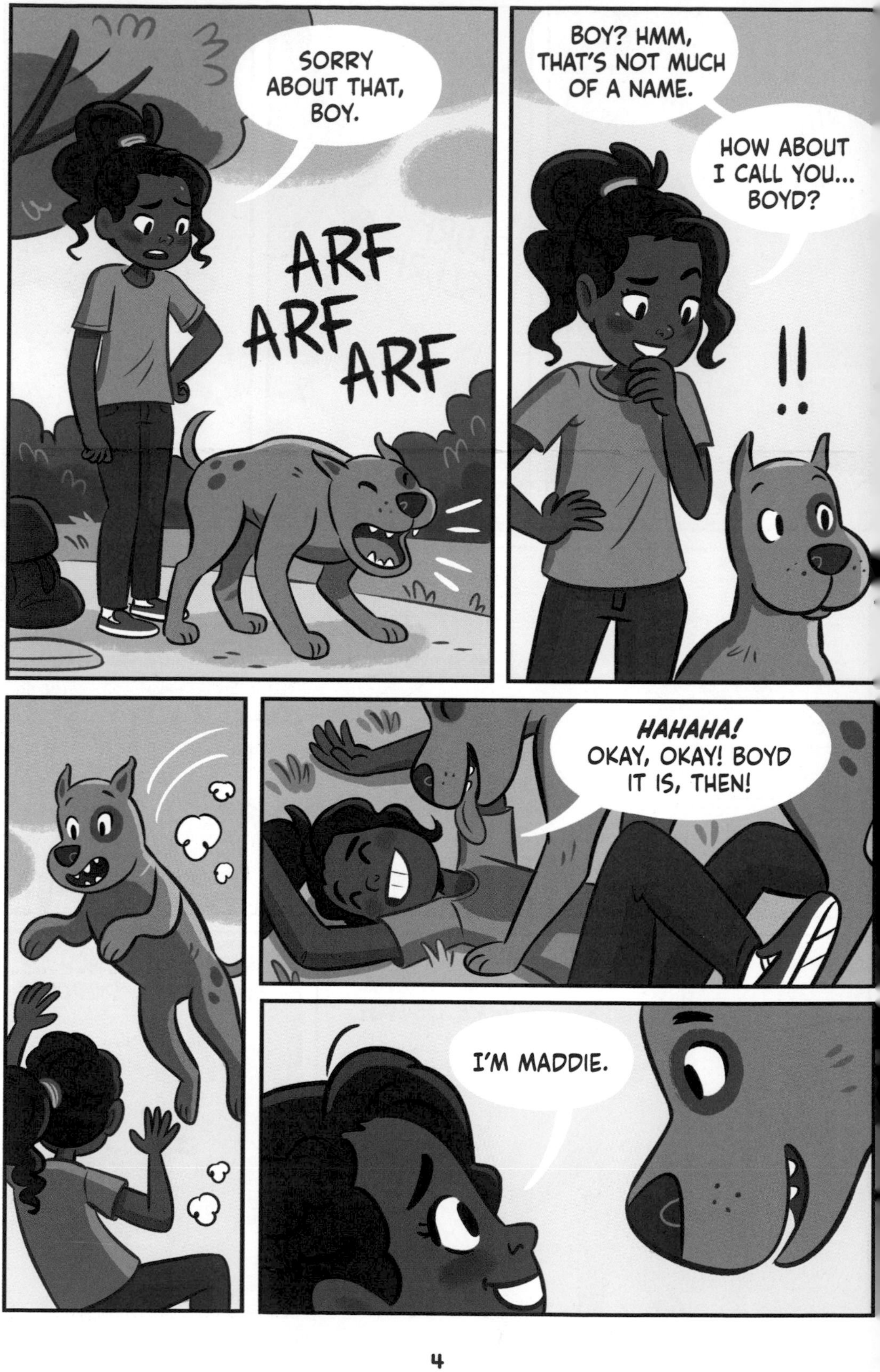
SORRY ABOUT THAT, BOY.
ARF ARF ARF
BOY? HMM, THAT'S NOT MUCH OF A NAME.
HOW ABOUT I CALL YOU... BOYD?
!!
HAHAHA! OKAY, OKAY! BOYD IT IS, THEN!
I'M MADDIE.

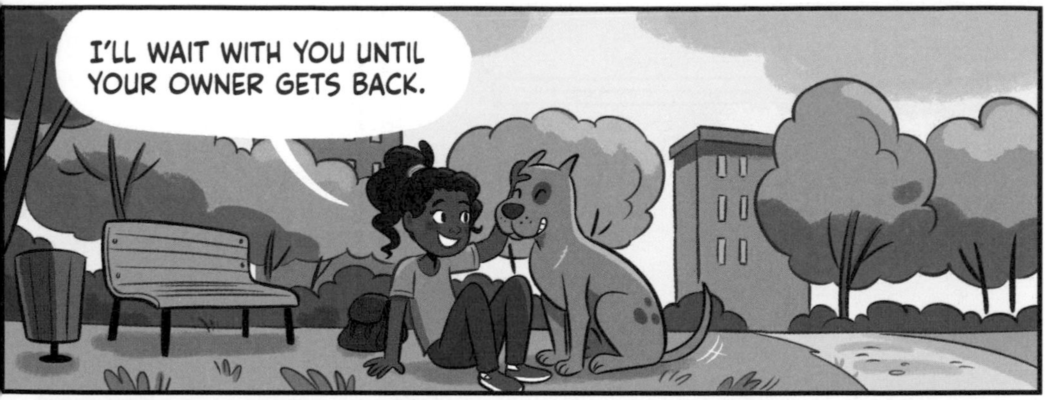
I'LL WAIT WITH YOU UNTIL YOUR OWNER GETS BACK.

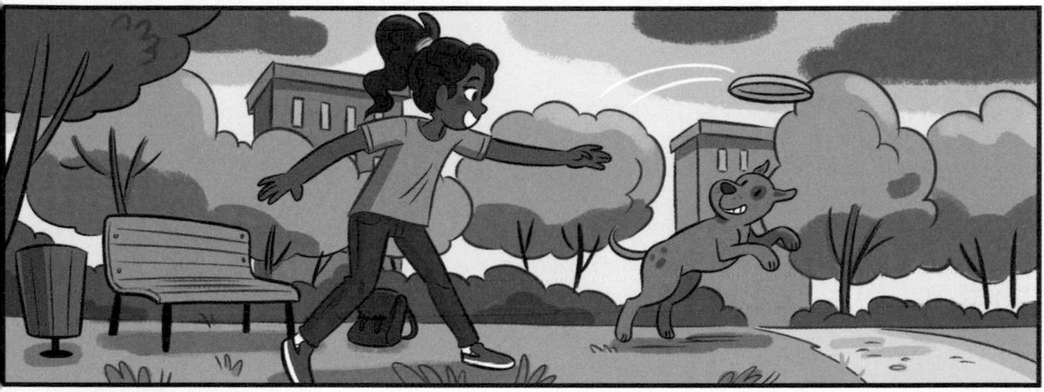

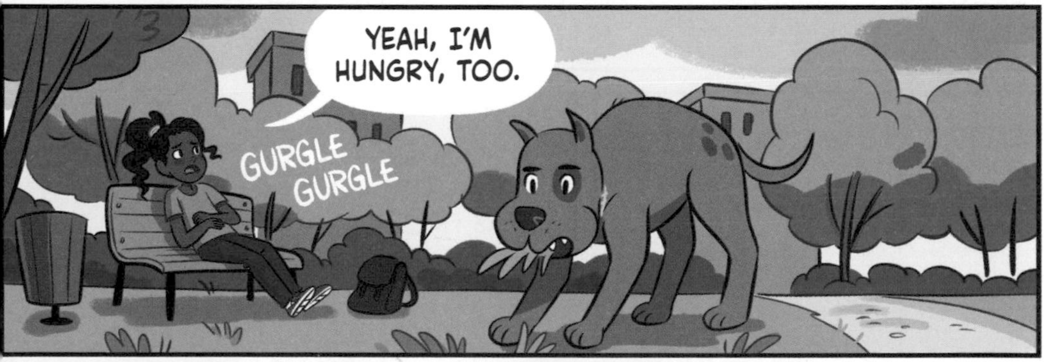
YEAH, I'M HUNGRY, TOO.
GURGLE GURGLE

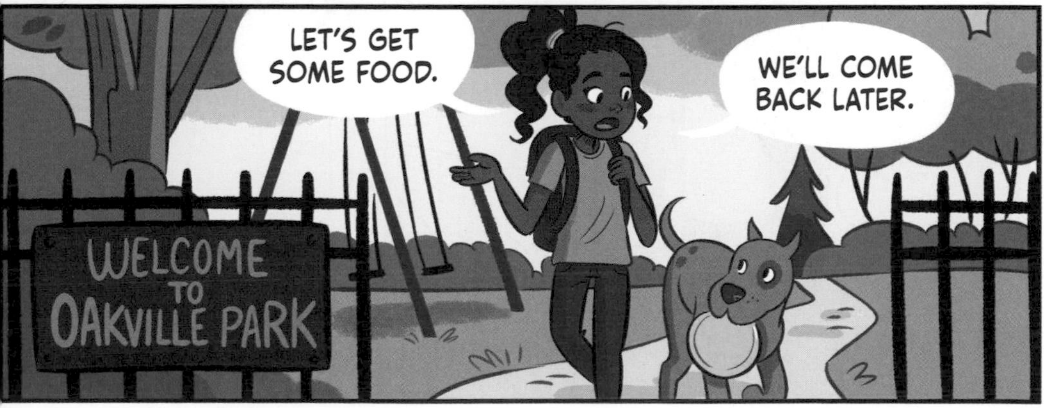
WELCOME TO OAKVILLE PARK
LET'S GET SOME FOOD.
WE'LL COME BACK LATER.

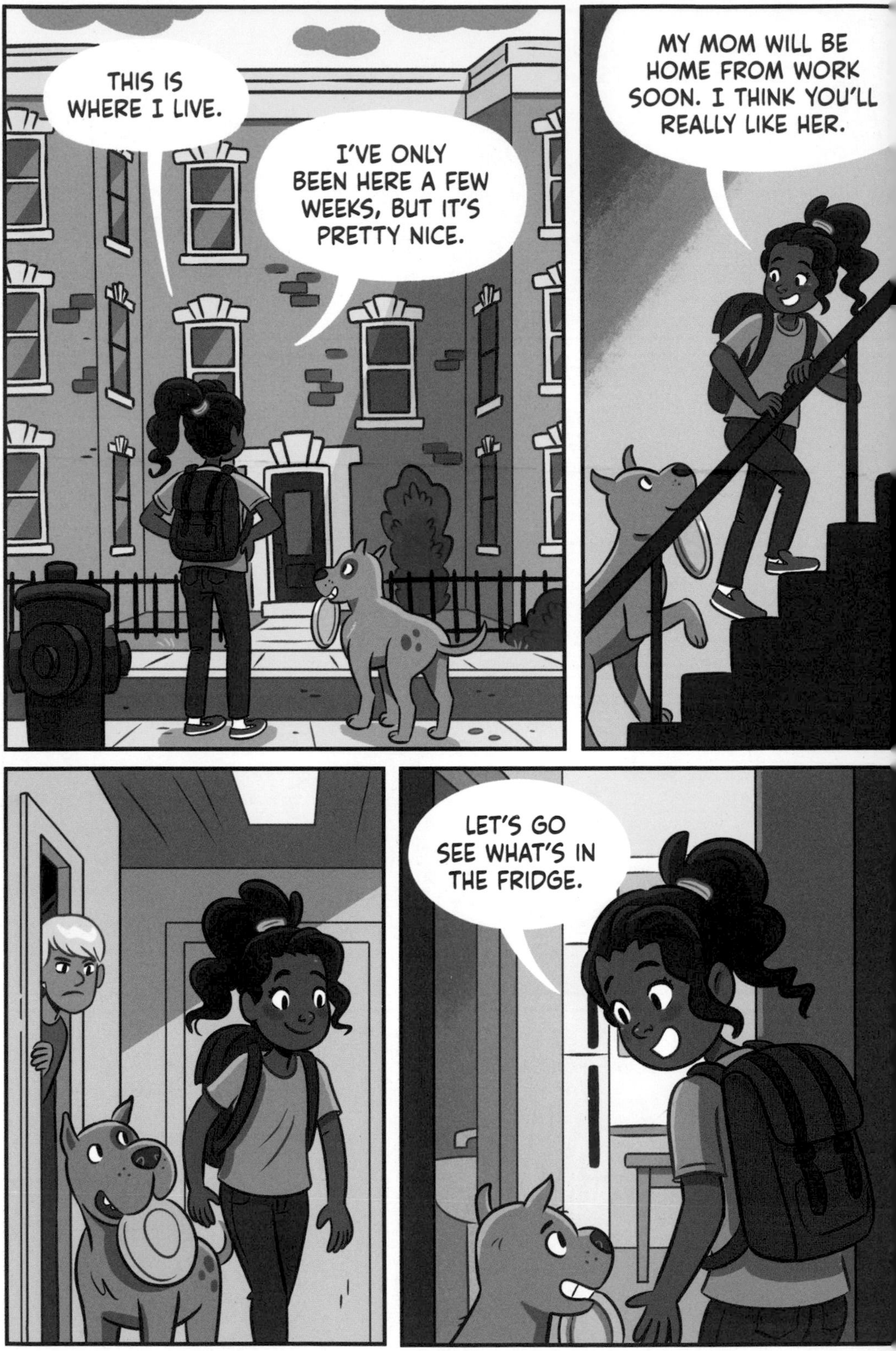
THIS IS WHERE I LIVE.
I'VE ONLY BEEN HERE A FEW WEEKS, BUT IT'S PRETTY NICE.
MY MOM WILL BE HOME FROM WORK SOON. I THINK YOU'LL REALLY LIKE HER.
LET'S GO SEE WHAT'S IN THE FRIDGE.

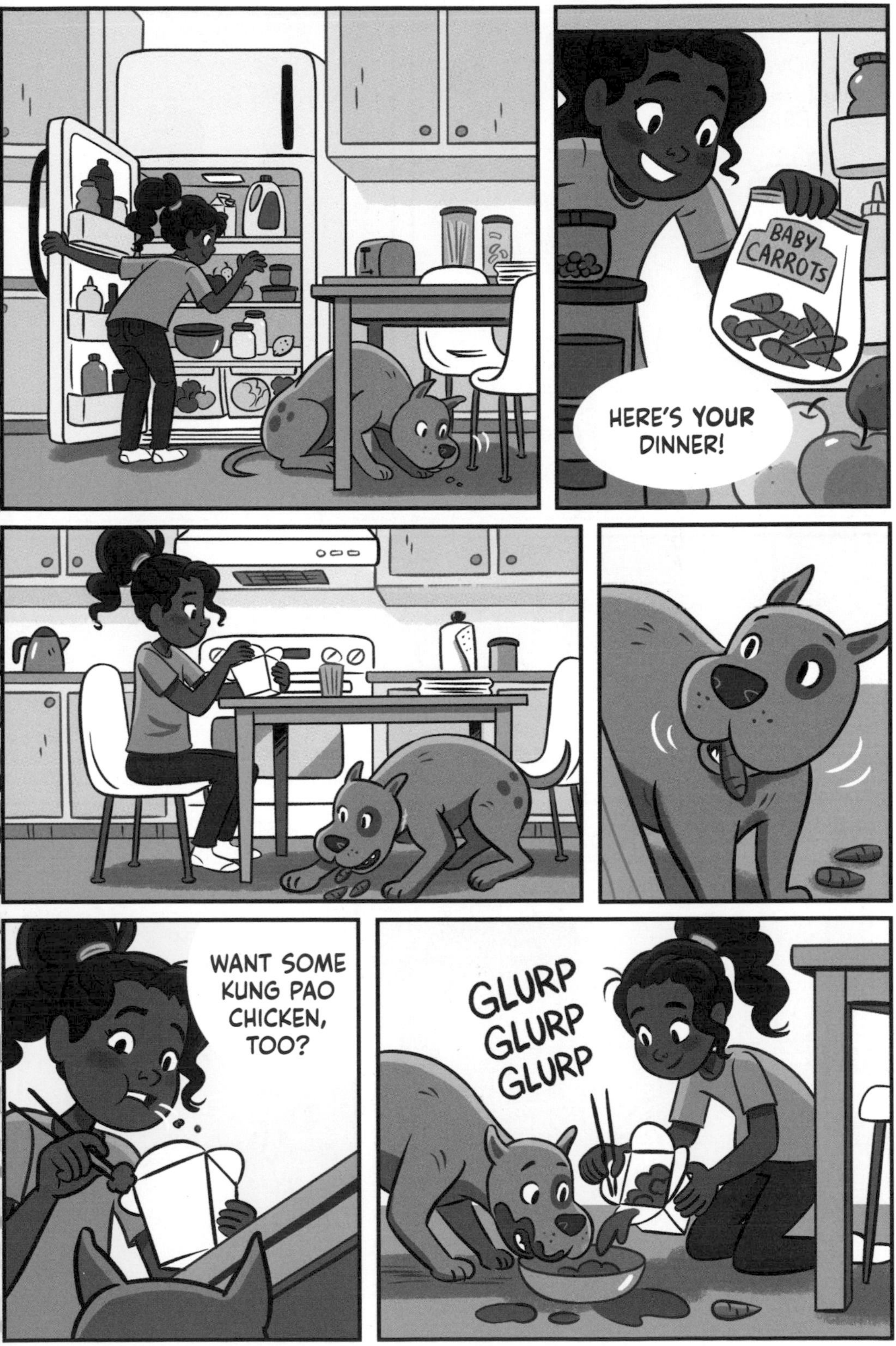
BABY CARROTS
HERE'S YOUR DINNER!
WANT SOME KUNG PAO CHICKEN, TOO?
GLURP GLURP GLURP

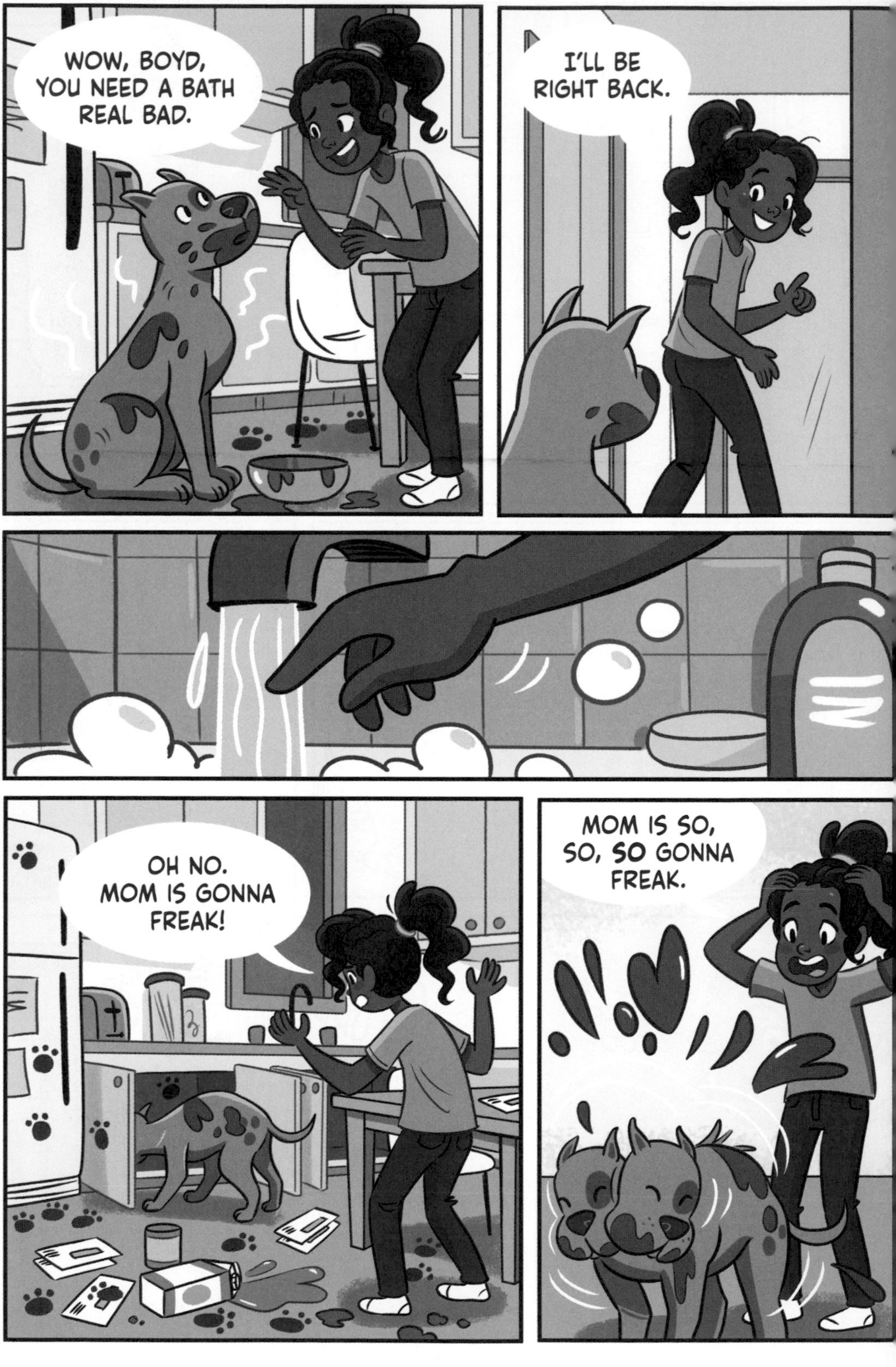
WOW, BOYD, YOU NEED A BATH REAL BAD.
I'LL BE RIGHT BACK.
OH NO. MOM IS GONNA FREAK!
MOM IS SO, SO, **SO** GONNA FREAK.

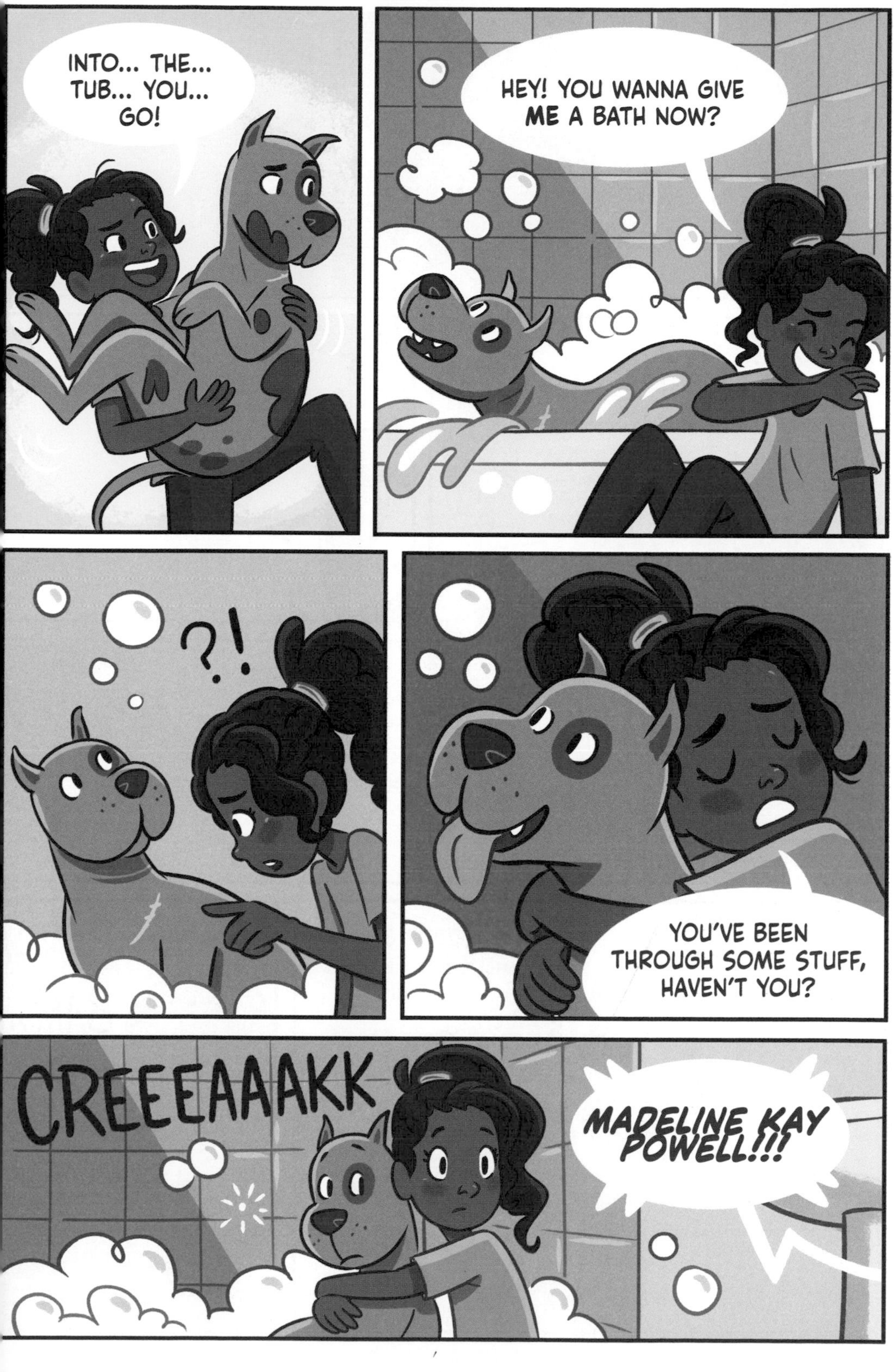
INTO... THE... TUB... YOU... GO!
HEY! YOU WANNA GIVE ME A BATH NOW?
?!
YOU'VE BEEN THROUGH SOME STUFF, HAVEN'T YOU?
CREEEAAAKK
MADELINE KAY POWELL!!!

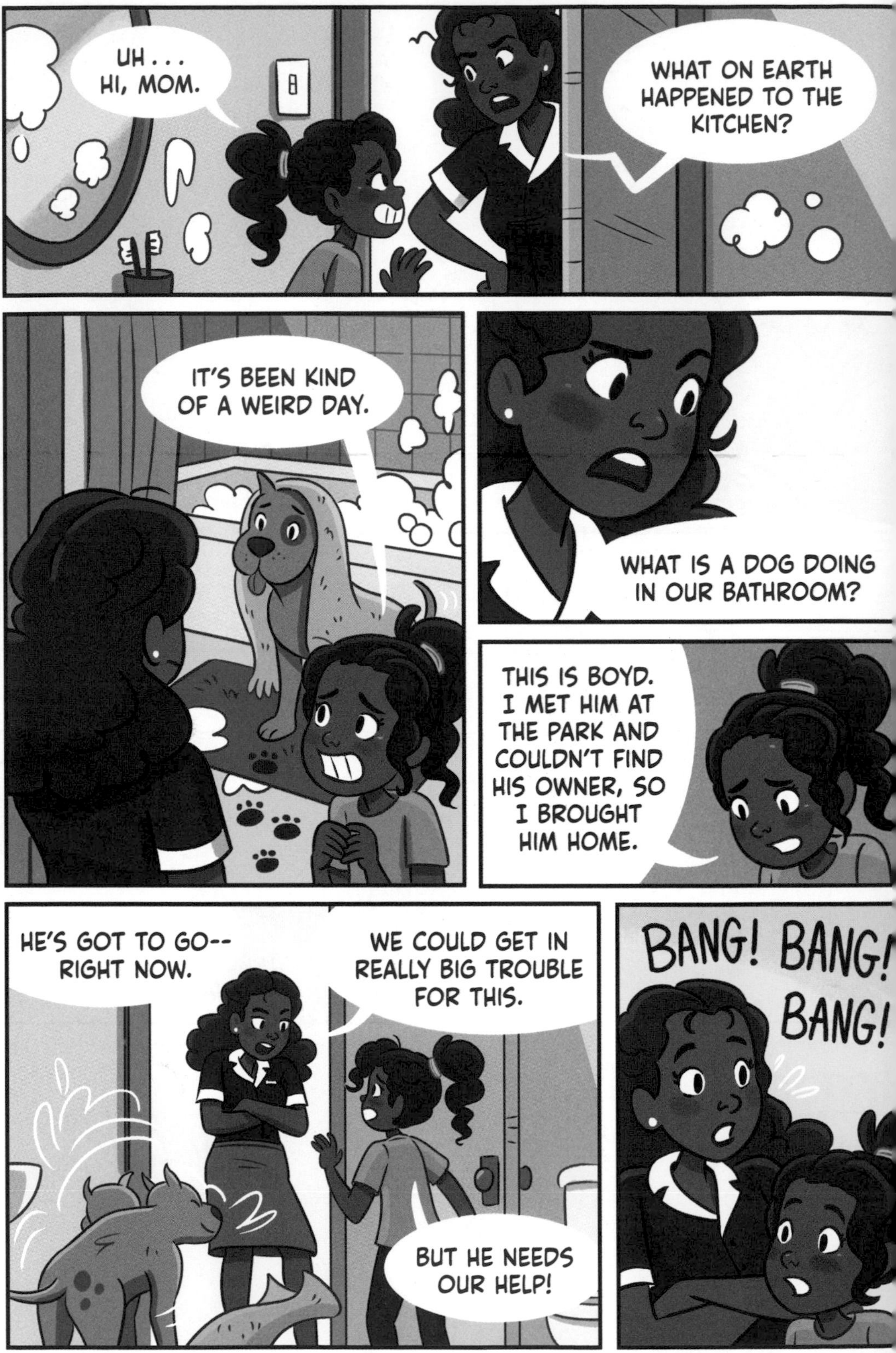
UH . . .
HI, MOM.
WHAT ON EARTH HAPPENED TO THE KITCHEN?
IT'S BEEN KIND OF A WEIRD DAY.
WHAT IS A DOG DOING IN OUR BATHROOM?
THIS IS BOYD. I MET HIM AT THE PARK AND COULDN'T FIND HIS OWNER, SO I BROUGHT HIM HOME.
HE'S GOT TO GO-- RIGHT NOW.
WE COULD GET IN REALLY BIG TROUBLE FOR THIS.
BUT HE NEEDS OUR HELP!
BANG! BANG!
BANG!

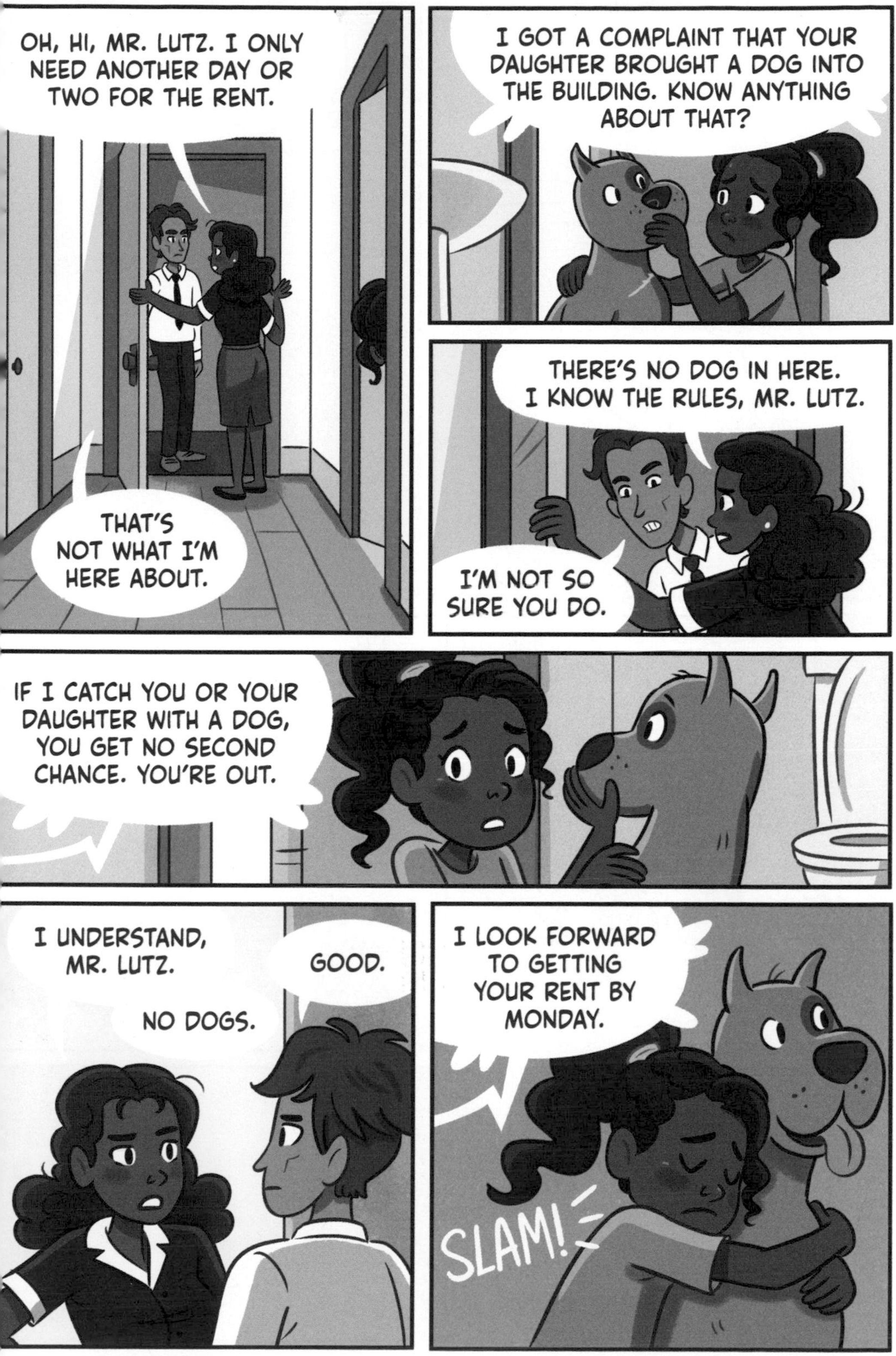

OH, HI, MR. LUTZ. I ONLY NEED ANOTHER DAY OR TWO FOR THE RENT.
THAT'S NOT WHAT I'M HERE ABOUT.
I GOT A COMPLAINT THAT YOUR DAUGHTER BROUGHT A DOG INTO THE BUILDING. KNOW ANYTHING ABOUT THAT?
THERE'S NO DOG IN HERE. I KNOW THE RULES, MR. LUTZ.
I'M NOT SO SURE YOU DO.
IF I CATCH YOU OR YOUR DAUGHTER WITH A DOG, YOU GET NO SECOND CHANCE. YOU'RE OUT.
I UNDERSTAND, MR. LUTZ.
GOOD.
NO DOGS.
I LOOK FORWARD TO GETTING YOUR RENT BY MONDAY.
SLAM!

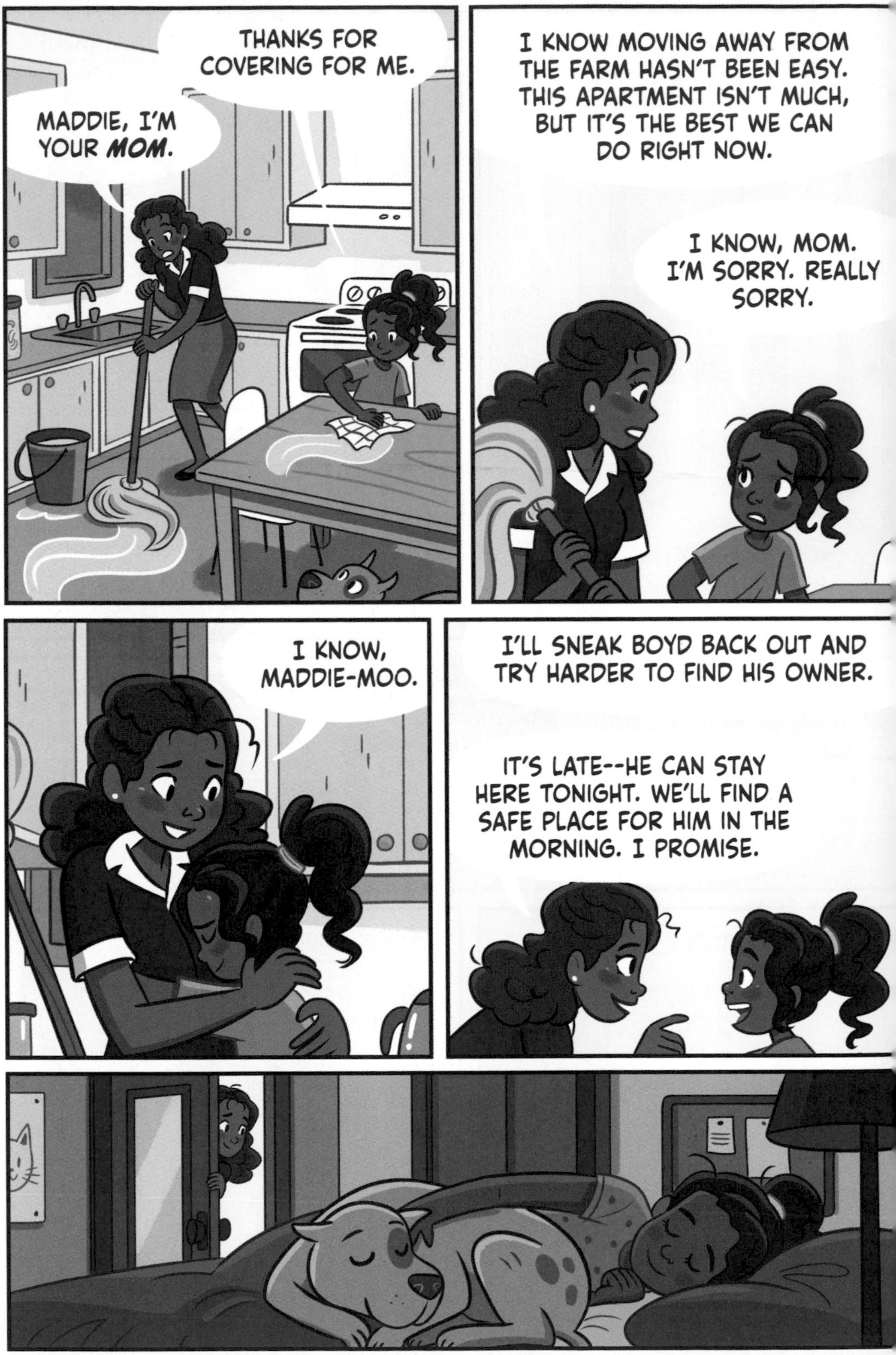
MADDIE, I'M YOUR *MOM*.
THANKS FOR COVERING FOR ME.
I KNOW MOVING AWAY FROM THE FARM HASN'T BEEN EASY. THIS APARTMENT ISN'T MUCH, BUT IT'S THE BEST WE CAN DO RIGHT NOW.
I KNOW, MOM. I'M SORRY. REALLY SORRY.
I KNOW, MADDIE-MOO.
I'LL SNEAK BOYD BACK OUT AND TRY HARDER TO FIND HIS OWNER.
IT'S LATE--HE CAN STAY HERE TONIGHT. WE'LL FIND A SAFE PLACE FOR HIM IN THE MORNING. I PROMISE.

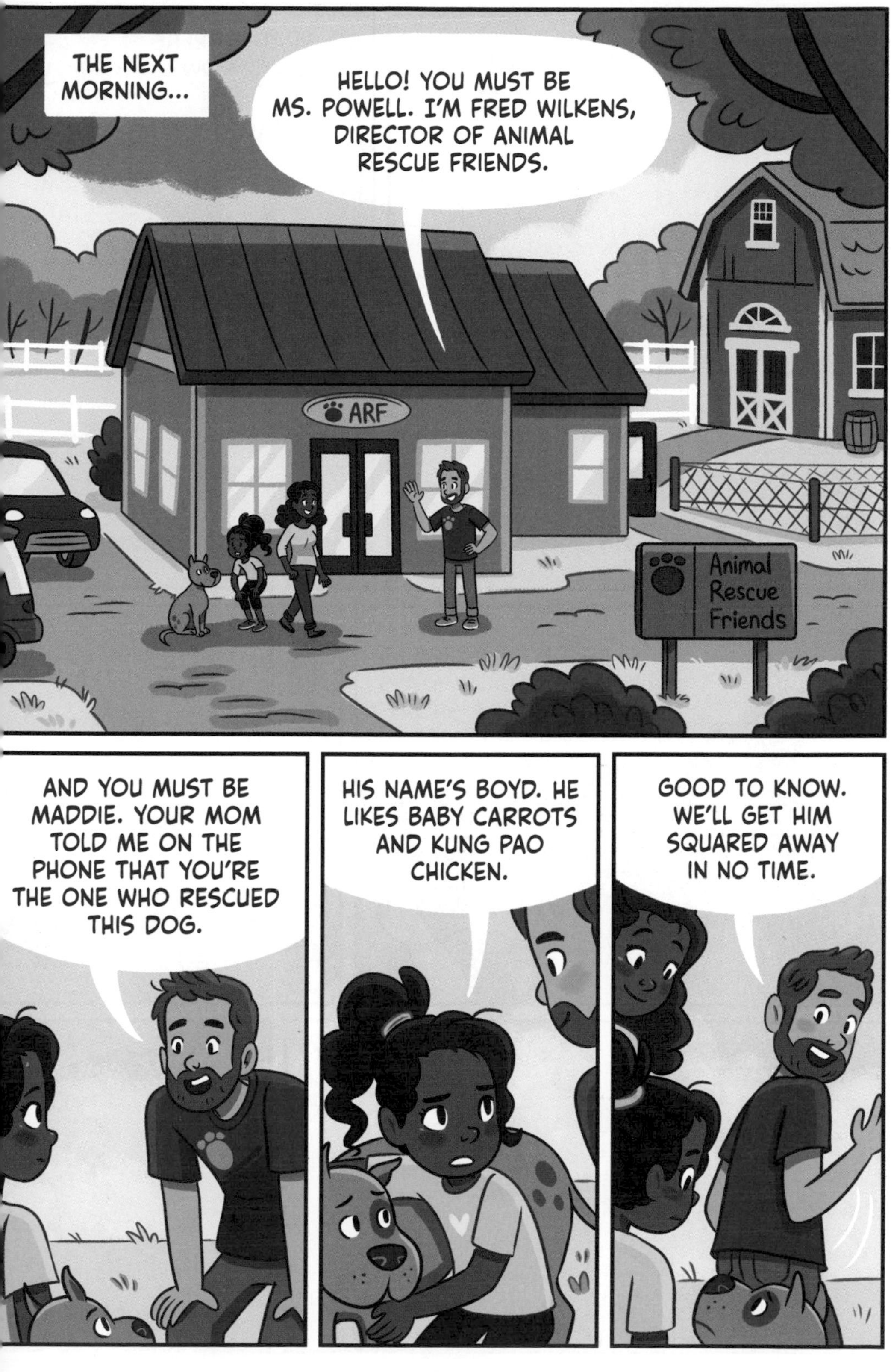
THE NEXT MORNING...
HELLO! YOU MUST BE MS. POWELL. I'M FRED WILKENS, DIRECTOR OF ANIMAL RESCUE FRIENDS.
ARF
Animal Rescue Friends
AND YOU MUST BE MADDIE. YOUR MOM TOLD ME ON THE PHONE THAT YOU'RE THE ONE WHO RESCUED THIS DOG.
HIS NAME'S BOYD. HE LIKES BABY CARROTS AND KUNG PAO CHICKEN.
GOOD TO KNOW. WE'LL GET HIM SQUARED AWAY IN NO TIME.

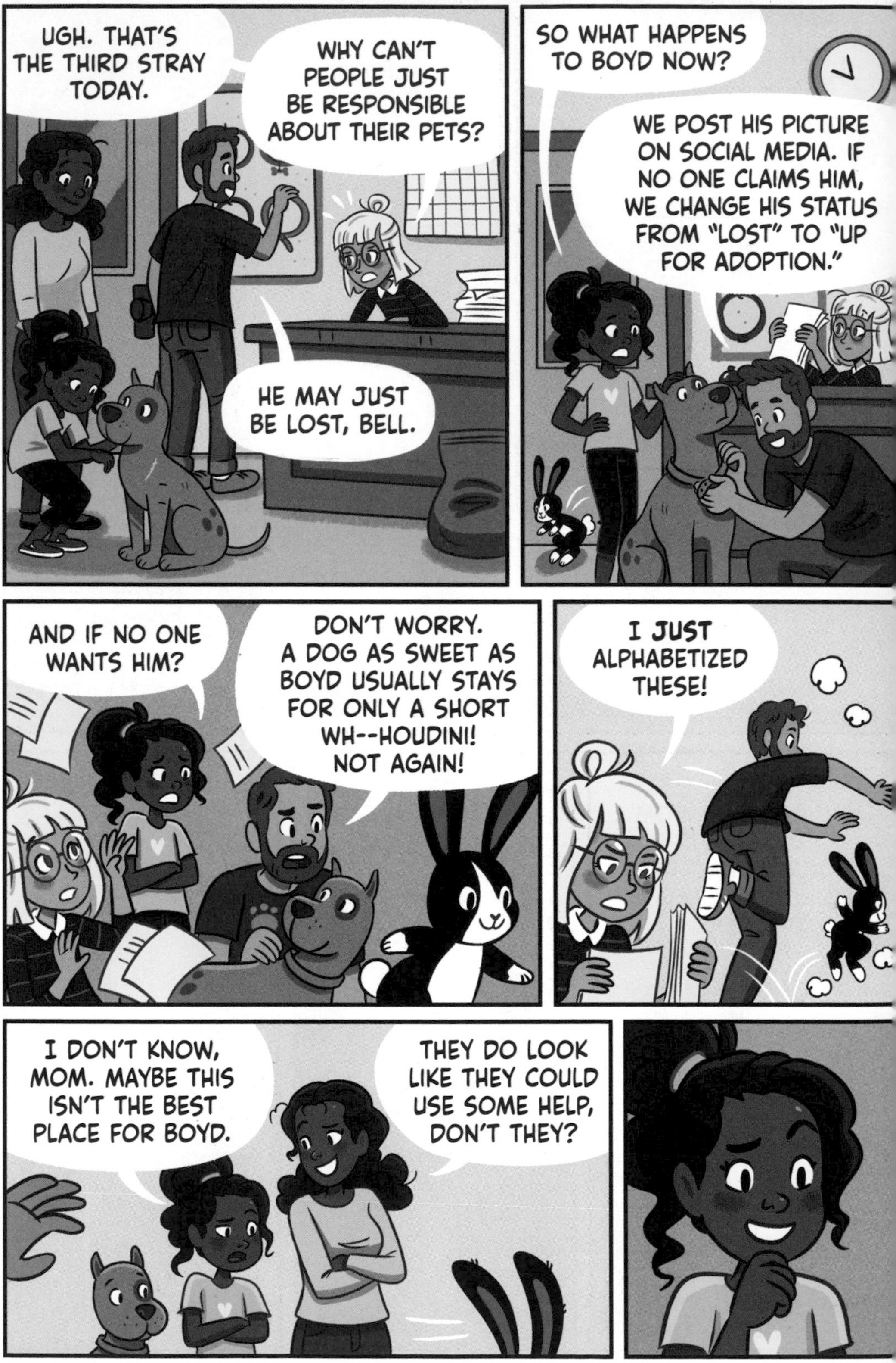
UGH. THAT'S THE THIRD STRAY TODAY.
WHY CAN'T PEOPLE JUST BE RESPONSIBLE ABOUT THEIR PETS?
HE MAY JUST BE LOST, BELL.
SO WHAT HAPPENS TO BOYD NOW?
WE POST HIS PICTURE ON SOCIAL MEDIA. IF NO ONE CLAIMS HIM, WE CHANGE HIS STATUS FROM "LOST" TO "UP FOR ADOPTION."
AND IF NO ONE WANTS HIM?
DON'T WORRY. A DOG AS SWEET AS BOYD USUALLY STAYS FOR ONLY A SHORT WH--HOUDINI! NOT AGAIN!
I **JUST** ALPHABETIZED THESE!
I DON'T KNOW, MOM. MAYBE THIS ISN'T THE BEST PLACE FOR BOYD.
THEY DO LOOK LIKE THEY COULD USE SOME HELP, DON'T THEY?

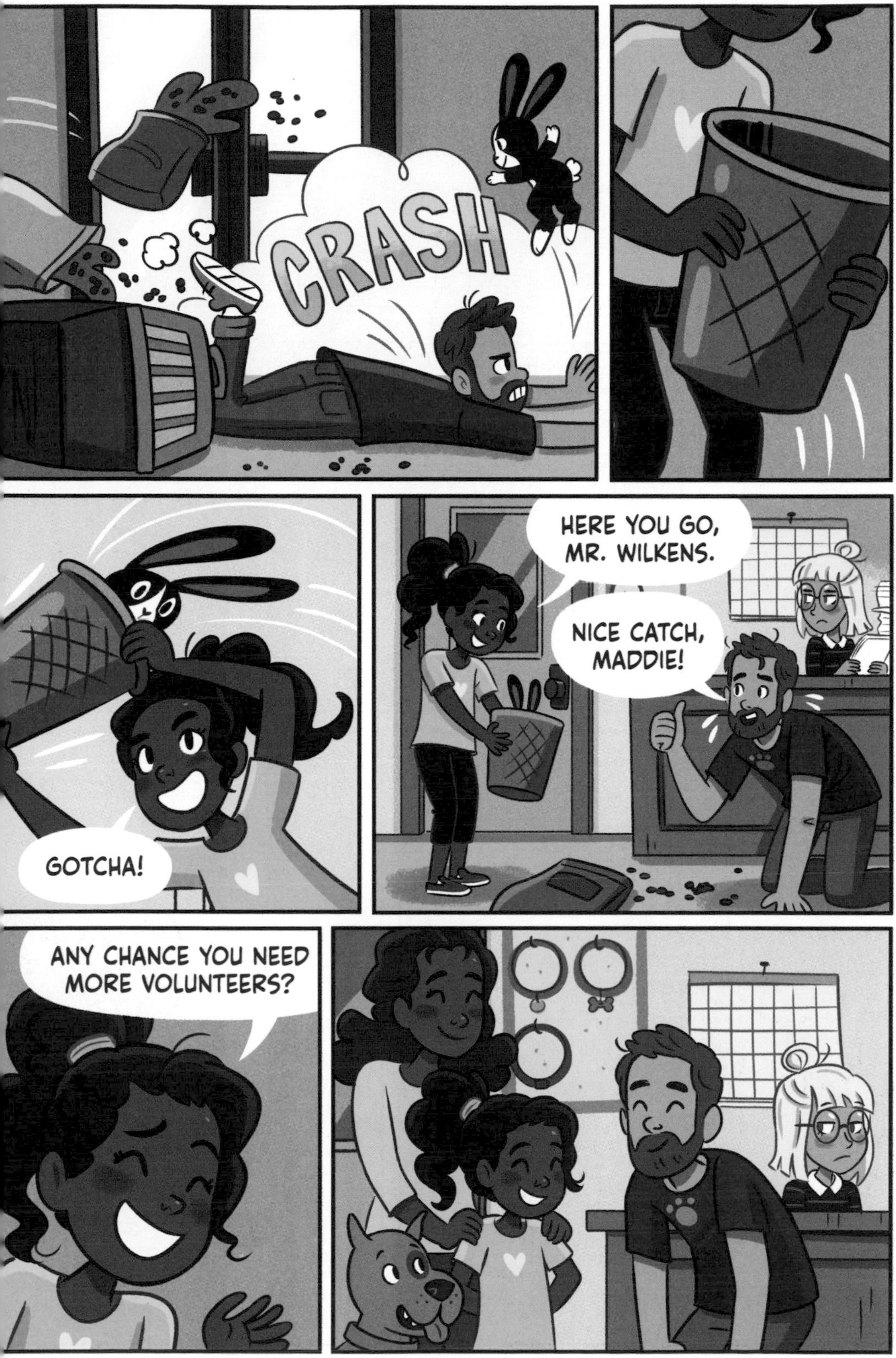

CRASH
GOTCHA!
HERE YOU GO, MR. WILKENS.
NICE CATCH, MADDIE!
ANY CHANCE YOU NEED MORE VOLUNTEERS?

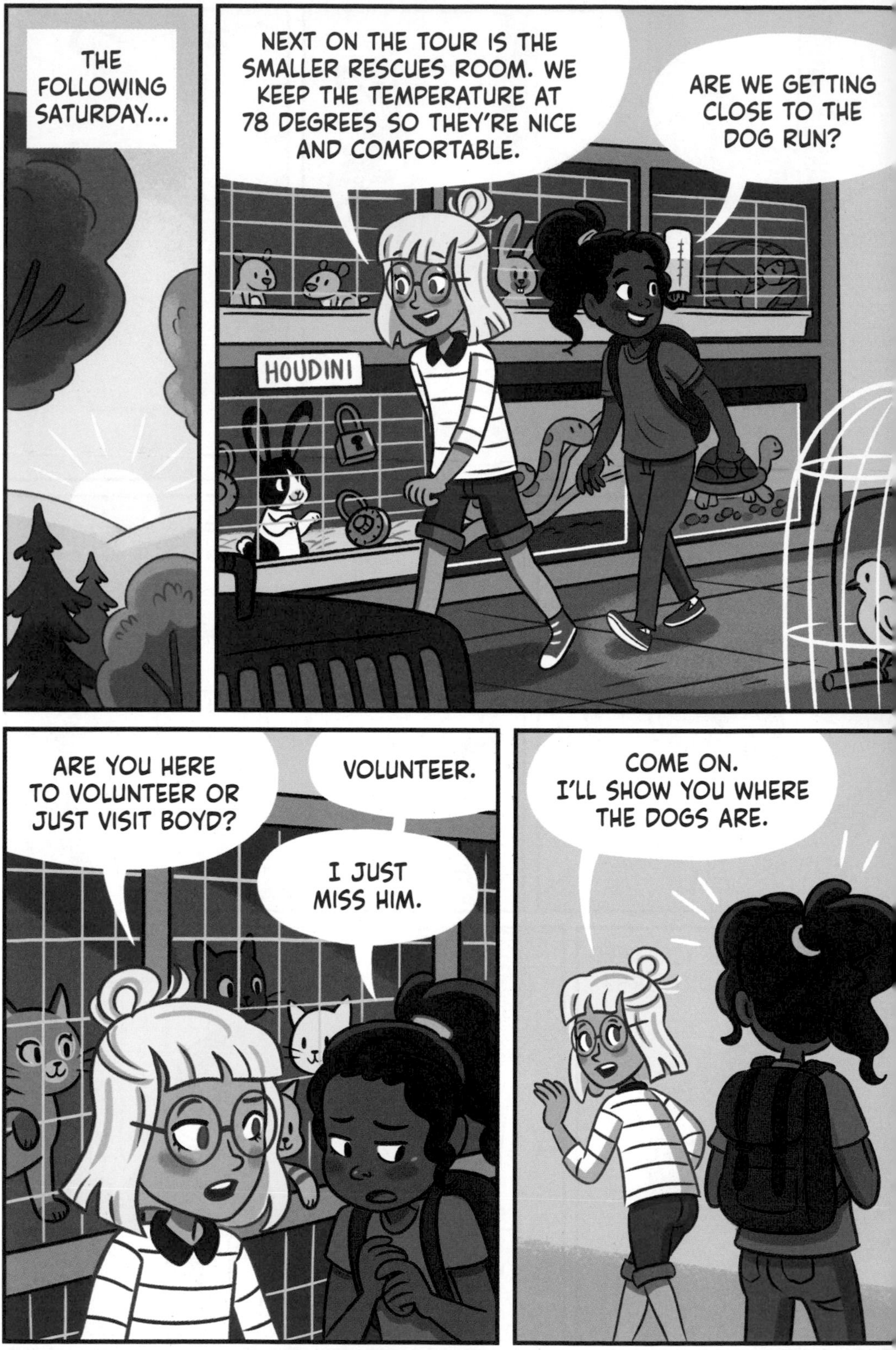
THE FOLLOWING SATURDAY...
NEXT ON THE TOUR IS THE SMALLER RESCUES ROOM. WE KEEP THE TEMPERATURE AT 78 DEGREES SO THEY'RE NICE AND COMFORTABLE.
ARE WE GETTING CLOSE TO THE DOG RUN?
HOUDINI
ARE YOU HERE TO VOLUNTEER OR JUST VISIT BOYD?
VOLUNTEER.
I JUST MISS HIM.
COME ON. I'LL SHOW YOU WHERE THE DOGS ARE.

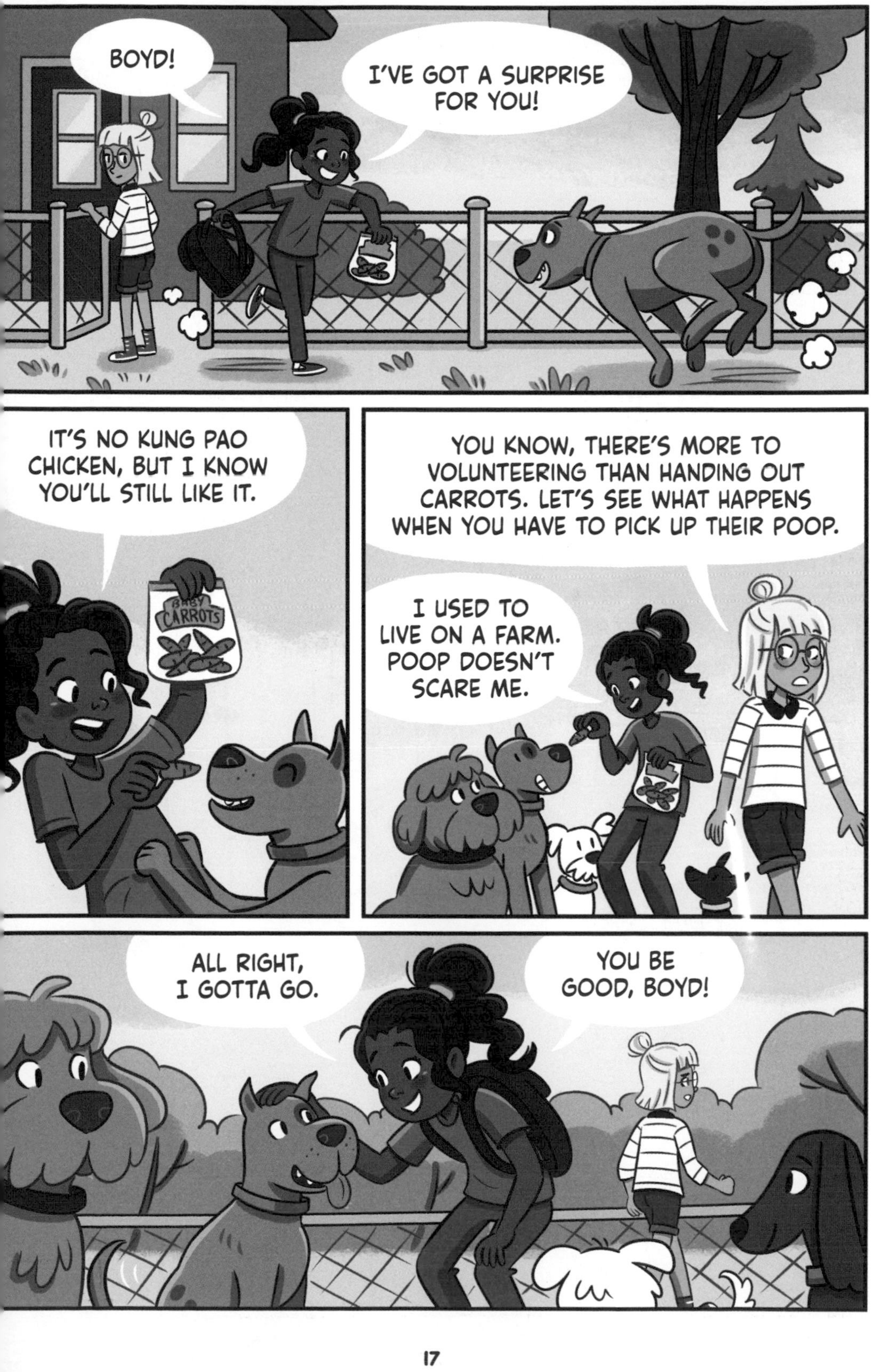
BOYD!
I'VE GOT A SURPRISE FOR YOU!
IT'S NO KUNG PAO CHICKEN, BUT I KNOW YOU'LL STILL LIKE IT.
BABY CARROTS
YOU KNOW, THERE'S MORE TO VOLUNTEERING THAN HANDING OUT CARROTS. LET'S SEE WHAT HAPPENS WHEN YOU HAVE TO PICK UP THEIR POOP.
I USED TO LIVE ON A FARM. POOP DOESN'T SCARE ME.
ALL RIGHT, I GOTTA GO.
YOU BE GOOD, BOYD!

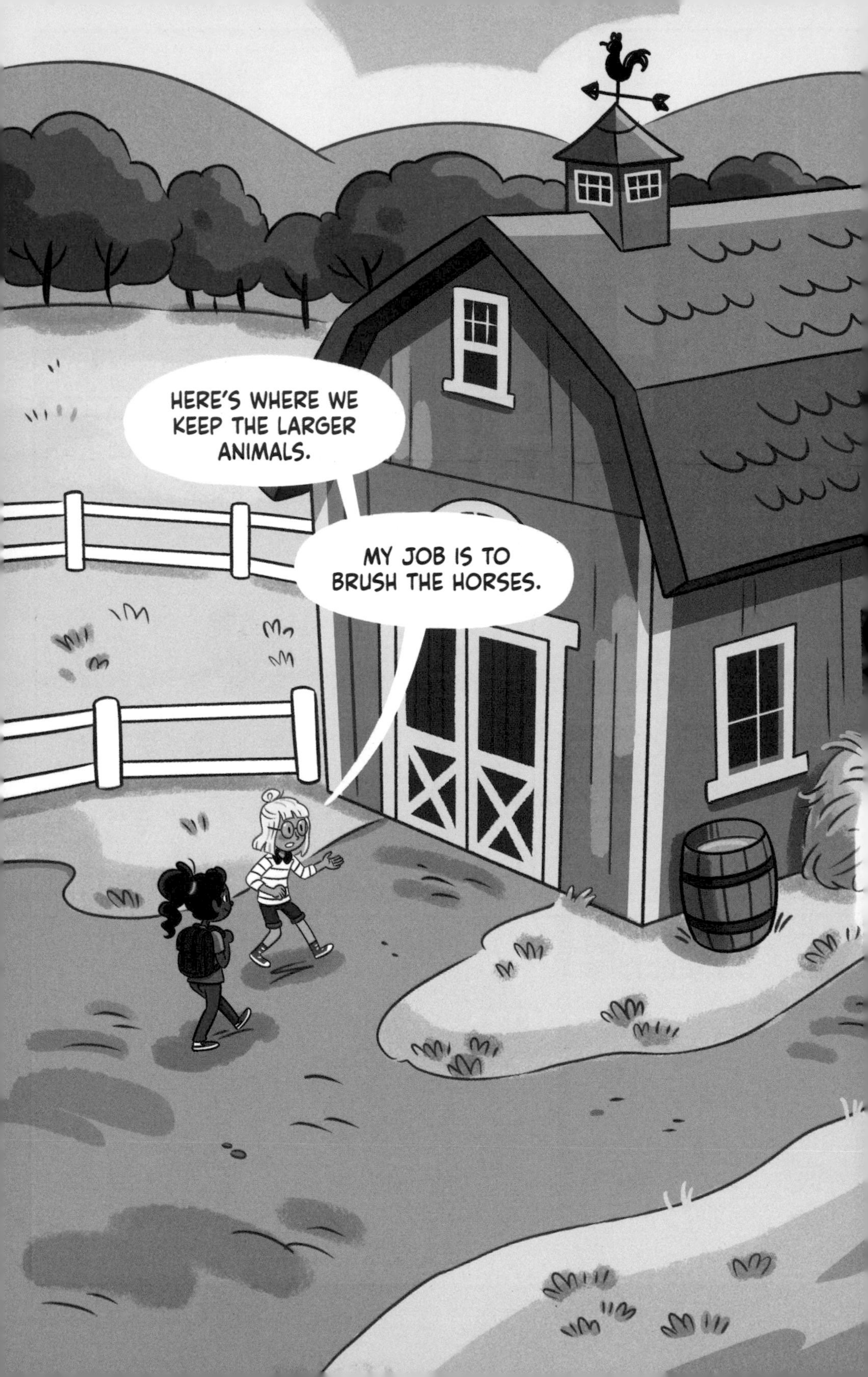
HERE'S WHERE WE KEEP THE LARGER ANIMALS.
MY JOB IS TO BRUSH THE HORSES.

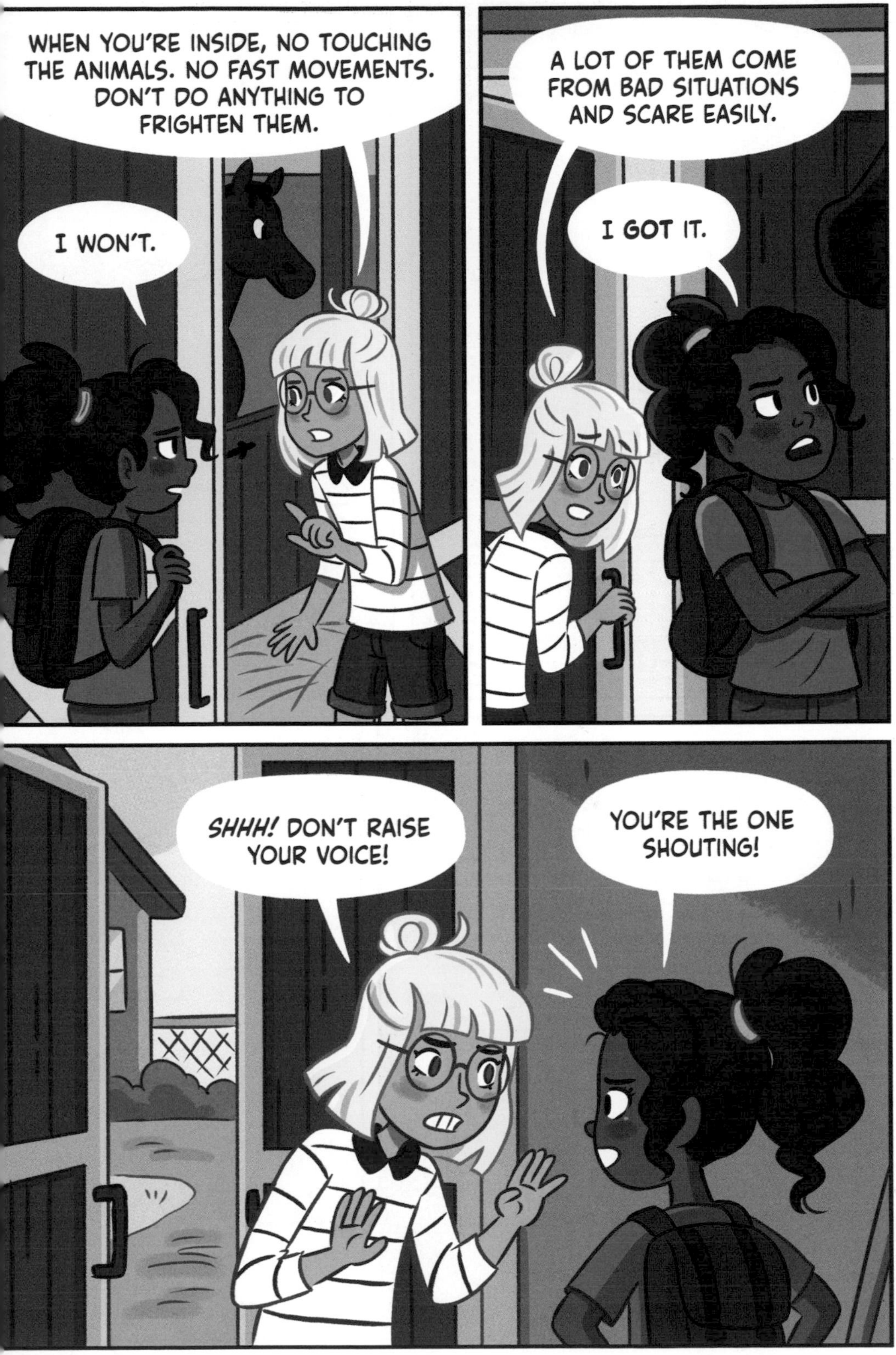
WHEN YOU'RE INSIDE, NO TOUCHING THE ANIMALS. NO FAST MOVEMENTS. DON'T DO ANYTHING TO FRIGHTEN THEM.
I WON'T.
A LOT OF THEM COME FROM BAD SITUATIONS AND SCARE EASILY.
I GOT IT.
SHHH! DON'T RAISE YOUR VOICE!
YOU'RE THE ONE SHOUTING!

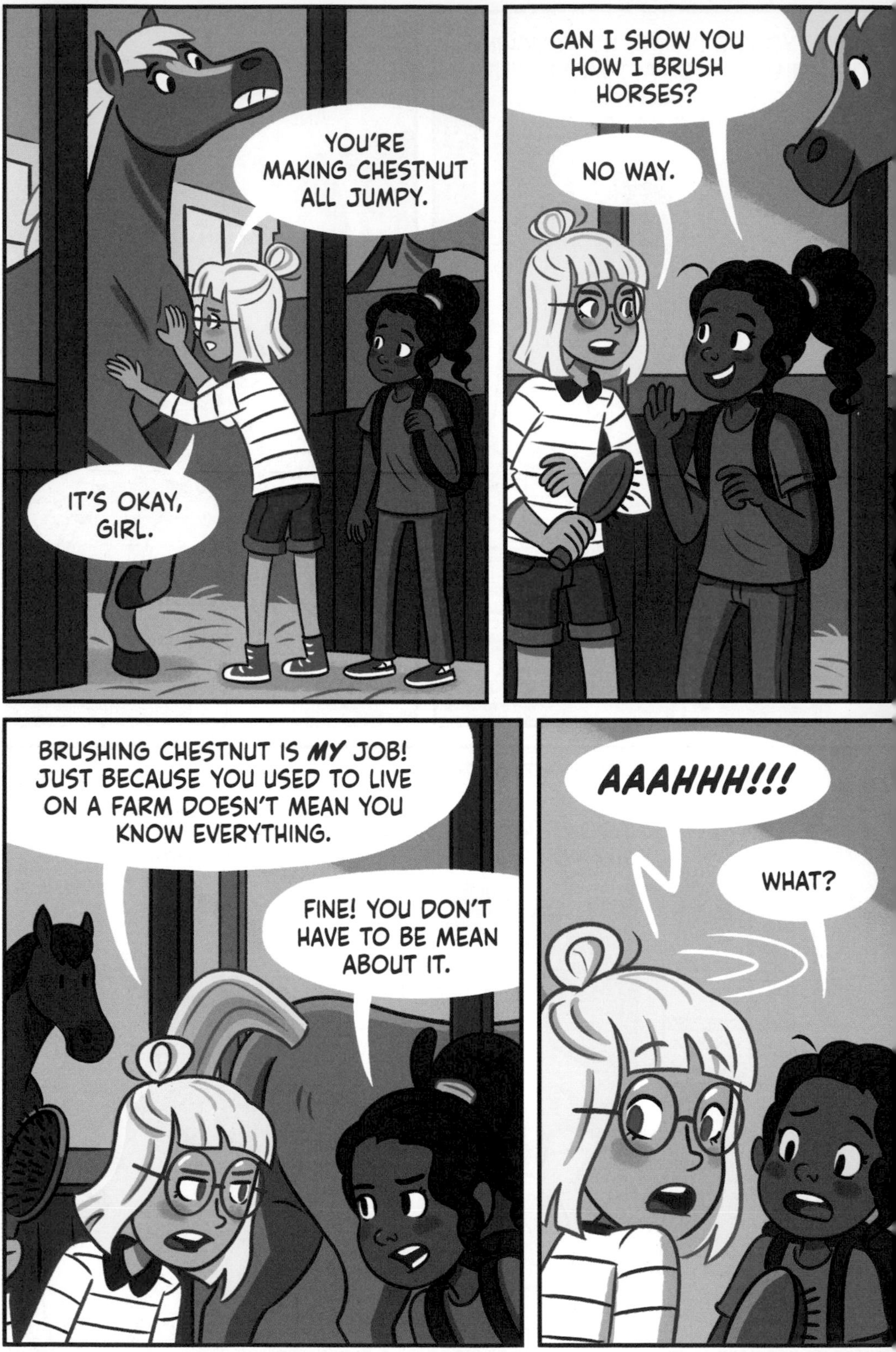
YOU'RE MAKING CHESTNUT ALL JUMPY.
IT'S OKAY, GIRL.
CAN I SHOW YOU HOW I BRUSH HORSES?
NO WAY.
BRUSHING CHESTNUT IS *MY* JOB! JUST BECAUSE YOU USED TO LIVE ON A FARM DOESN'T MEAN YOU KNOW EVERYTHING.
FINE! YOU DON'T HAVE TO BE MEAN ABOUT IT.
AAAHHH!!!
WHAT?

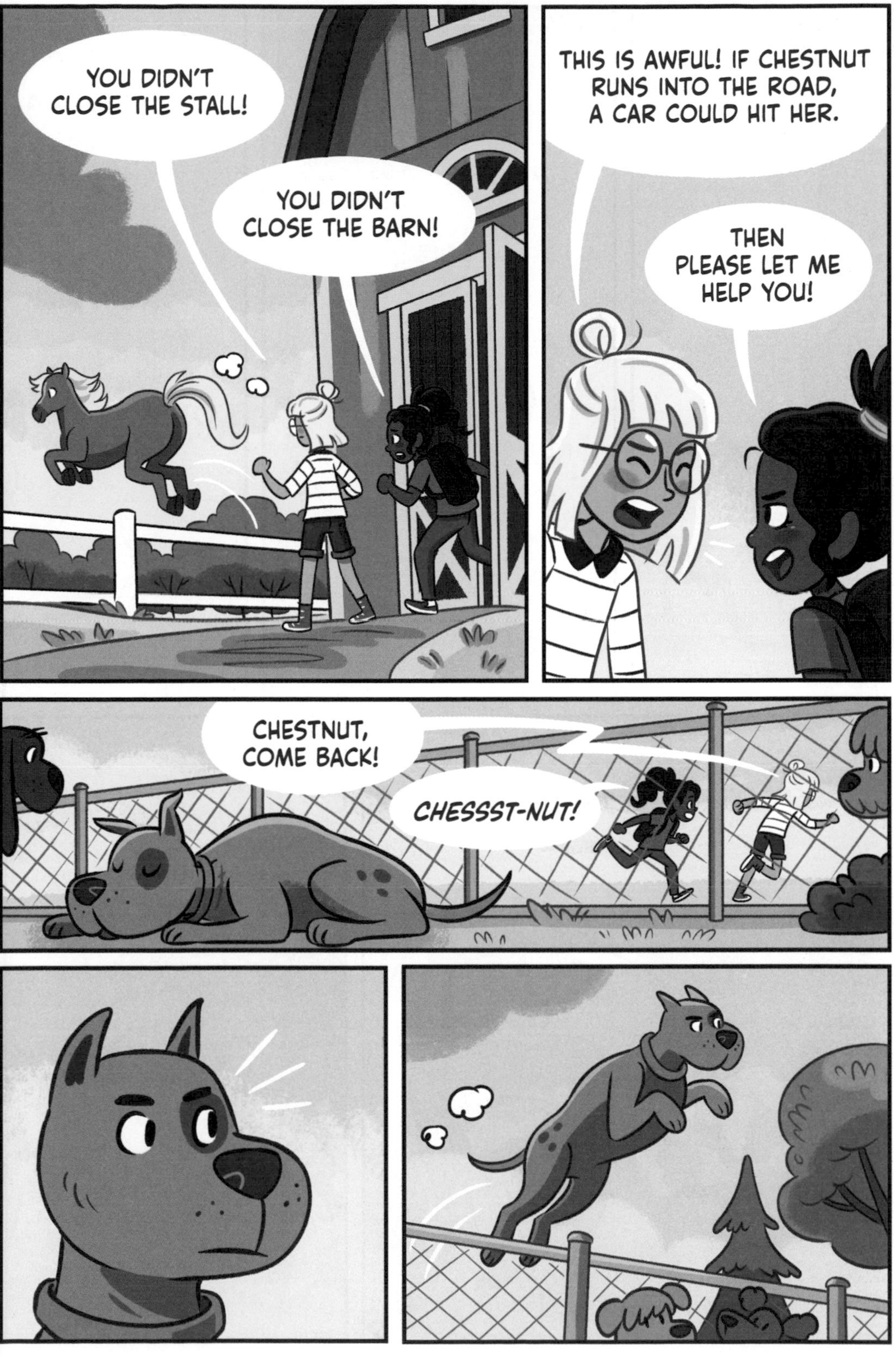
YOU DIDN'T CLOSE THE STALL!
YOU DIDN'T CLOSE THE BARN!
THIS IS AWFUL! IF CHESTNUT RUNS INTO THE ROAD, A CAR COULD HIT HER.
THEN PLEASE LET ME HELP YOU!
CHESTNUT, COME BACK!
CHESSST-NUT!

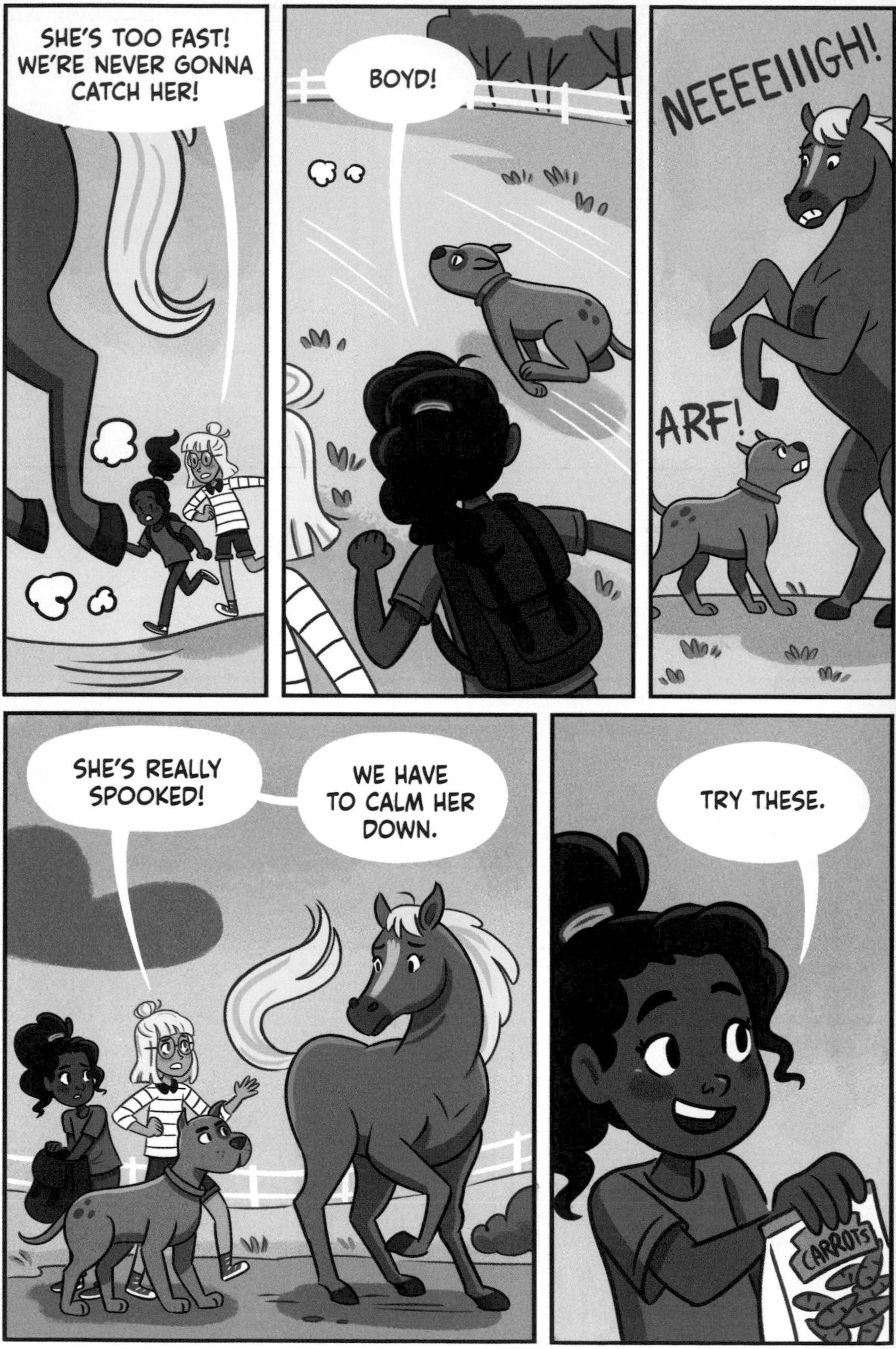
SHE'S TOO FAST! WE'RE NEVER GONNA CATCH HER!
BOYD!
NEEEEIIIIGH!
ARF!
SHE'S REALLY SPOOKED!
WE HAVE TO CALM HER DOWN.
TRY THESE.
CARROTS

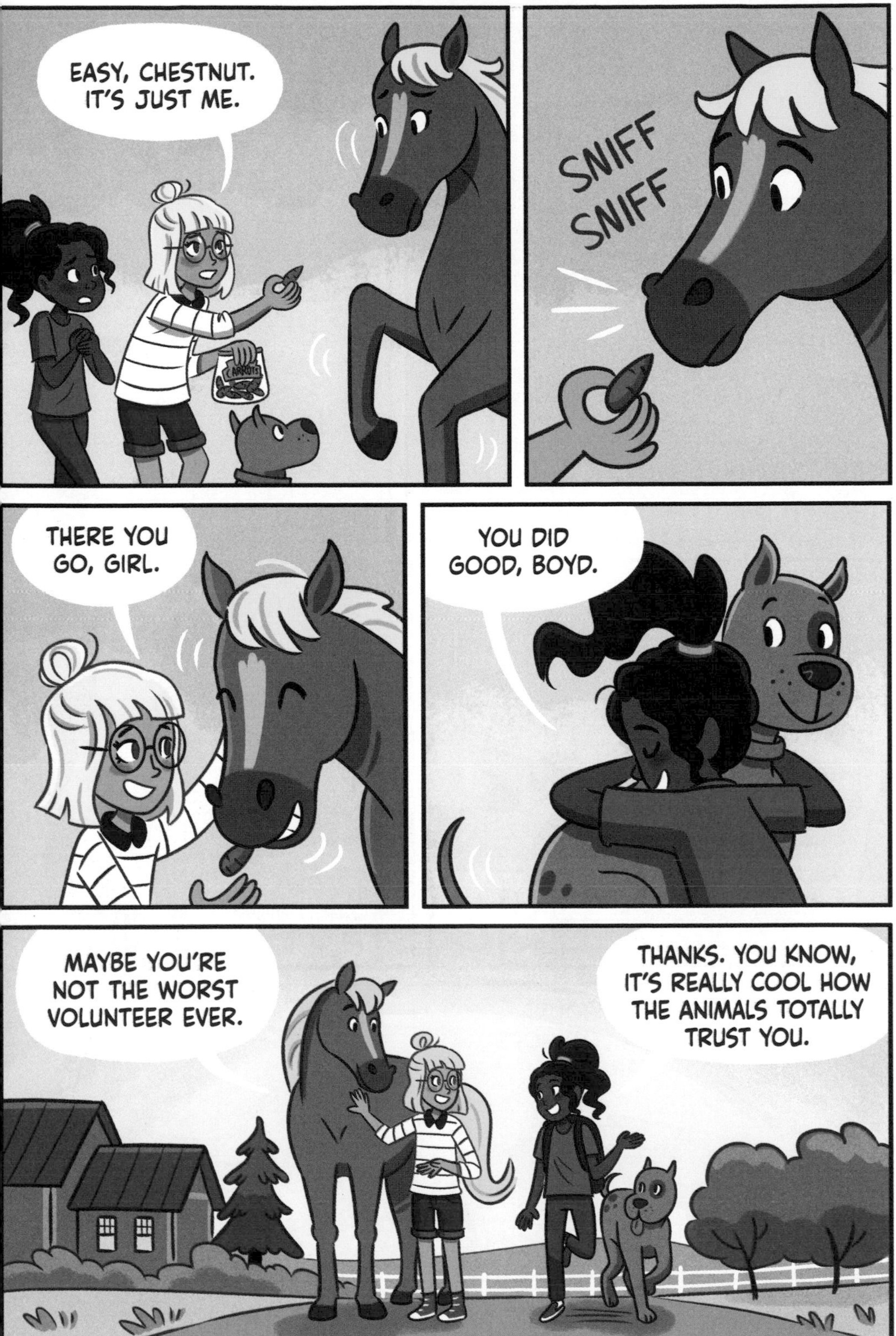
EASY, CHESTNUT. IT'S JUST ME.
CARROTS
SNIFF SNIFF
THERE YOU GO, GIRL.
YOU DID GOOD, BOYD.
MAYBE YOU'RE NOT THE WORST VOLUNTEER EVER.
THANKS. YOU KNOW, IT'S REALLY COOL HOW THE ANIMALS TOTALLY TRUST YOU.

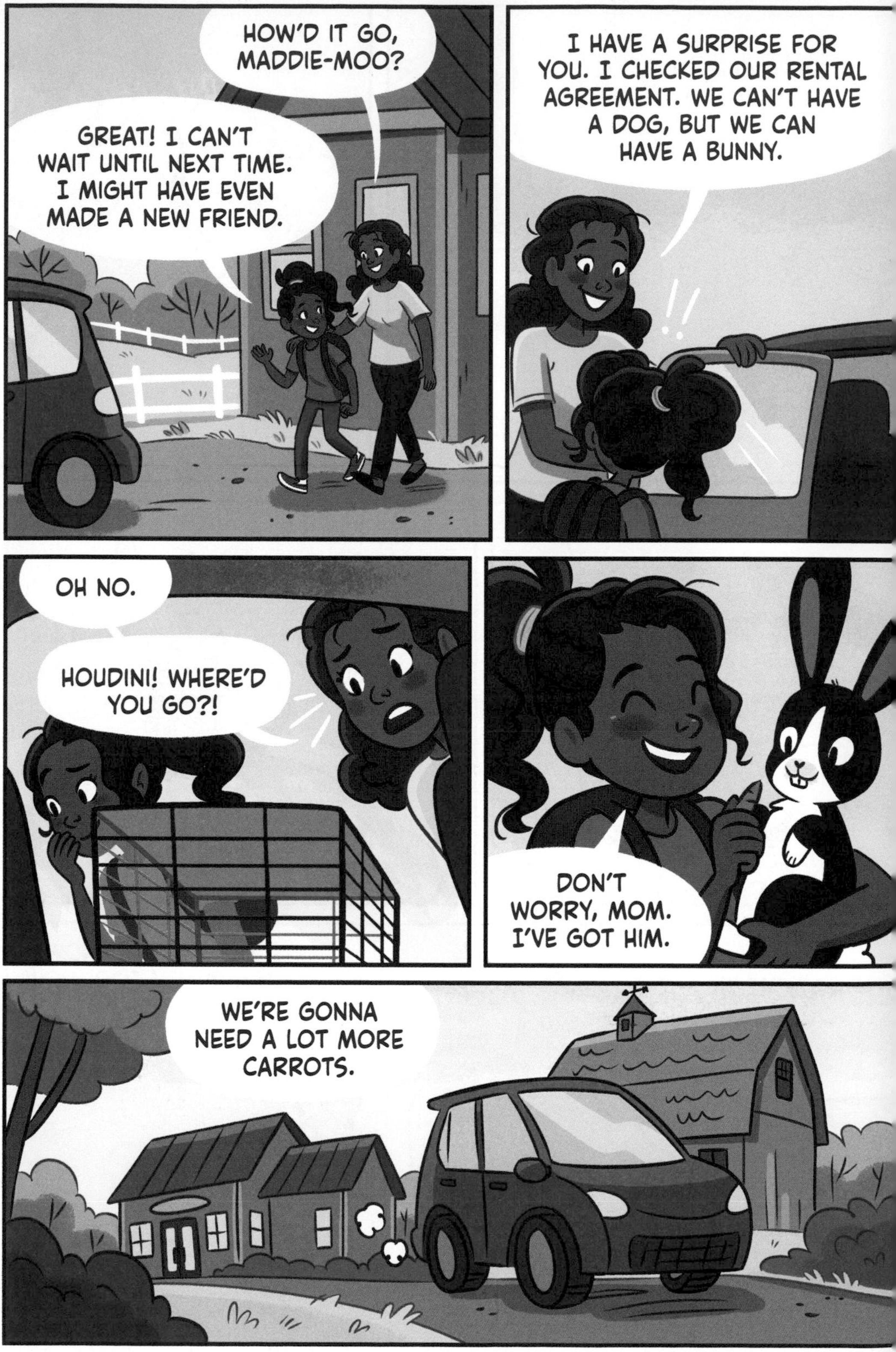
HOW'D IT GO, MADDIE-MOO?
GREAT! I CAN'T WAIT UNTIL NEXT TIME. I MIGHT HAVE EVEN MADE A NEW FRIEND.
I HAVE A SURPRISE FOR YOU. I CHECKED OUR RENTAL AGREEMENT. WE CAN'T HAVE A DOG, BUT WE CAN HAVE A BUNNY.
!!
OH NO.
HOUDINI! WHERE'D YOU GO?!
DON'T WORRY, MOM. I'VE GOT HIM.
WE'RE GONNA NEED A LOT MORE CARROTS.

Chapter 2

BELL AND KIKI

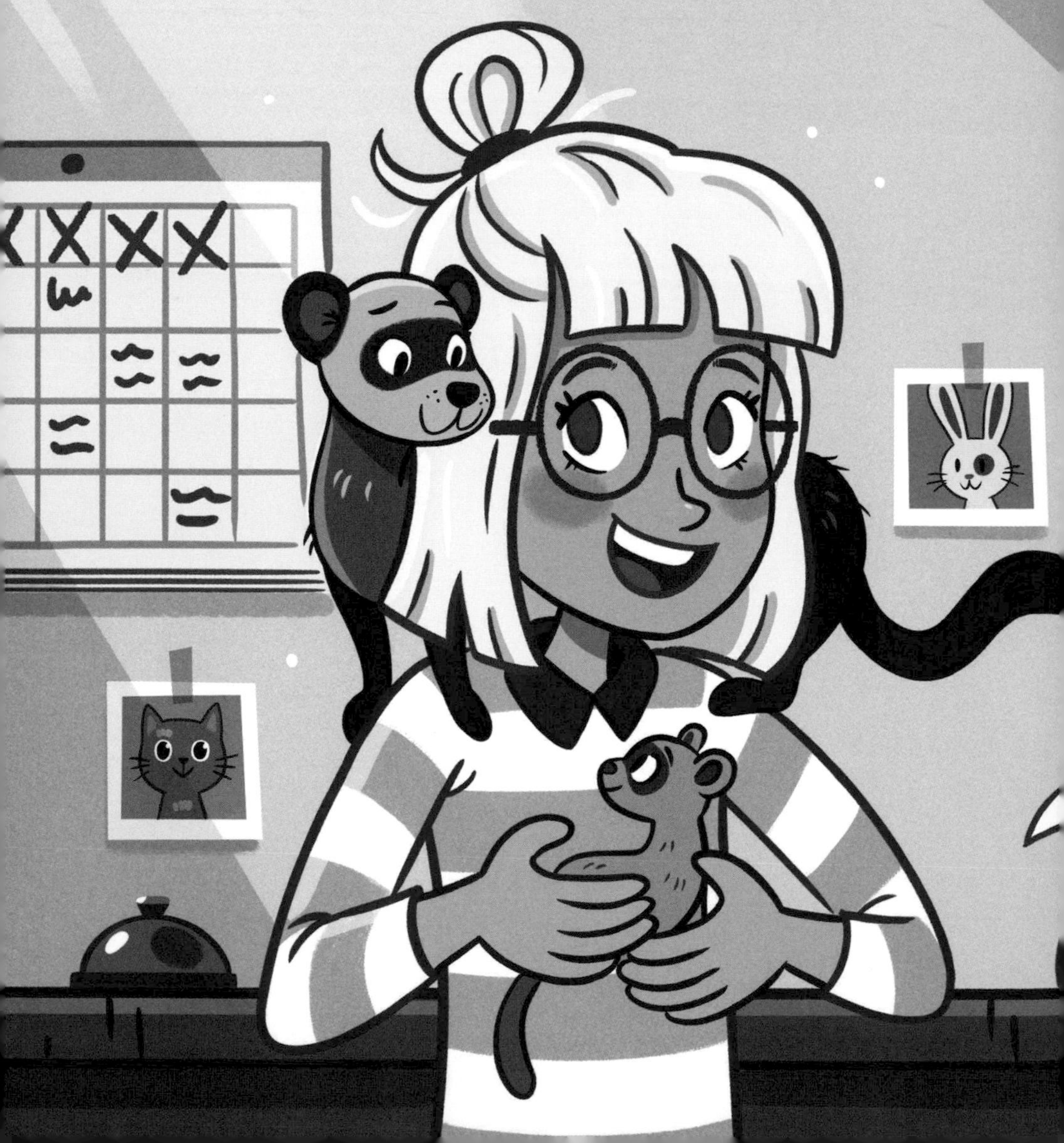

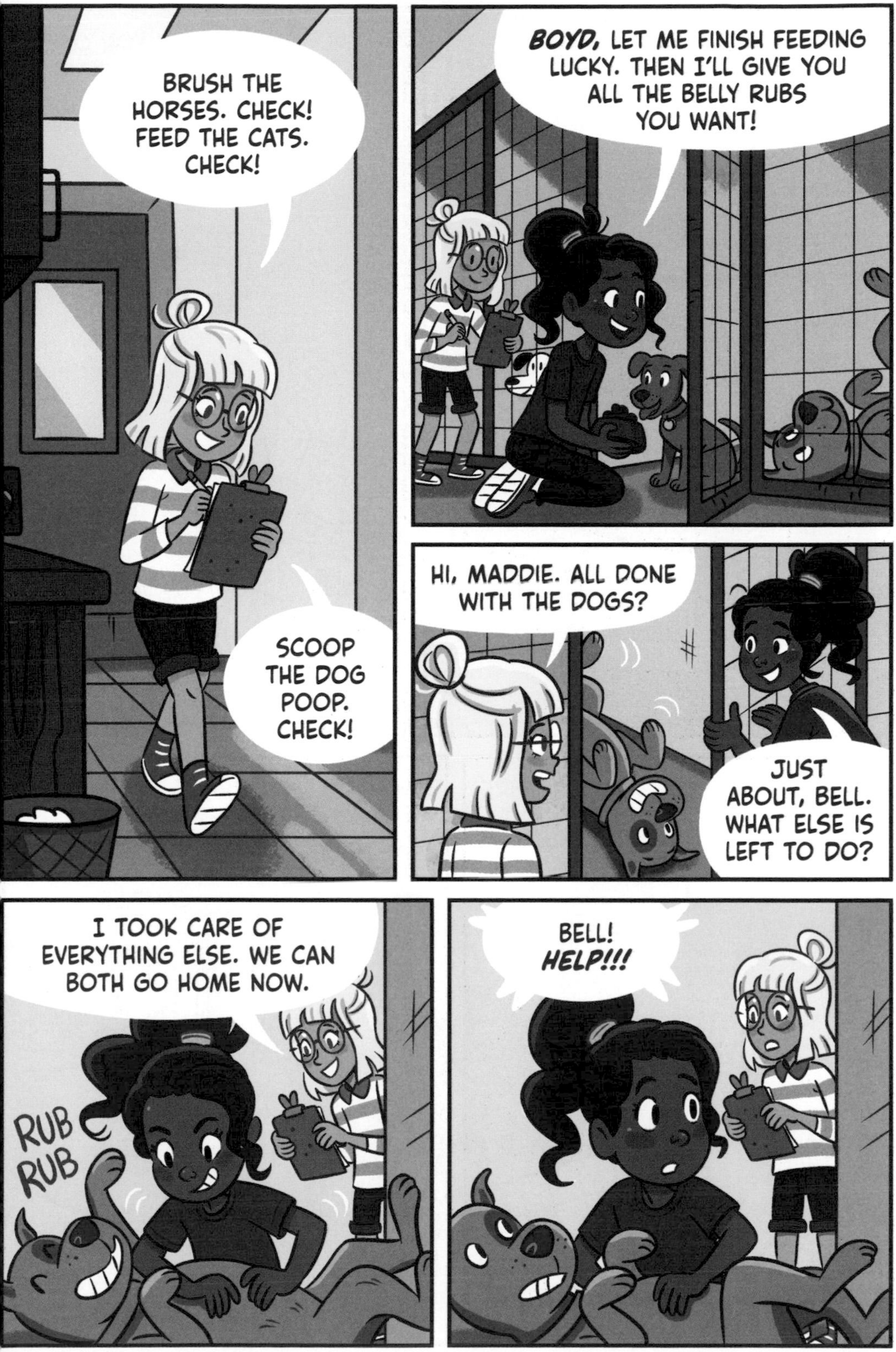
BRUSH THE HORSES. CHECK! FEED THE CATS. CHECK!
SCOOP THE DOG POOP. CHECK!
BOYD, LET ME FINISH FEEDING LUCKY. THEN I'LL GIVE YOU ALL THE BELLY RUBS YOU WANT!
HI, MADDIE. ALL DONE WITH THE DOGS?
JUST ABOUT, BELL. WHAT ELSE IS LEFT TO DO?
I TOOK CARE OF EVERYTHING ELSE. WE CAN BOTH GO HOME NOW.
RUB RUB
BELL! HELP!!!

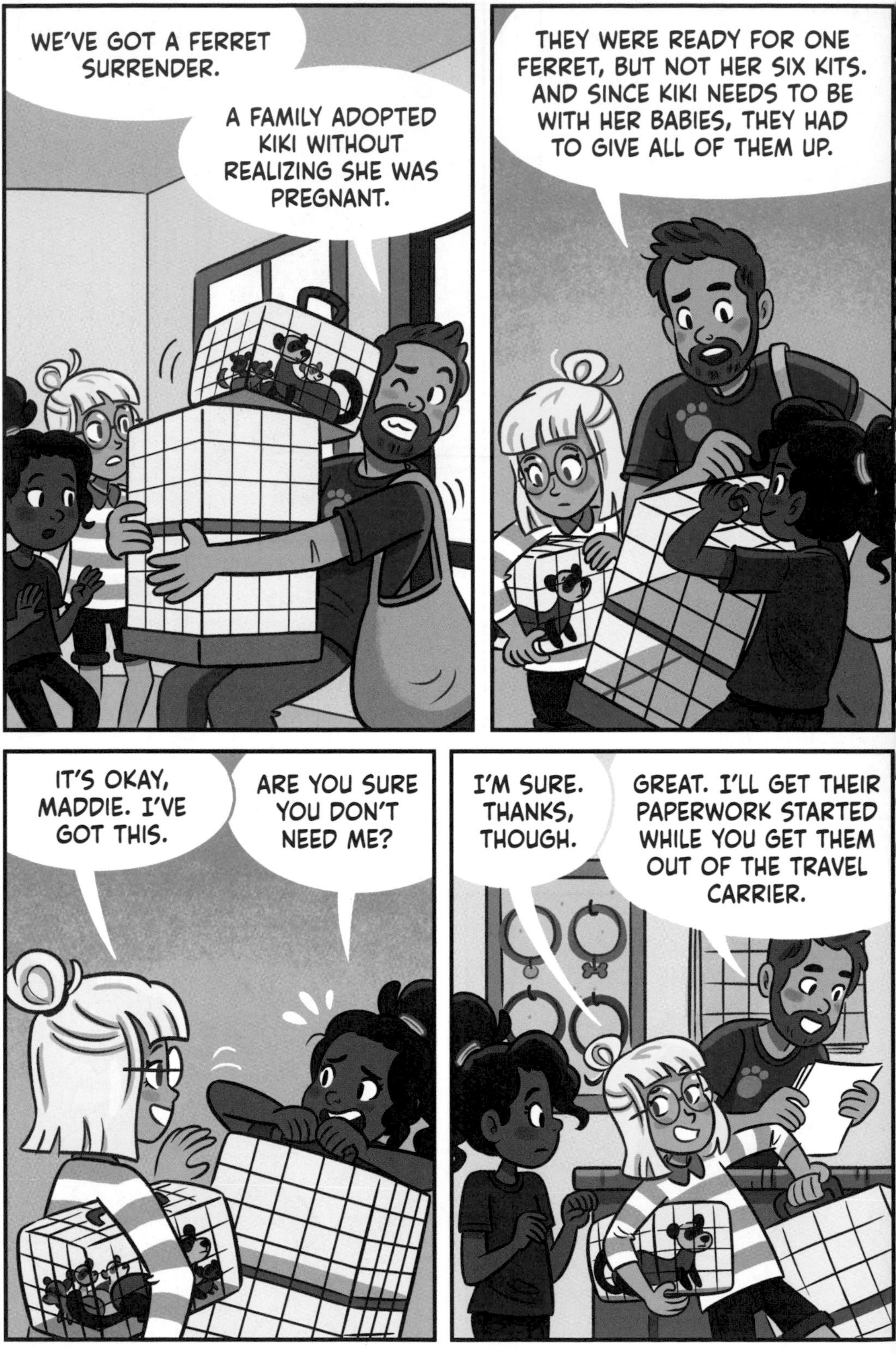
WE'VE GOT A FERRET SURRENDER.
A FAMILY ADOPTED KIKI WITHOUT REALIZING SHE WAS PREGNANT.
THEY WERE READY FOR ONE FERRET, BUT NOT HER SIX KITS. AND SINCE KIKI NEEDS TO BE WITH HER BABIES, THEY HAD TO GIVE ALL OF THEM UP.
IT'S OKAY, MADDIE. I'VE GOT THIS.
ARE YOU SURE YOU DON'T NEED ME?
I'M SURE. THANKS, THOUGH.
GREAT. I'LL GET THEIR PAPERWORK STARTED WHILE YOU GET THEM OUT OF THE TRAVEL CARRIER.

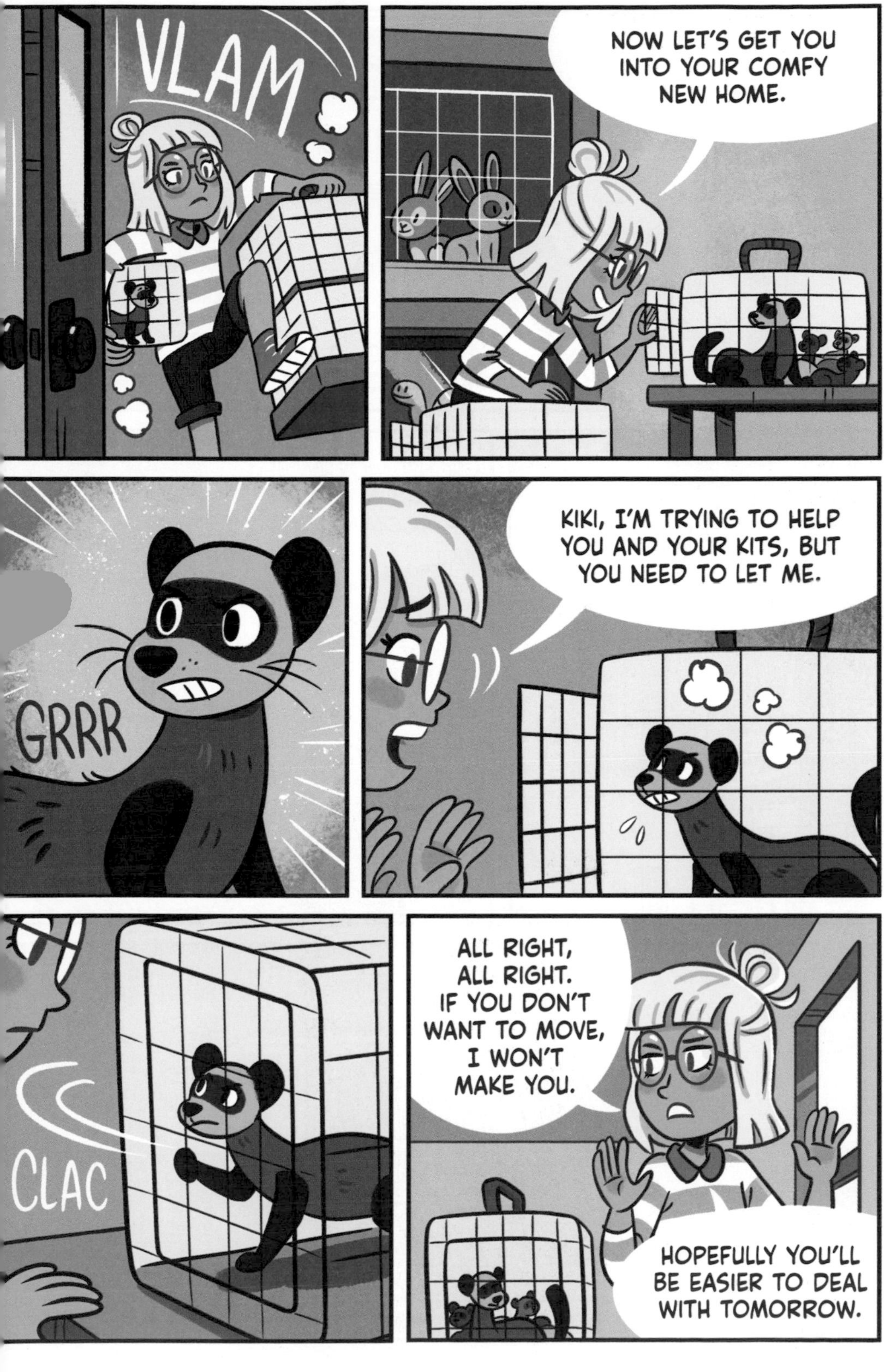
VLAM
NOW LET'S GET YOU INTO YOUR COMFY NEW HOME.
GRRR
KIKI, I'M TRYING TO HELP YOU AND YOUR KITS, BUT YOU NEED TO LET ME.
CLAC
ALL RIGHT, ALL RIGHT. IF YOU DON'T WANT TO MOVE, I WON'T MAKE YOU.
HOPEFULLY YOU'LL BE EASIER TO DEAL WITH TOMORROW.

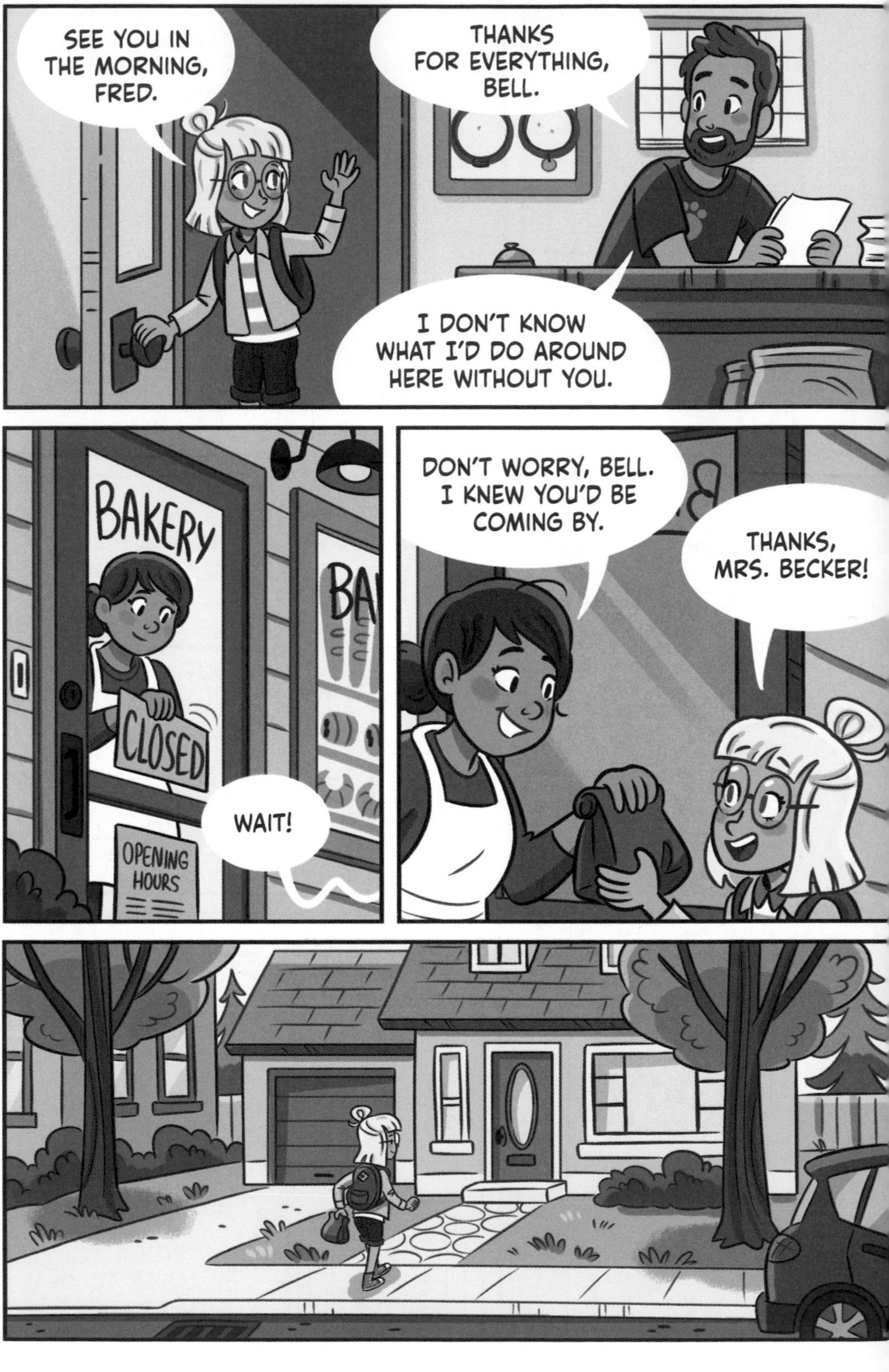
SEE YOU IN THE MORNING, FRED.
THANKS FOR EVERYTHING, BELL.
I DON'T KNOW WHAT I'D DO AROUND HERE WITHOUT YOU.
BAKERY
CLOSED
OPENING HOURS
WAIT!
DON'T WORRY, BELL. I KNEW YOU'D BE COMING BY.
THANKS, MRS. BECKER!

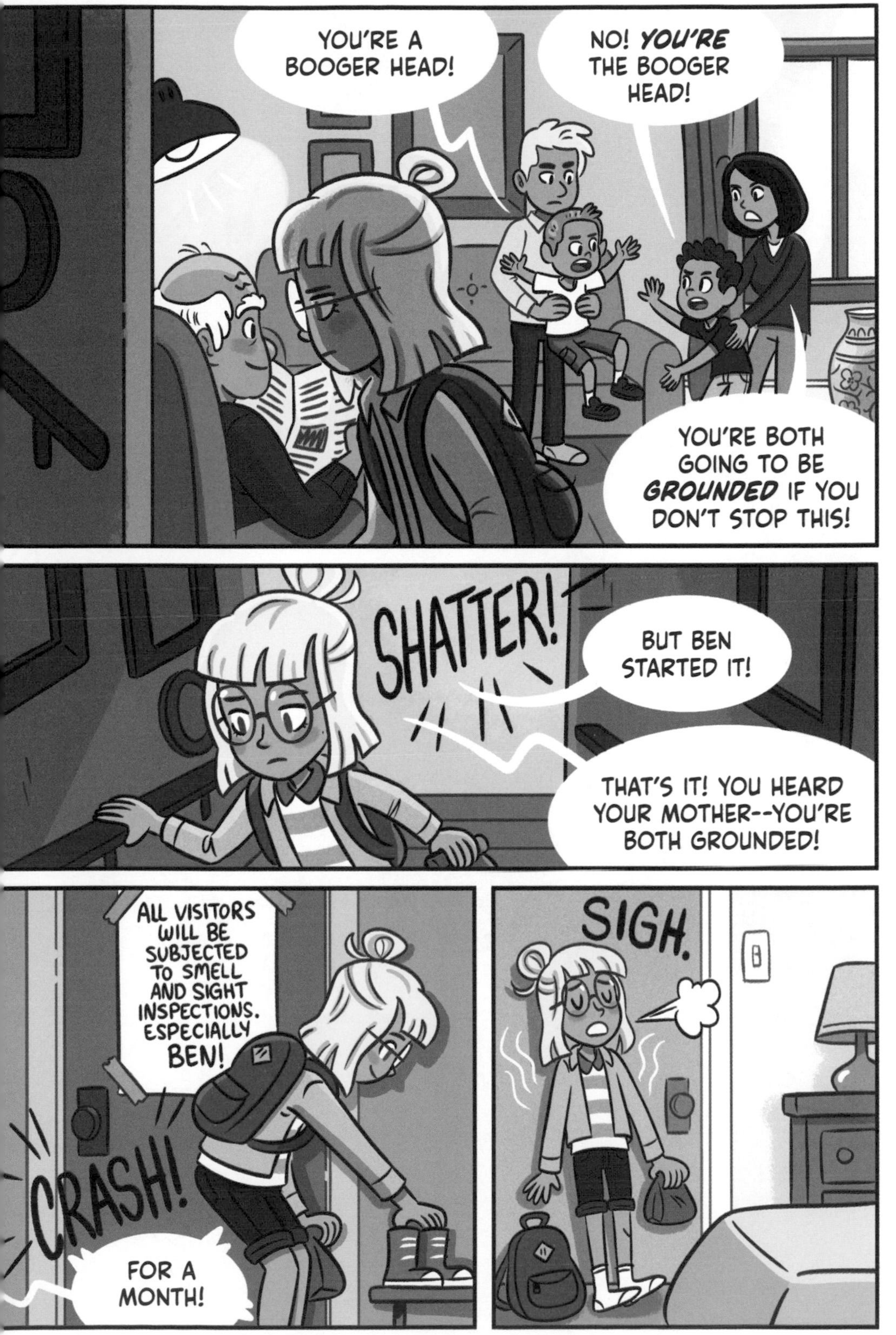

YOU'RE A BOOGER HEAD!
NO! ***YOU'RE*** THE BOOGER HEAD!
YOU'RE BOTH GOING TO BE ***GROUNDED*** IF YOU DON'T STOP THIS!
SHATTER!
BUT BEN STARTED IT!
THAT'S IT! YOU HEARD YOUR MOTHER--YOU'RE BOTH GROUNDED!
ALL VISITORS WILL BE SUBJECTED TO SMELL AND SIGHT INSPECTIONS. ESPECIALLY BEN!
CRASH!
FOR A MONTH!
SIGH.

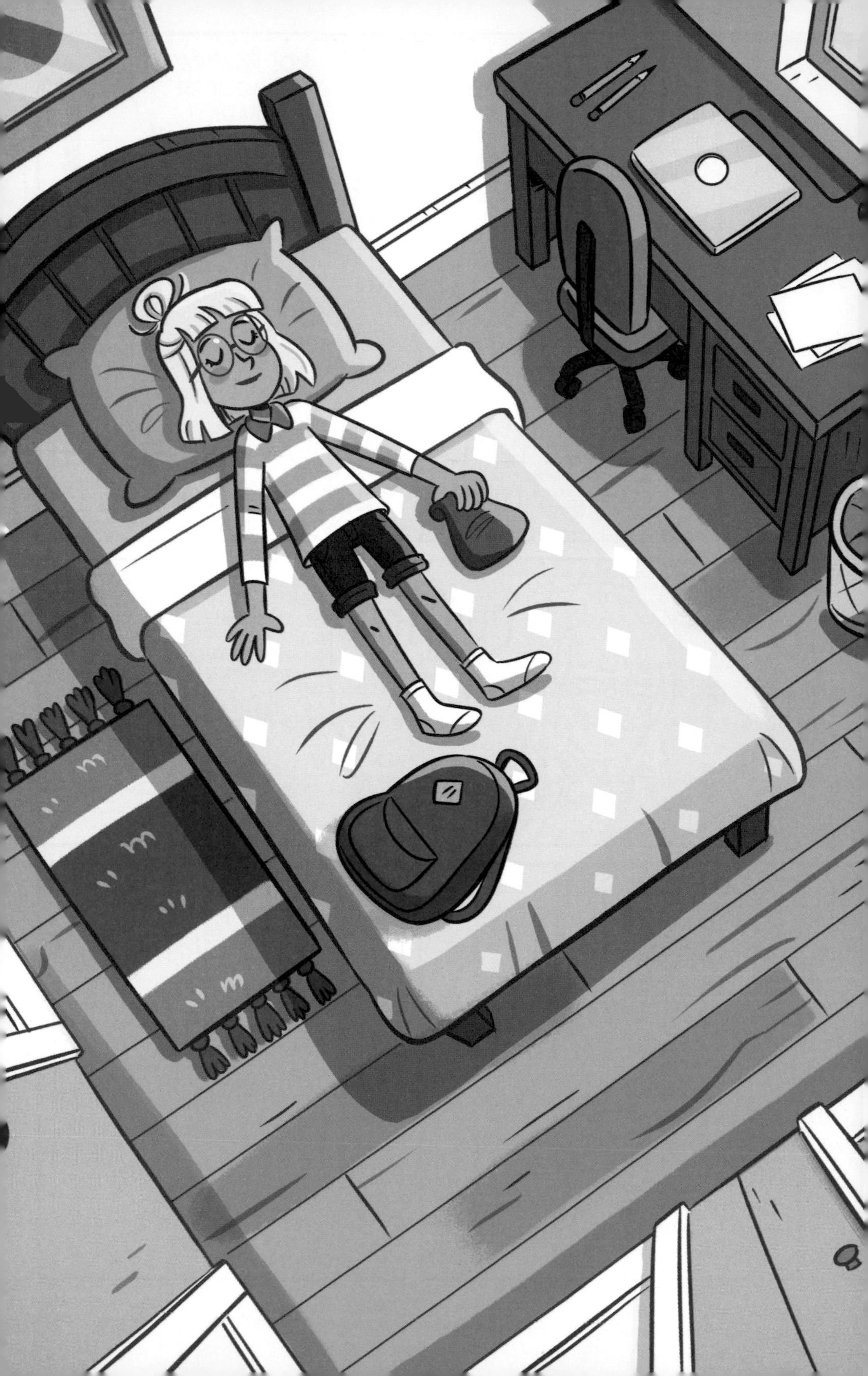

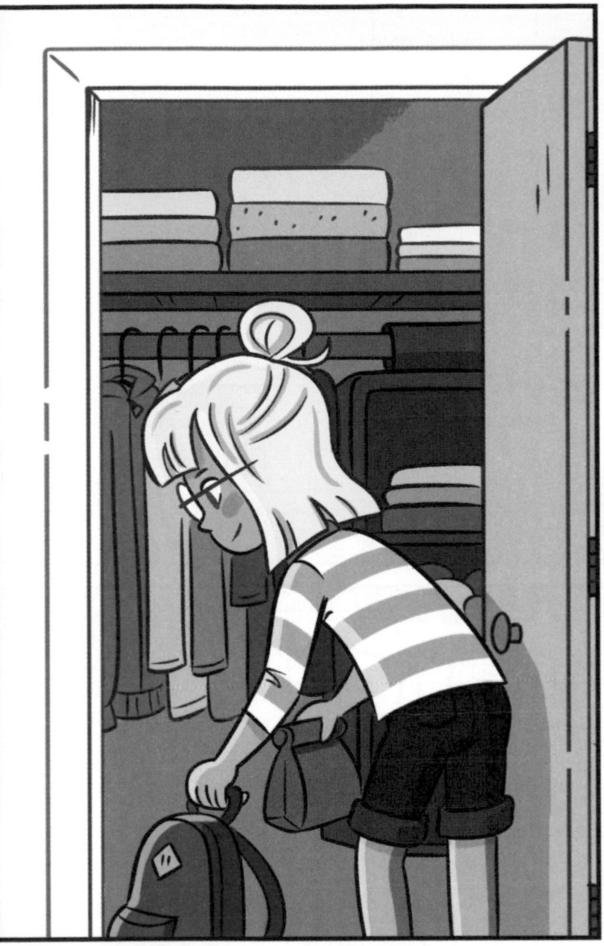

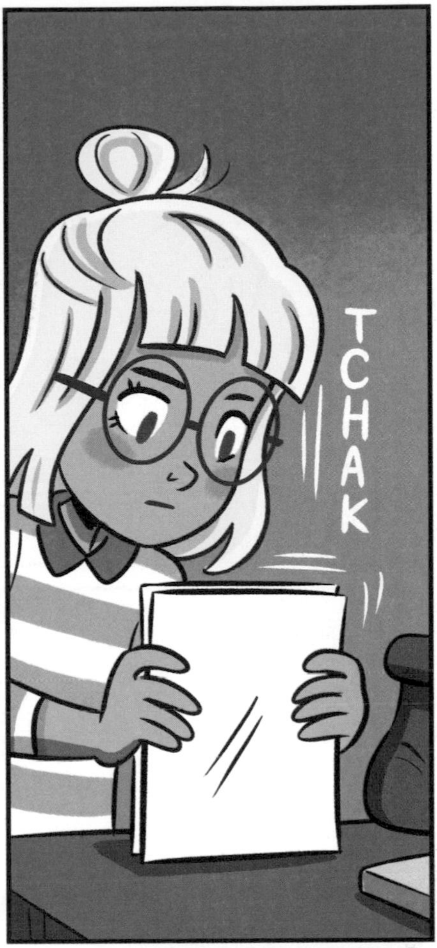

TCHAK

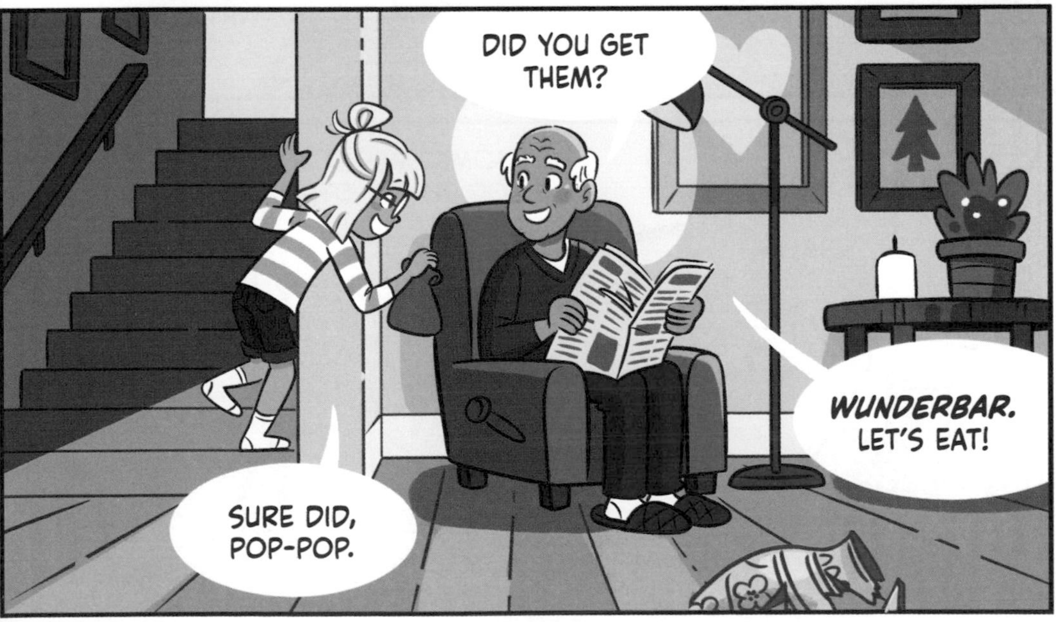

DID YOU GET THEM?
SURE DID, POP-POP.
WUNDERBAR. LET'S EAT!

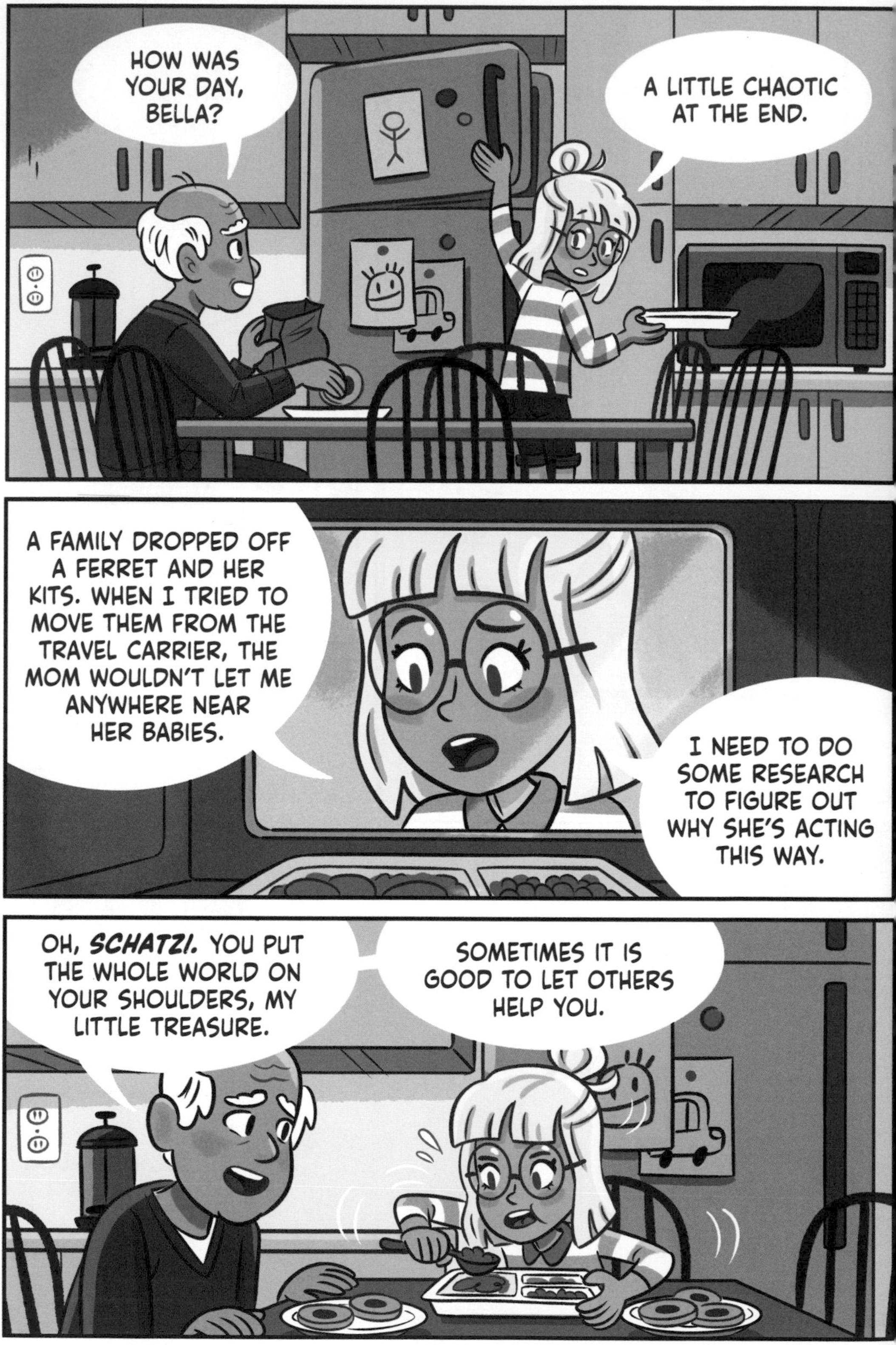
HOW WAS YOUR DAY, BELLA?
A LITTLE CHAOTIC AT THE END.
A FAMILY DROPPED OFF A FERRET AND HER KITS. WHEN I TRIED TO MOVE THEM FROM THE TRAVEL CARRIER, THE MOM WOULDN'T LET ME ANYWHERE NEAR HER BABIES.
I NEED TO DO SOME RESEARCH TO FIGURE OUT WHY SHE'S ACTING THIS WAY.
OH, *SCHATZI.* YOU PUT THE WHOLE WORLD ON YOUR SHOULDERS, MY LITTLE TREASURE.
SOMETIMES IT IS GOOD TO LET OTHERS HELP YOU.

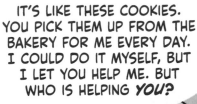
IT'S LIKE THESE COOKIES. YOU PICK THEM UP FROM THE BAKERY FOR ME EVERY DAY. I COULD DO IT MYSELF, BUT I LET YOU HELP ME. BUT WHO IS HELPING *YOU*?

IT'S NOT LIKE THAT. COOKIES ARE ONE THING, BUT THE SHELTER IS ANOTHER. I KNOW HOW TO DO THINGS RIGHT. IF I LET SOMEONE HELP, THEY COULD DO IT WRONG.

NIGHT, POP-POP.

NIGHT, BELLA. DON'T STAY UP TOO LATE.

MOTHER FERRETS DO NOT LIKE BEING SEPARATED FROM THEIR YOUNG.

1:00 A.M.

35

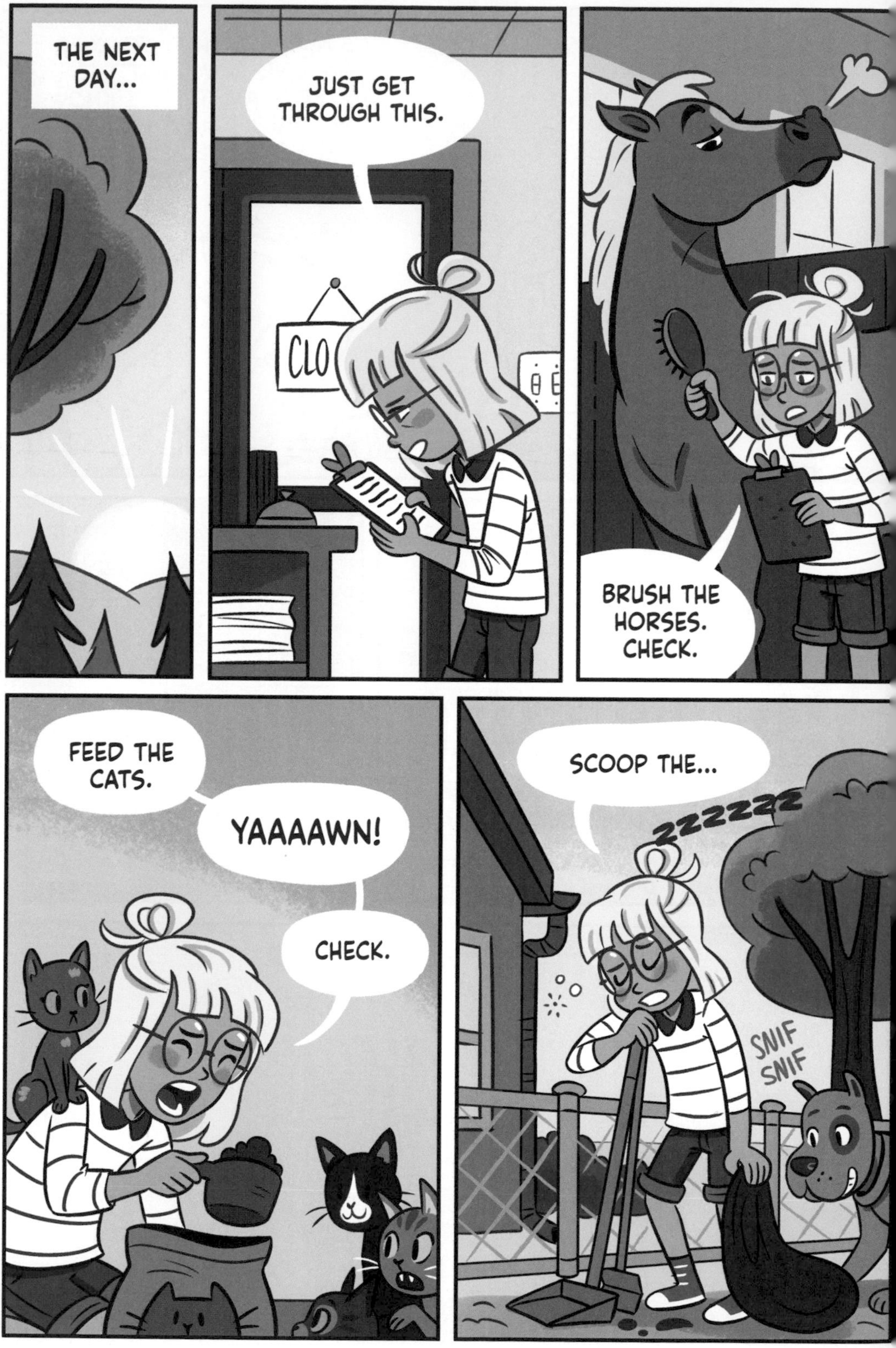
THE NEXT DAY...
JUST GET THROUGH THIS.
CLO
BRUSH THE HORSES. CHECK.
FEED THE CATS.
YAAAAWN!
CHECK.
SCOOP THE...
ZZZZZZ
SNIF SNIF

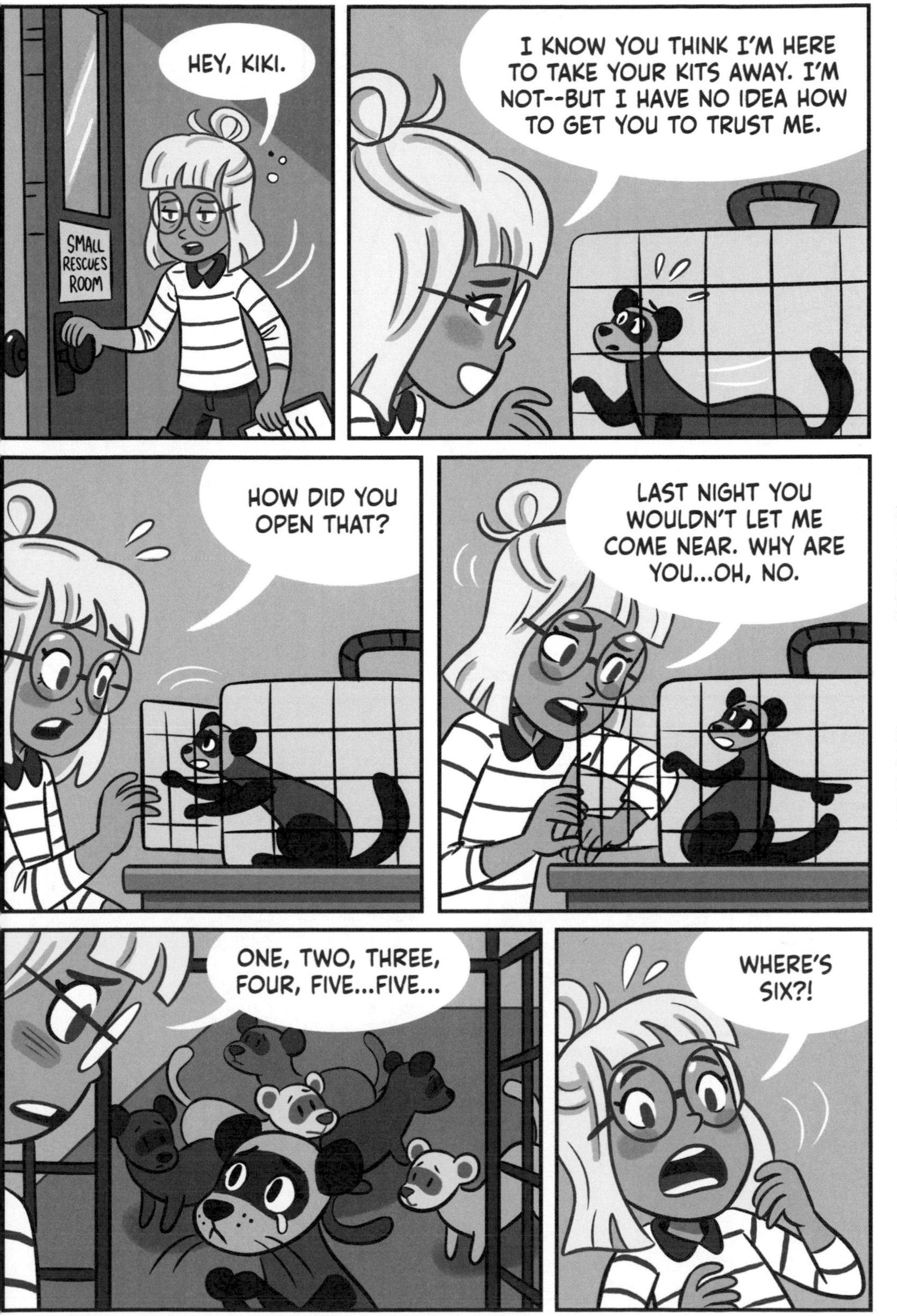
SMALL RESCUES ROOM
HEY, KIKI.
I KNOW YOU THINK I'M HERE TO TAKE YOUR KITS AWAY. I'M NOT--BUT I HAVE NO IDEA HOW TO GET YOU TO TRUST ME.
HOW DID YOU OPEN THAT?
LAST NIGHT YOU WOULDN'T LET ME COME NEAR. WHY ARE YOU...OH, NO.
ONE, TWO, THREE, FOUR, FIVE...FIVE...
WHERE'S SIX?!

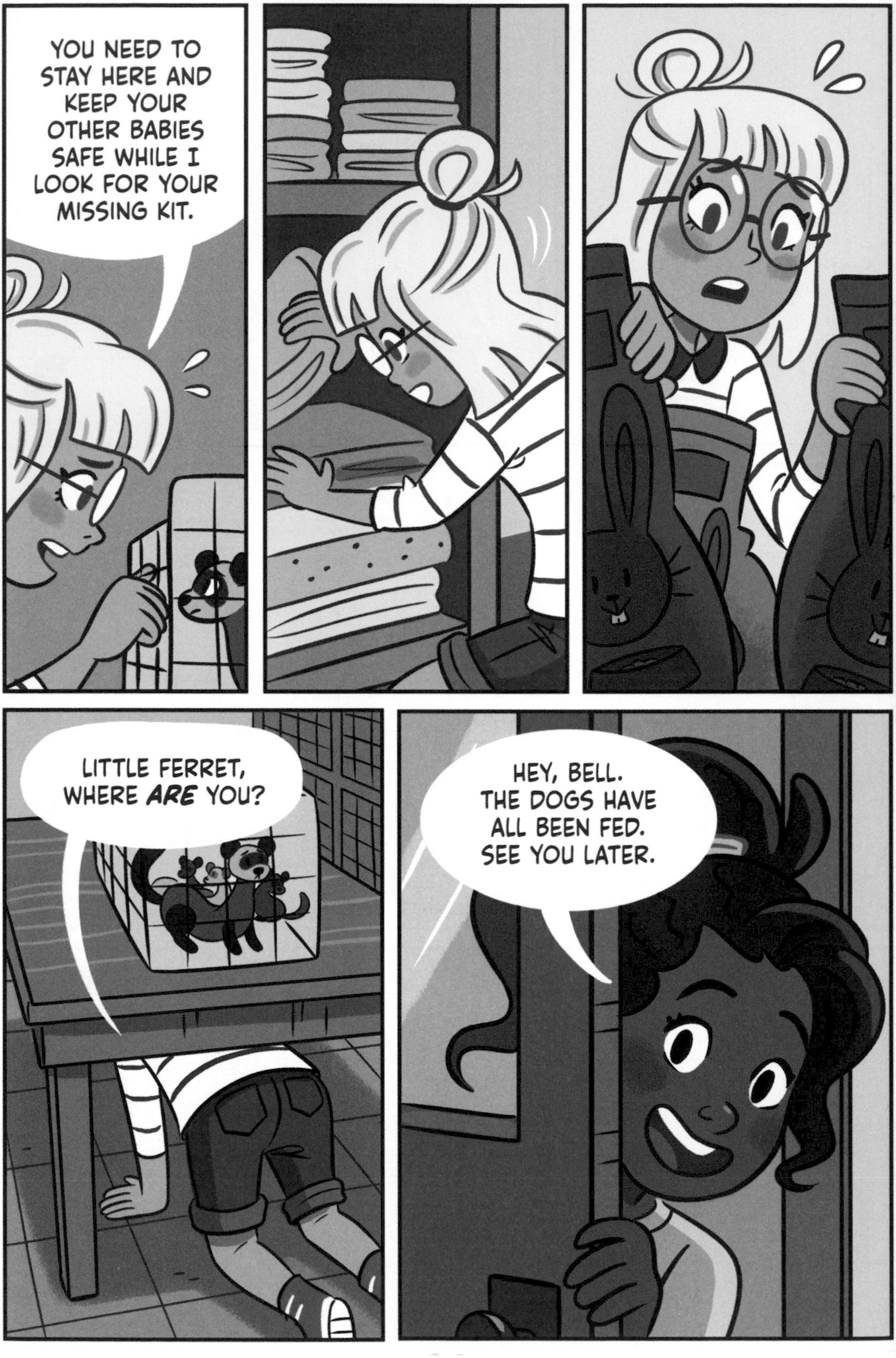
YOU NEED TO STAY HERE AND KEEP YOUR OTHER BABIES SAFE WHILE I LOOK FOR YOUR MISSING KIT.
LITTLE FERRET, WHERE *ARE* YOU?
HEY, BELL. THE DOGS HAVE ALL BEEN FED. SEE YOU LATER.

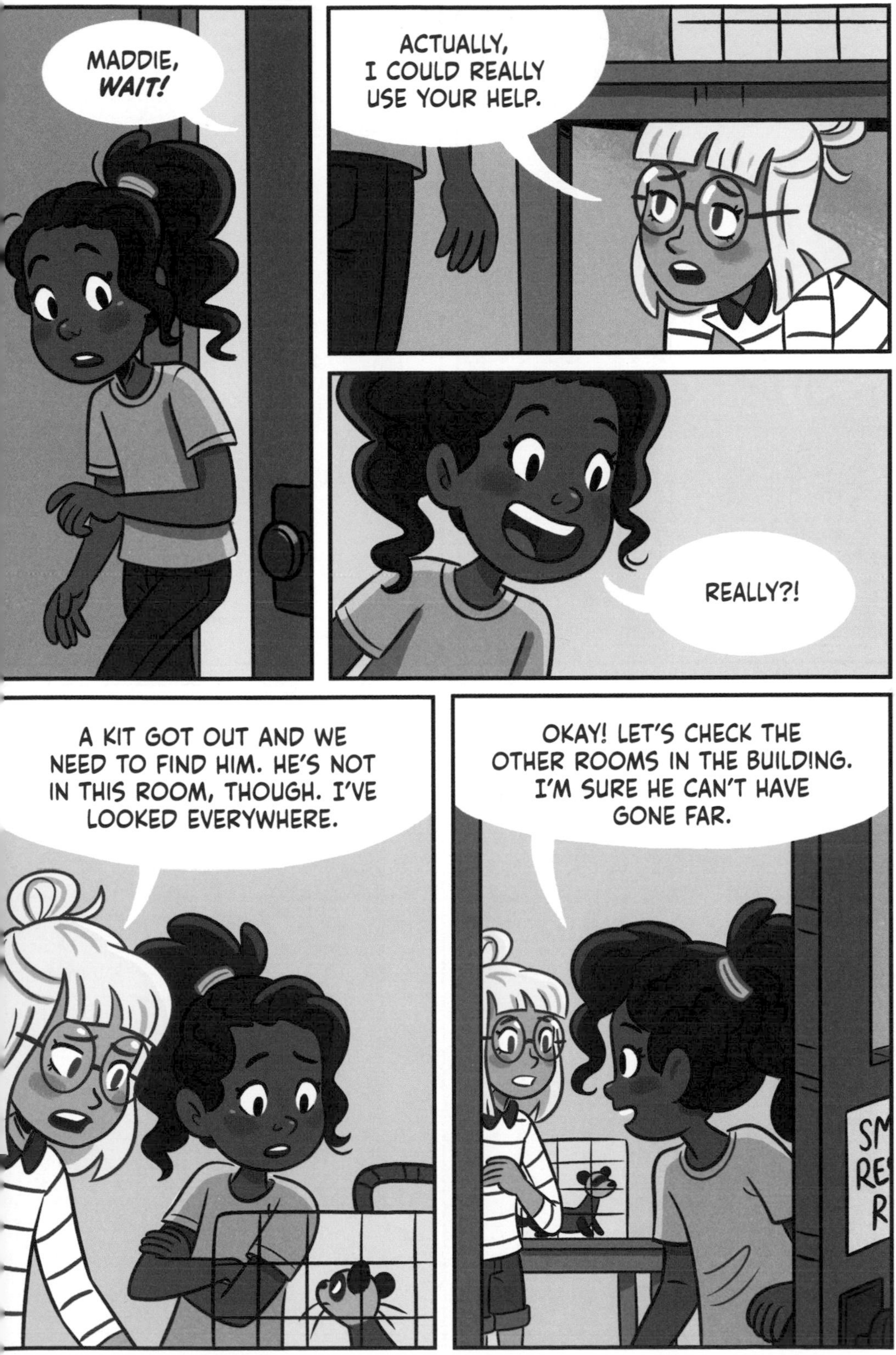
MADDIE, *WAIT!*
ACTUALLY, I COULD REALLY USE YOUR HELP.
REALLY?!
A KIT GOT OUT AND WE NEED TO FIND HIM. HE'S NOT IN THIS ROOM, THOUGH. I'VE LOOKED EVERYWHERE.
OKAY! LET'S CHECK THE OTHER ROOMS IN THE BUILDING. I'M SURE HE CAN'T HAVE GONE FAR.

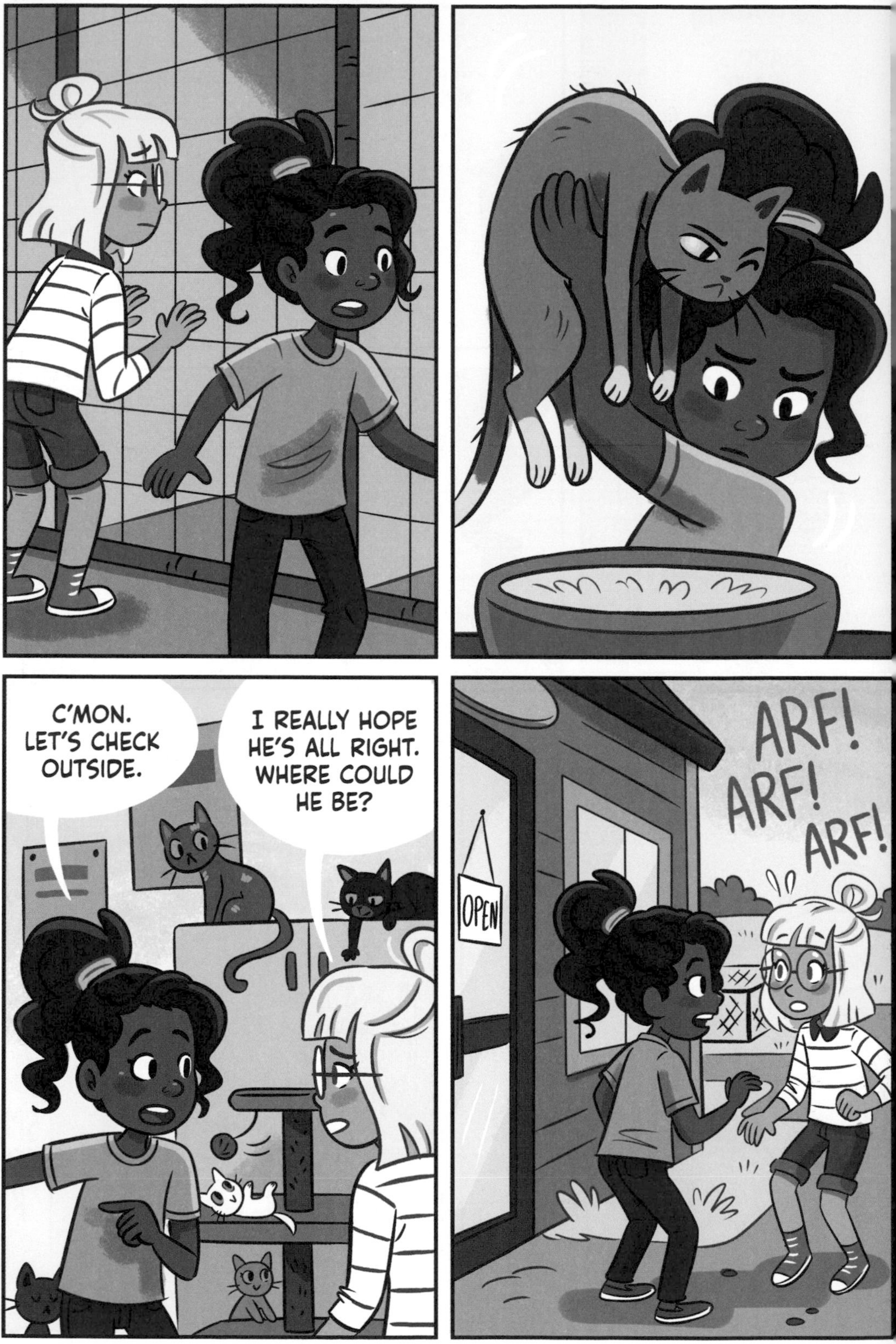
C'MON. LET'S CHECK OUTSIDE.
I REALLY HOPE HE'S ALL RIGHT. WHERE COULD HE BE?
OPEN
ARF!
ARF!
ARF!

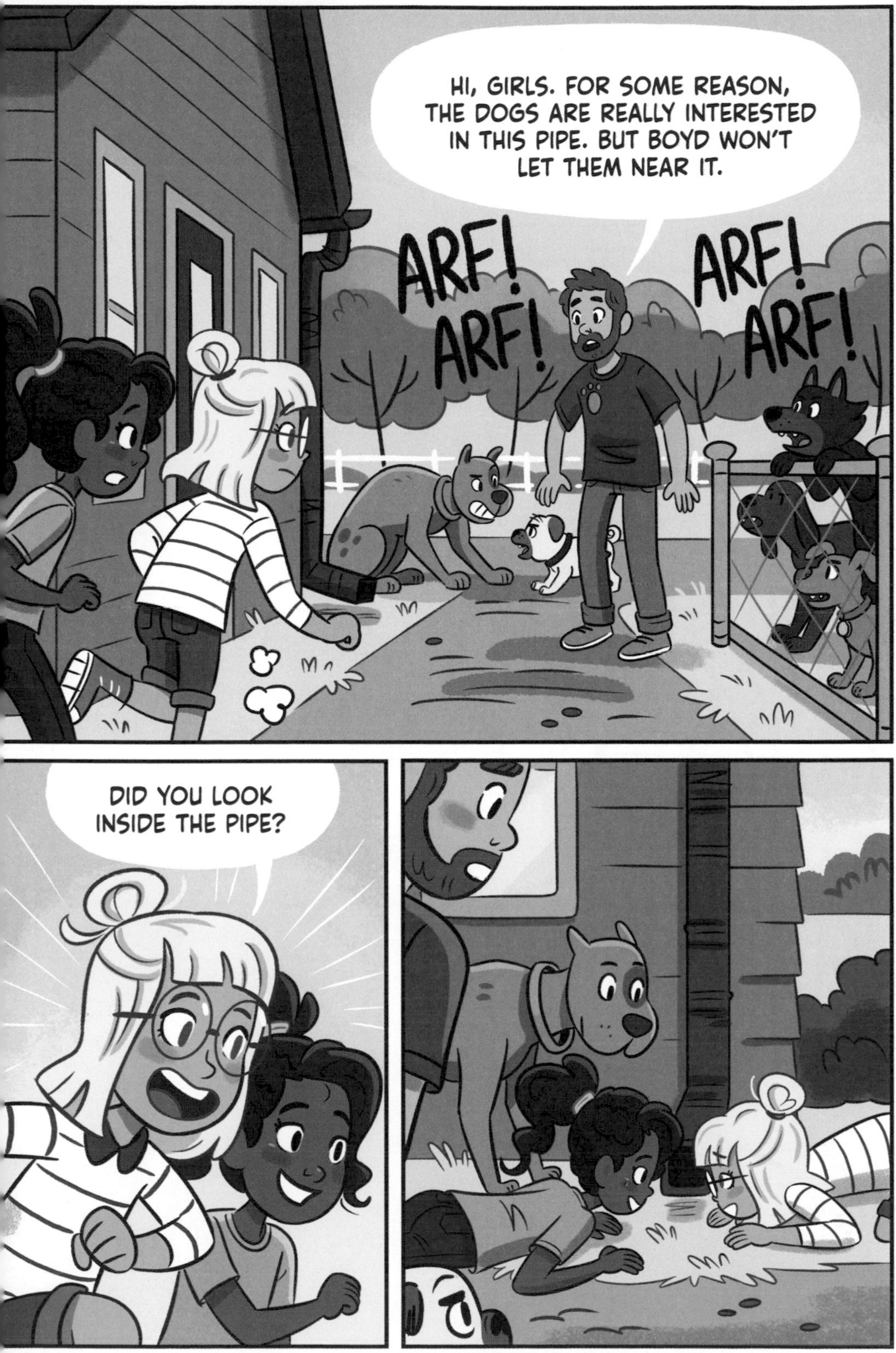
HI, GIRLS. FOR SOME REASON, THE DOGS ARE REALLY INTERESTED IN THIS PIPE. BUT BOYD WON'T LET THEM NEAR IT.
ARF! ARF!
ARF! ARF!
DID YOU LOOK INSIDE THE PIPE?

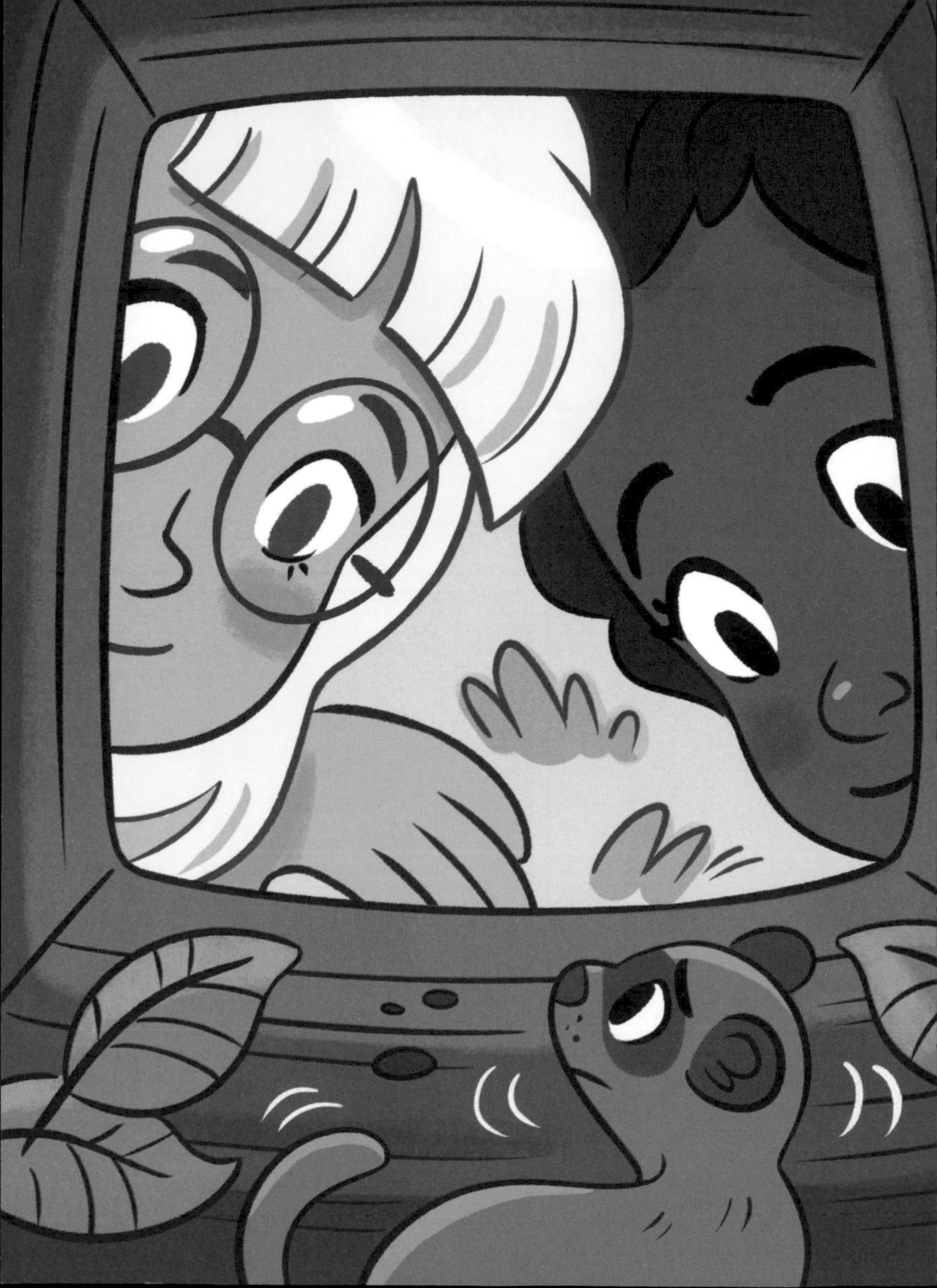

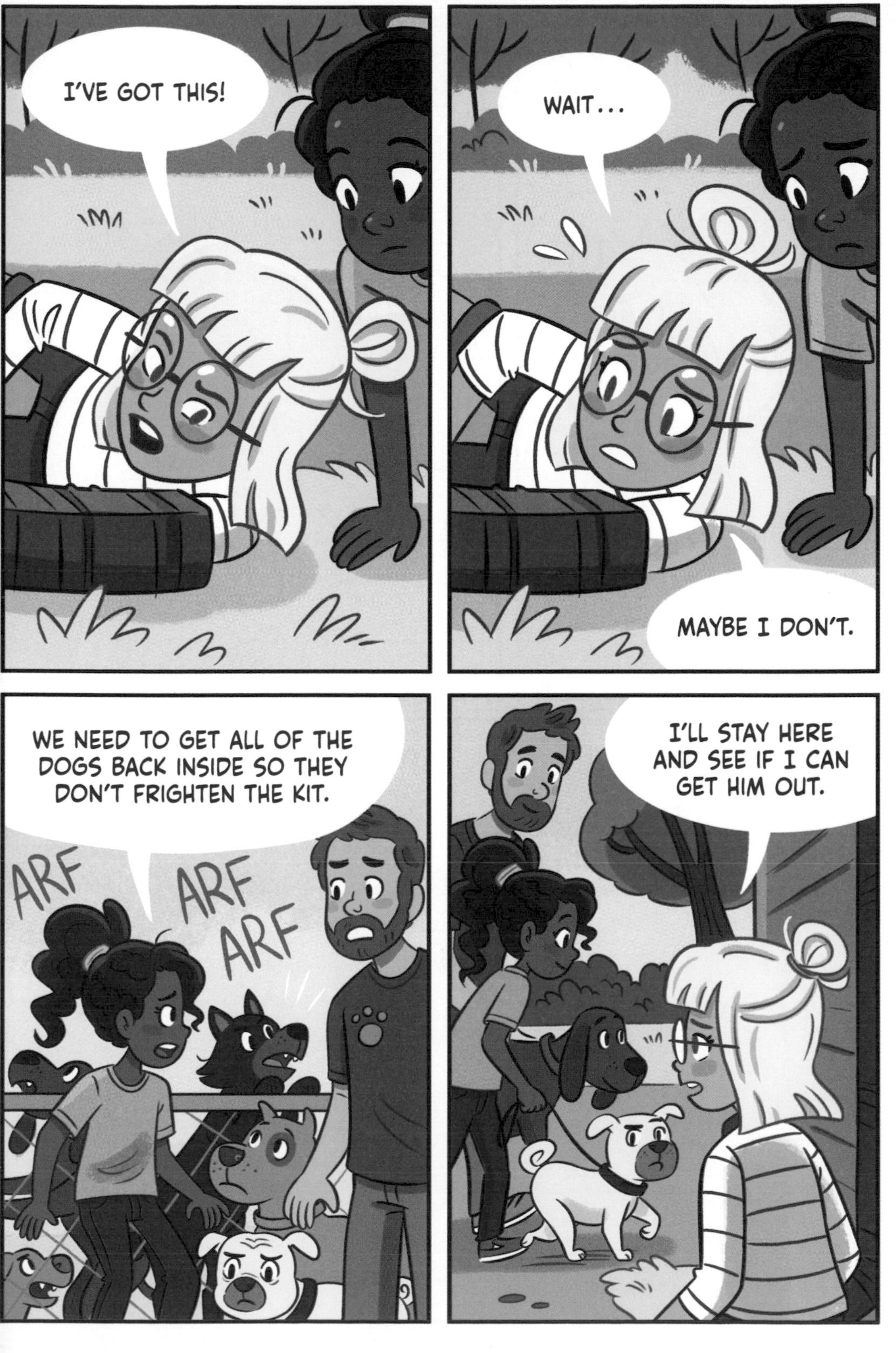
I'VE GOT THIS!
WAIT...
MAYBE I DON'T.
WE NEED TO GET ALL OF THE DOGS BACK INSIDE SO THEY DON'T FRIGHTEN THE KIT.
ARF
ARF
ARF
I'LL STAY HERE AND SEE IF I CAN GET HIM OUT.

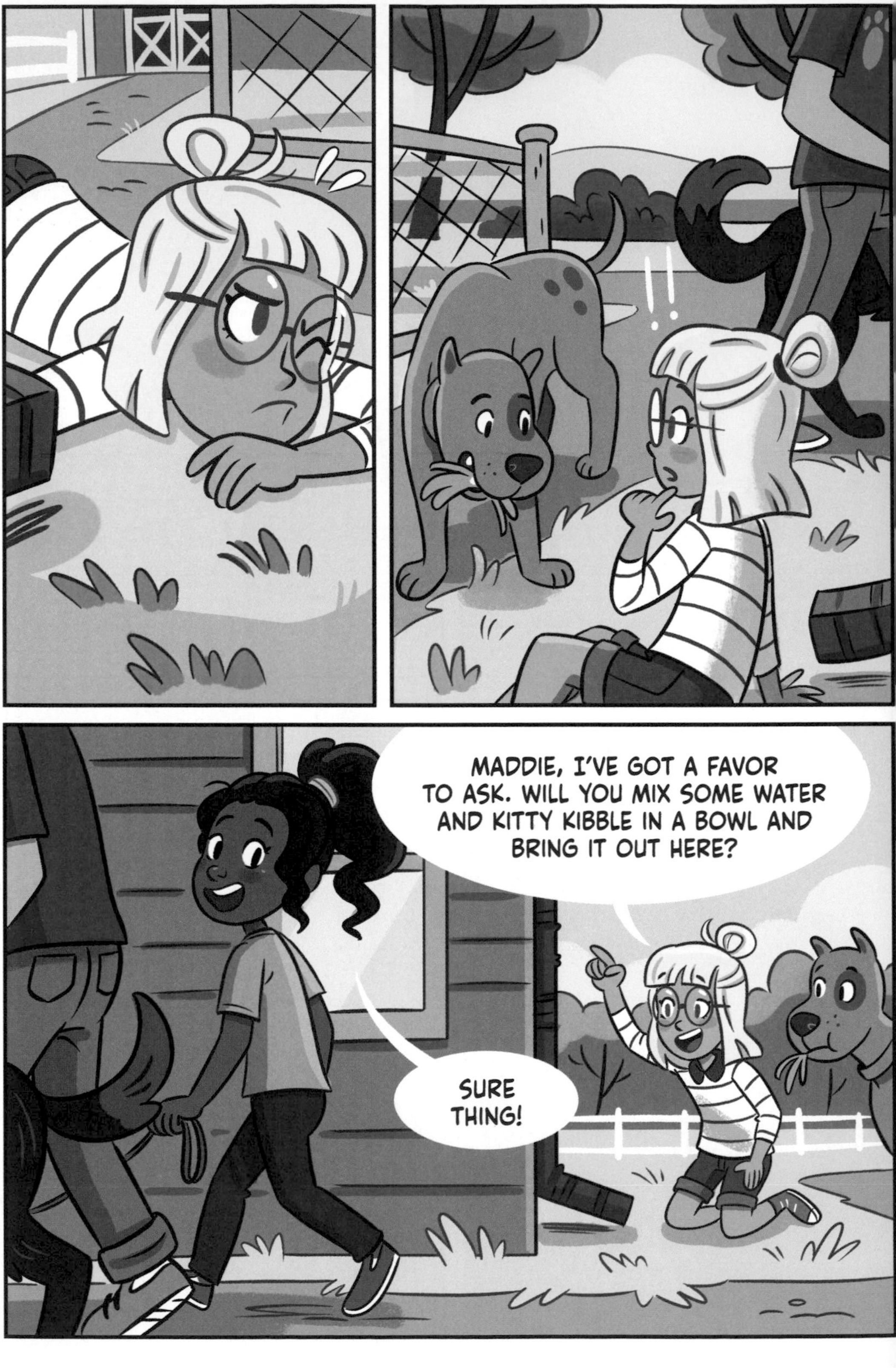
MADDIE, I'VE GOT A FAVOR TO ASK. WILL YOU MIX SOME WATER AND KITTY KIBBLE IN A BOWL AND BRING IT OUT HERE?
SURE THING!

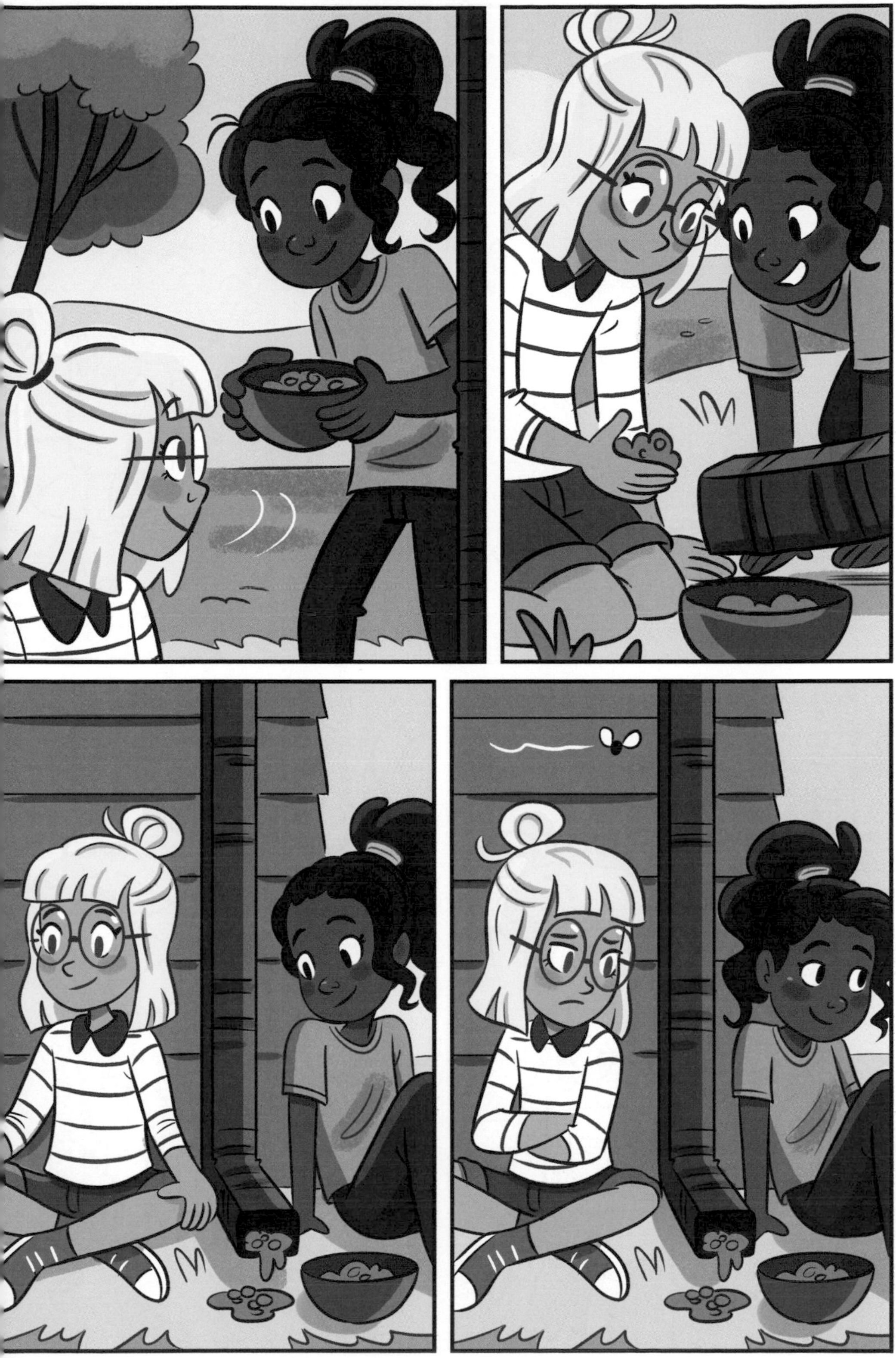

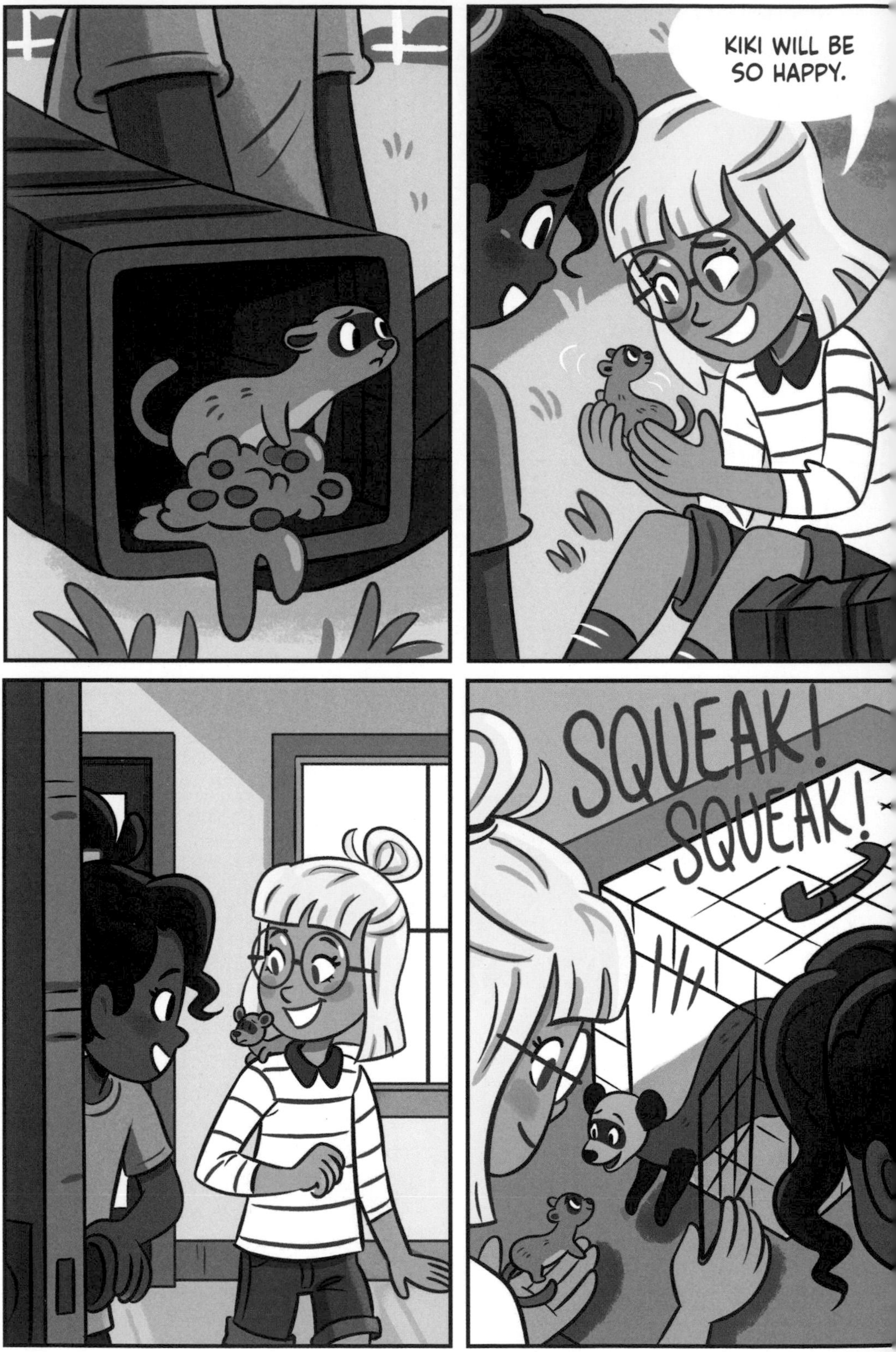
KIKI WILL BE SO HAPPY.
SQUEAK!
SQUEAK!

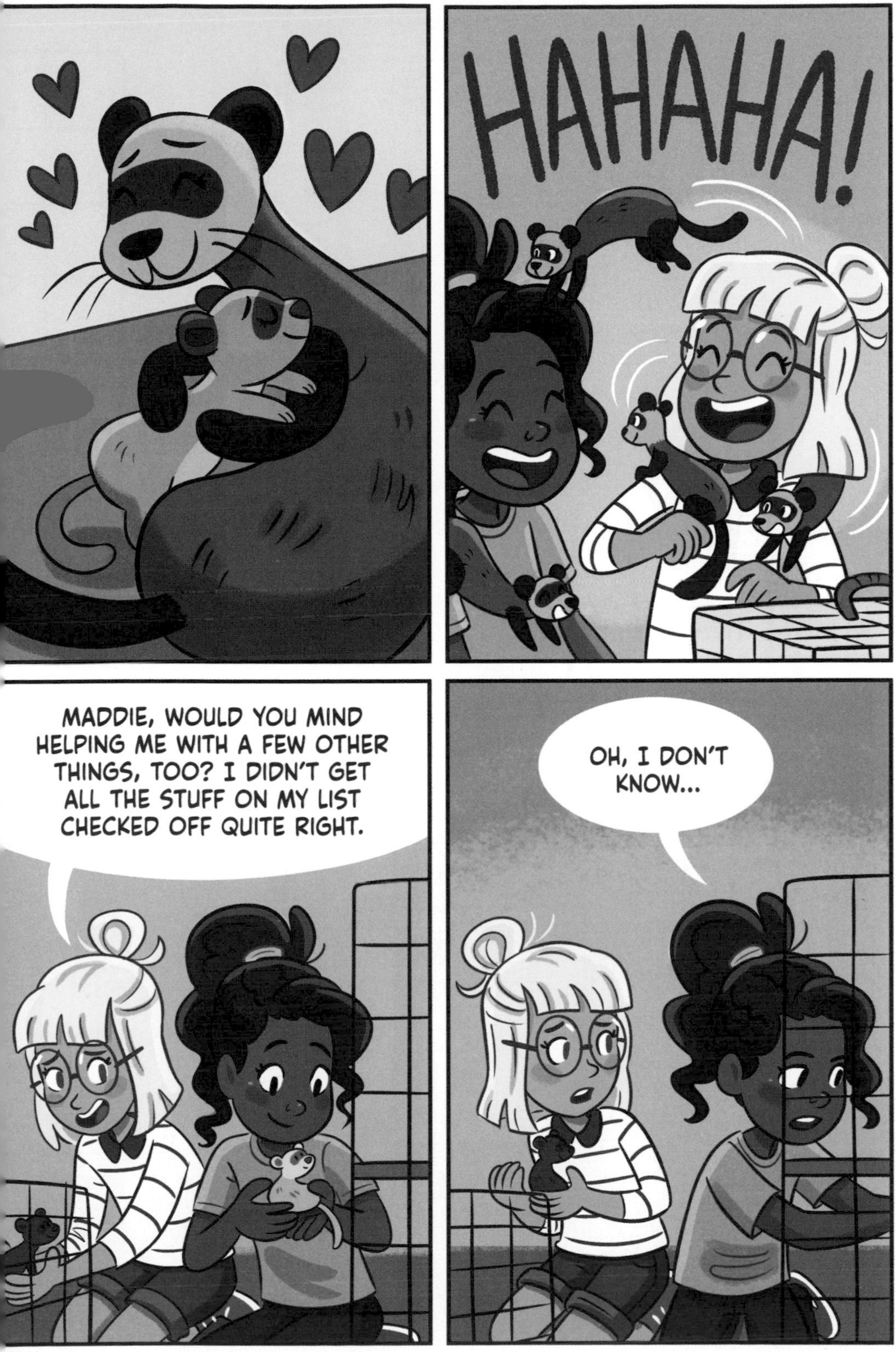
HAHAHA!
MADDIE, WOULD YOU MIND HELPING ME WITH A FEW OTHER THINGS, TOO? I DIDN'T GET ALL THE STUFF ON MY LIST CHECKED OFF QUITE RIGHT.
OH, I DON'T KNOW...

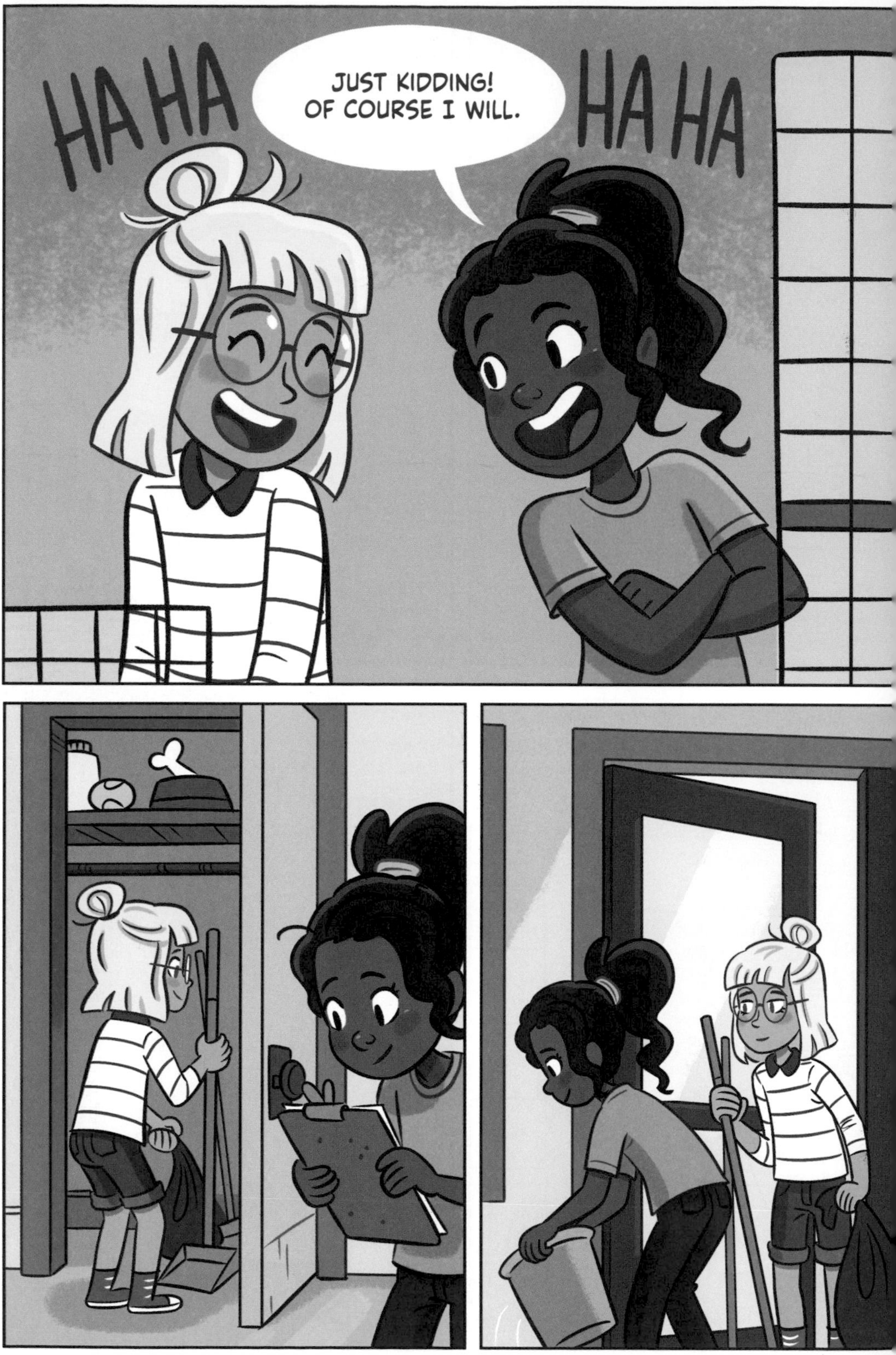
HA HA
JUST KIDDING! OF COURSE I WILL.
HA HA

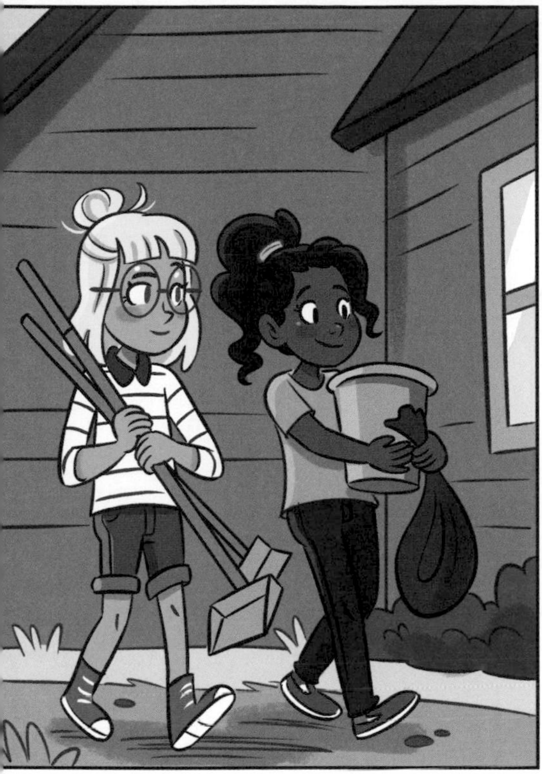

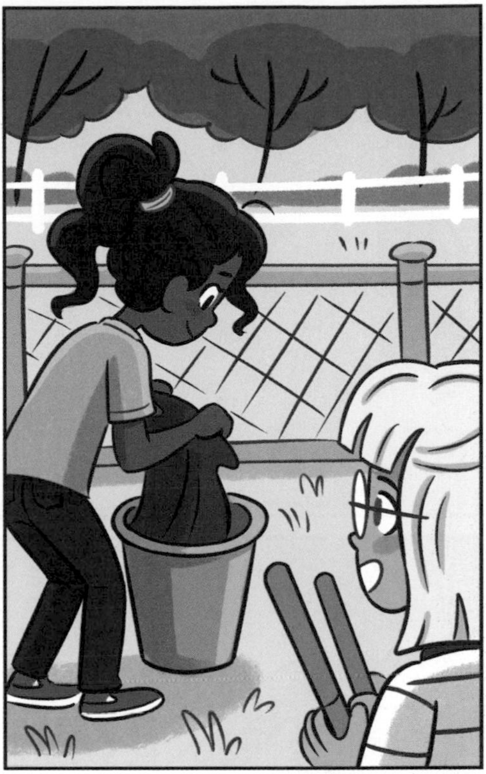

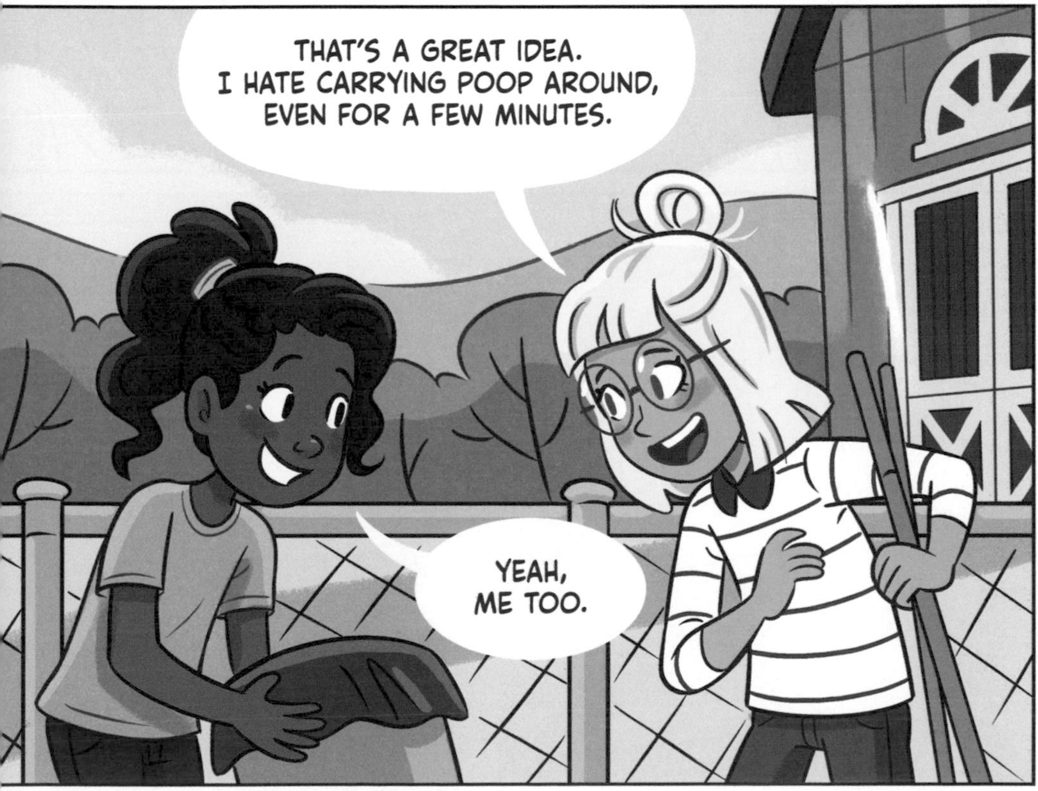
THAT'S A GREAT IDEA. I HATE CARRYING POOP AROUND, EVEN FOR A FEW MINUTES.
YEAH, ME TOO.

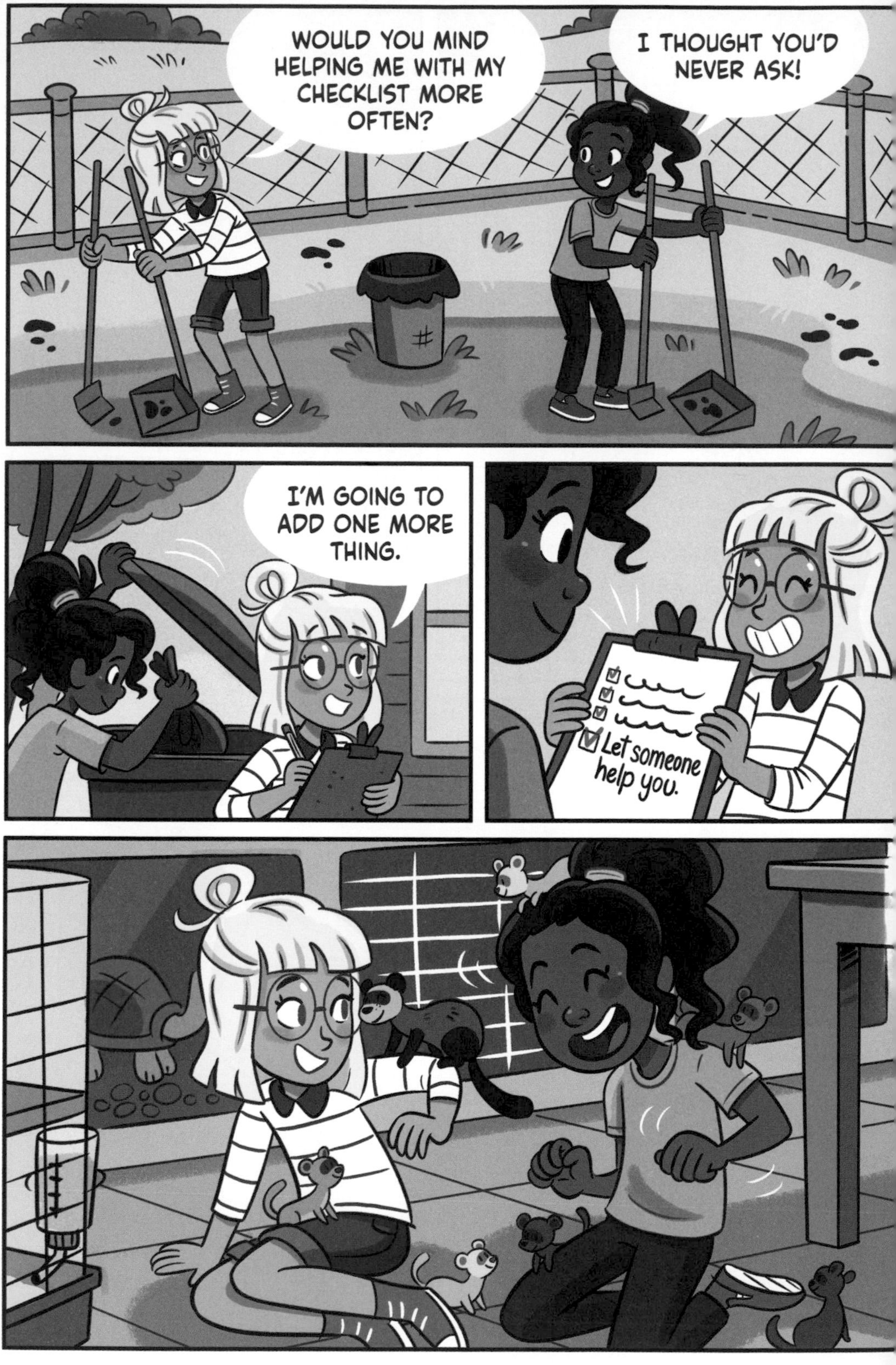
WOULD YOU MIND HELPING ME WITH MY CHECKLIST MORE OFTEN?
I THOUGHT YOU'D NEVER ASK!
I'M GOING TO ADD ONE MORE THING.
Let someone help you.

Chapter 3

MIKEY AND HOPPER

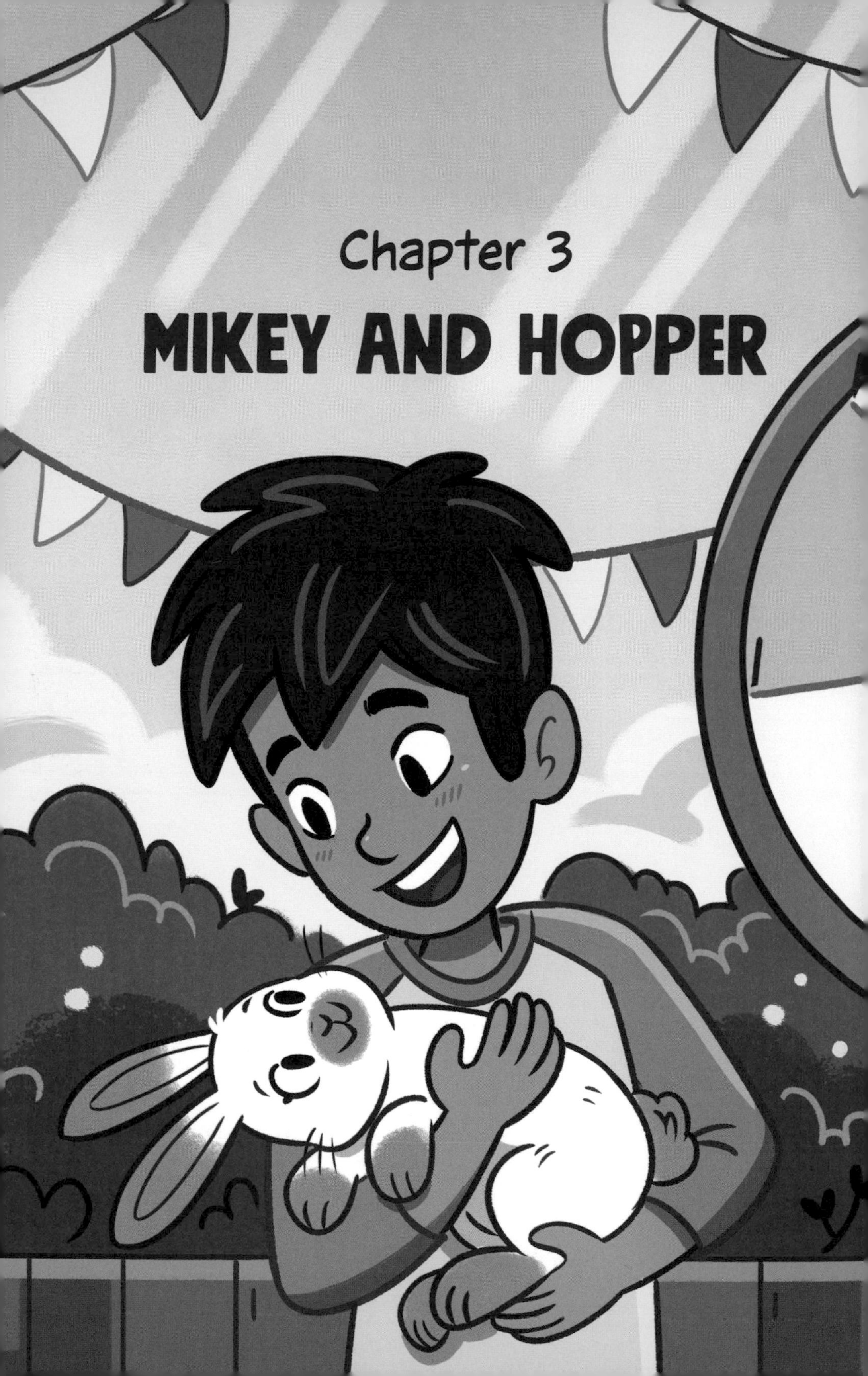

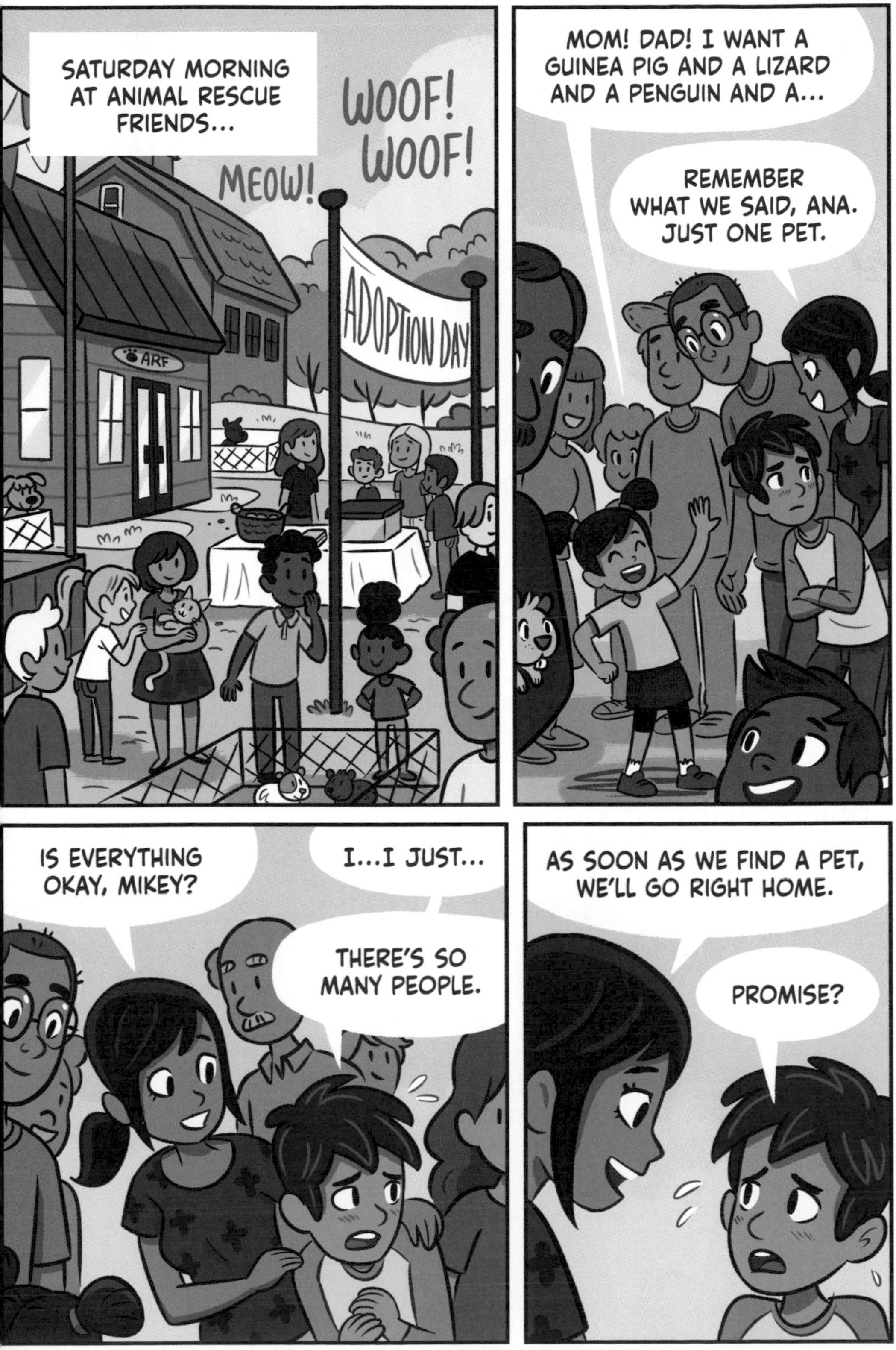
SATURDAY MORNING AT ANIMAL RESCUE FRIENDS...
WOOF! WOOF!
MEOW!
ARF
ADOPTION DAY
MOM! DAD! I WANT A GUINEA PIG AND A LIZARD AND A PENGUIN AND A...
REMEMBER WHAT WE SAID, ANA. JUST ONE PET.
IS EVERYTHING OKAY, MIKEY?
I...I JUST...
THERE'S SO MANY PEOPLE.
AS SOON AS WE FIND A PET, WE'LL GO RIGHT HOME.
PROMISE?

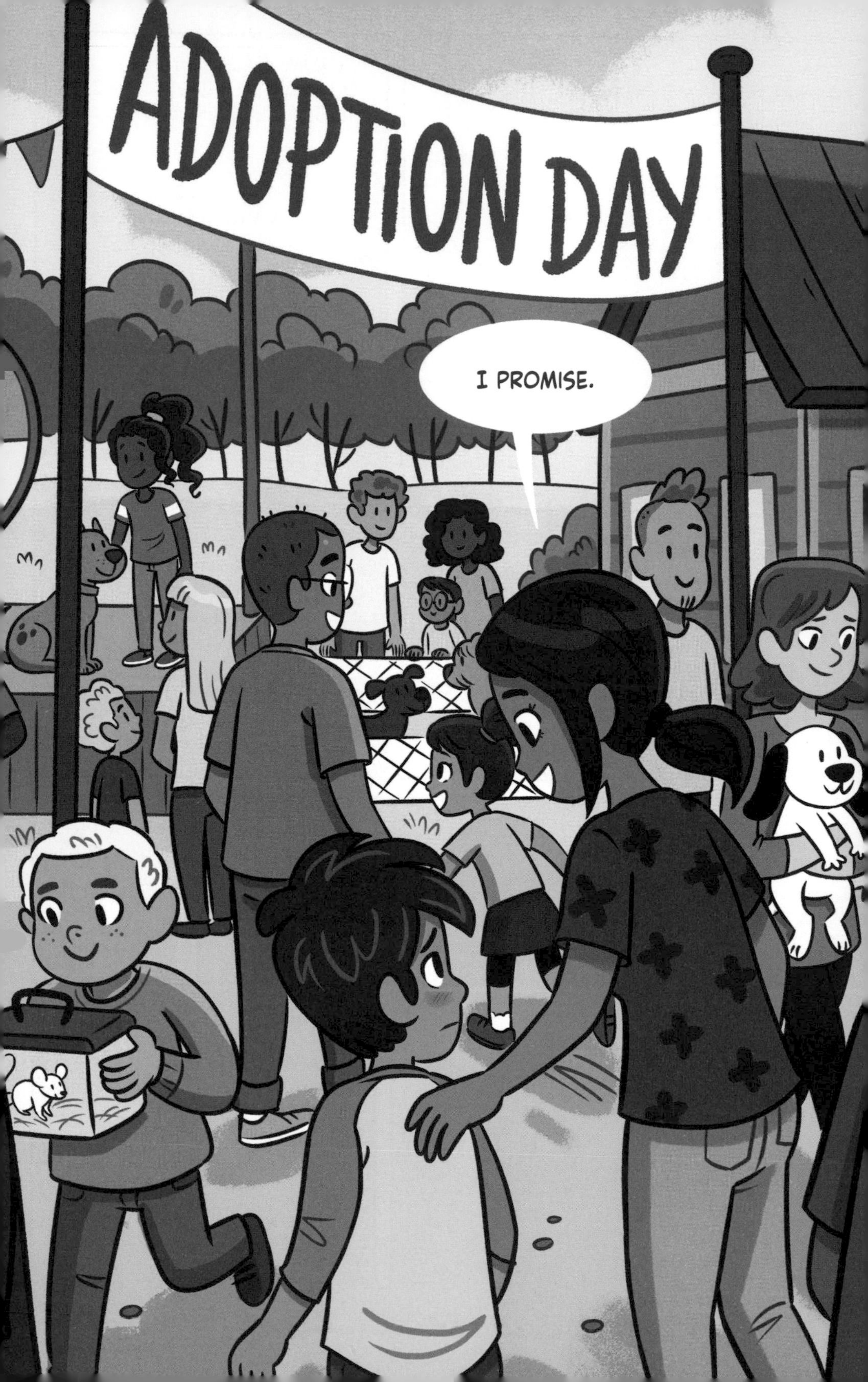
ADOPTION DAY
I PROMISE.

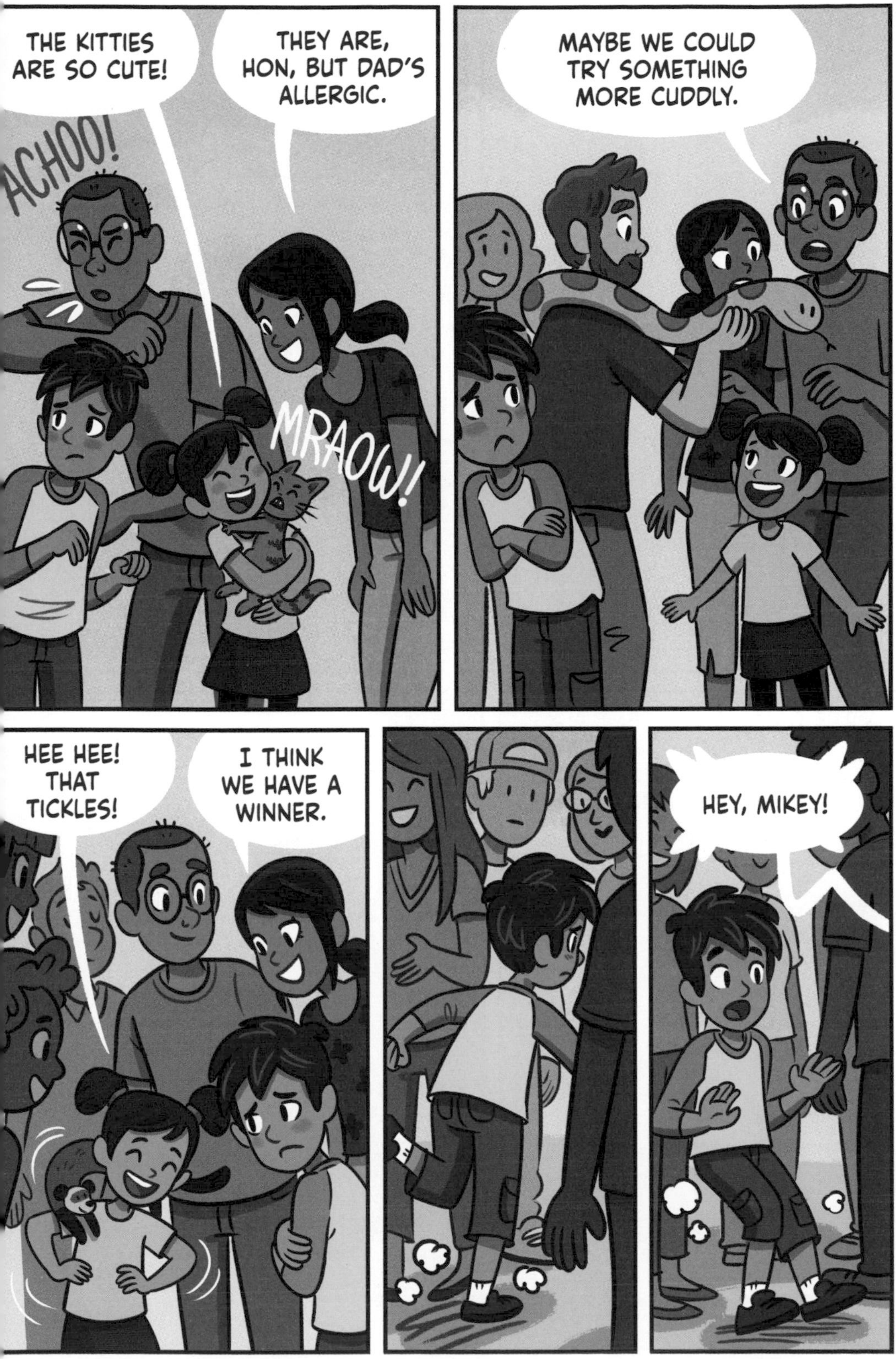
THE KITTIES ARE SO CUTE!
THEY ARE, HON, BUT DAD'S ALLERGIC.
ACHOO!
MRAOW!
MAYBE WE COULD TRY SOMETHING MORE CUDDLY.
HEE HEE! THAT TICKLES!
I THINK WE HAVE A WINNER.
HEY, MIKEY!

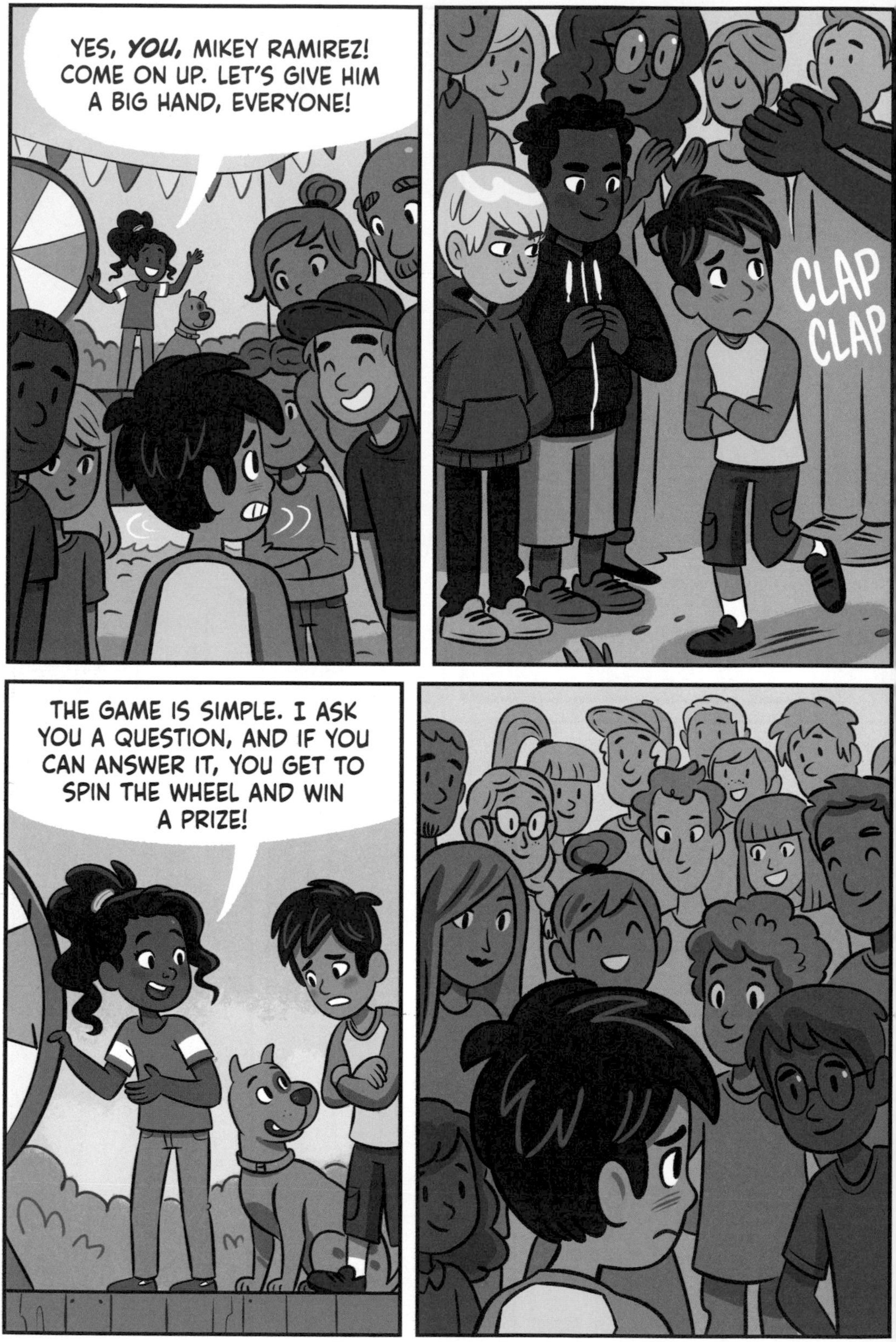
YES, ***YOU,*** MIKEY RAMIREZ! COME ON UP. LET'S GIVE HIM A BIG HAND, EVERYONE!
CLAP CLAP
THE GAME IS SIMPLE. I ASK YOU A QUESTION, AND IF YOU CAN ANSWER IT, YOU GET TO SPIN THE WHEEL AND WIN A PRIZE!

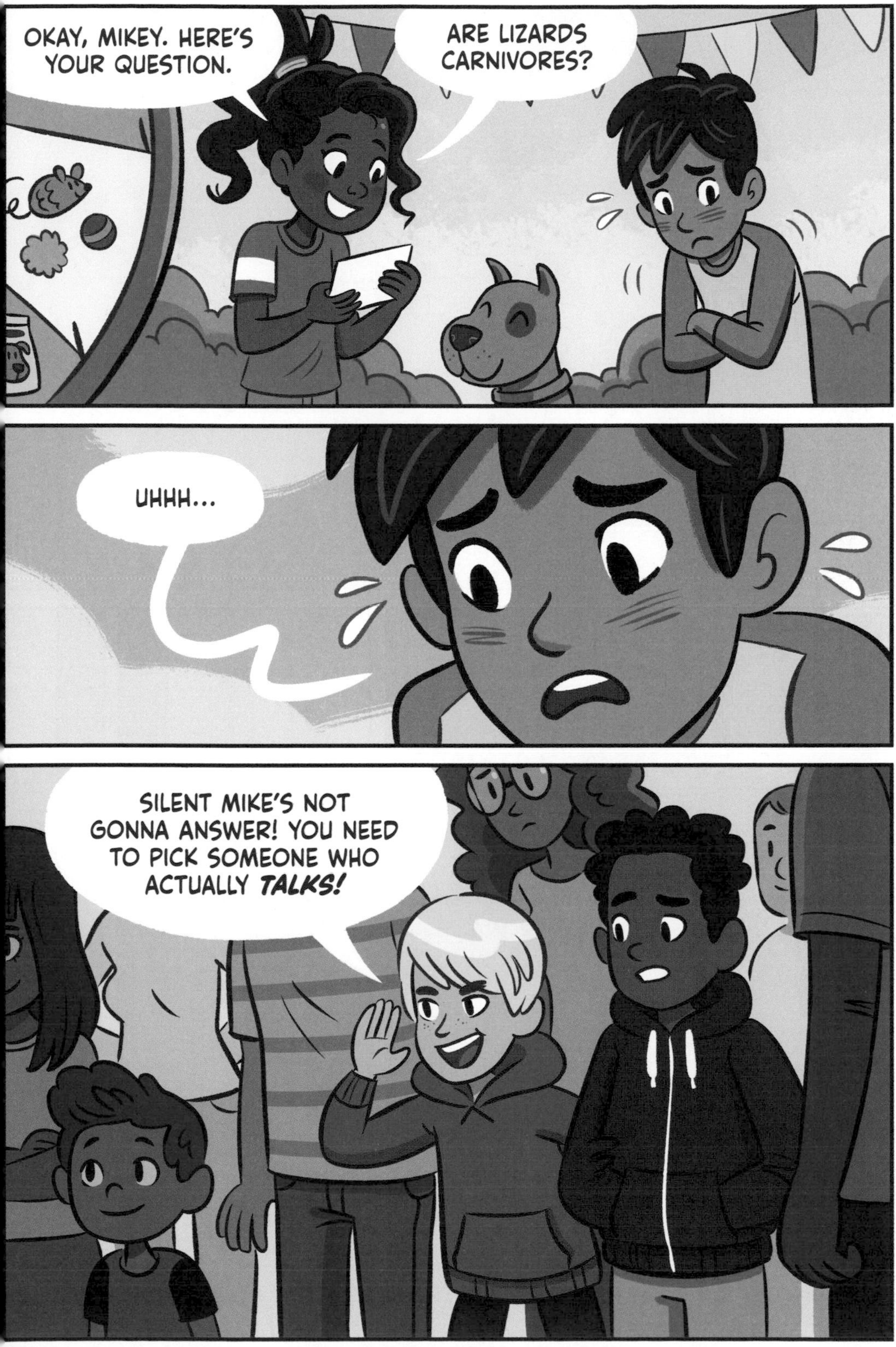
OKAY, MIKEY. HERE'S YOUR QUESTION.
ARE LIZARDS CARNIVORES?
UHHH...
SILENT MIKE'S NOT GONNA ANSWER! YOU NEED TO PICK SOMEONE WHO ACTUALLY ***TALKS!***

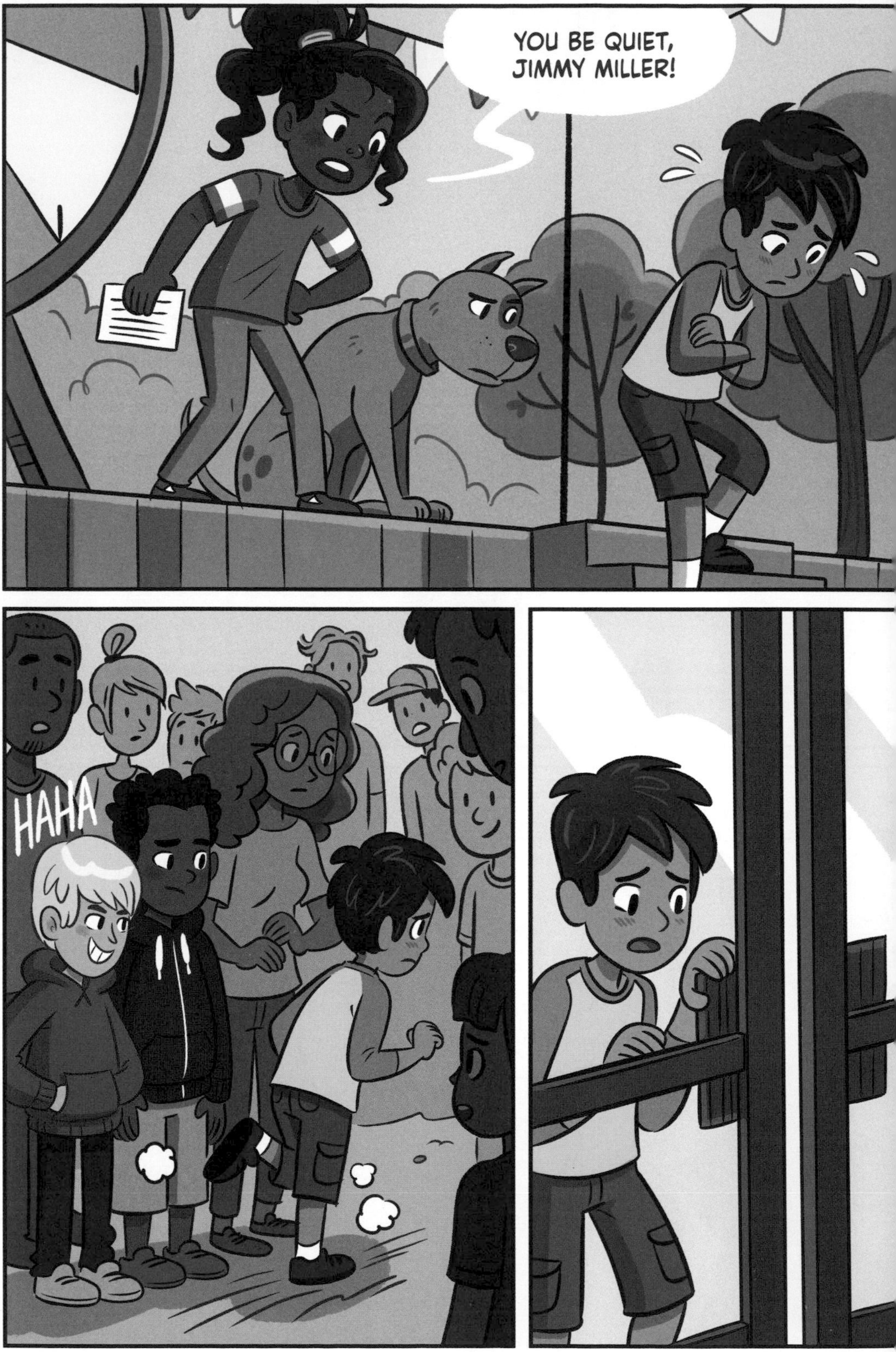
YOU BE QUIET, JIMMY MILLER!
HAHA

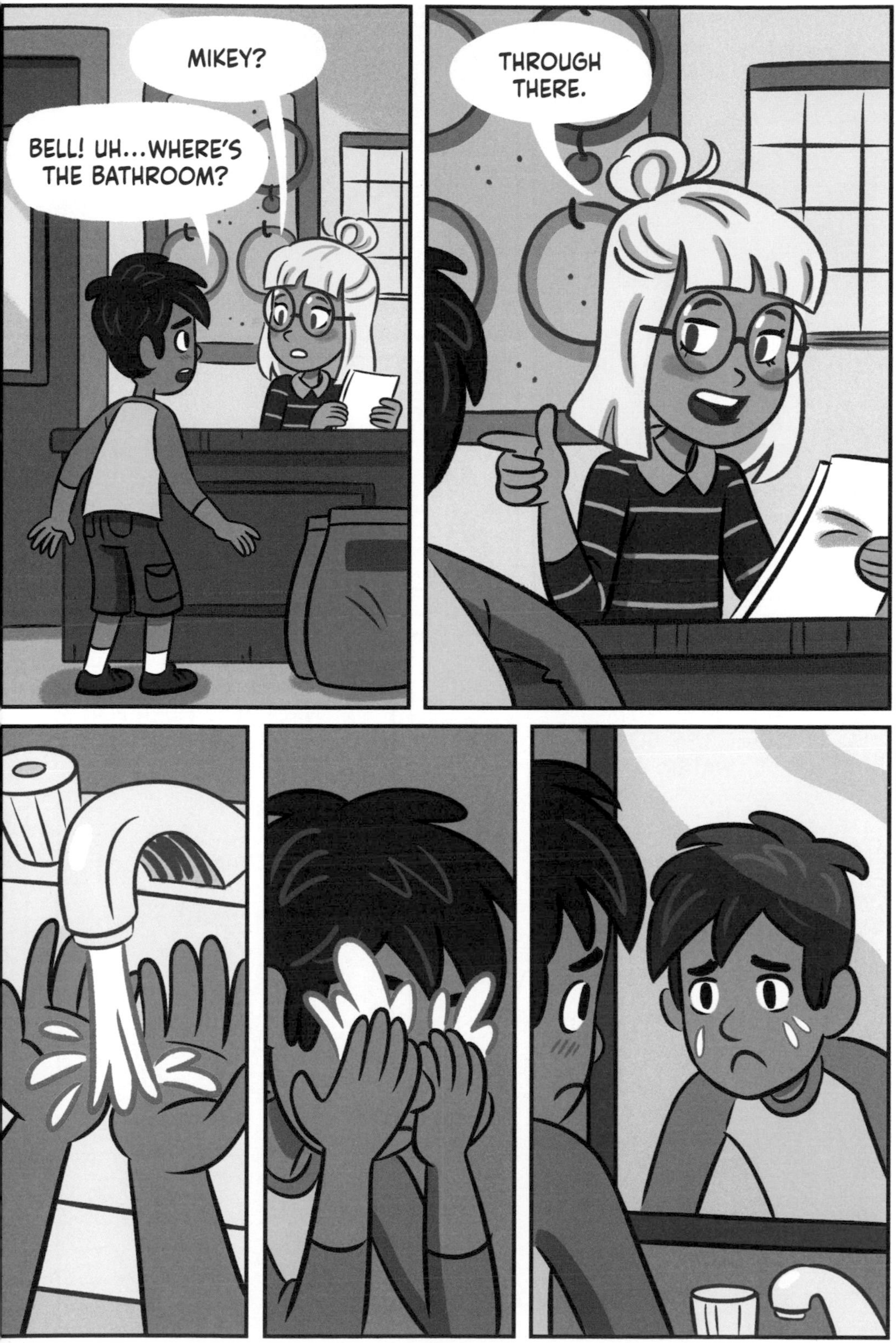
MIKEY?
BELL! UH...WHERE'S THE BATHROOM?
THROUGH THERE.

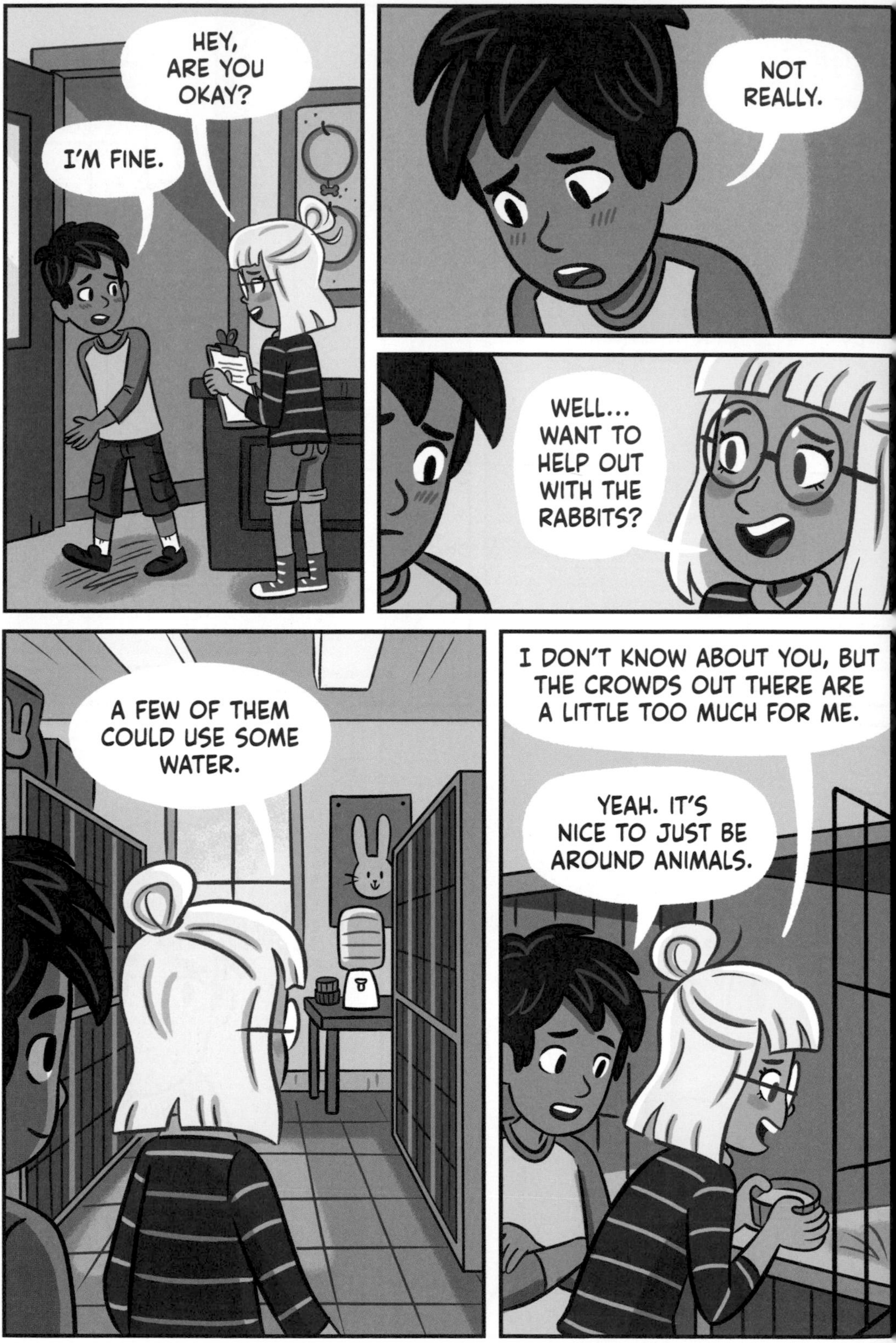
HEY, ARE YOU OKAY?
I'M FINE.
NOT REALLY.
WELL... WANT TO HELP OUT WITH THE RABBITS?
A FEW OF THEM COULD USE SOME WATER.
I DON'T KNOW ABOUT YOU, BUT THE CROWDS OUT THERE ARE A LITTLE TOO MUCH FOR ME.
YEAH. IT'S NICE TO JUST BE AROUND ANIMALS.

IS THIS ONE OKAY?

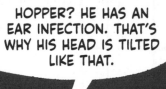

HOPPER? HE HAS AN EAR INFECTION. THAT'S WHY HIS HEAD IS TILTED LIKE THAT.

IS HE IN ANY PAIN?

NO. HE'S BEEN GETTING BETTER, BUT EVEN IF HOPPER HAD HEAD TILT FOREVER, HE'D BE OKAY.

RABBITS CAN LIVE HAPPY LIVES, EVEN OFF-BALANCE.

HUH.

I HAVE TO CHECK ON THE FRONT DESK. DO YOU WANT TO STAY AND GIVE THE RABBITS SOME HAY?

SURE!

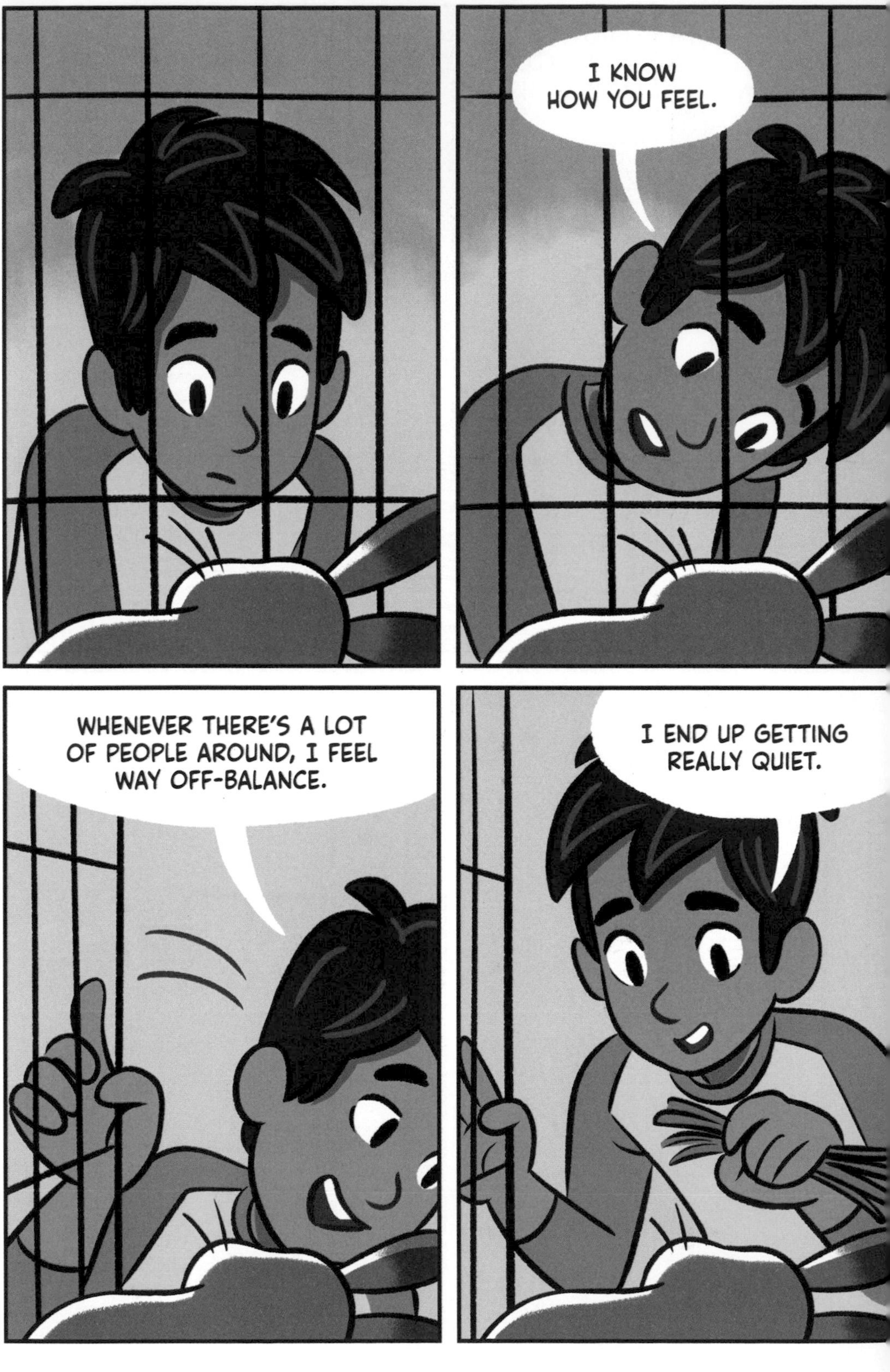
I KNOW HOW YOU FEEL.
WHENEVER THERE'S A LOT OF PEOPLE AROUND, I FEEL WAY OFF-BALANCE.
I END UP GETTING REALLY QUIET.

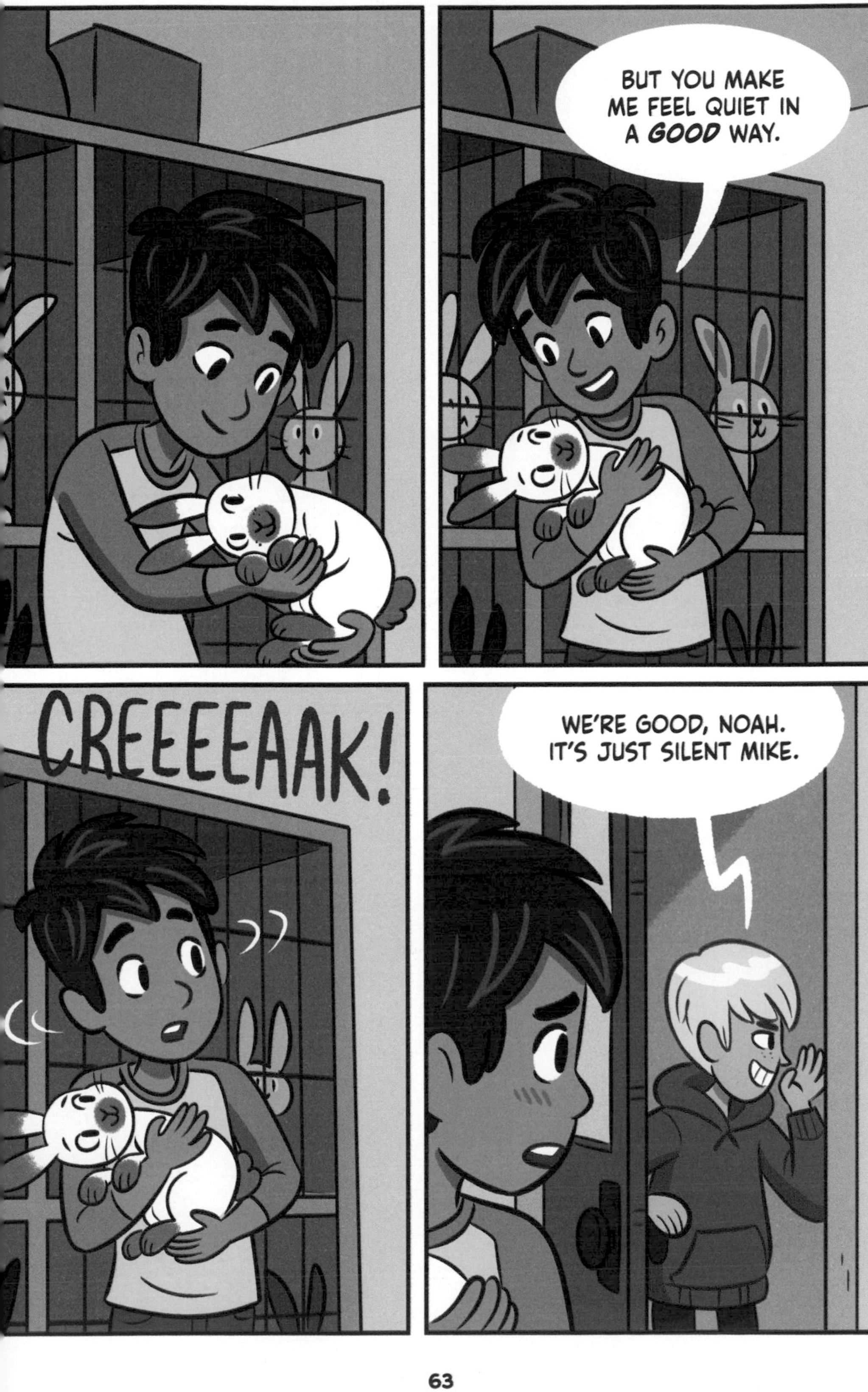
BUT YOU MAKE ME FEEL QUIET IN A *GOOD* WAY.
CREEEEAAK!
WE'RE GOOD, NOAH. IT'S JUST SILENT MIKE.

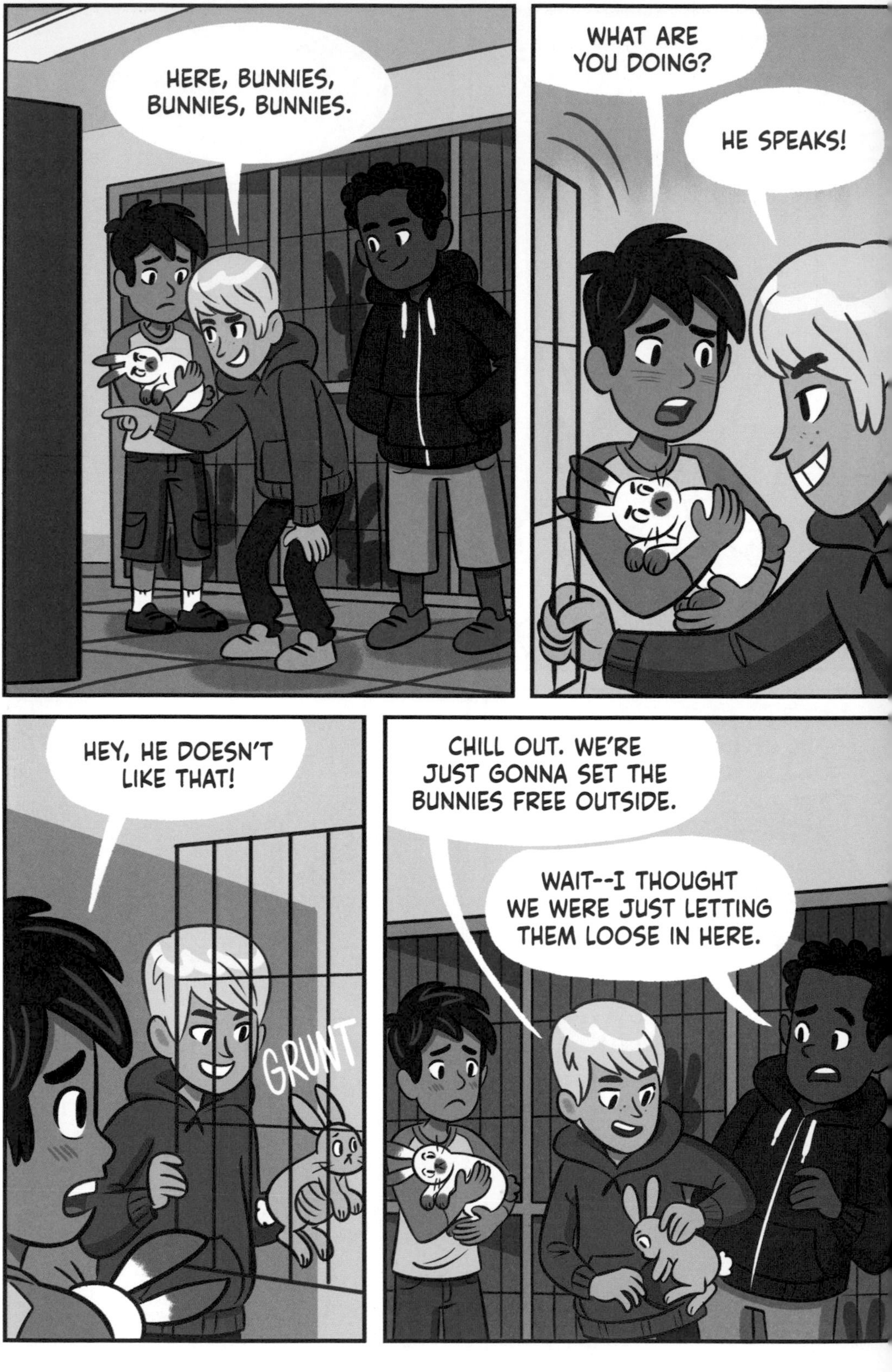
HERE, BUNNIES, BUNNIES, BUNNIES.
WHAT ARE YOU DOING?
HE SPEAKS!
HEY, HE DOESN'T LIKE THAT!
GRUNT
CHILL OUT. WE'RE JUST GONNA SET THE BUNNIES FREE OUTSIDE.
WAIT--I THOUGHT WE WERE JUST LETTING THEM LOOSE IN HERE.

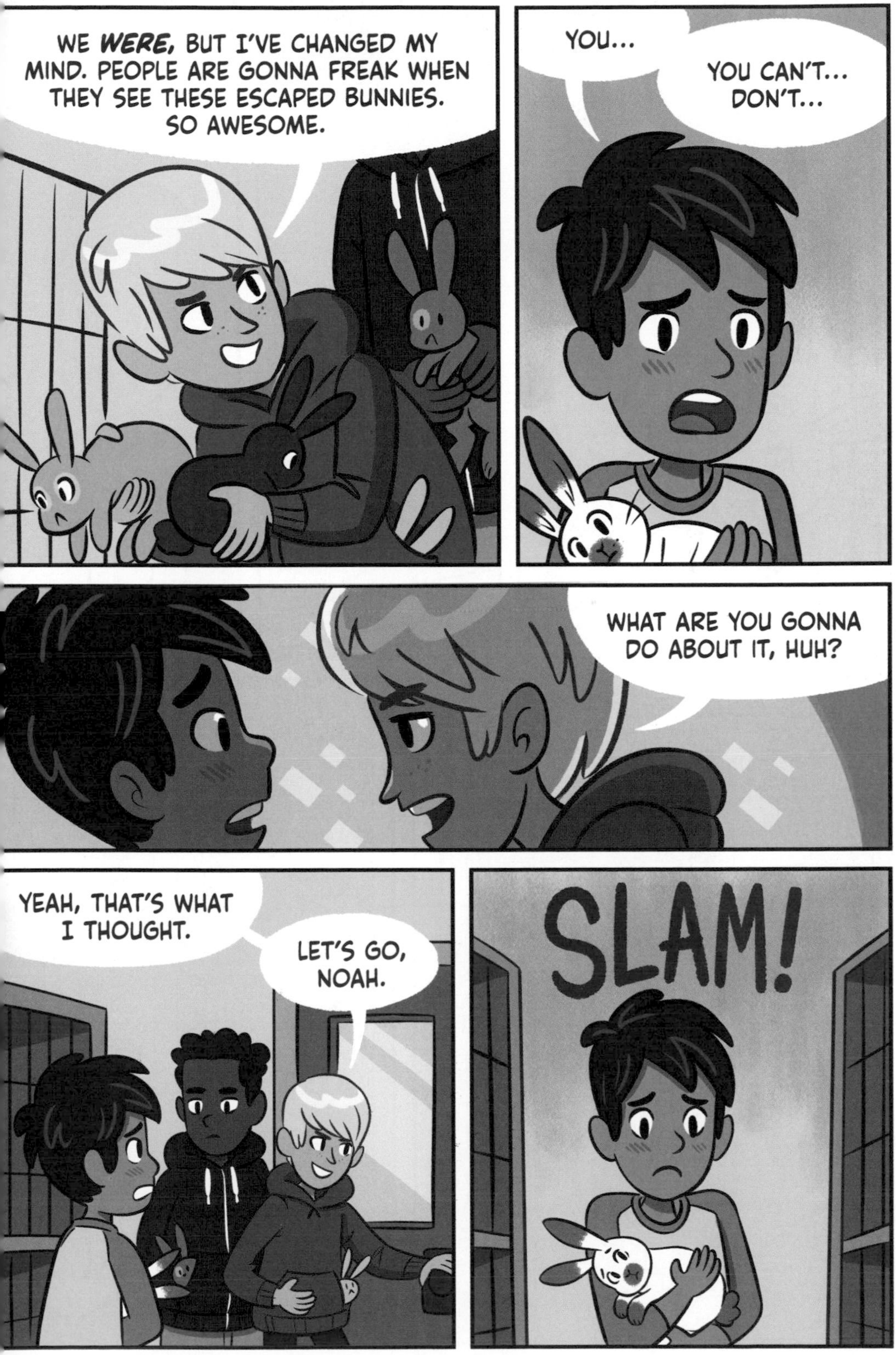
WE *WERE,* BUT I'VE CHANGED MY MIND. PEOPLE ARE GONNA FREAK WHEN THEY SEE THESE ESCAPED BUNNIES. SO AWESOME.
YOU...
YOU CAN'T... DON'T...
WHAT ARE YOU GONNA DO ABOUT IT, HUH?
YEAH, THAT'S WHAT I THOUGHT.
LET'S GO, NOAH.
SLAM!

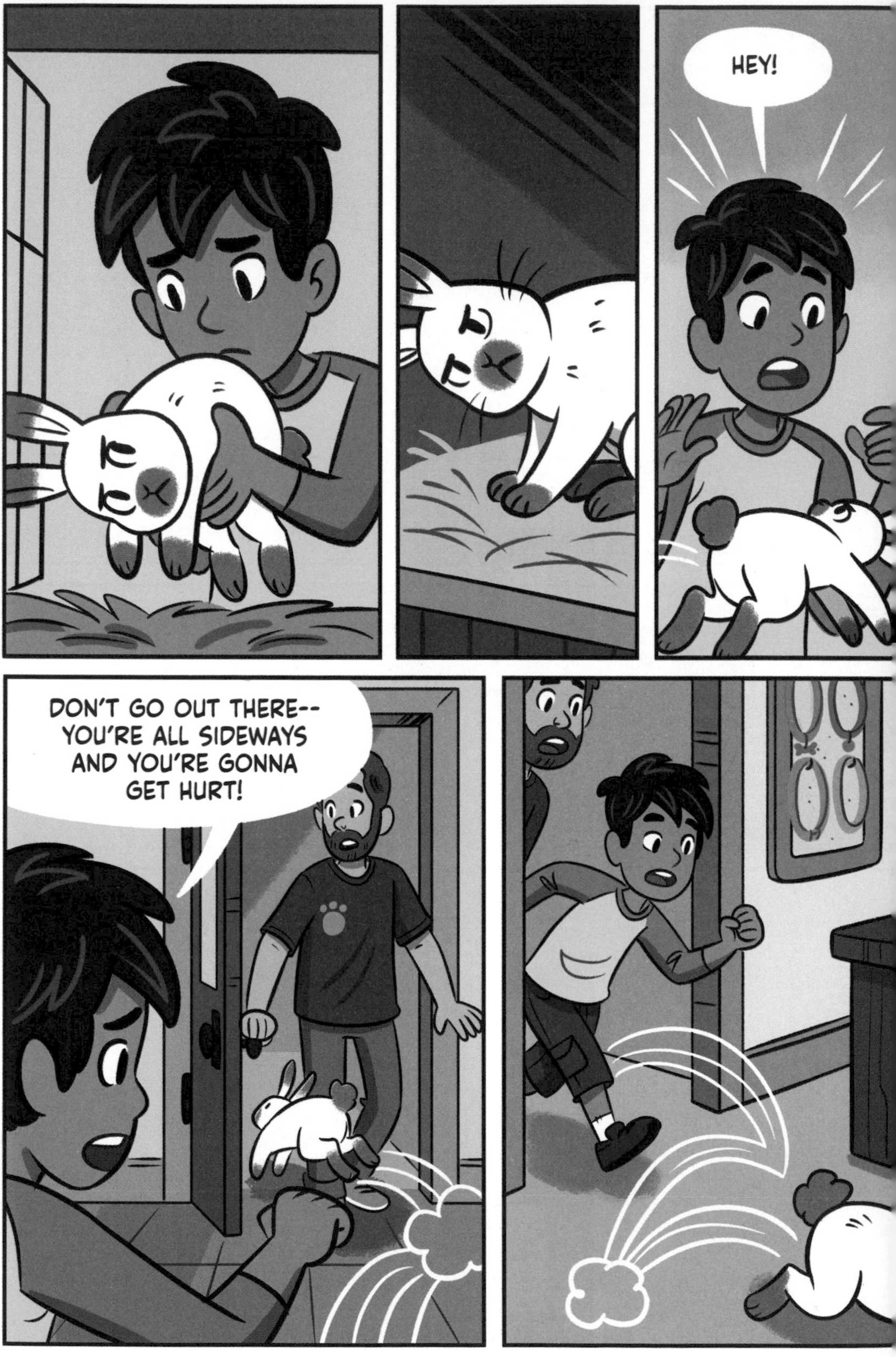
HEY!
DON'T GO OUT THERE-- YOU'RE ALL SIDEWAYS AND YOU'RE GONNA GET HURT!

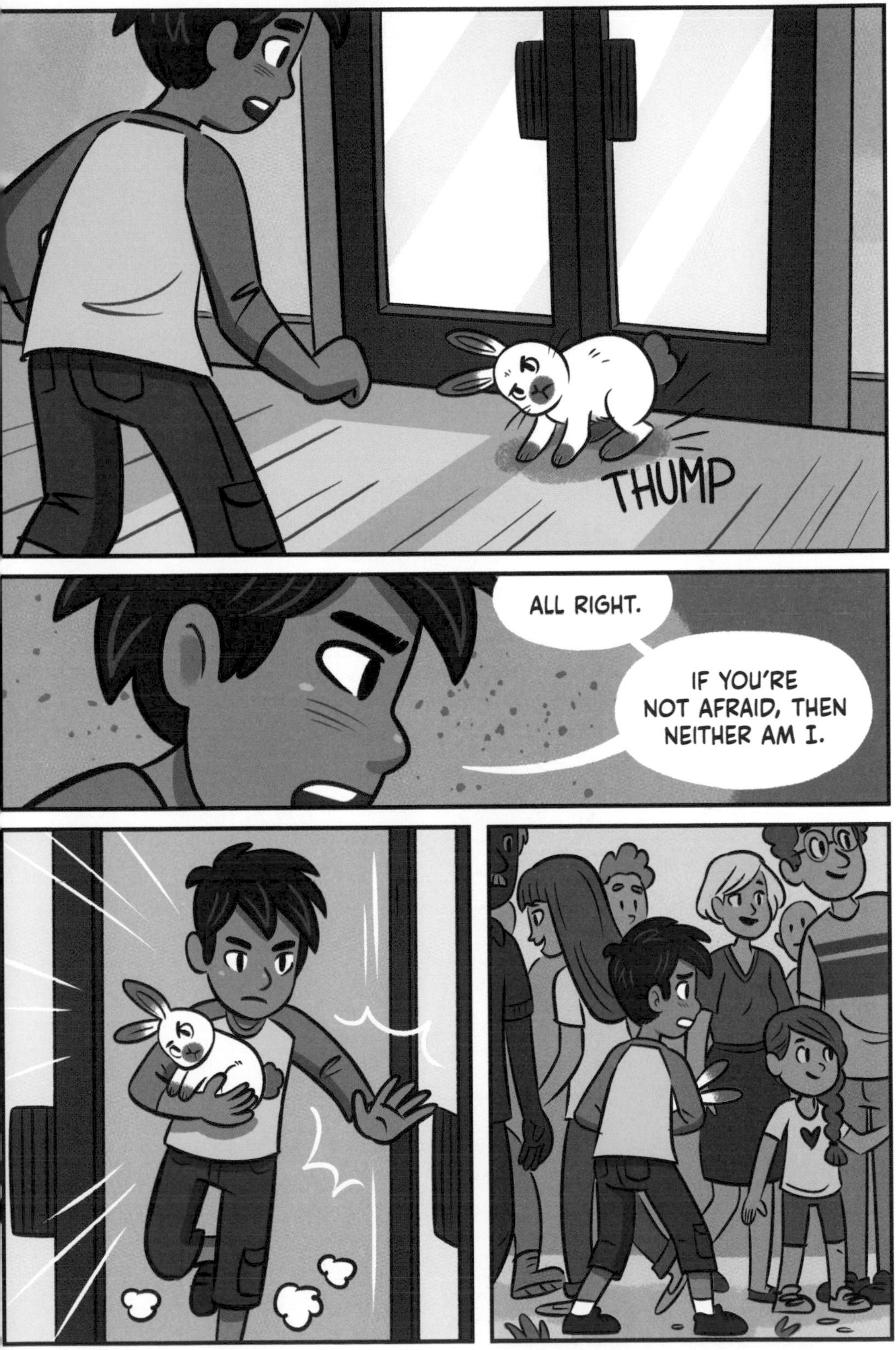
THUMP
ALL RIGHT.
IF YOU'RE NOT AFRAID, THEN NEITHER AM I.

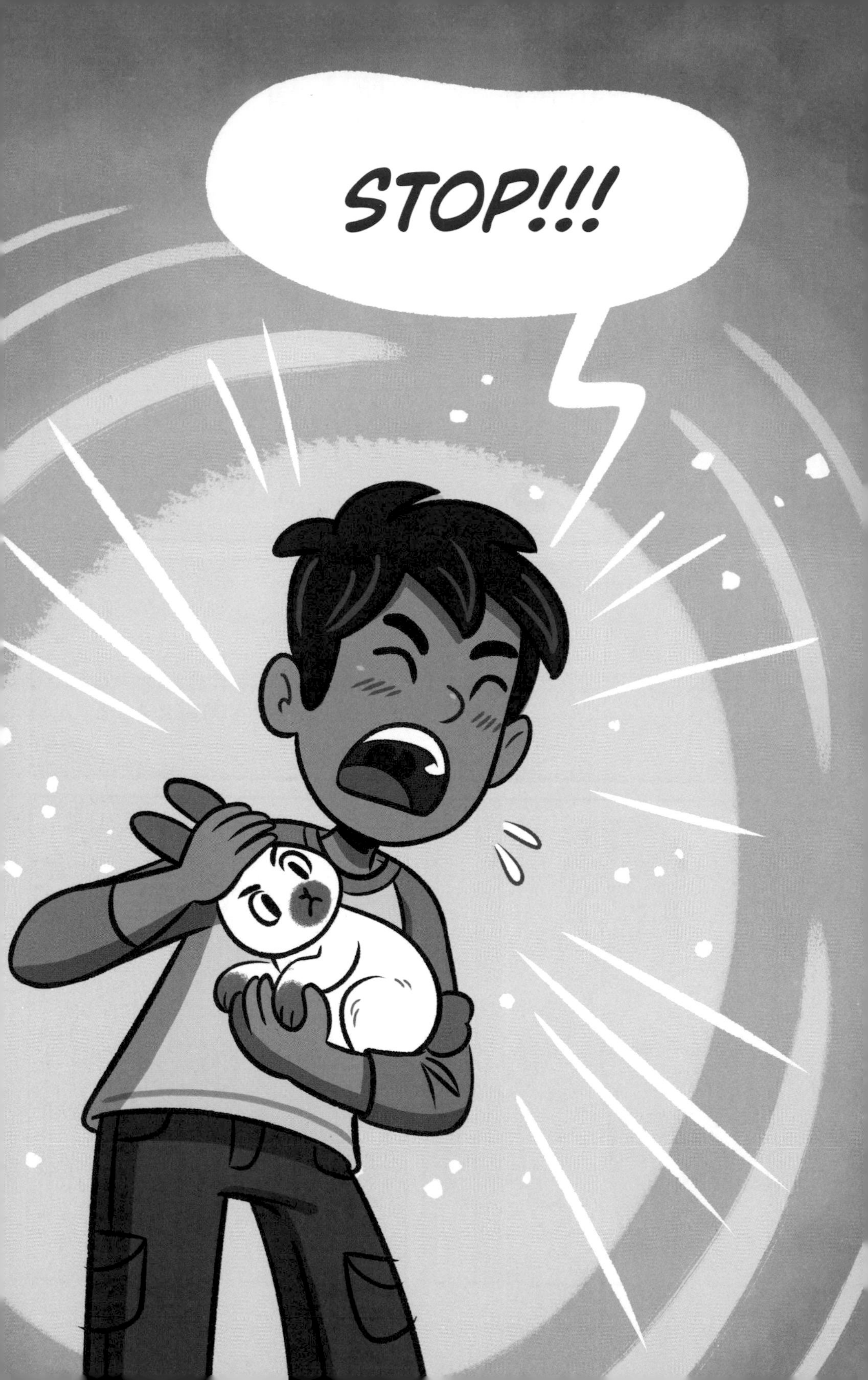
STOP!!!

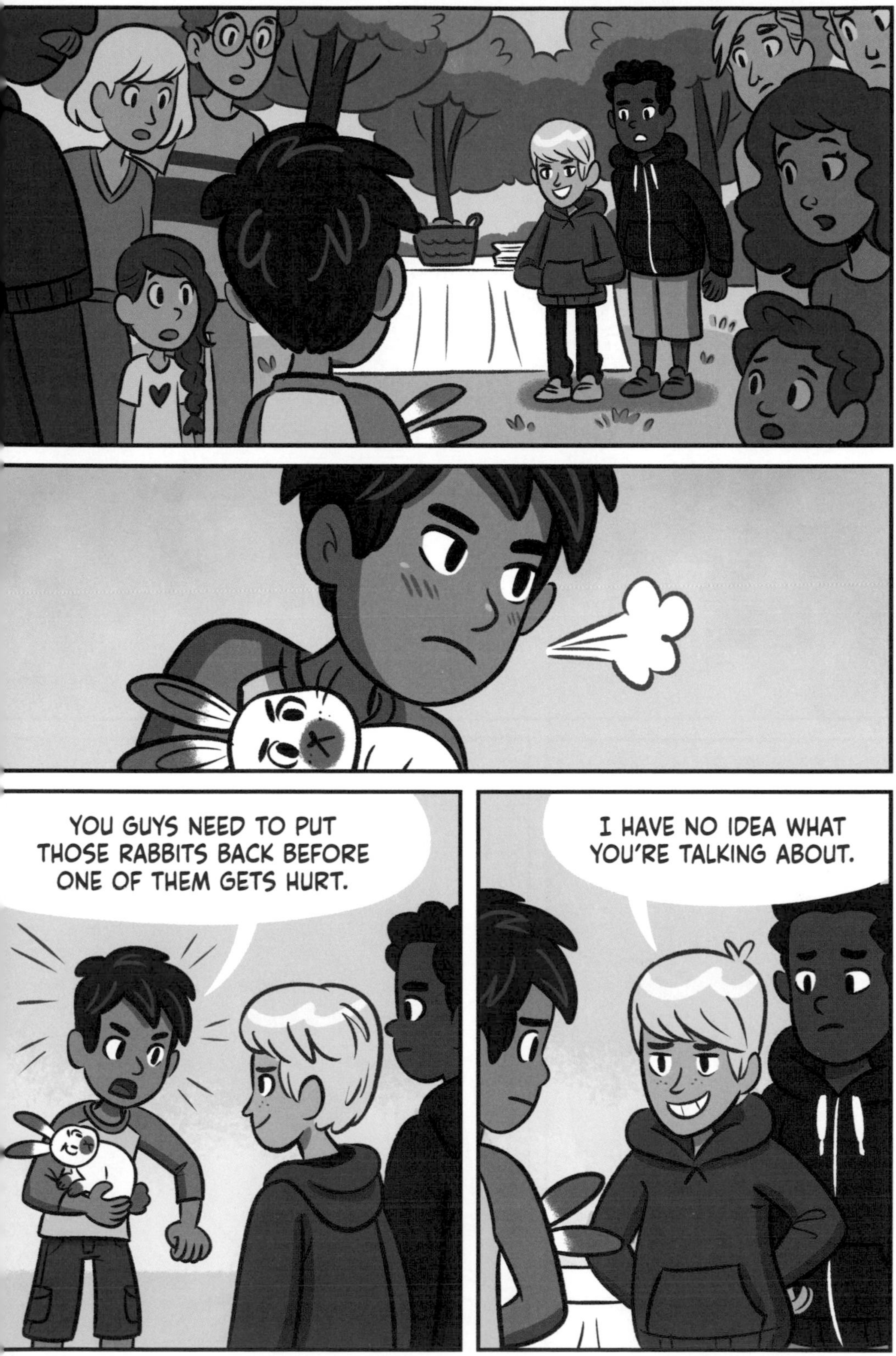
YOU GUYS NEED TO PUT THOSE RABBITS BACK BEFORE ONE OF THEM GETS HURT.
I HAVE NO IDEA WHAT YOU'RE TALKING ABOUT.

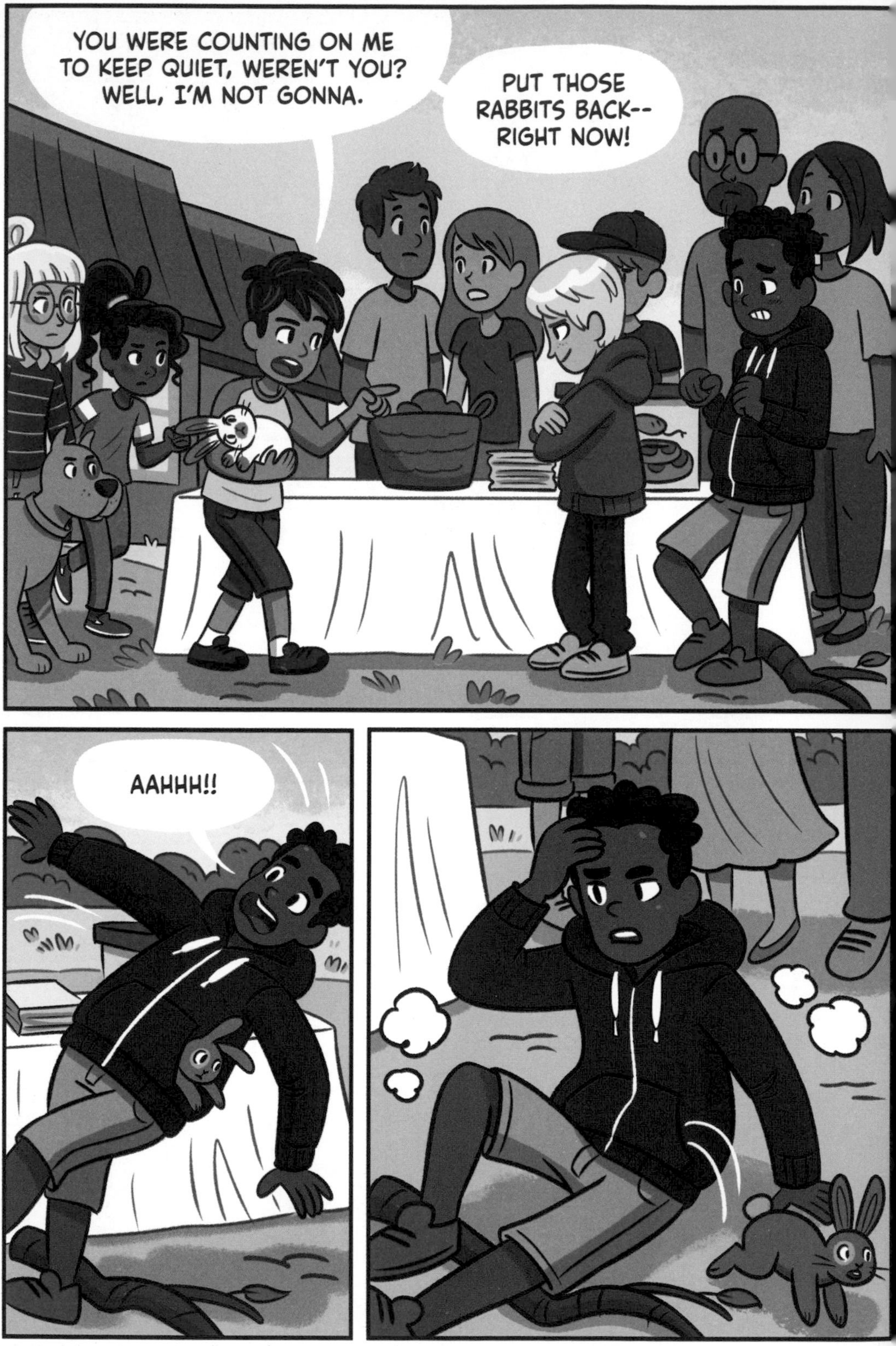
YOU WERE COUNTING ON ME TO KEEP QUIET, WEREN'T YOU? WELL, I'M NOT GONNA.
PUT THOSE RABBITS BACK-- RIGHT NOW!
AAHHH!!

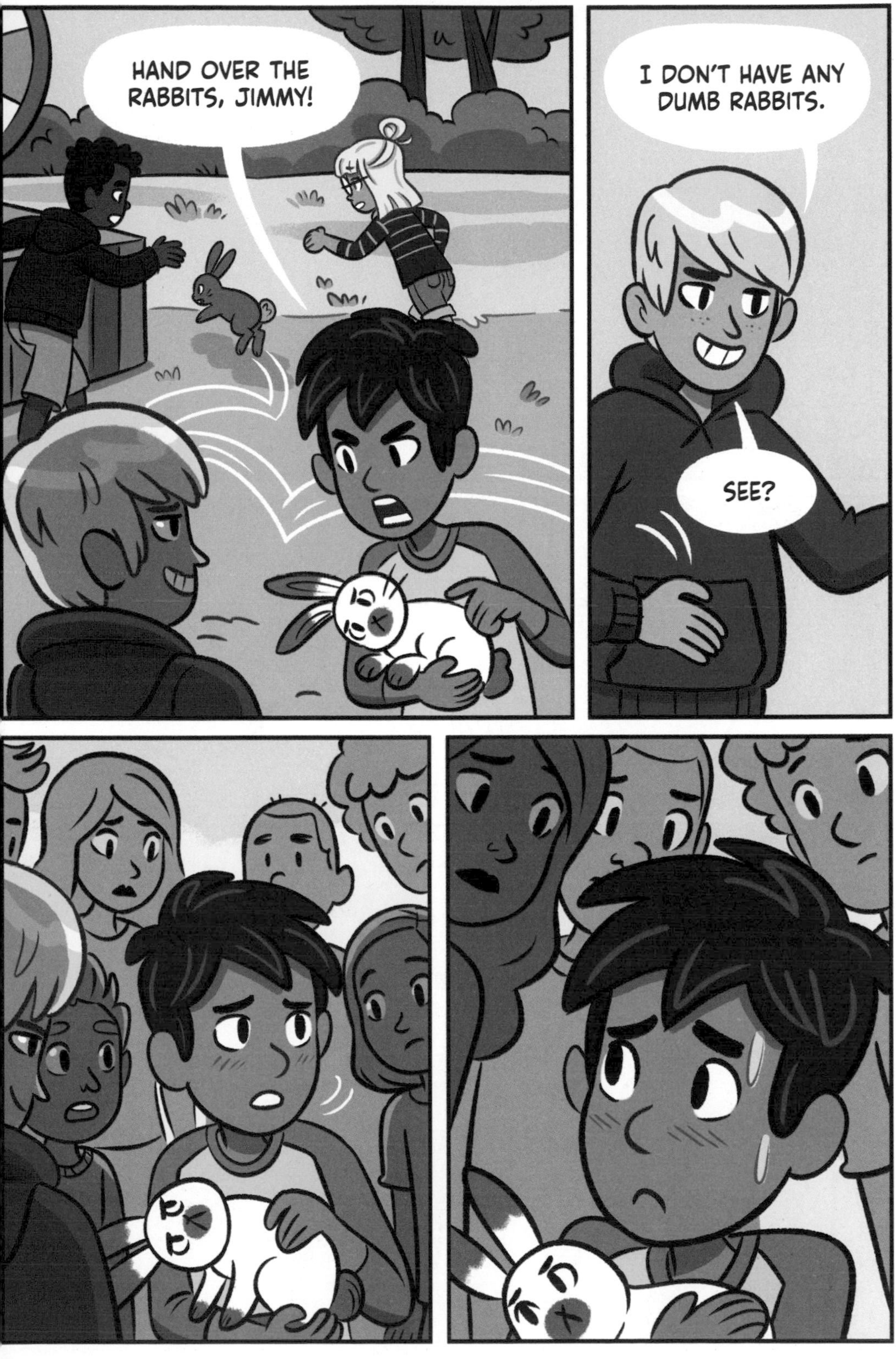
HAND OVER THE RABBITS, JIMMY!
I DON'T HAVE ANY DUMB RABBITS.
SEE?

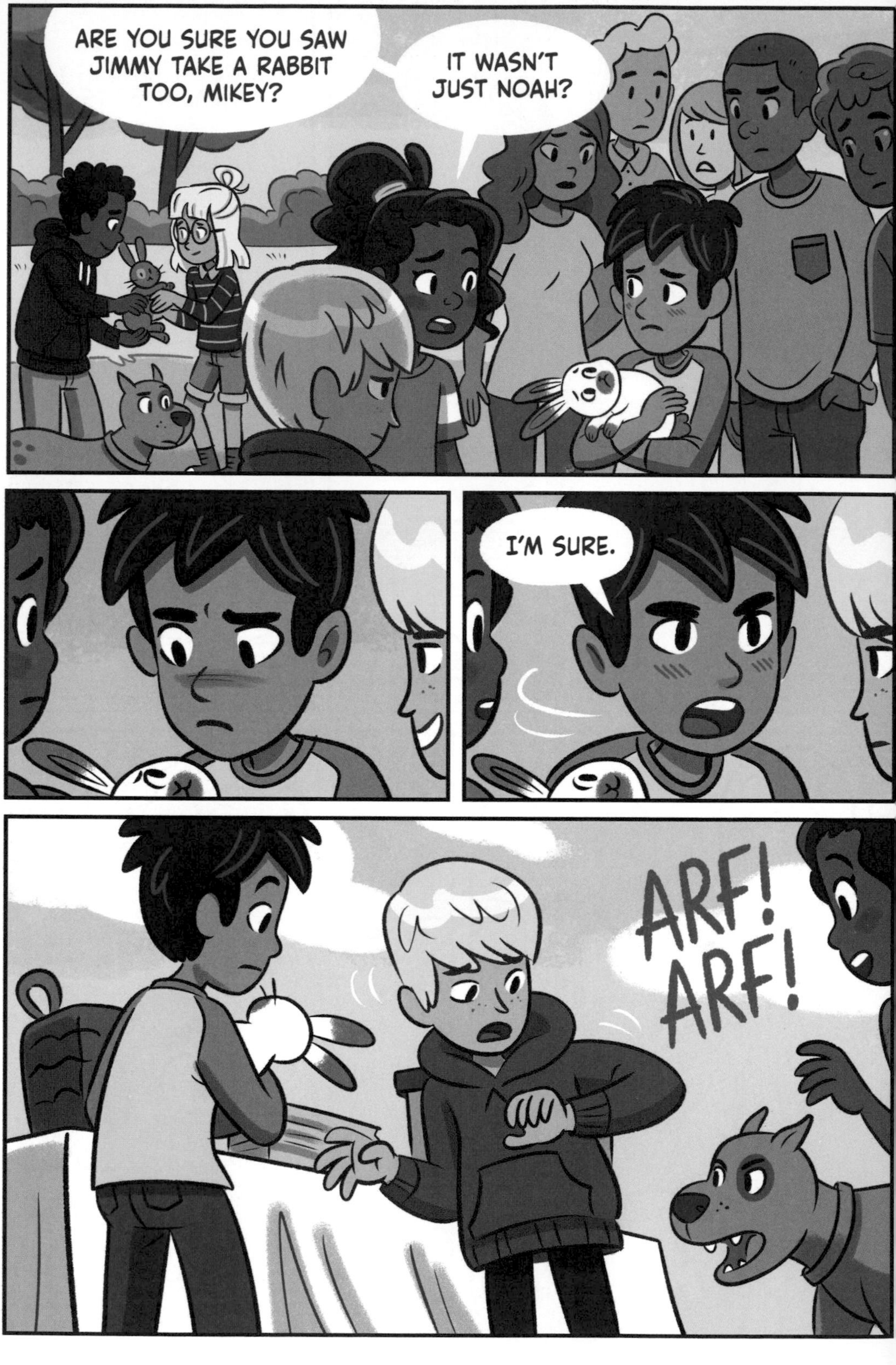
ARE YOU SURE YOU SAW JIMMY TAKE A RABBIT TOO, MIKEY?
IT WASN'T JUST NOAH?
I'M SURE.
ARF! ARF!

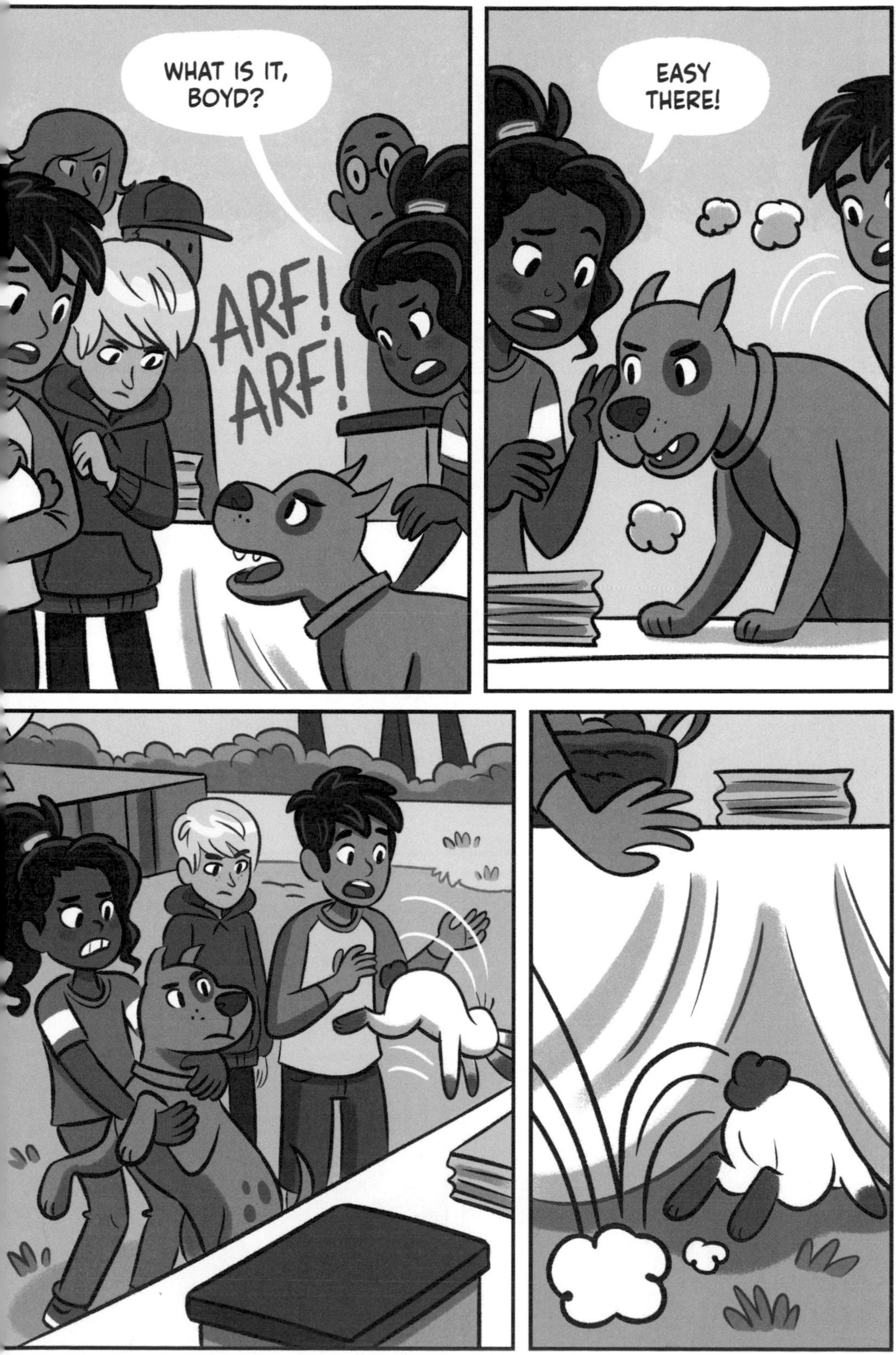
WHAT IS IT, BOYD?
ARF! ARF!
EASY THERE!

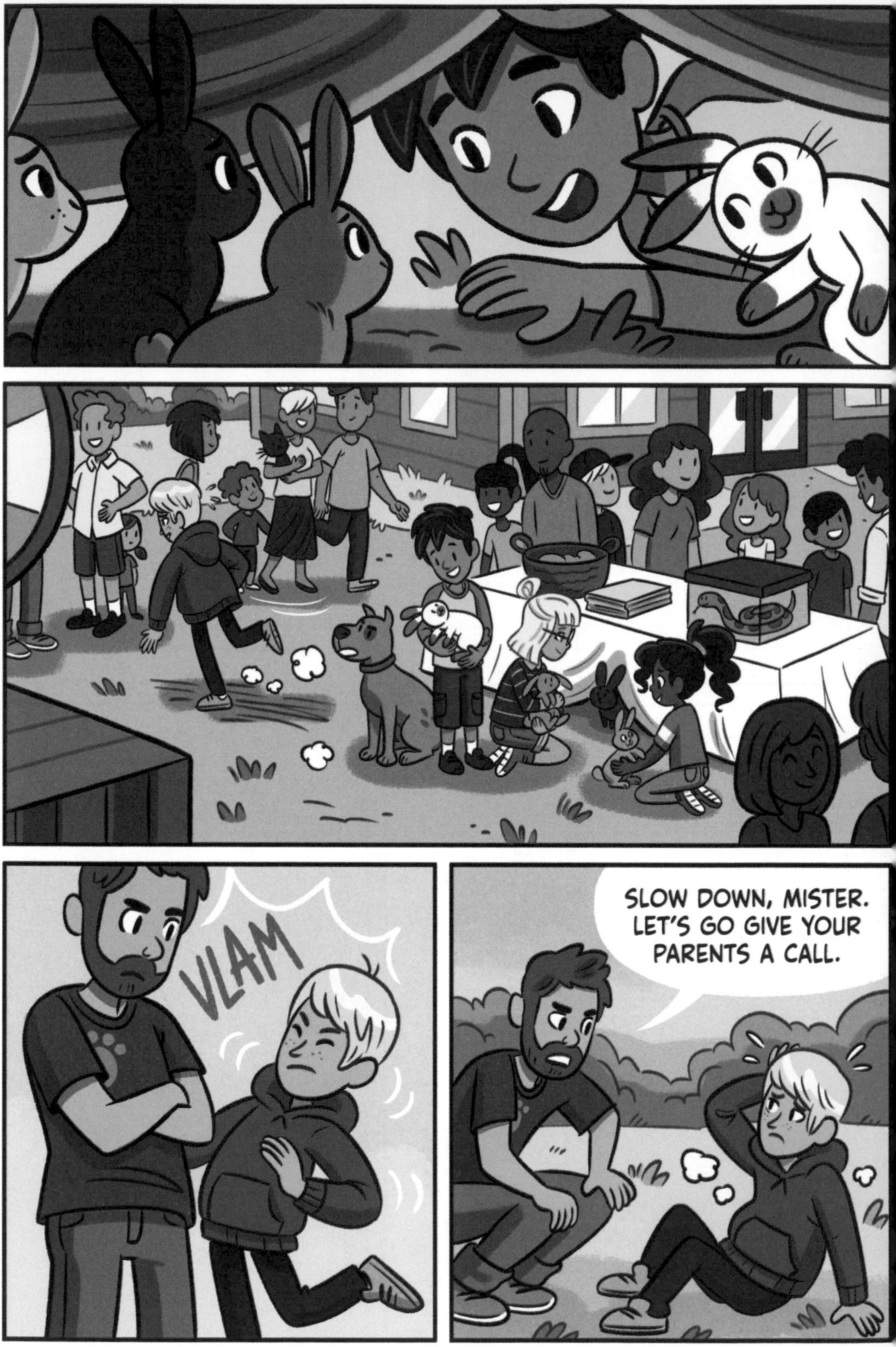
VLAM
SLOW DOWN, MISTER. LET'S GO GIVE YOUR PARENTS A CALL.

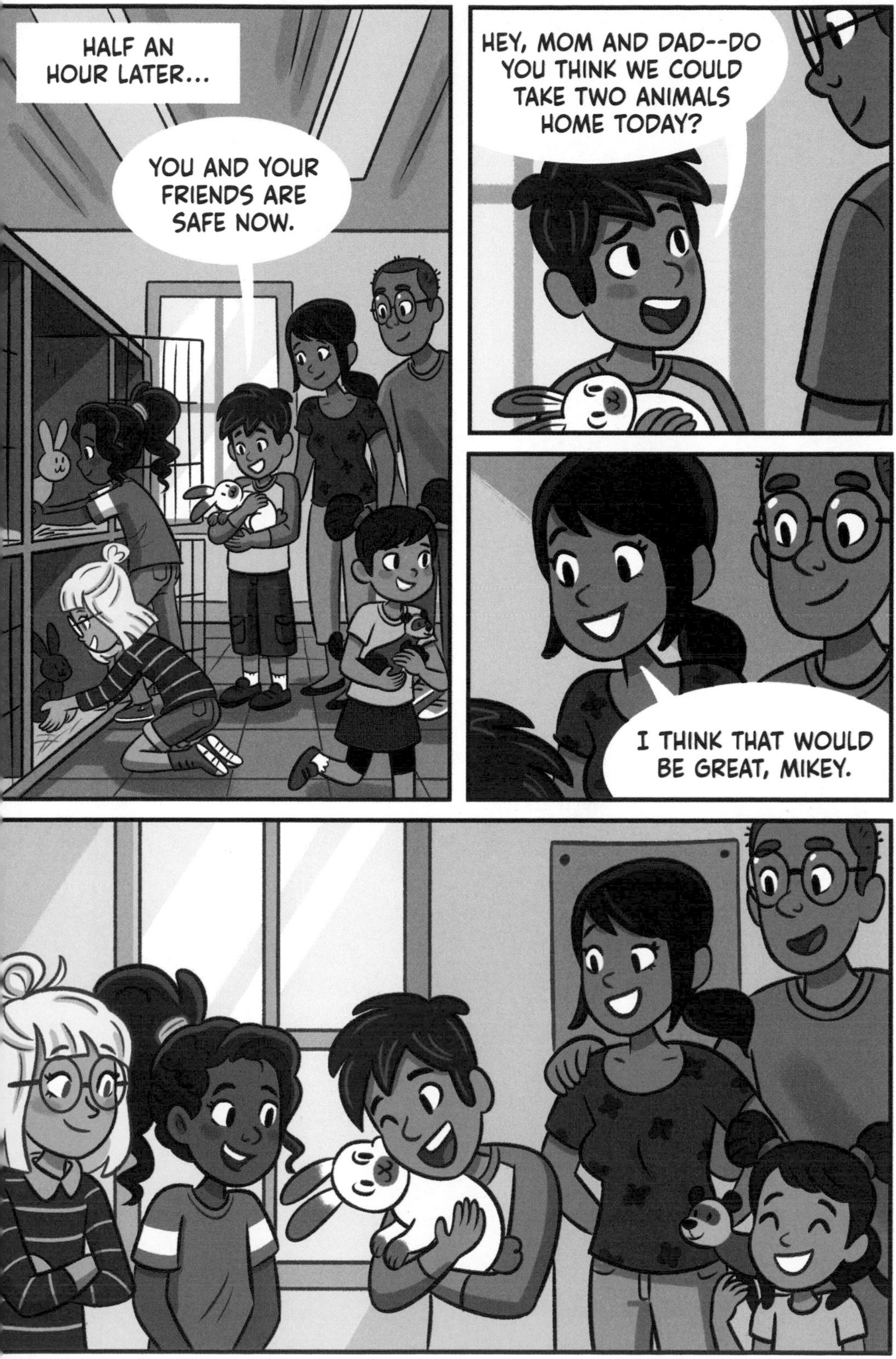
HALF AN HOUR LATER...
YOU AND YOUR FRIENDS ARE SAFE NOW.
HEY, MOM AND DAD--DO YOU THINK WE COULD TAKE TWO ANIMALS HOME TODAY?
I THINK THAT WOULD BE GREAT, MIKEY.

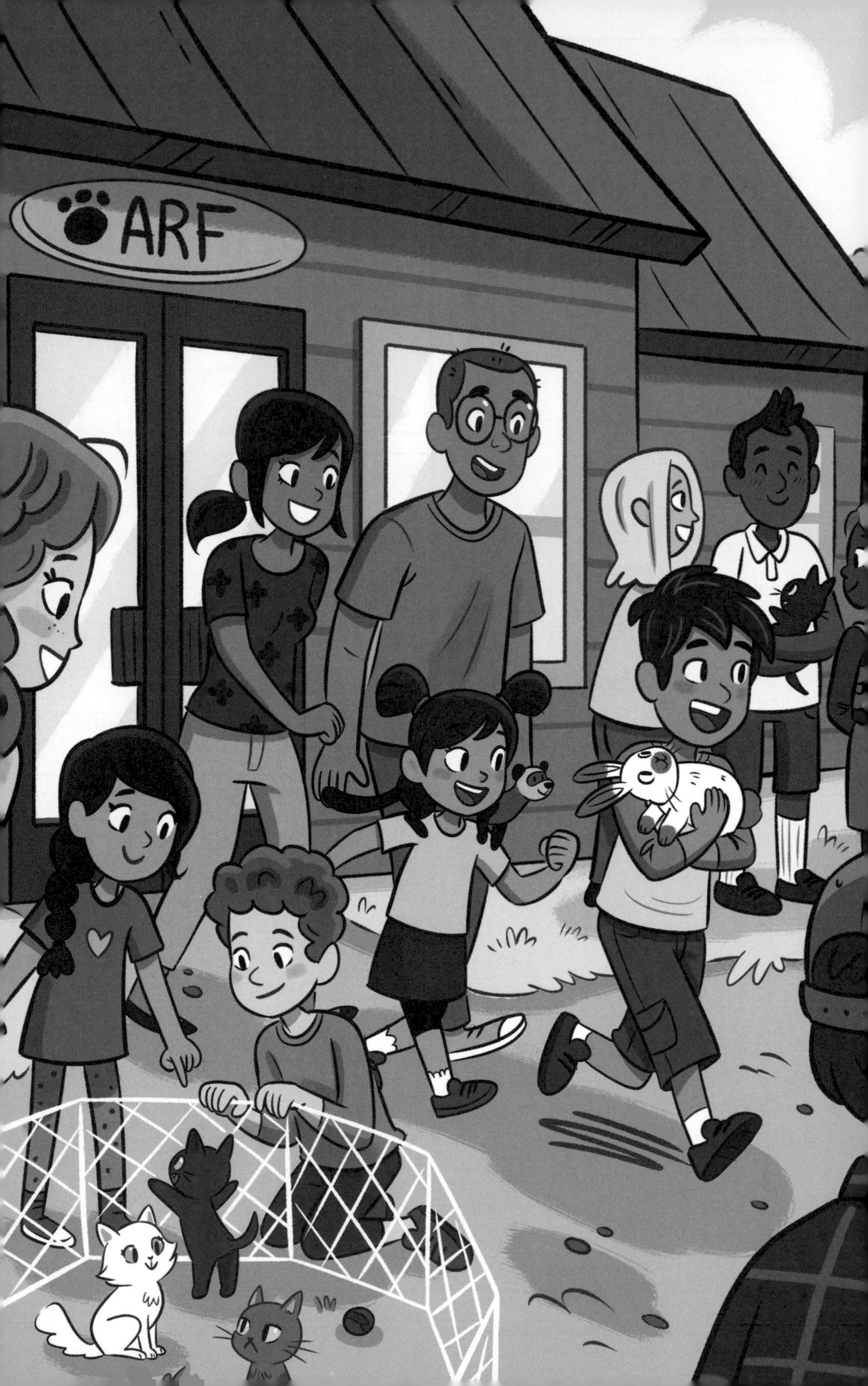
ARF

Chapter 4

NOAH AND PEPPER

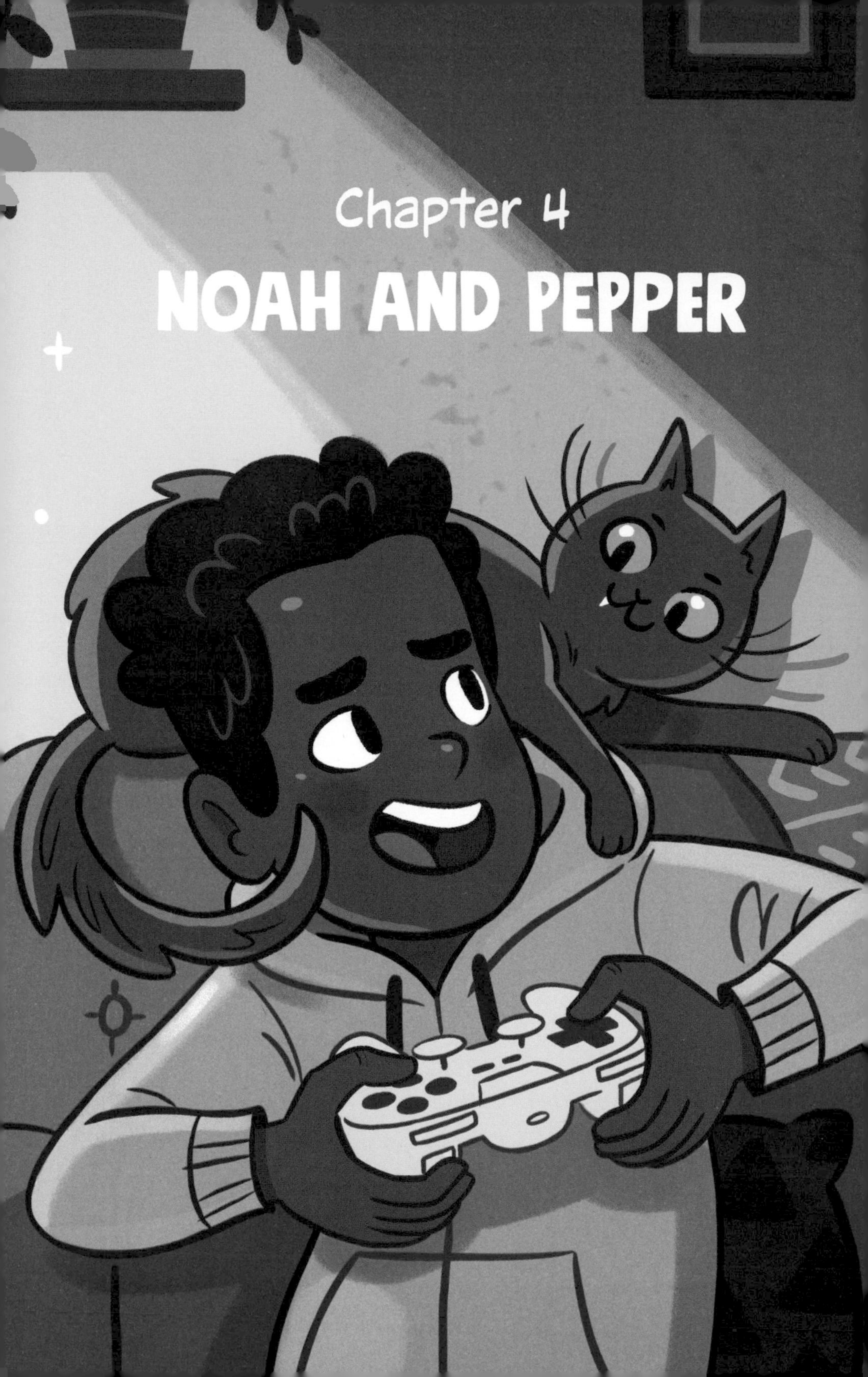

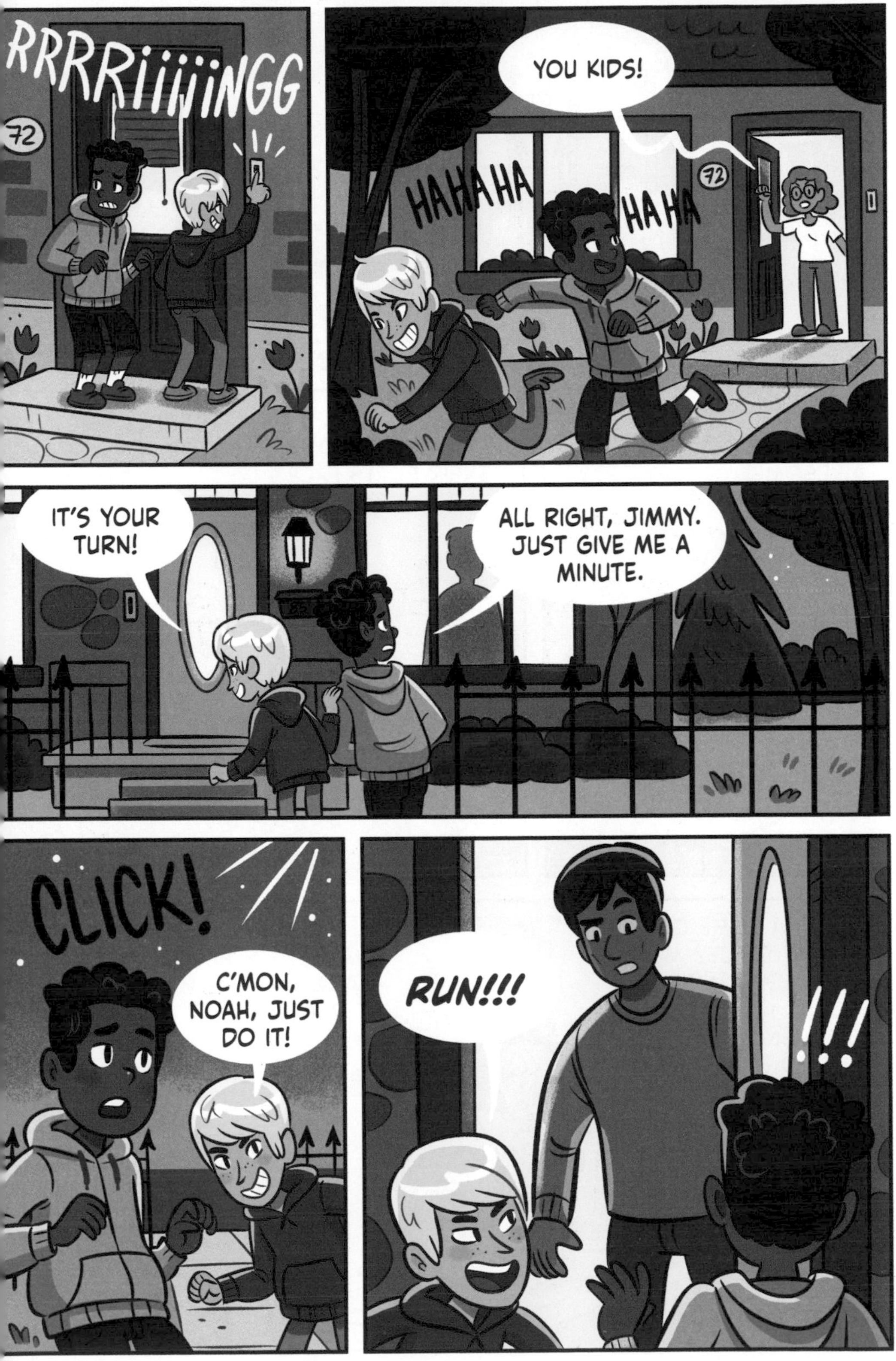
RRRRiiijjiNGG
72
YOU KIDS!
HAHAHA
72
HAHA
IT'S YOUR TURN!
ALL RIGHT, JIMMY. JUST GIVE ME A MINUTE.
CLICK!
C'MON, NOAH, JUST DO IT!
RUN!!!
!!!

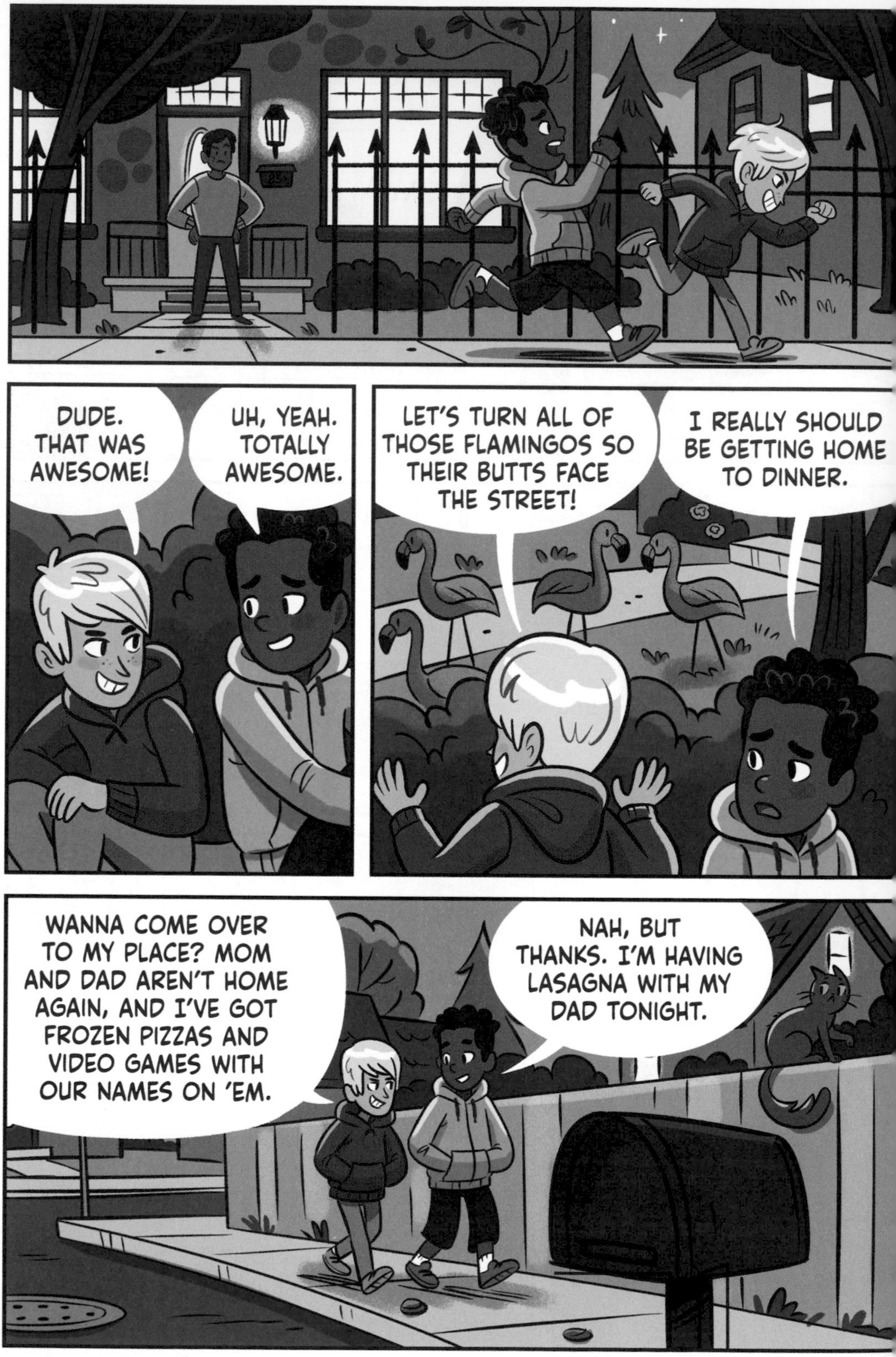
DUDE. THAT WAS AWESOME!
UH, YEAH. TOTALLY AWESOME.
LET'S TURN ALL OF THOSE FLAMINGOS SO THEIR BUTTS FACE THE STREET!
I REALLY SHOULD BE GETTING HOME TO DINNER.
WANNA COME OVER TO MY PLACE? MOM AND DAD AREN'T HOME AGAIN, AND I'VE GOT FROZEN PIZZAS AND VIDEO GAMES WITH OUR NAMES ON 'EM.
NAH, BUT THANKS. I'M HAVING LASAGNA WITH MY DAD TONIGHT.

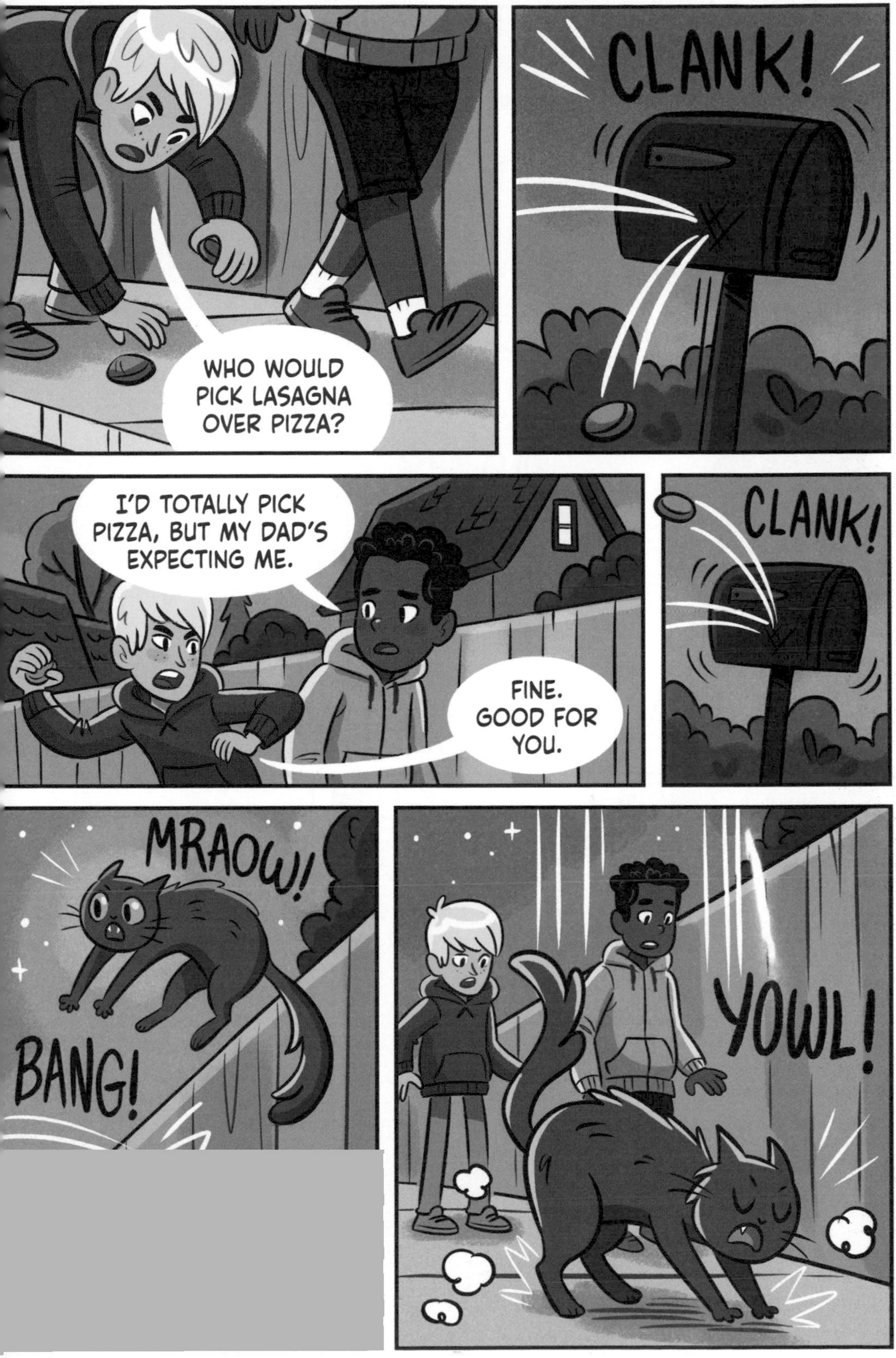
WHO WOULD PICK LASAGNA OVER PIZZA?
CLANK!
I'D TOTALLY PICK PIZZA, BUT MY DAD'S EXPECTING ME.
FINE. GOOD FOR YOU.
CLANK!
MRAOW!
BANG!
YOWL!

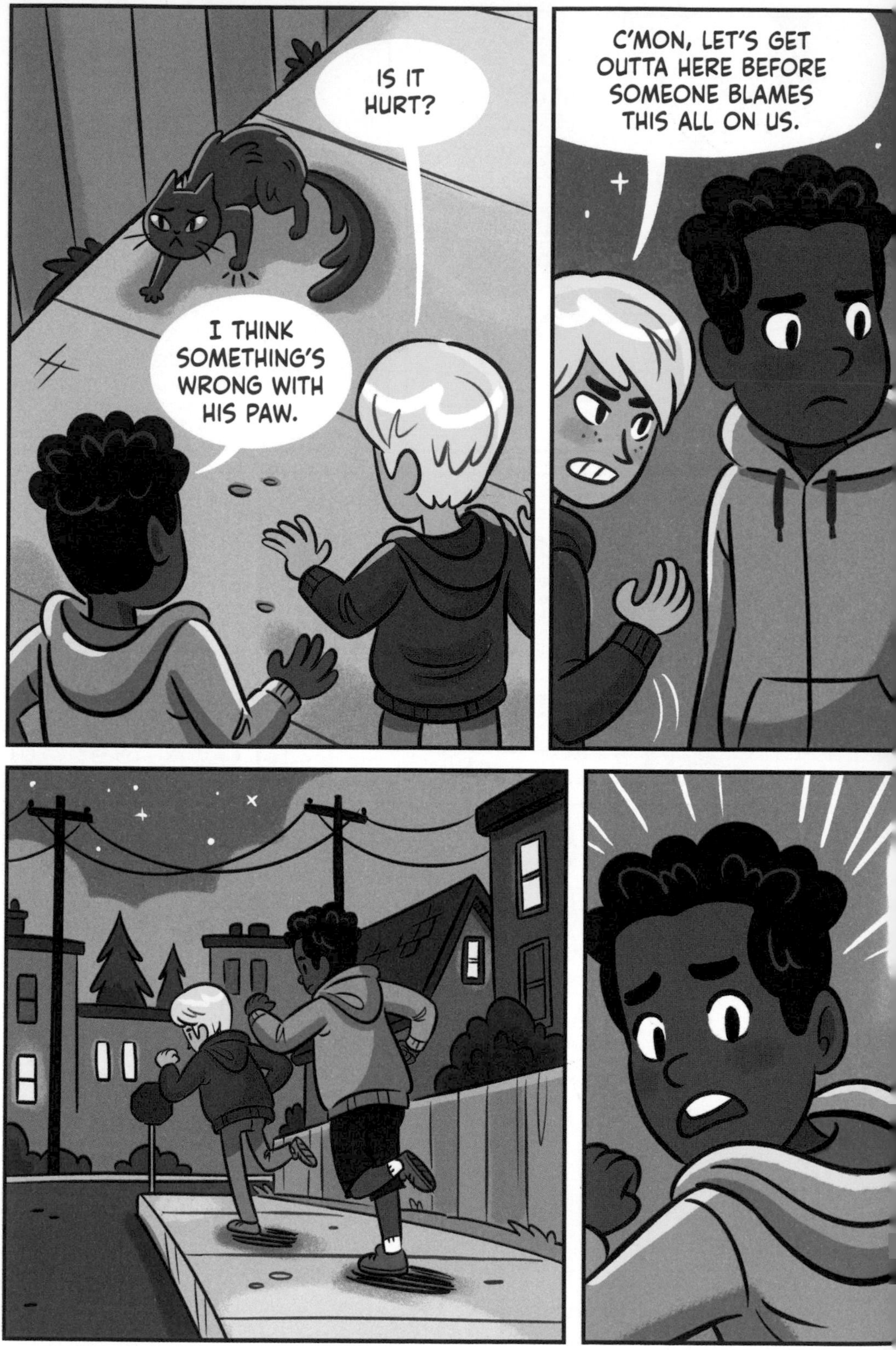
IS IT HURT?
I THINK SOMETHING'S WRONG WITH HIS PAW.
C'MON, LET'S GET OUTTA HERE BEFORE SOMEONE BLAMES THIS ALL ON US.

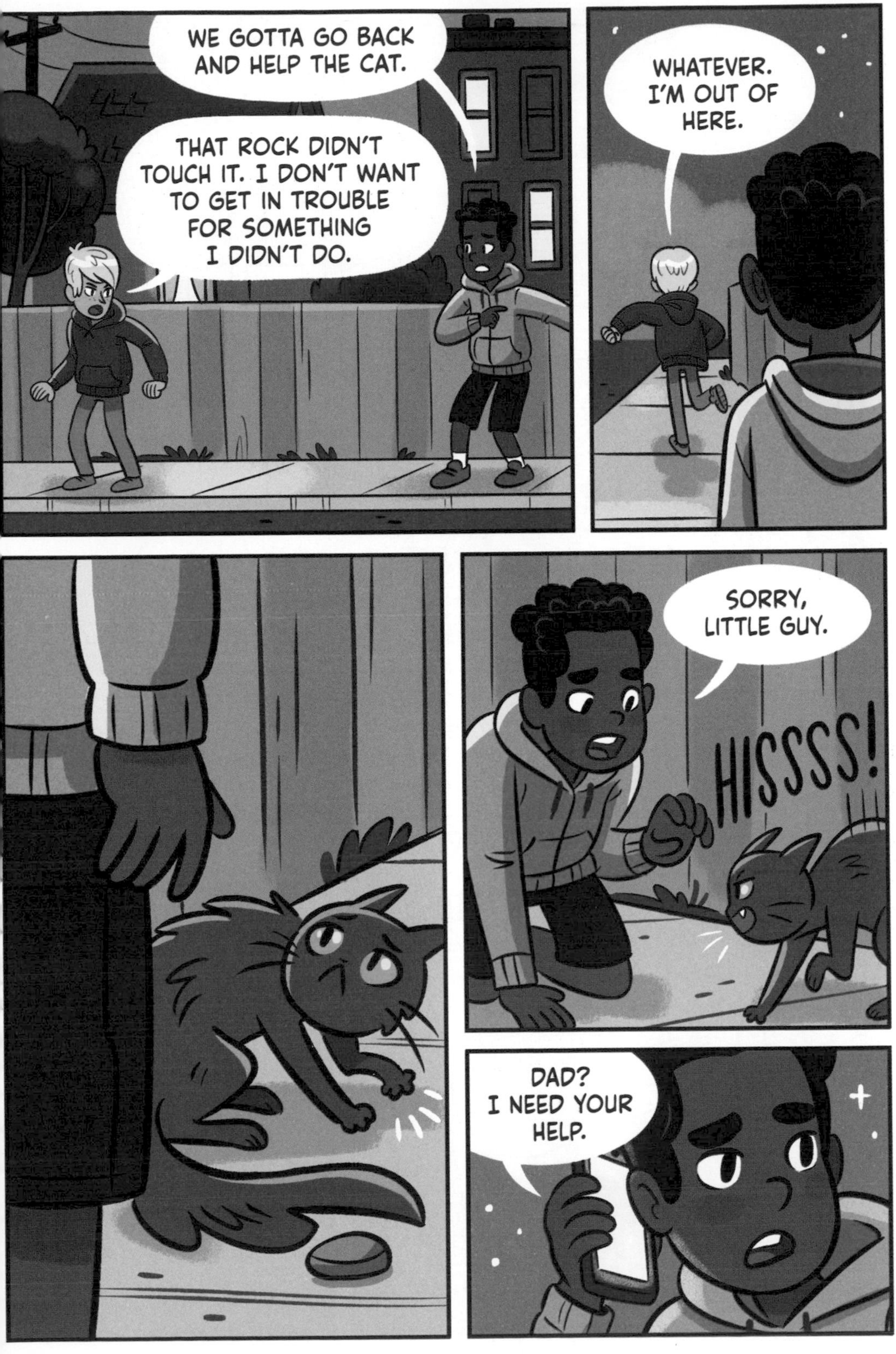
WE GOTTA GO BACK AND HELP THE CAT.
THAT ROCK DIDN'T TOUCH IT. I DON'T WANT TO GET IN TROUBLE FOR SOMETHING I DIDN'T DO.
WHATEVER. I'M OUT OF HERE.
SORRY, LITTLE GUY.
HISSSS!
DAD? I NEED YOUR HELP.

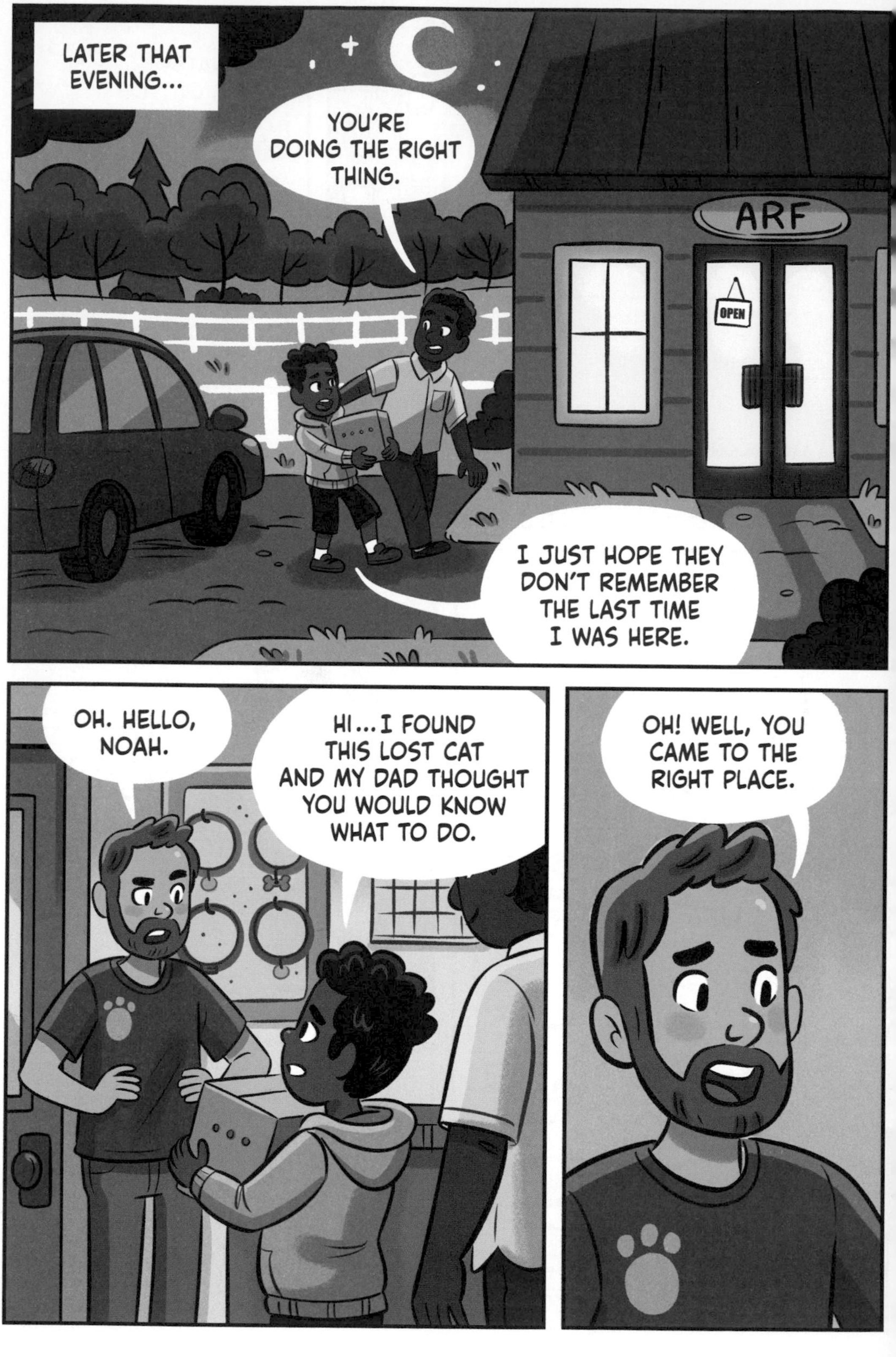
LATER THAT EVENING...
YOU'RE DOING THE RIGHT THING.
ARF
OPEN
I JUST HOPE THEY DON'T REMEMBER THE LAST TIME I WAS HERE.
OH. HELLO, NOAH.
HI...I FOUND THIS LOST CAT AND MY DAD THOUGHT YOU WOULD KNOW WHAT TO DO.
OH! WELL, YOU CAME TO THE RIGHT PLACE.

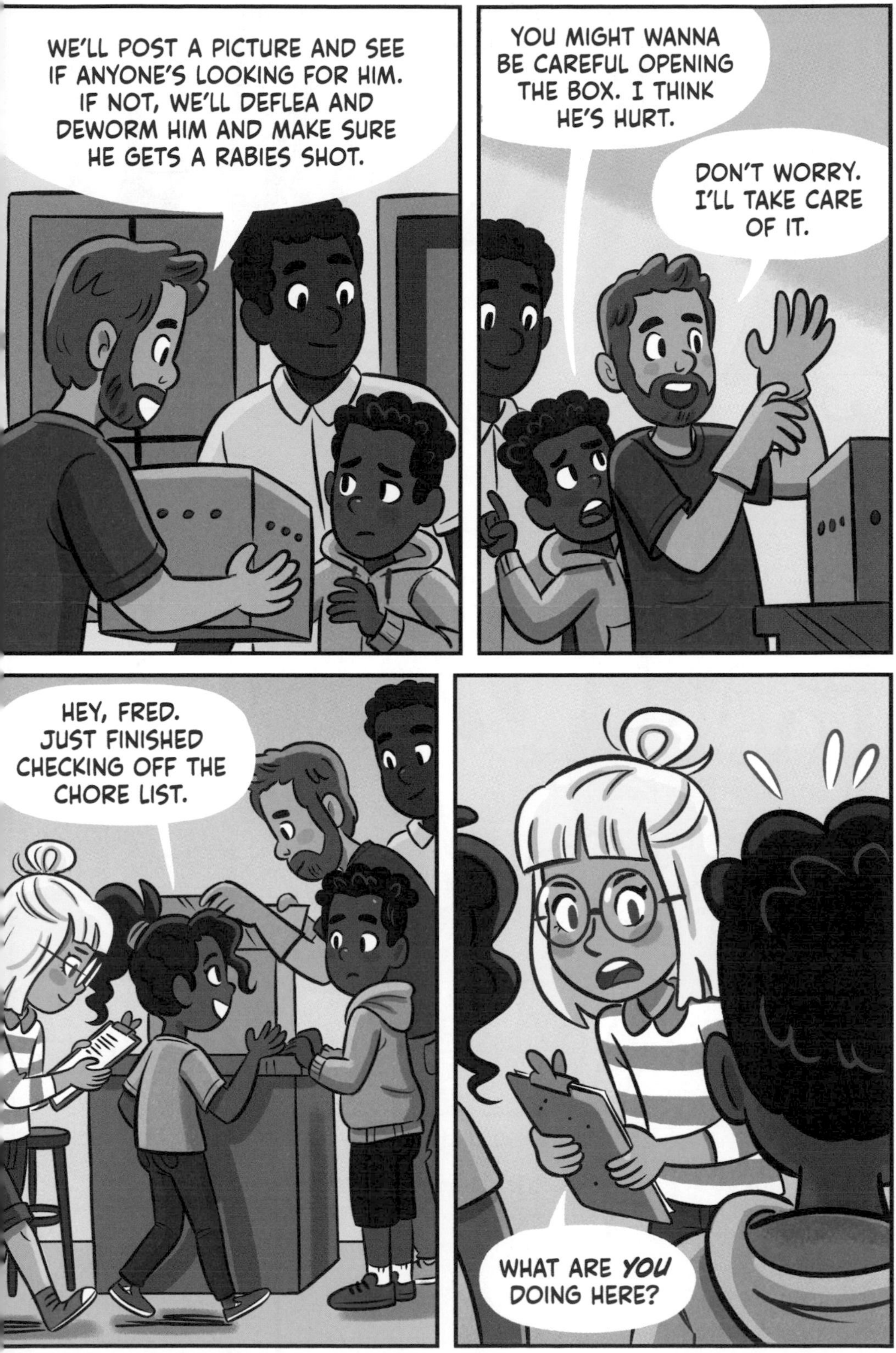
WE'LL POST A PICTURE AND SEE IF ANYONE'S LOOKING FOR HIM. IF NOT, WE'LL DEFLEA AND DEWORM HIM AND MAKE SURE HE GETS A RABIES SHOT.
YOU MIGHT WANNA BE CAREFUL OPENING THE BOX. I THINK HE'S HURT.
DON'T WORRY. I'LL TAKE CARE OF IT.
HEY, FRED. JUST FINISHED CHECKING OFF THE CHORE LIST.
WHAT ARE *YOU* DOING HERE?

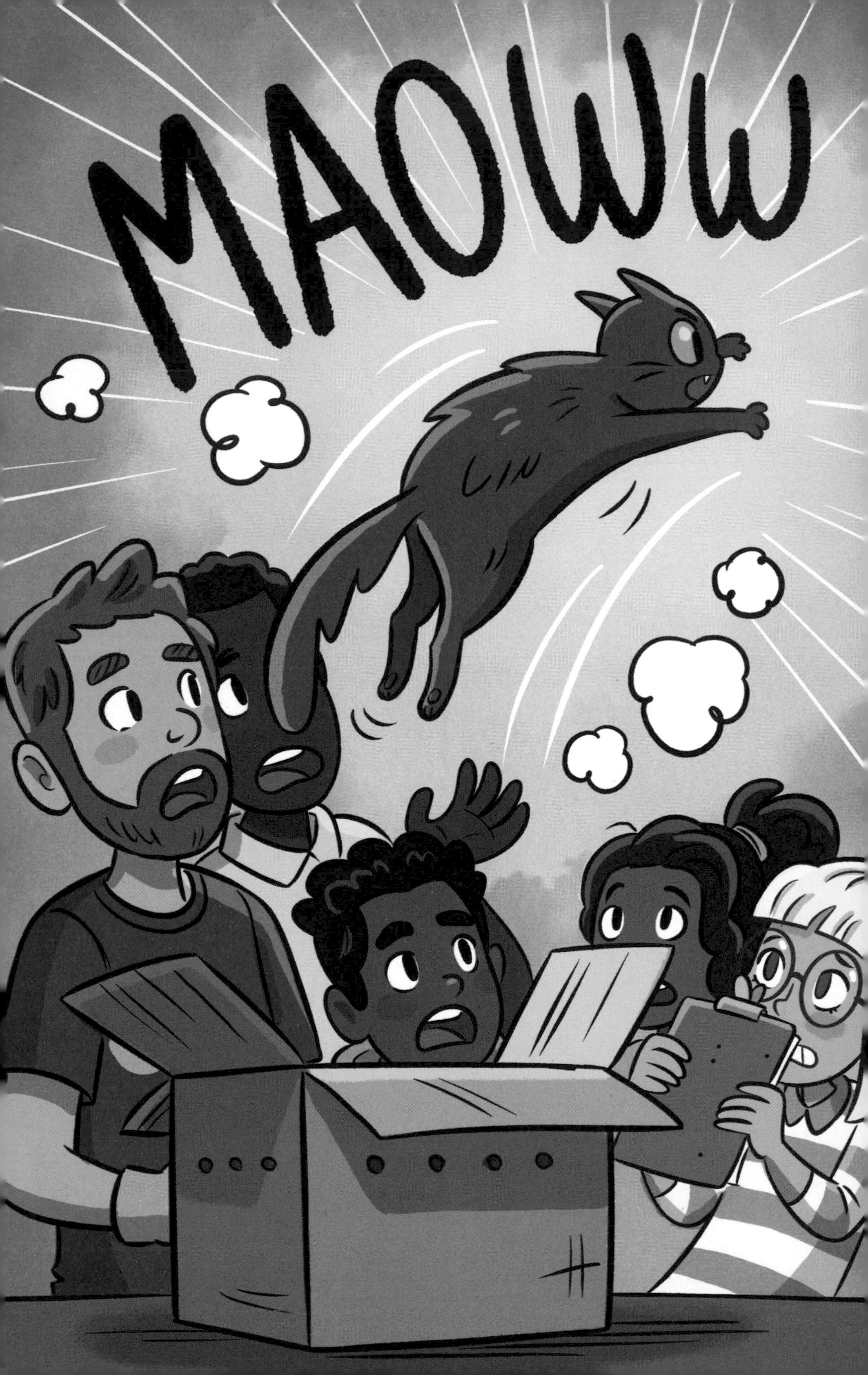
MAOWW

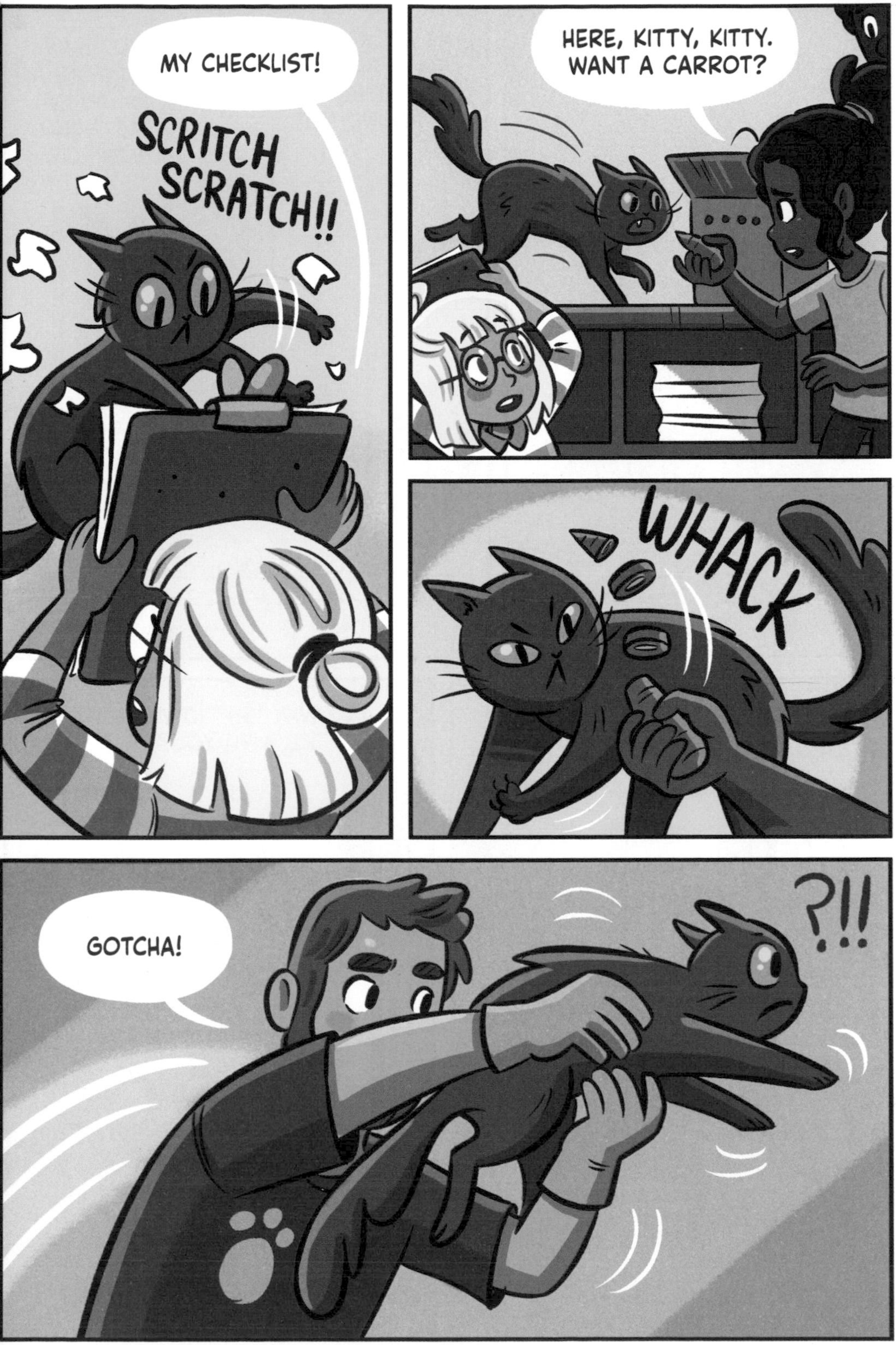

MY CHECKLIST!
SCRITCH SCRATCH!!
HERE, KITTY, KITTY. WANT A CARROT?
WHACK
GOTCHA!
?!!

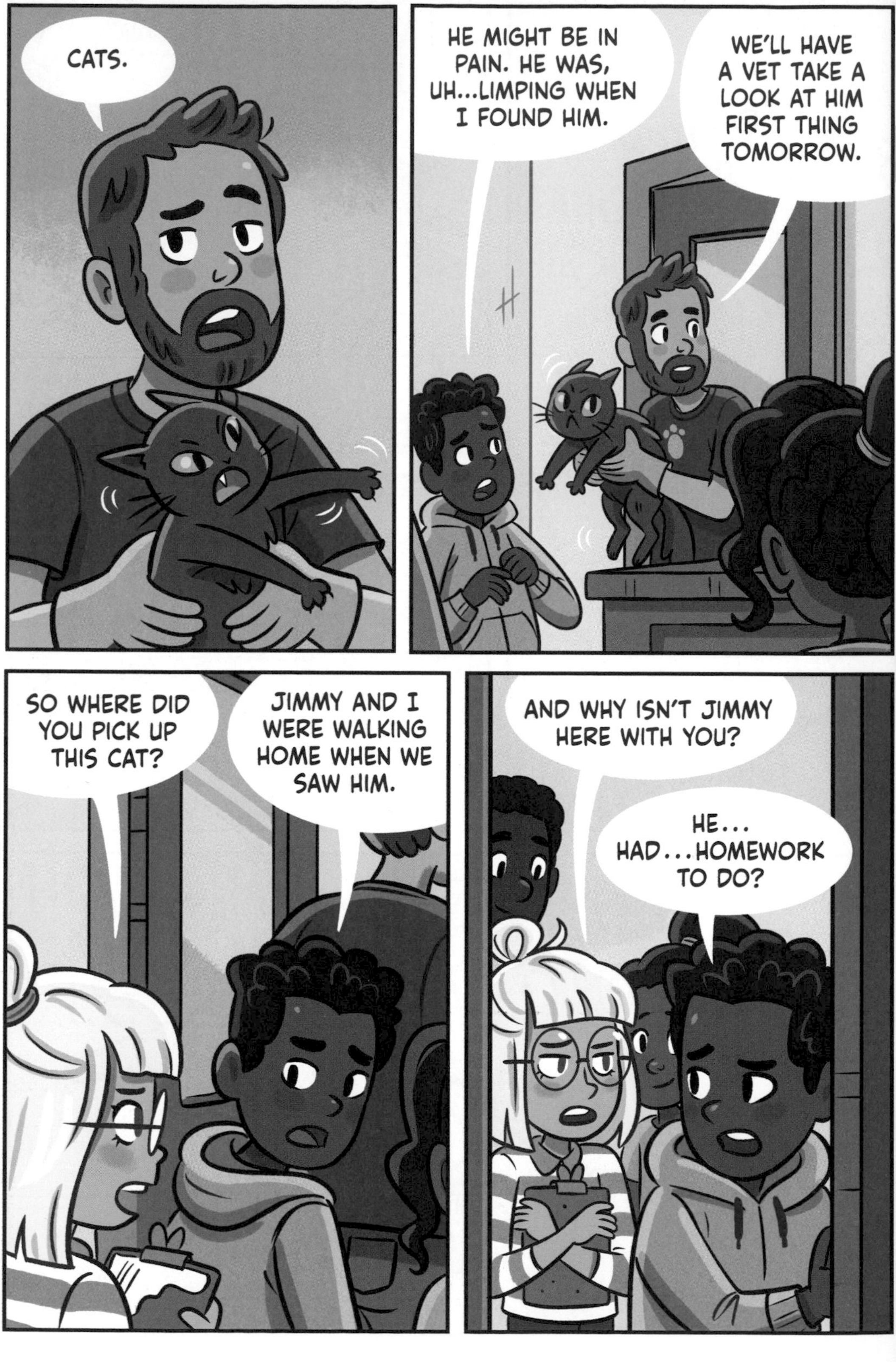
CATS.
HE MIGHT BE IN PAIN. HE WAS, UH...LIMPING WHEN I FOUND HIM.
WE'LL HAVE A VET TAKE A LOOK AT HIM FIRST THING TOMORROW.
SO WHERE DID YOU PICK UP THIS CAT?
JIMMY AND I WERE WALKING HOME WHEN WE SAW HIM.
AND WHY ISN'T JIMMY HERE WITH YOU?
HE... HAD...HOMEWORK TO DO?

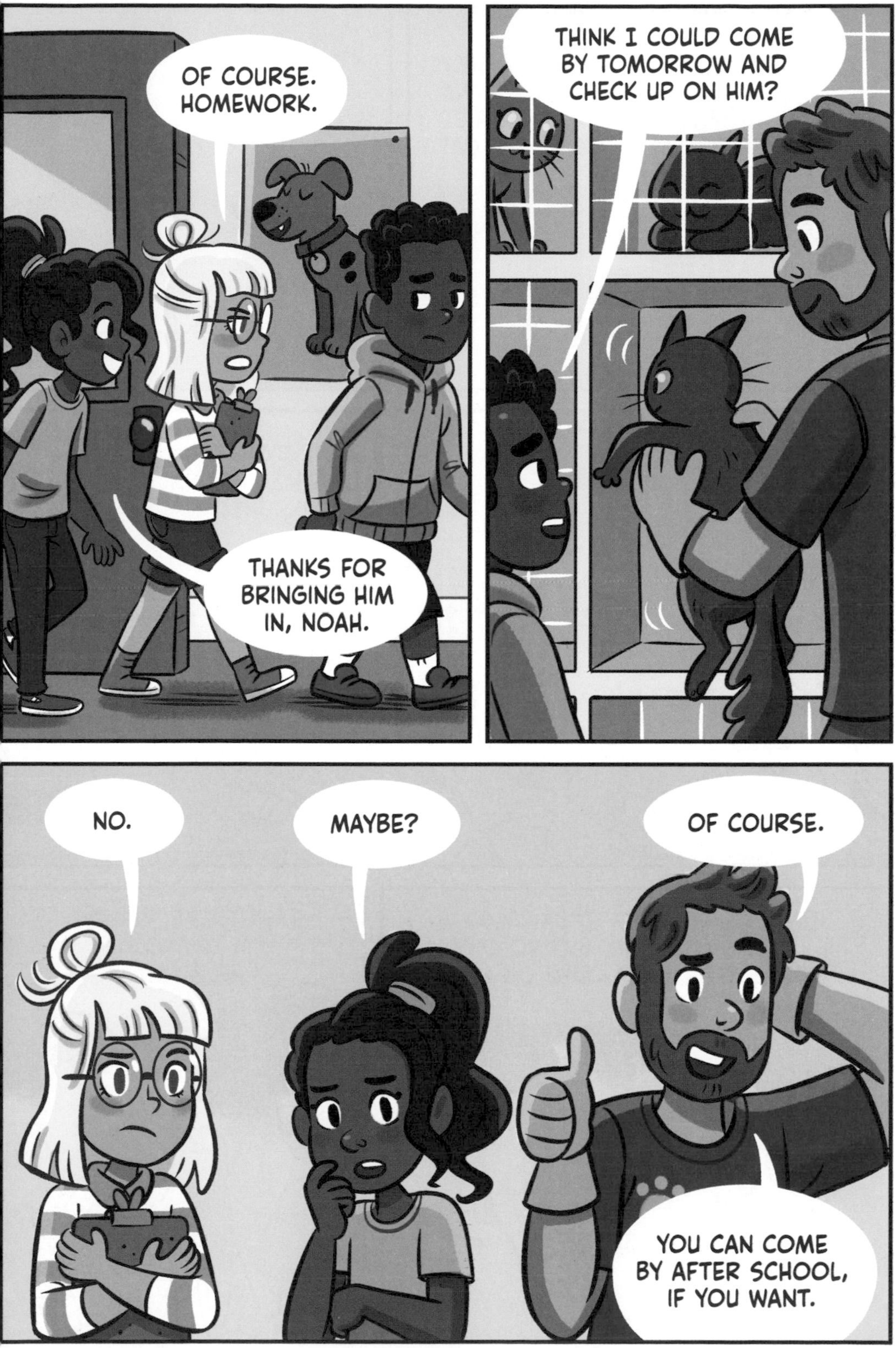
OF COURSE. HOMEWORK.
THANKS FOR BRINGING HIM IN, NOAH.
THINK I COULD COME BY TOMORROW AND CHECK UP ON HIM?
NO.
MAYBE?
OF COURSE.
YOU CAN COME BY AFTER SCHOOL, IF YOU WANT.

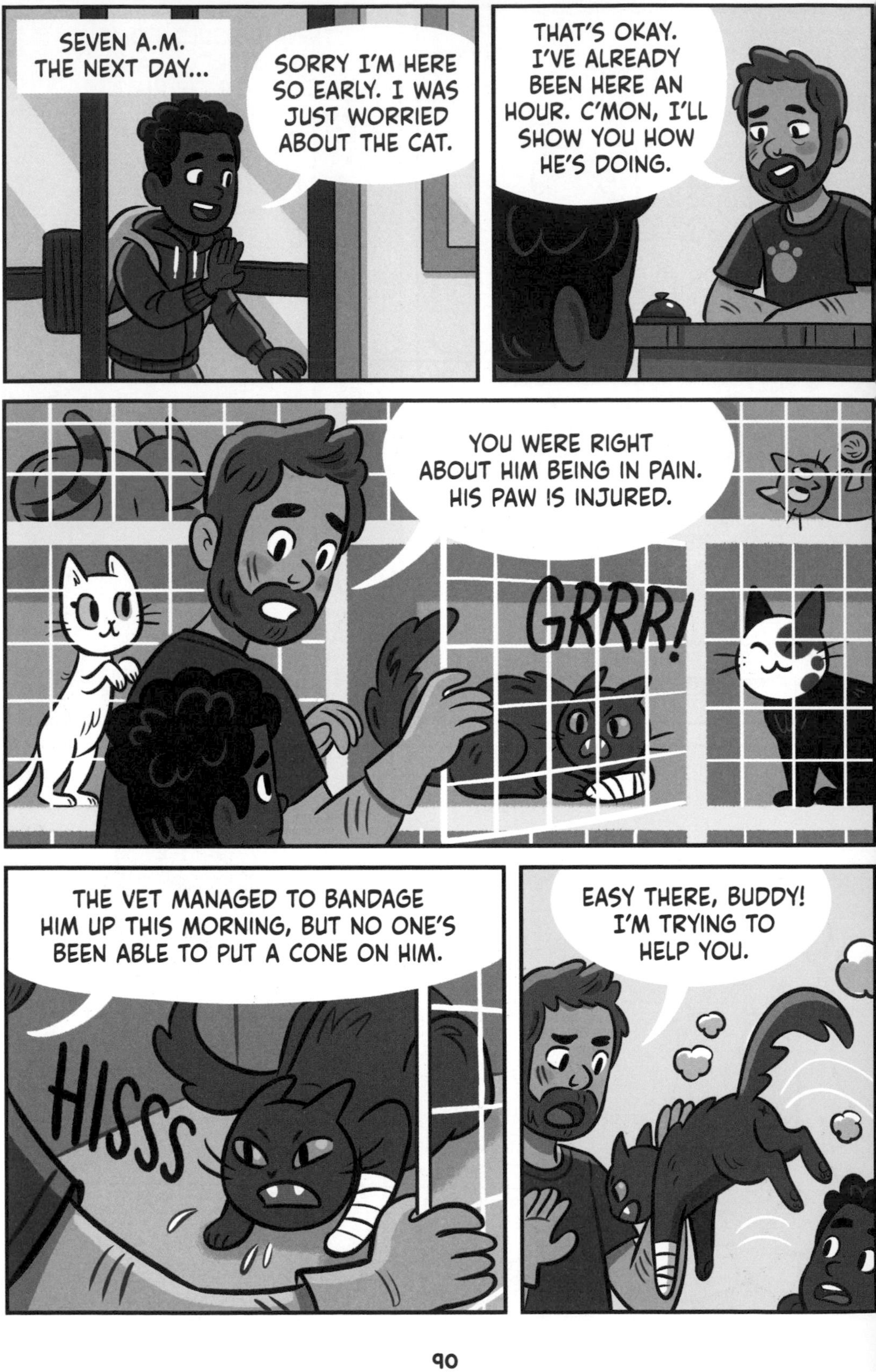
SEVEN A.M. THE NEXT DAY...
SORRY I'M HERE SO EARLY. I WAS JUST WORRIED ABOUT THE CAT.
THAT'S OKAY. I'VE ALREADY BEEN HERE AN HOUR. C'MON, I'LL SHOW YOU HOW HE'S DOING.
YOU WERE RIGHT ABOUT HIM BEING IN PAIN. HIS PAW IS INJURED.
GRRR!
THE VET MANAGED TO BANDAGE HIM UP THIS MORNING, BUT NO ONE'S BEEN ABLE TO PUT A CONE ON HIM.
HISSS
EASY THERE, BUDDY! I'M TRYING TO HELP YOU.

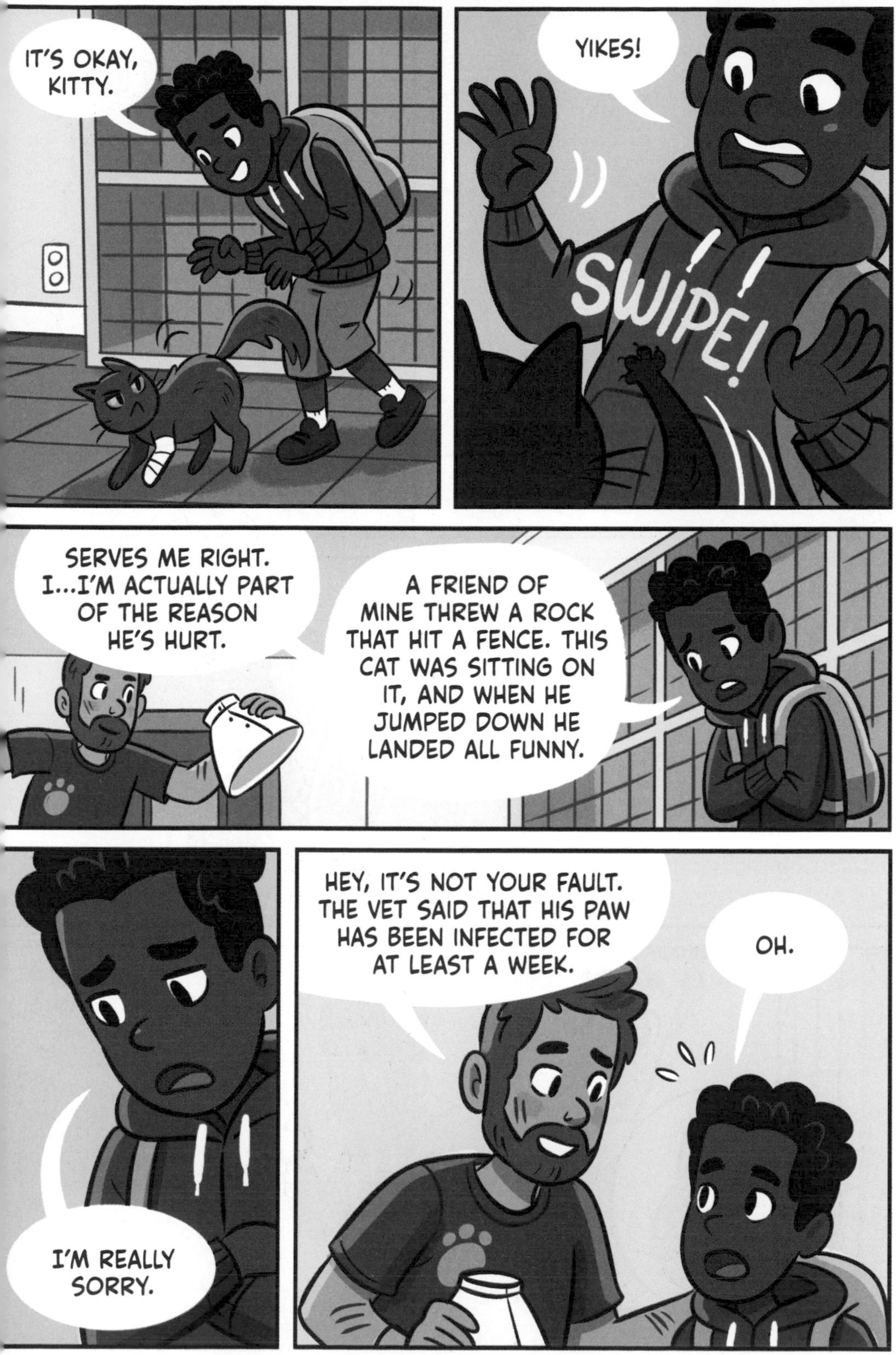
IT'S OKAY, KITTY.
YIKES!
SWIPE!
SERVES ME RIGHT. I...I'M ACTUALLY PART OF THE REASON HE'S HURT.
A FRIEND OF MINE THREW A ROCK THAT HIT A FENCE. THIS CAT WAS SITTING ON IT, AND WHEN HE JUMPED DOWN HE LANDED ALL FUNNY.
I'M REALLY SORRY.
HEY, IT'S NOT YOUR FAULT. THE VET SAID THAT HIS PAW HAS BEEN INFECTED FOR AT LEAST A WEEK.
OH.

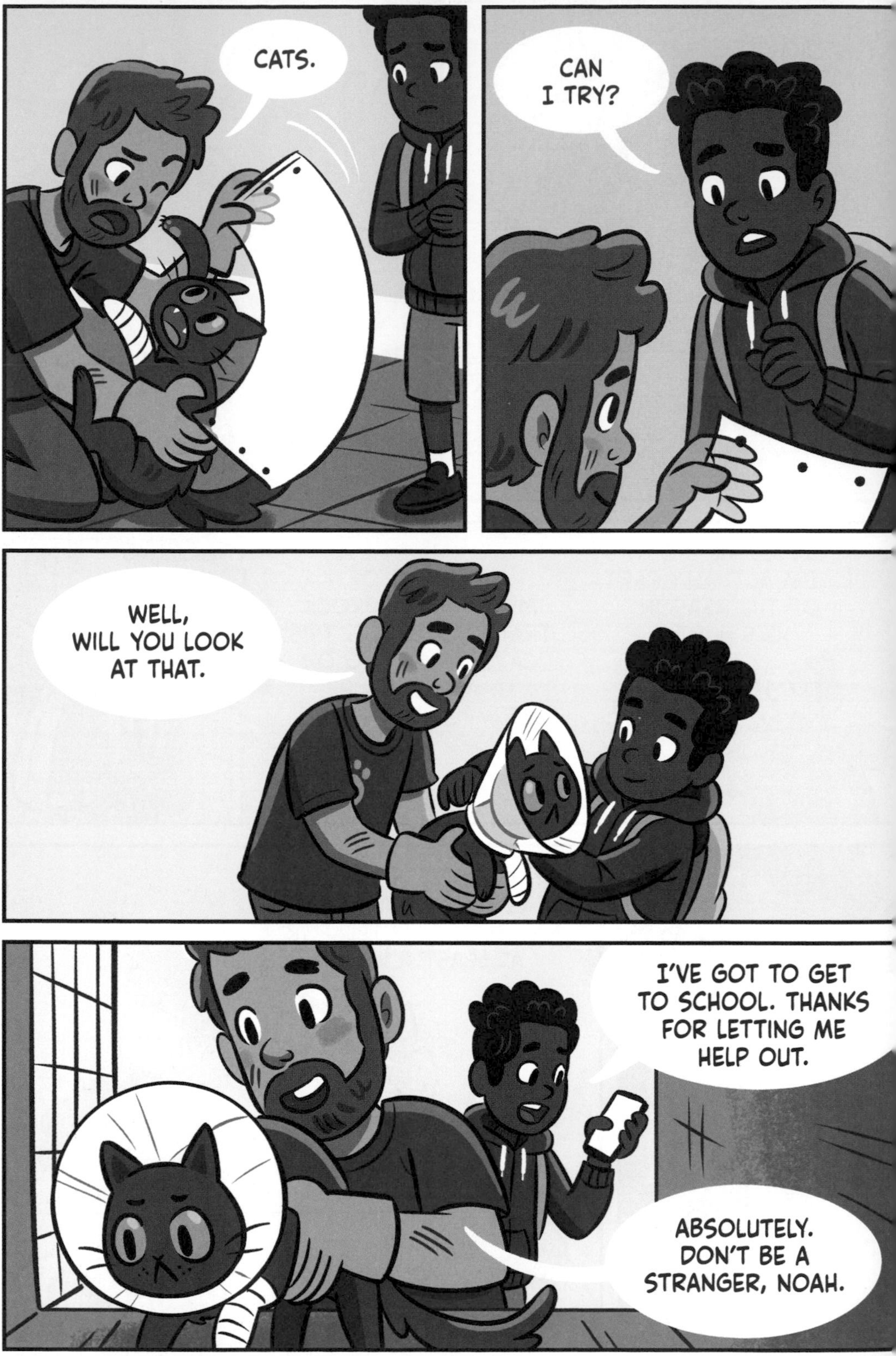
CATS.
CAN I TRY?
WELL, WILL YOU LOOK AT THAT.
I'VE GOT TO GET TO SCHOOL. THANKS FOR LETTING ME HELP OUT.
ABSOLUTELY. DON'T BE A STRANGER, NOAH.

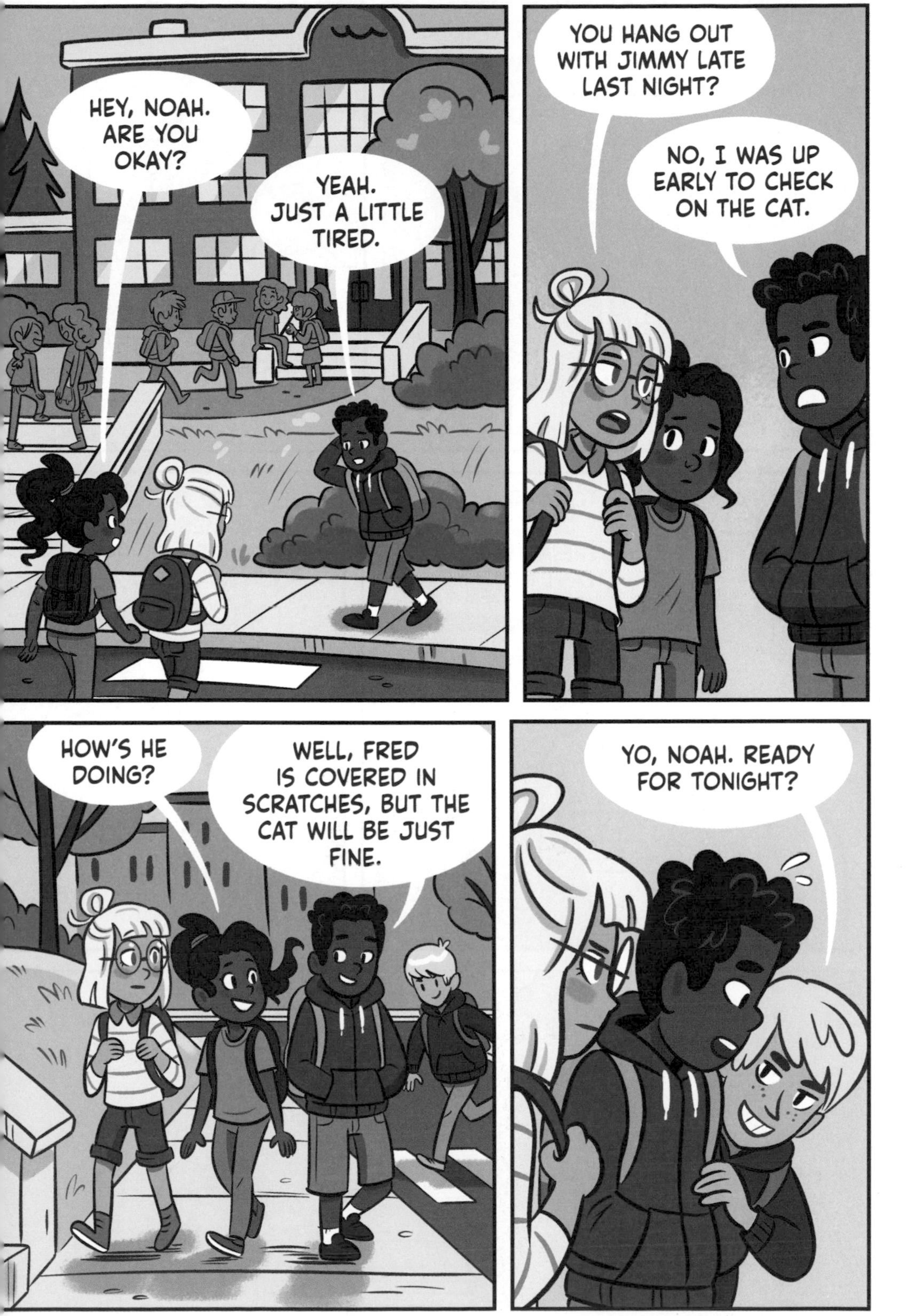
HEY, NOAH. ARE YOU OKAY?
YEAH. JUST A LITTLE TIRED.
YOU HANG OUT WITH JIMMY LATE LAST NIGHT?
NO, I WAS UP EARLY TO CHECK ON THE CAT.
HOW'S HE DOING?
WELL, FRED IS COVERED IN SCRATCHES, BUT THE CAT WILL BE JUST FINE.
YO, NOAH. READY FOR TONIGHT?

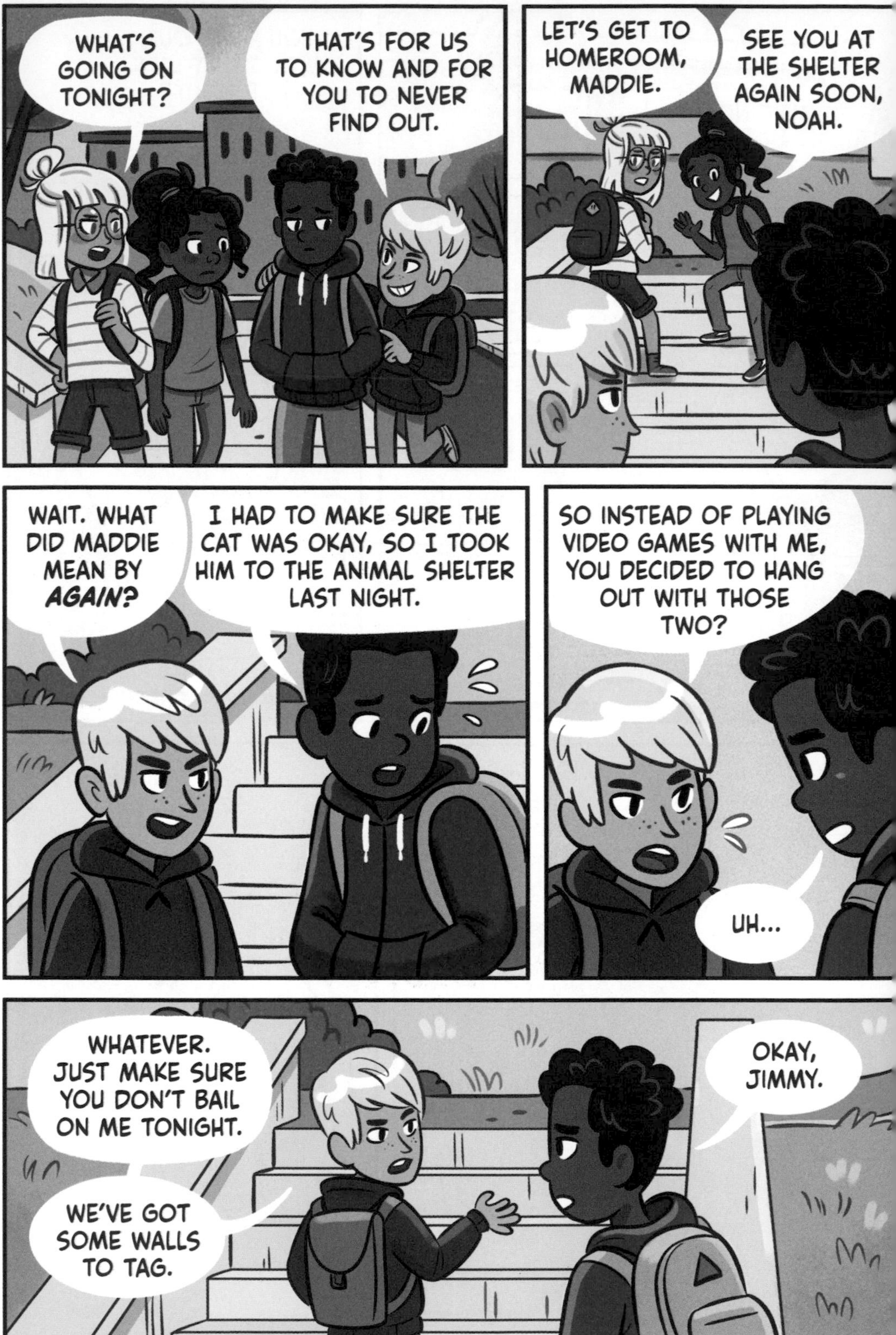
WHAT'S GOING ON TONIGHT?
THAT'S FOR US TO KNOW AND FOR YOU TO NEVER FIND OUT.
LET'S GET TO HOMEROOM, MADDIE.
SEE YOU AT THE SHELTER AGAIN SOON, NOAH.
WAIT. WHAT DID MADDIE MEAN BY *AGAIN?*
I HAD TO MAKE SURE THE CAT WAS OKAY, SO I TOOK HIM TO THE ANIMAL SHELTER LAST NIGHT.
SO INSTEAD OF PLAYING VIDEO GAMES WITH ME, YOU DECIDED TO HANG OUT WITH THOSE TWO?
UH...
WHATEVER. JUST MAKE SURE YOU DON'T BAIL ON ME TONIGHT.
WE'VE GOT SOME WALLS TO TAG.
OKAY, JIMMY.

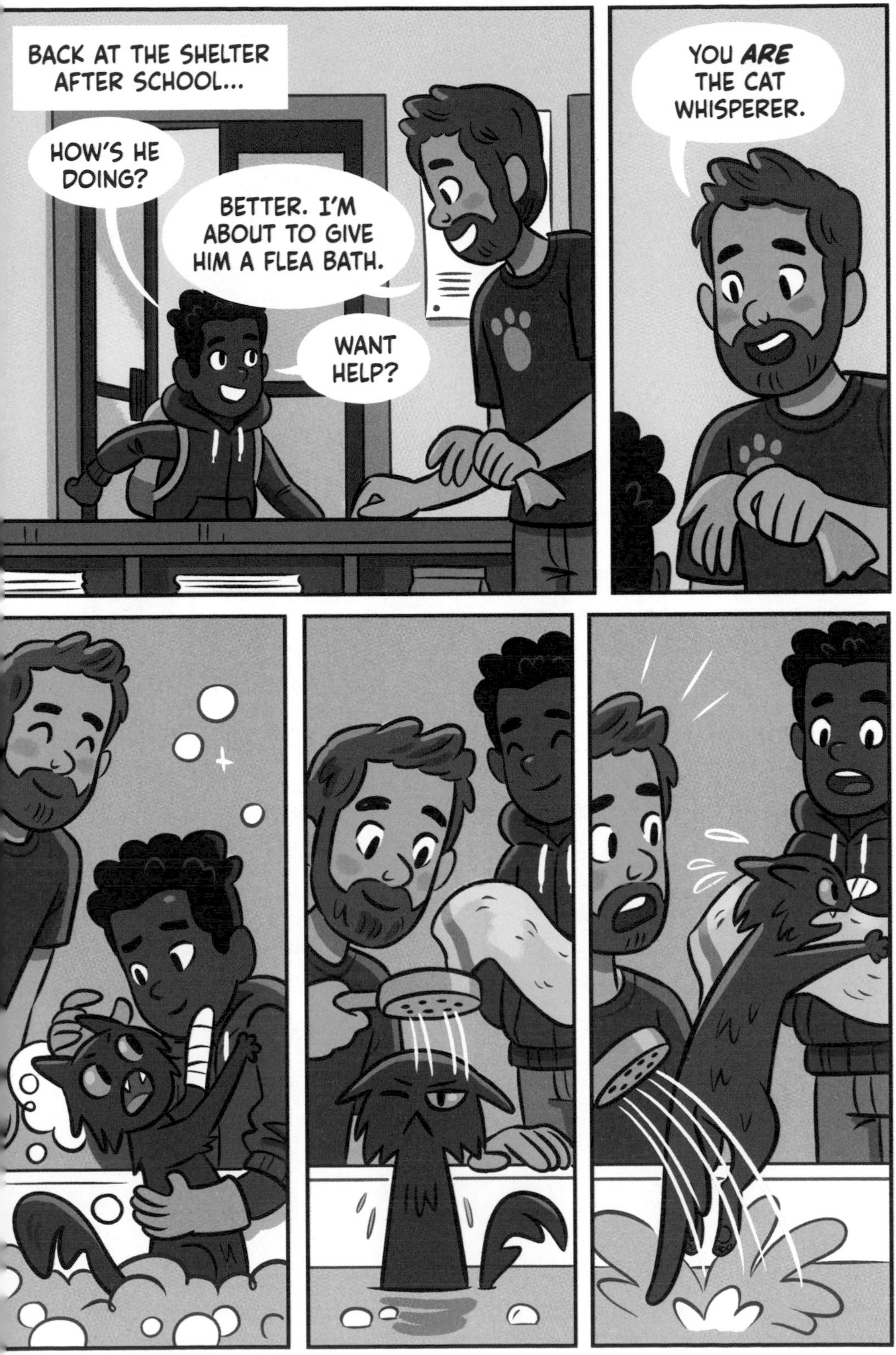
BACK AT THE SHELTER AFTER SCHOOL...
HOW'S HE DOING?
BETTER. I'M ABOUT TO GIVE HIM A FLEA BATH.
WANT HELP?
YOU *ARE* THE CAT WHISPERER.

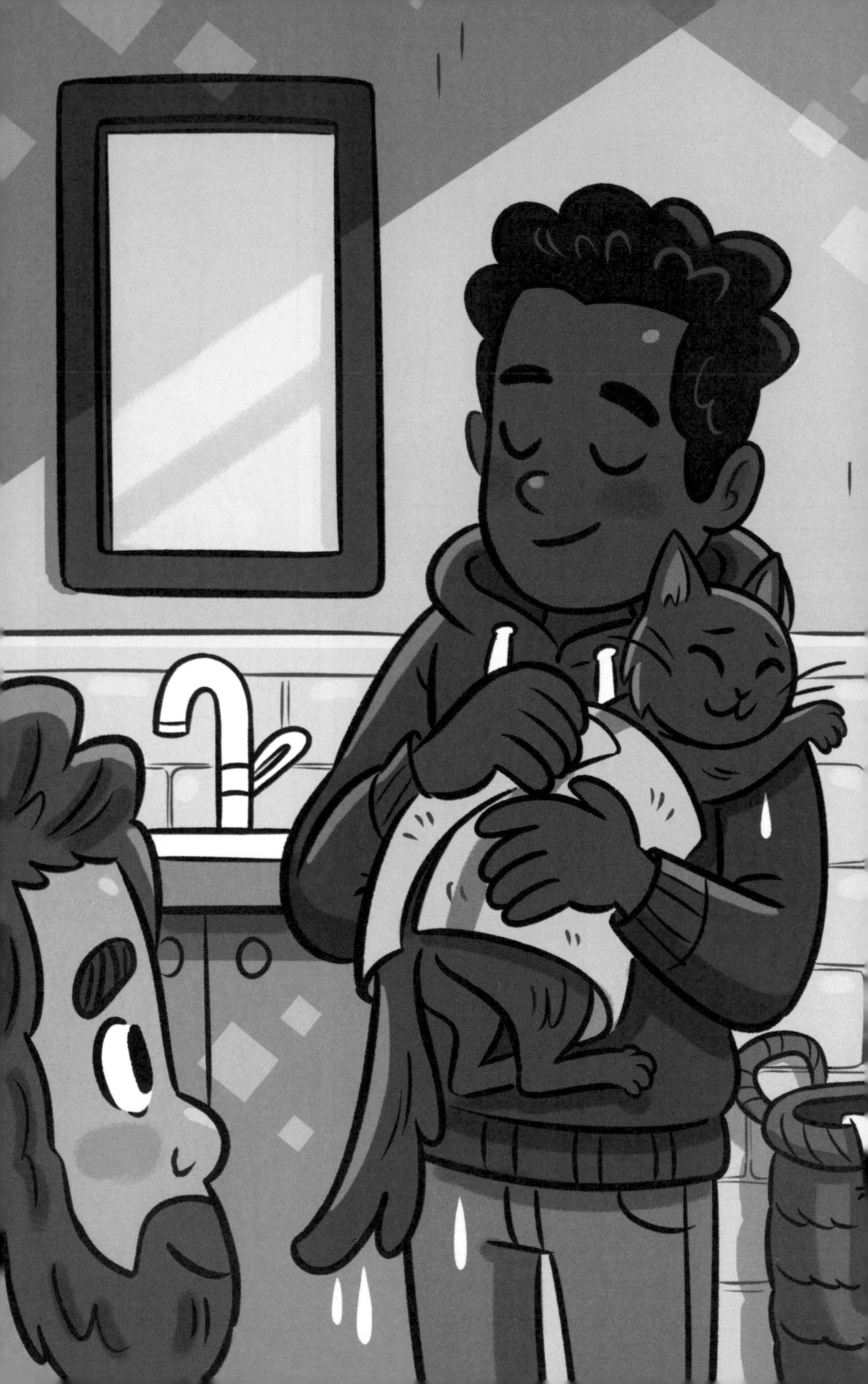

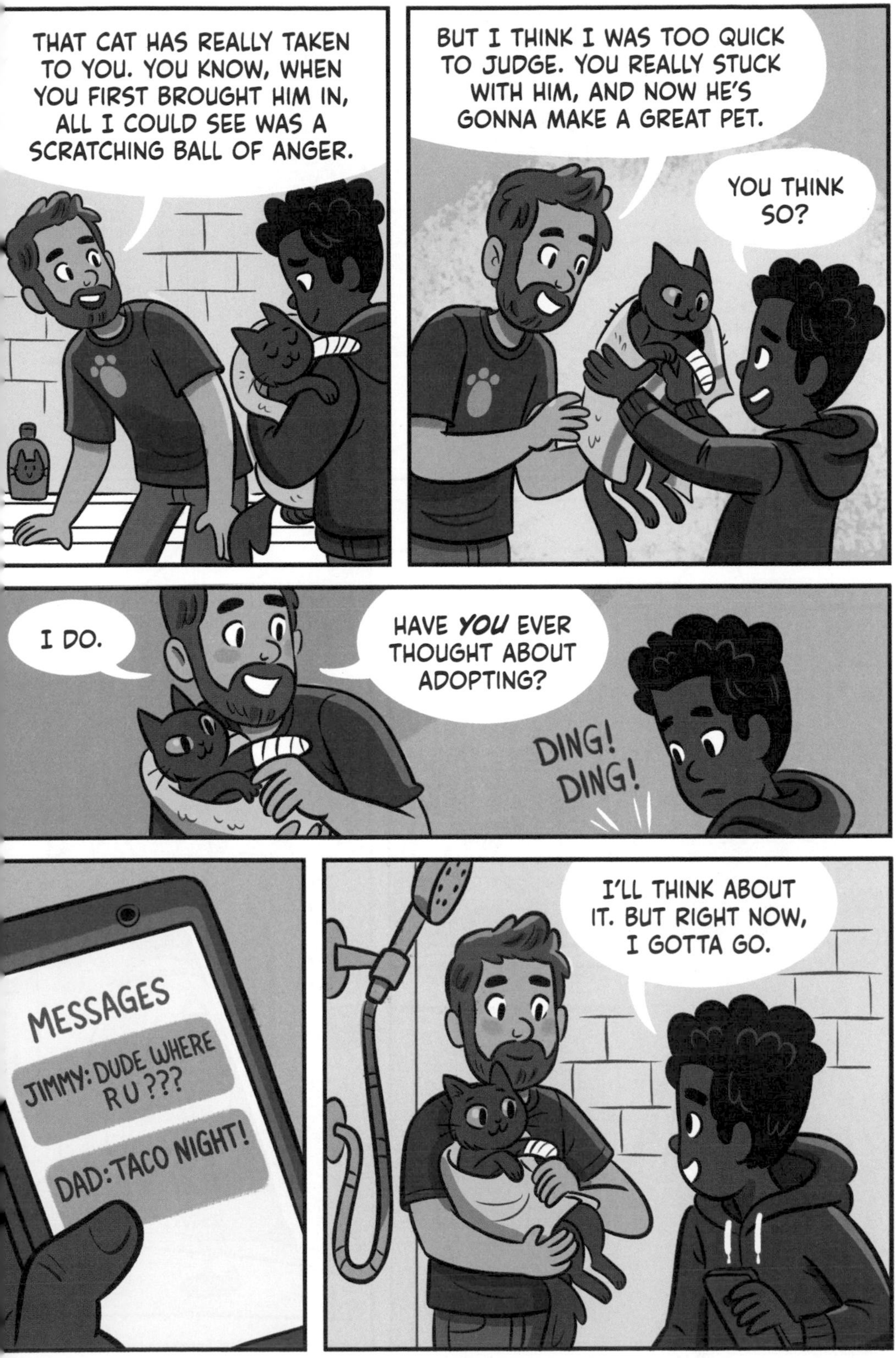
THAT CAT HAS REALLY TAKEN TO YOU. YOU KNOW, WHEN YOU FIRST BROUGHT HIM IN, ALL I COULD SEE WAS A SCRATCHING BALL OF ANGER.
BUT I THINK I WAS TOO QUICK TO JUDGE. YOU REALLY STUCK WITH HIM, AND NOW HE'S GONNA MAKE A GREAT PET.
YOU THINK SO?
I DO.
HAVE *YOU* EVER THOUGHT ABOUT ADOPTING?
DING! DING!
MESSAGES
JIMMY: DUDE WHERE R U ???
DAD: TACO NIGHT!
I'LL THINK ABOUT IT. BUT RIGHT NOW, I GOTTA GO.

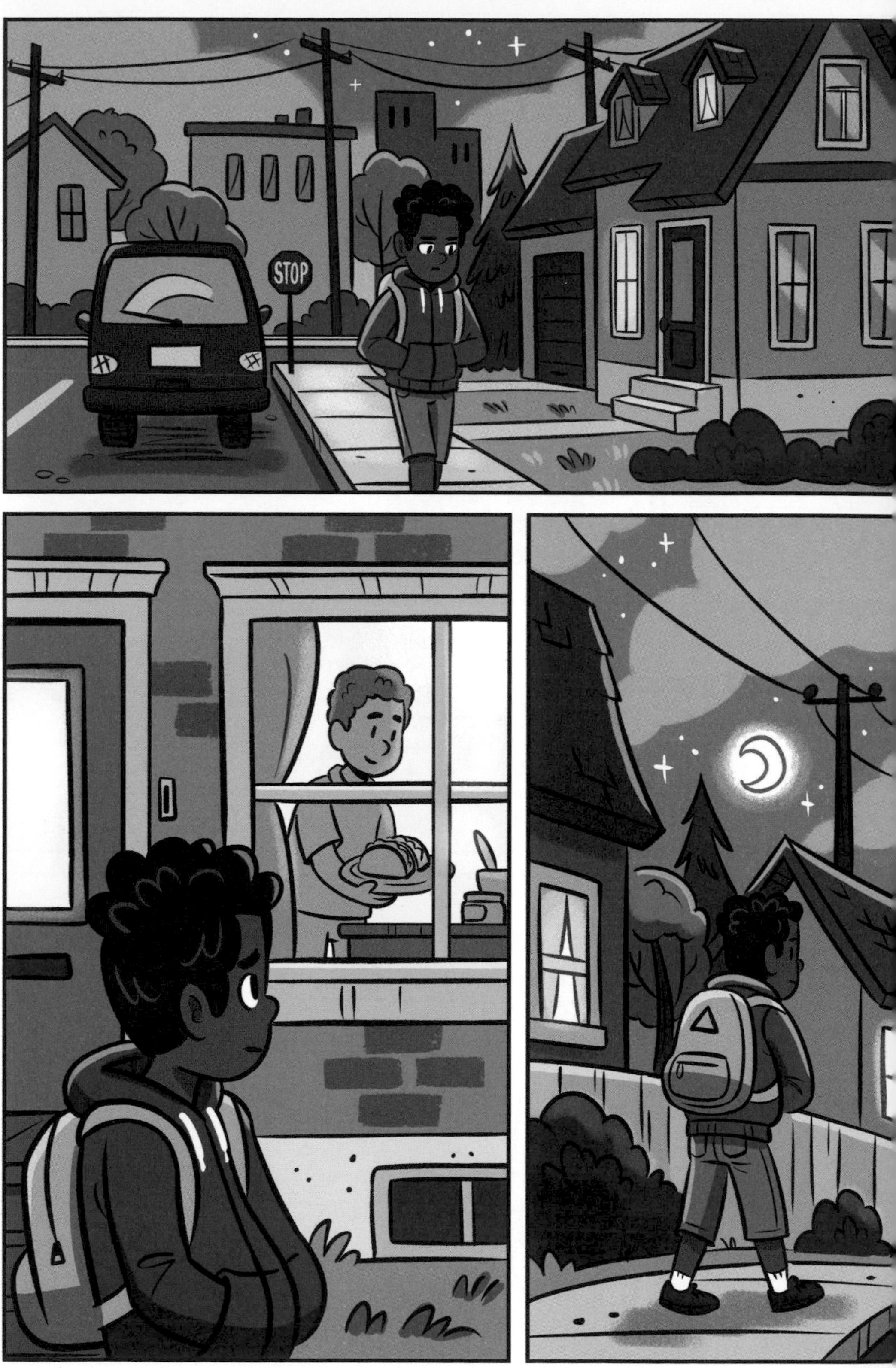
STOP

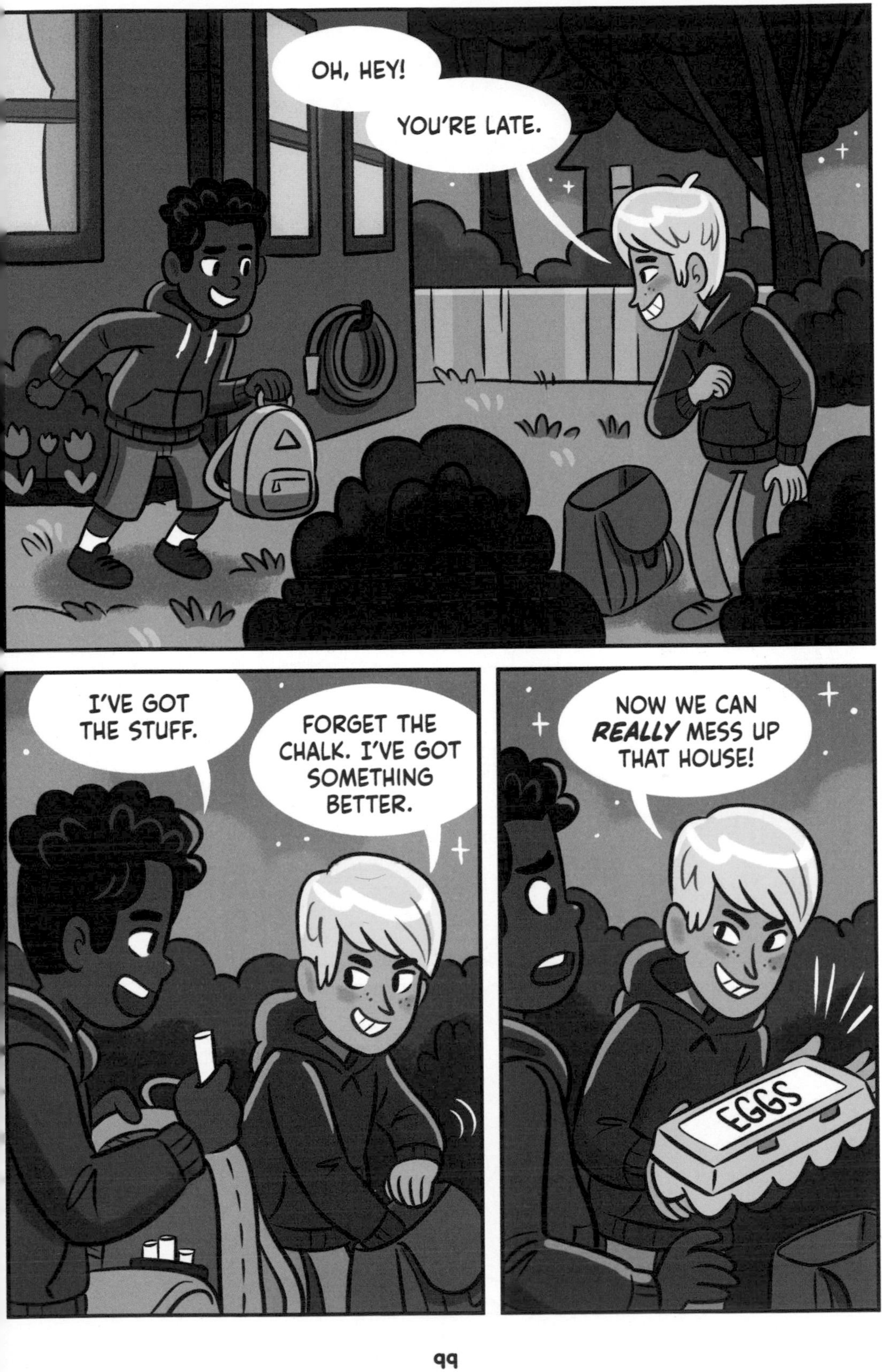
OH, HEY!
YOU'RE LATE.
I'VE GOT THE STUFF.
FORGET THE CHALK. I'VE GOT SOMETHING BETTER.
NOW WE CAN *REALLY* MESS UP THAT HOUSE!
EGGS

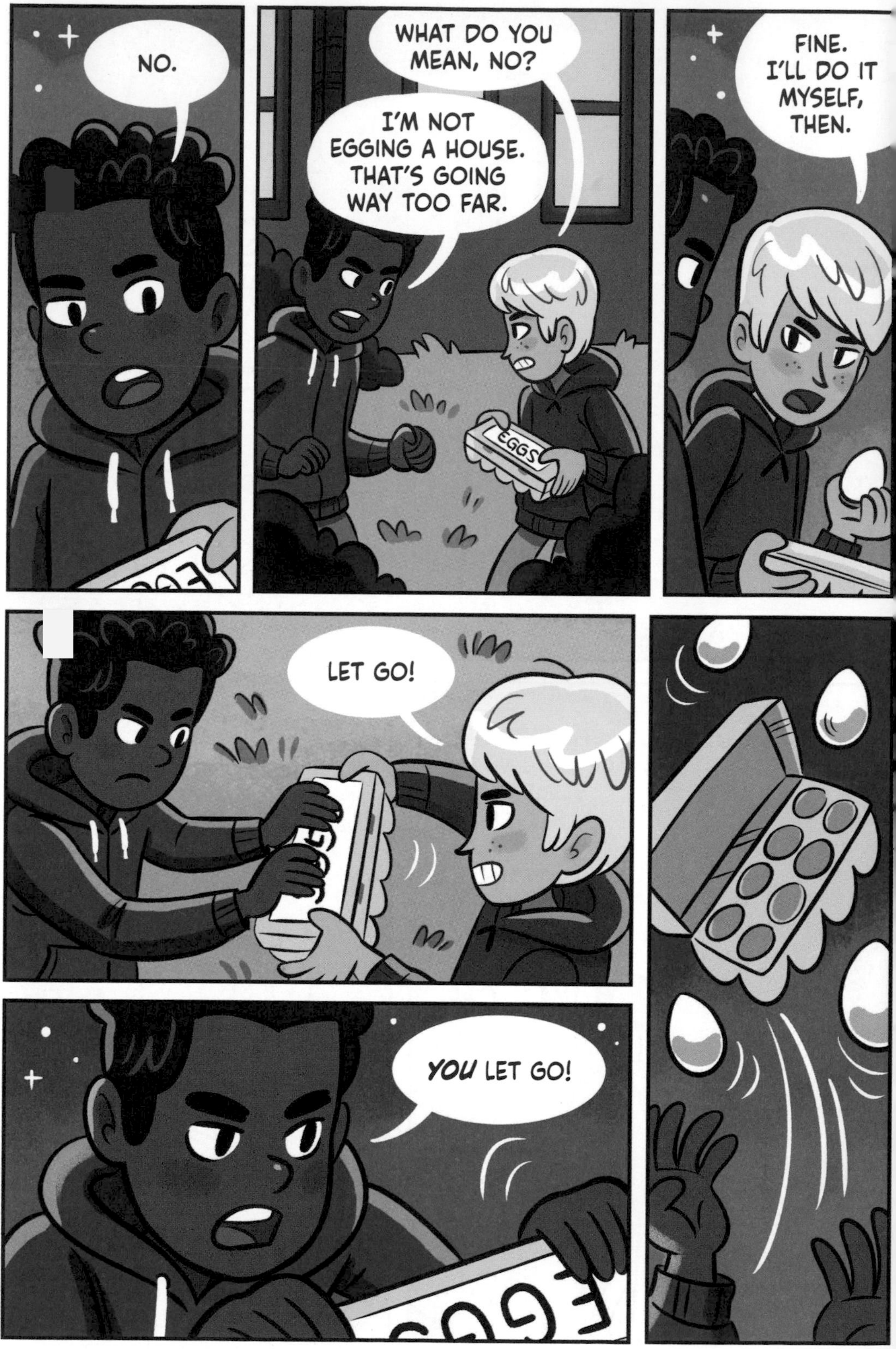
NO.
WHAT DO YOU MEAN, NO?
I'M NOT EGGING A HOUSE. THAT'S GOING WAY TOO FAR.
EGGS
FINE. I'LL DO IT MYSELF, THEN.
LET GO!
YOU LET GO!

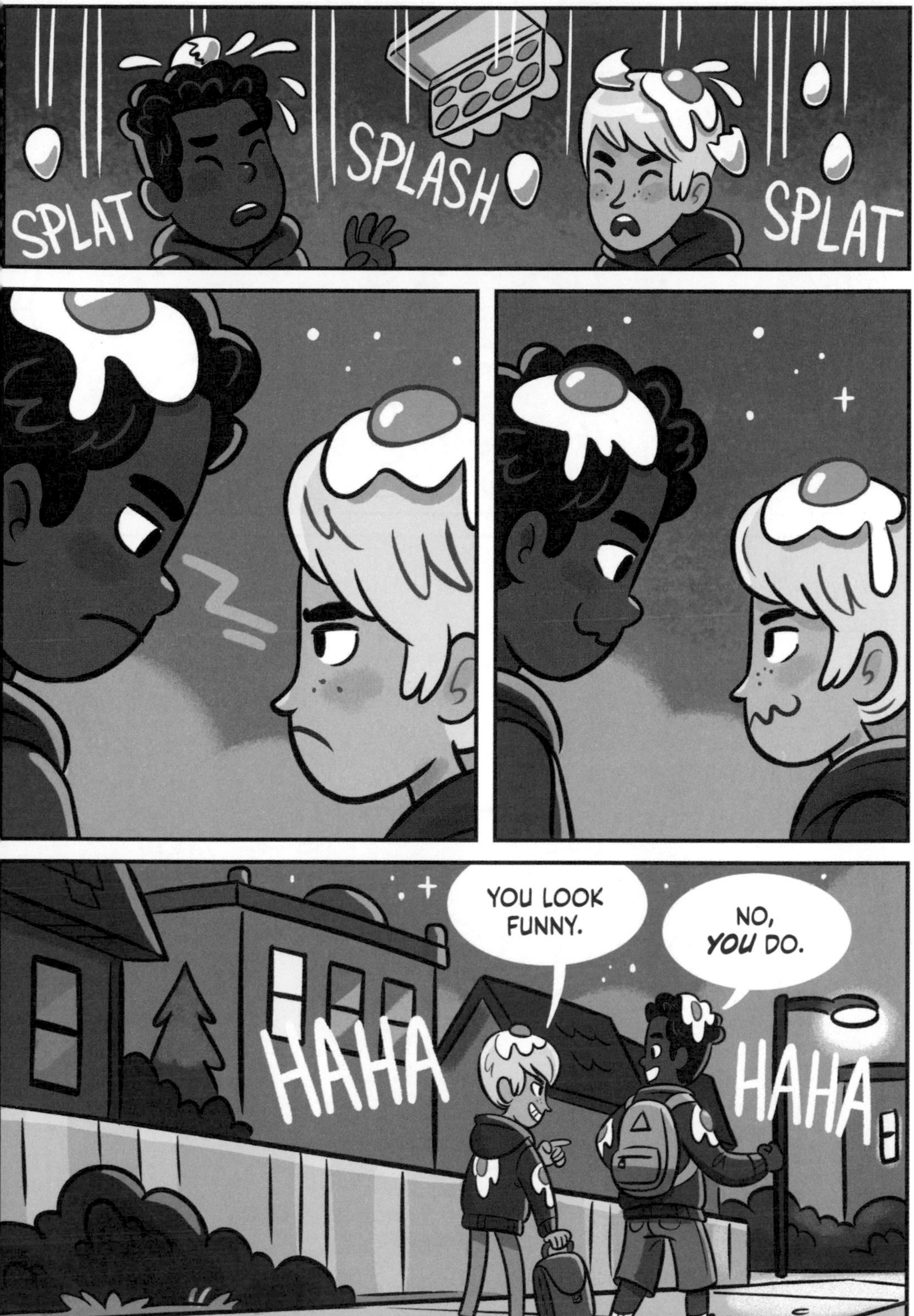

SPLAT
SPLASH
SPLAT
YOU LOOK FUNNY.
HAHA
NO, *YOU* DO.
HAHA

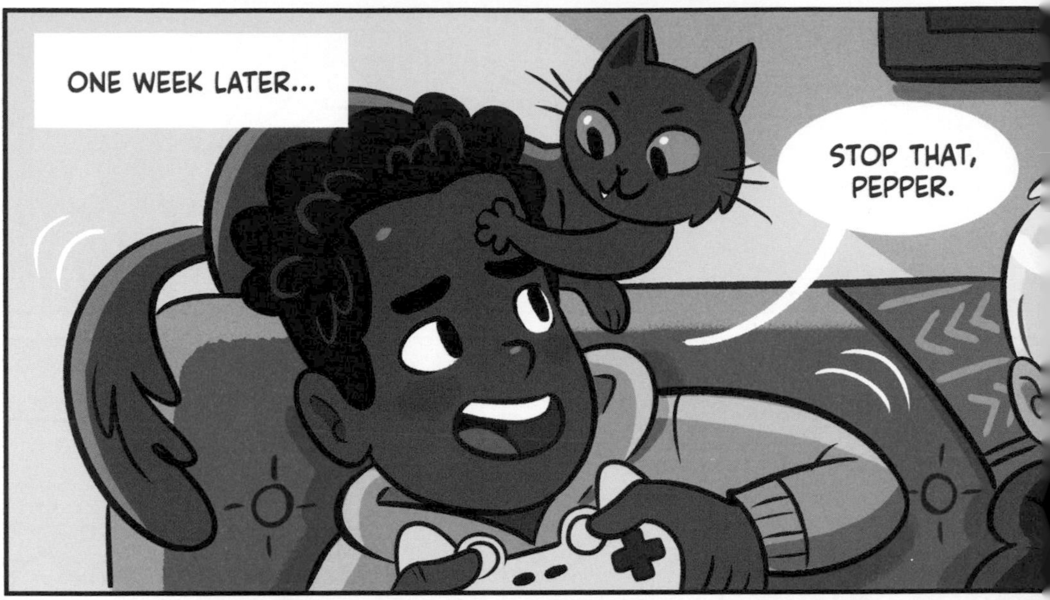
ONE WEEK LATER...
STOP THAT, PEPPER.

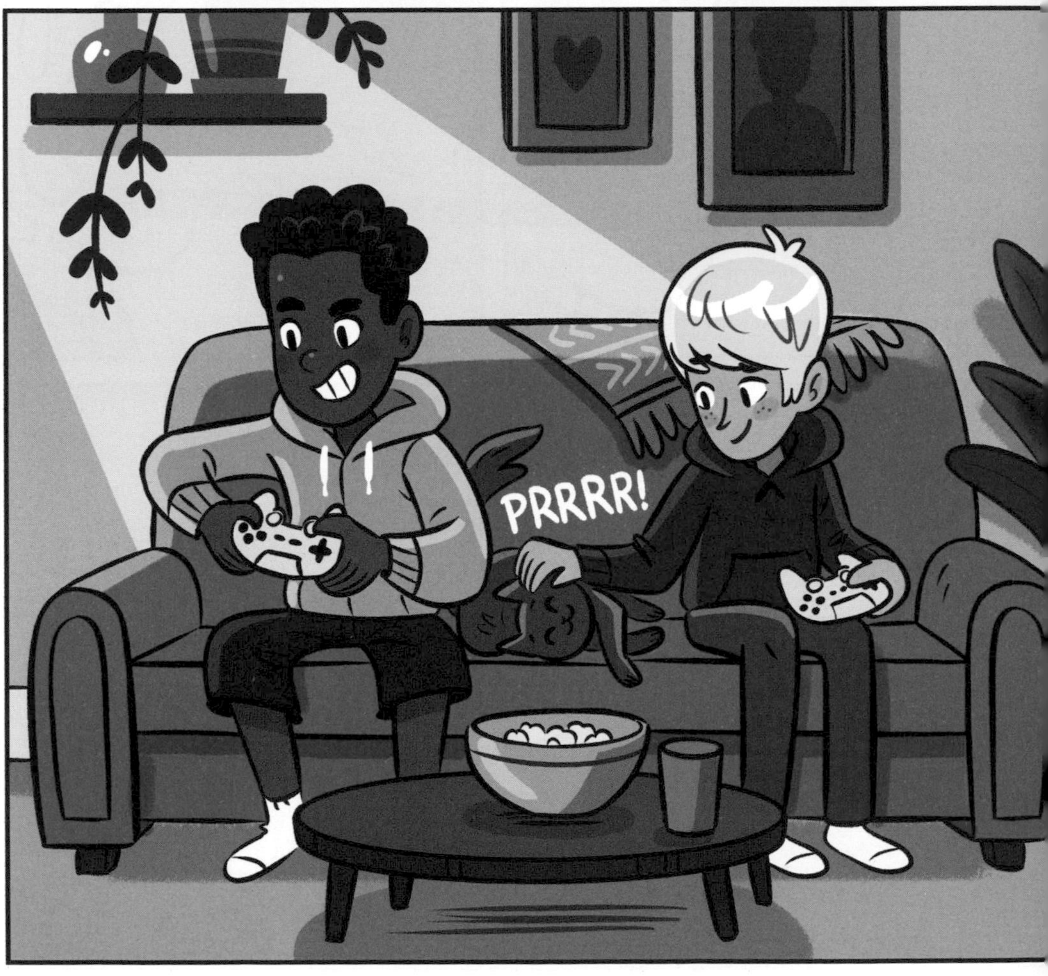
PRRRR!

Chapter 5

MADDIE AND PAXTON

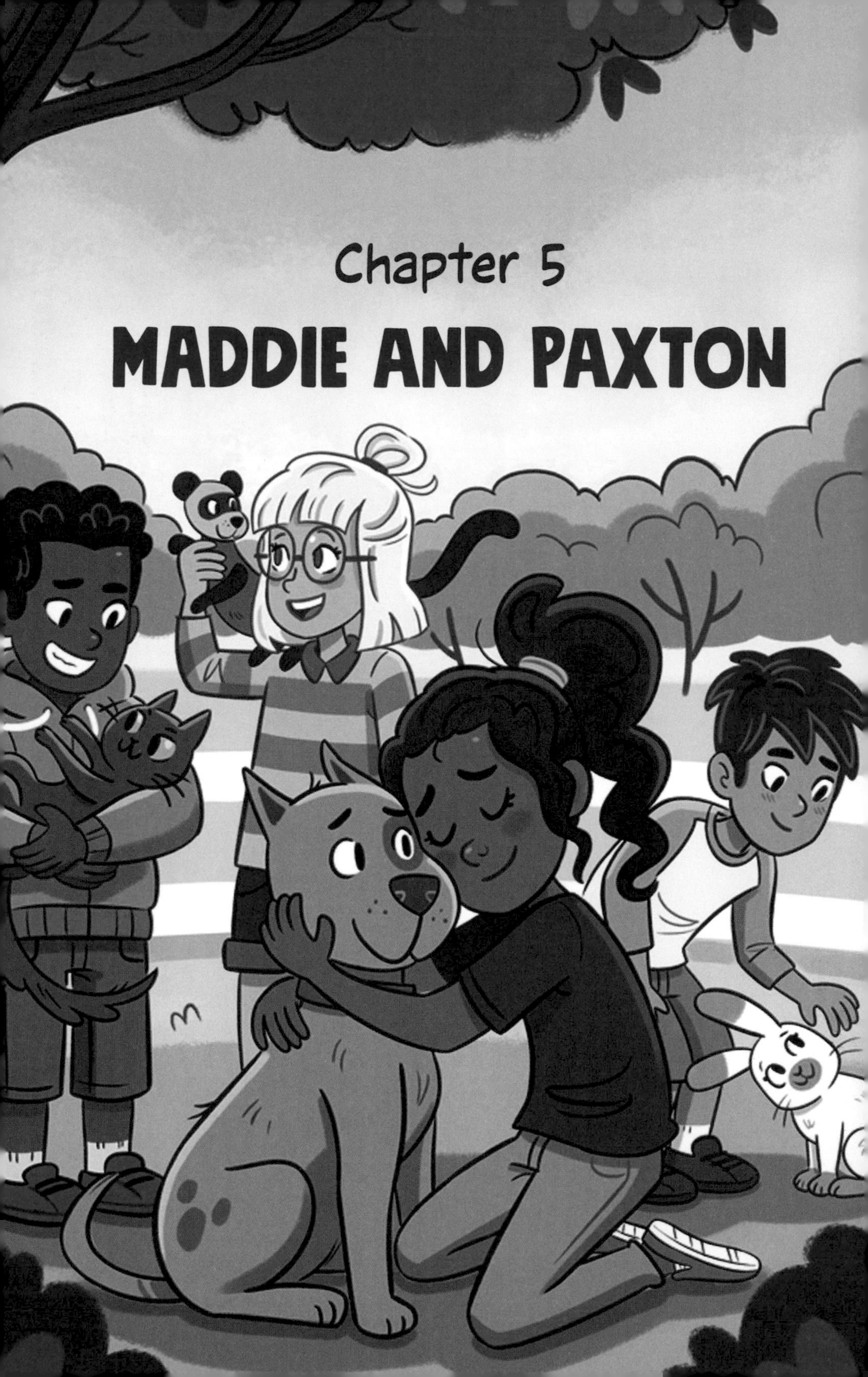

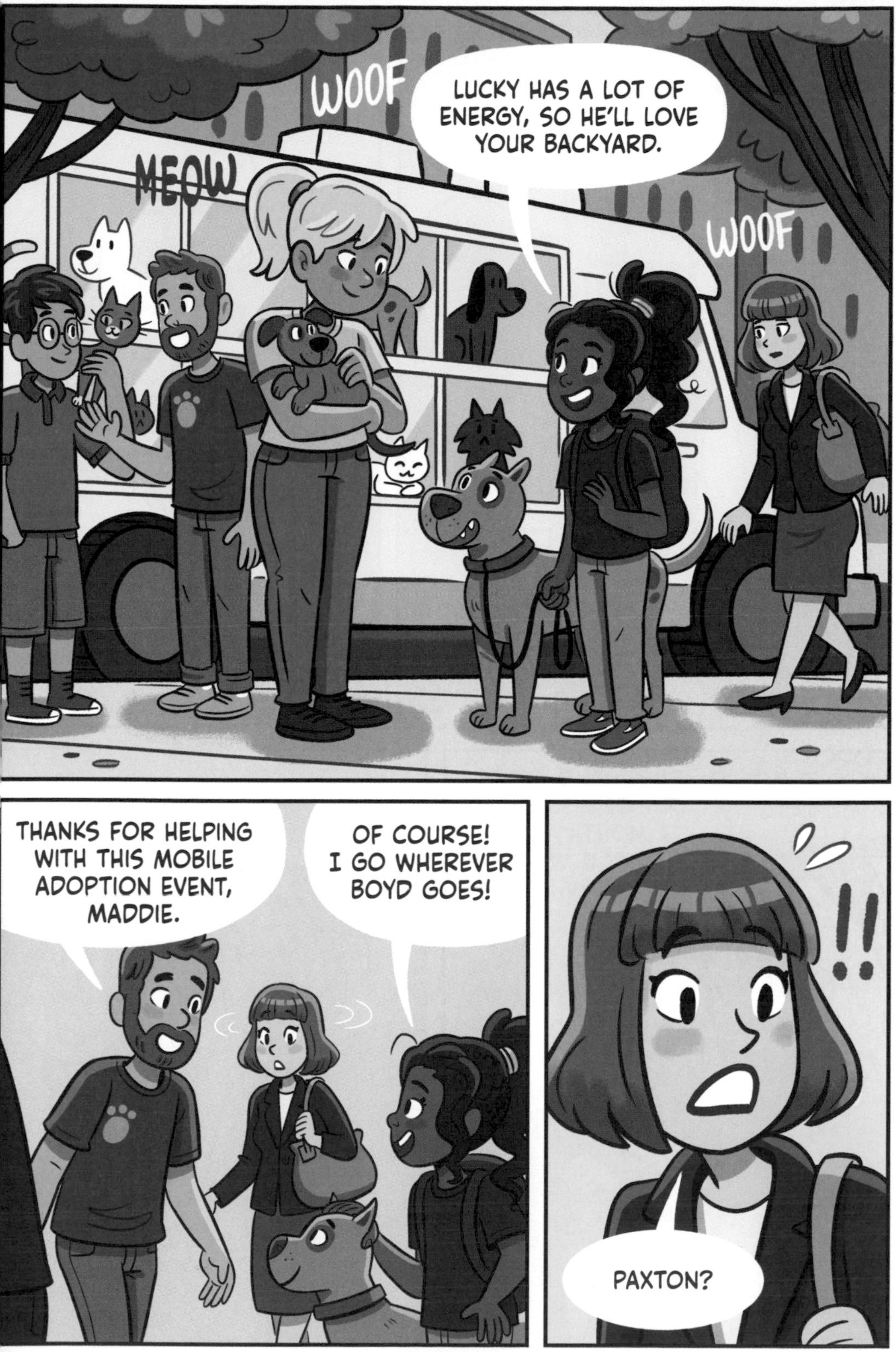
WOOF
LUCKY HAS A LOT OF ENERGY, SO HE'LL LOVE YOUR BACKYARD.
MEOW
WOOF
THANKS FOR HELPING WITH THIS MOBILE ADOPTION EVENT, MADDIE.
OF COURSE! I GO WHEREVER BOYD GOES!
!!
PAXTON?

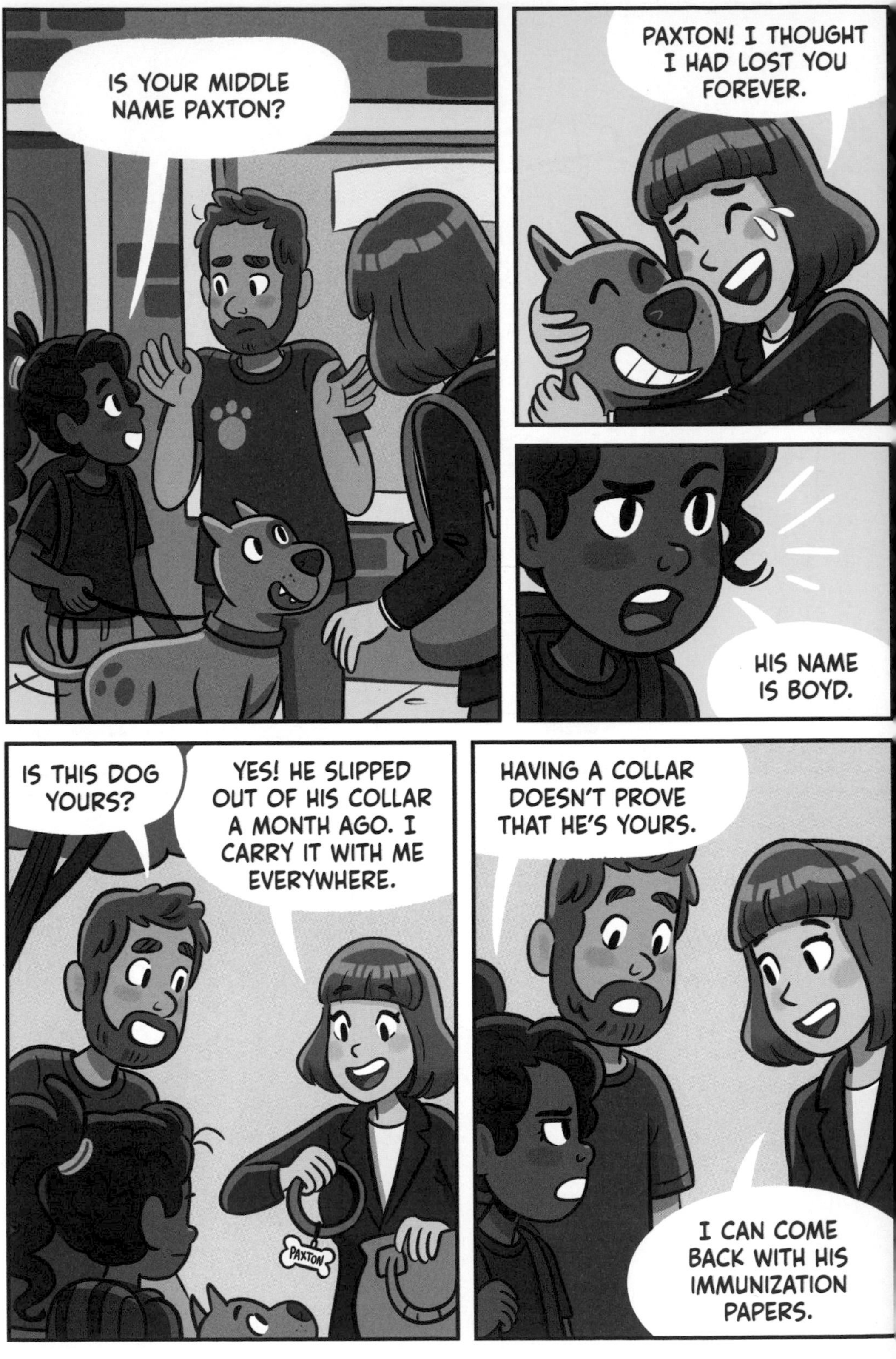
IS YOUR MIDDLE NAME PAXTON?
PAXTON! I THOUGHT I HAD LOST YOU FOREVER.
HIS NAME IS BOYD.
IS THIS DOG YOURS?
YES! HE SLIPPED OUT OF HIS COLLAR A MONTH AGO. I CARRY IT WITH ME EVERYWHERE.
PAXTON
HAVING A COLLAR DOESN'T PROVE THAT HE'S YOURS.
I CAN COME BACK WITH HIS IMMUNIZATION PAPERS.

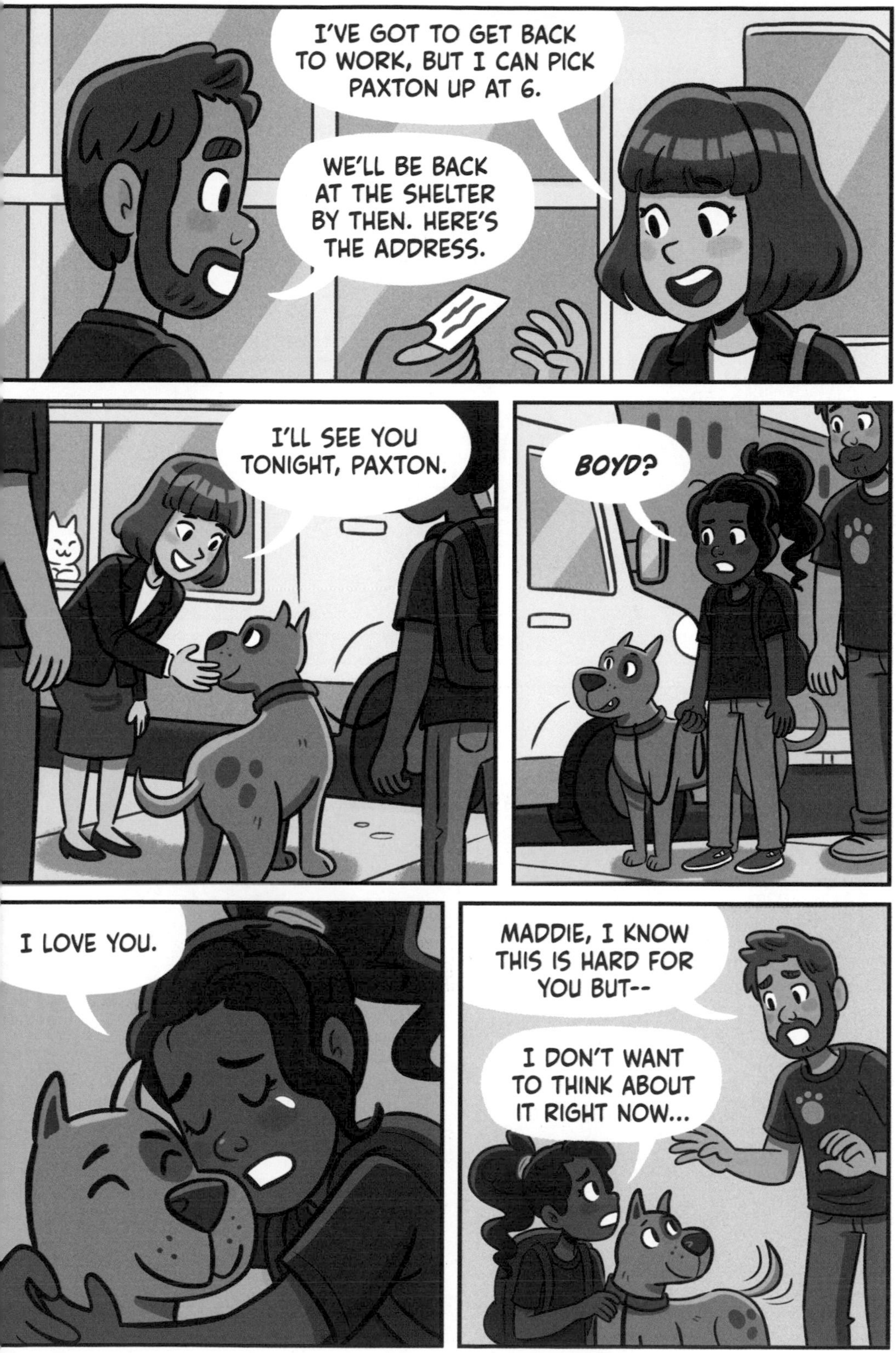
I'VE GOT TO GET BACK TO WORK, BUT I CAN PICK PAXTON UP AT 6.
WE'LL BE BACK AT THE SHELTER BY THEN. HERE'S THE ADDRESS.
I'LL SEE YOU TONIGHT, PAXTON.
BOYD?
I LOVE YOU.
MADDIE, I KNOW THIS IS HARD FOR YOU BUT--
I DON'T WANT TO THINK ABOUT IT RIGHT NOW...

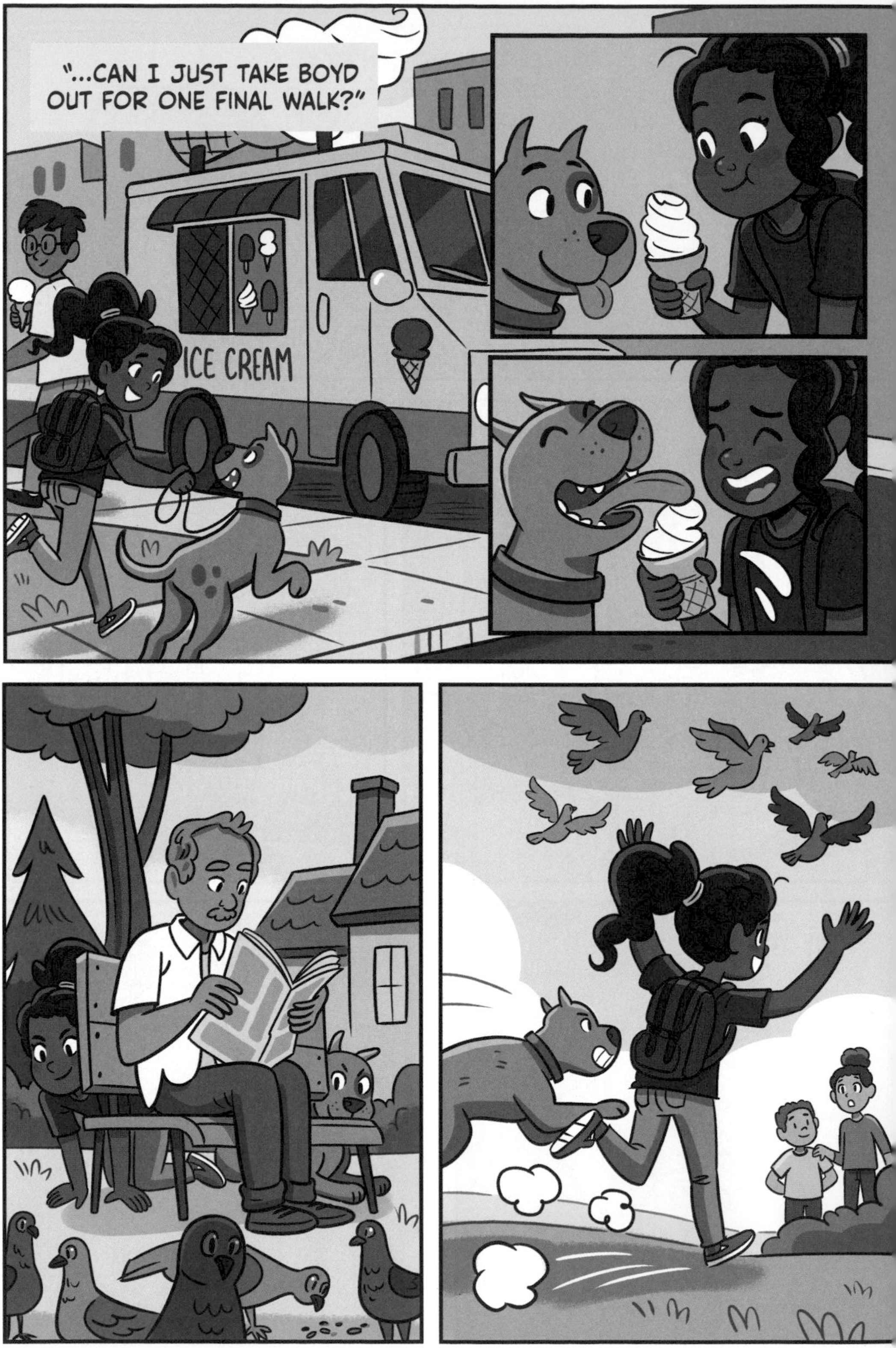
"...CAN I JUST TAKE BOYD OUT FOR ONE FINAL WALK?"
ICE CREAM

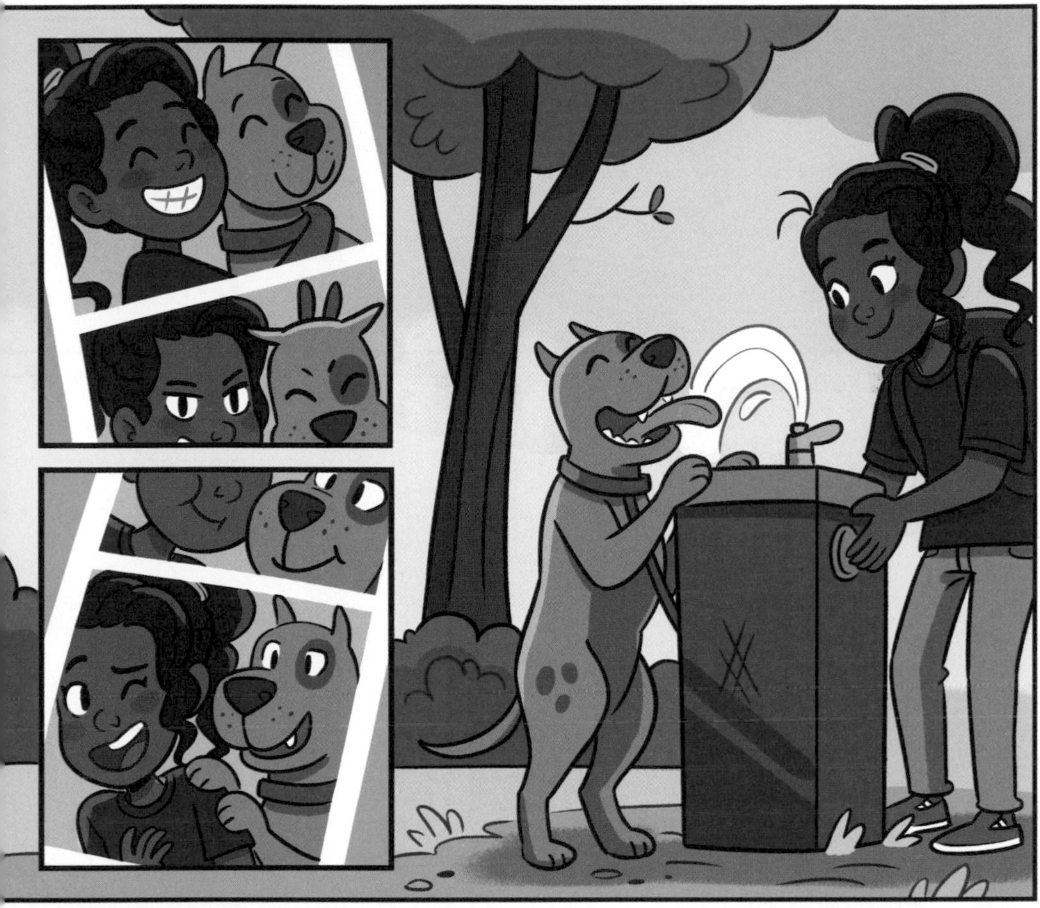
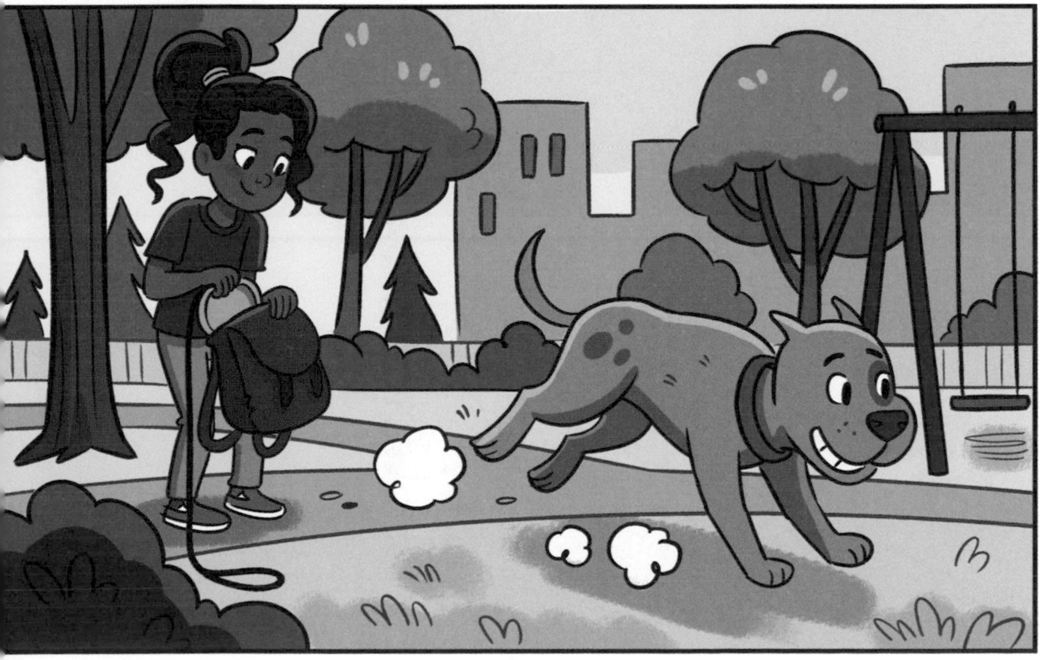

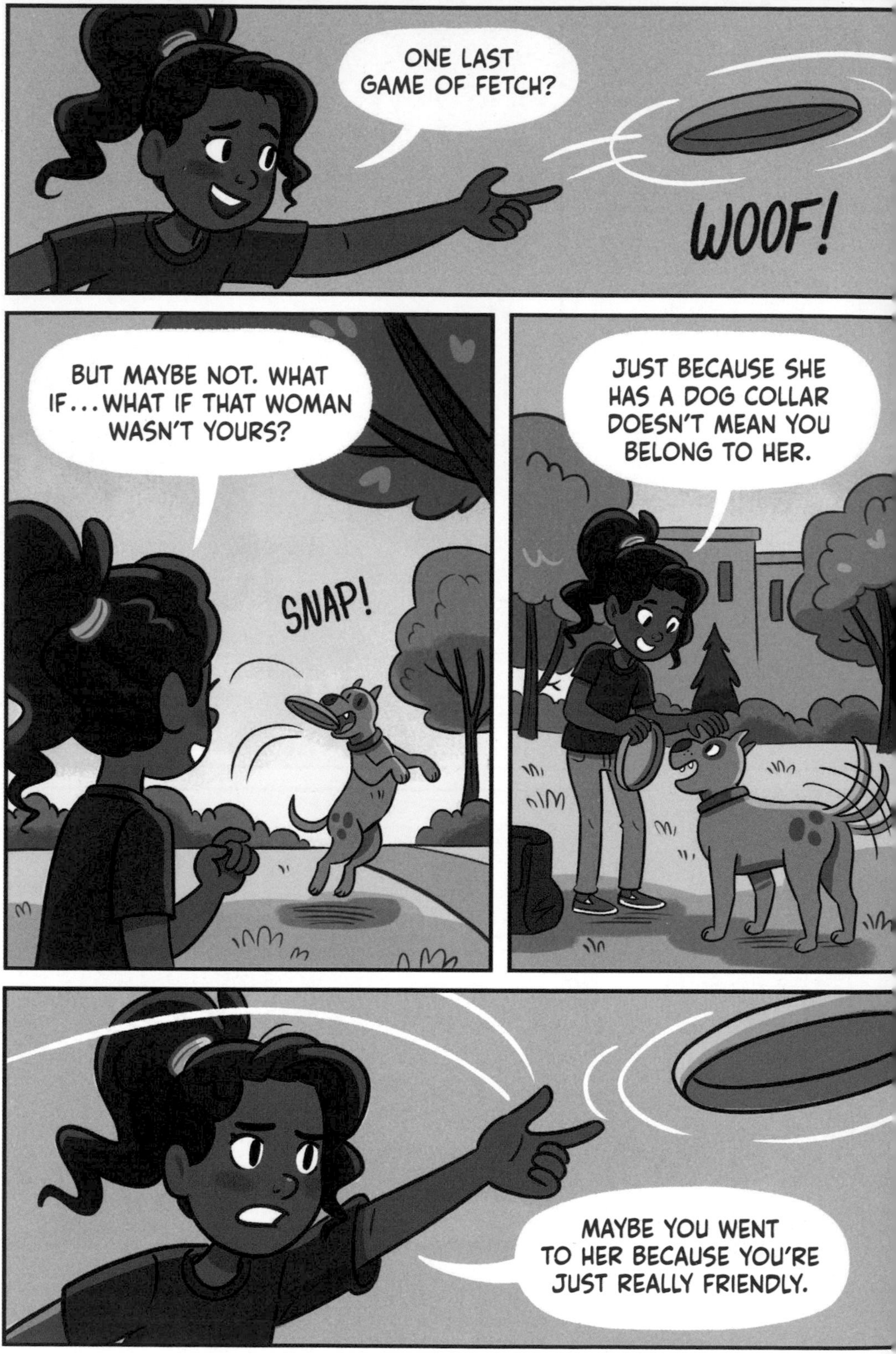
ONE LAST GAME OF FETCH?
WOOF!
BUT MAYBE NOT. WHAT IF...WHAT IF THAT WOMAN WASN'T YOURS?
SNAP!
JUST BECAUSE SHE HAS A DOG COLLAR DOESN'T MEAN YOU BELONG TO HER.
MAYBE YOU WENT TO HER BECAUSE YOU'RE JUST REALLY FRIENDLY.

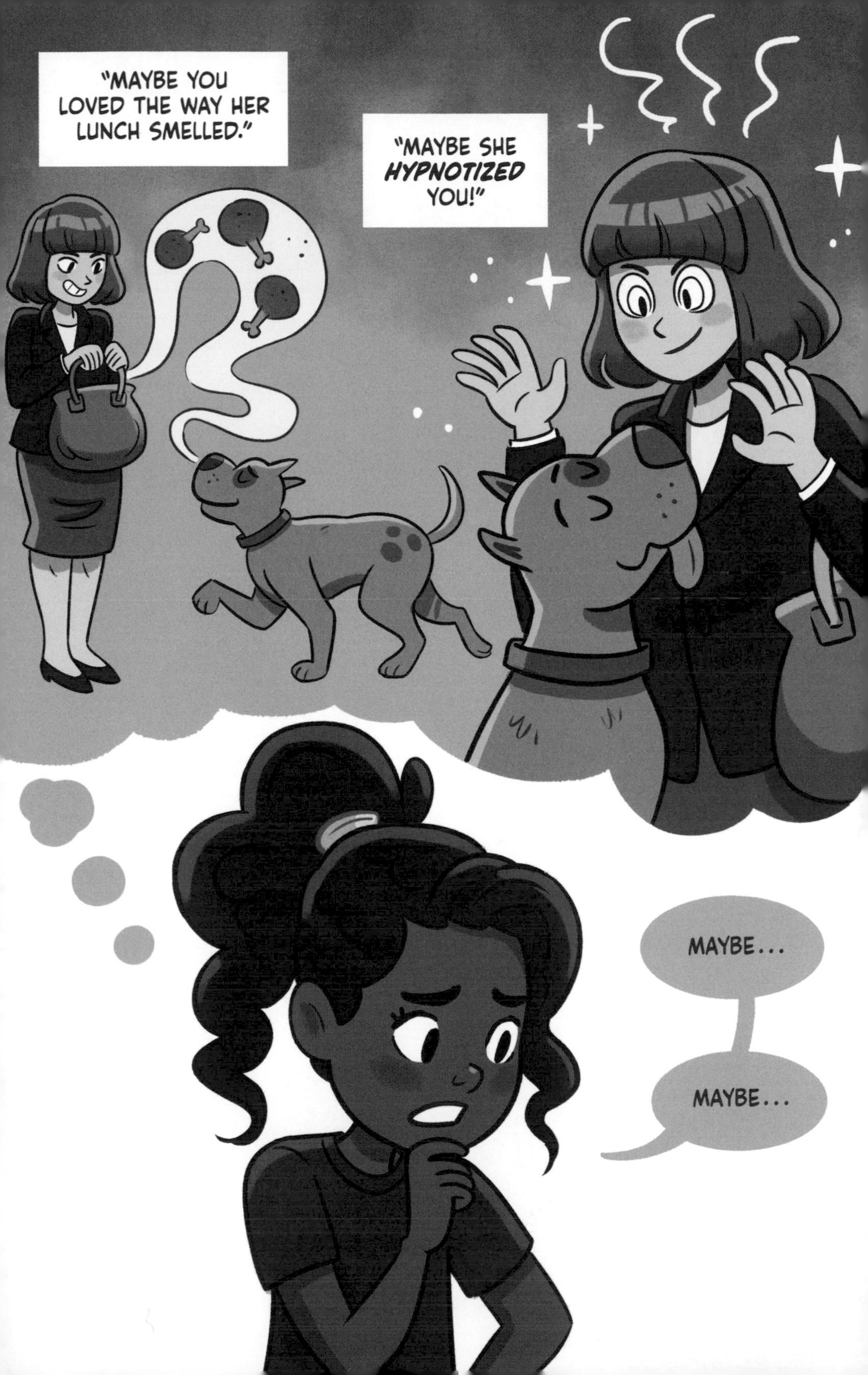
"MAYBE YOU LOVED THE WAY HER LUNCH SMELLED."
"MAYBE SHE *HYPNOTIZED* YOU!"
MAYBE...
MAYBE...

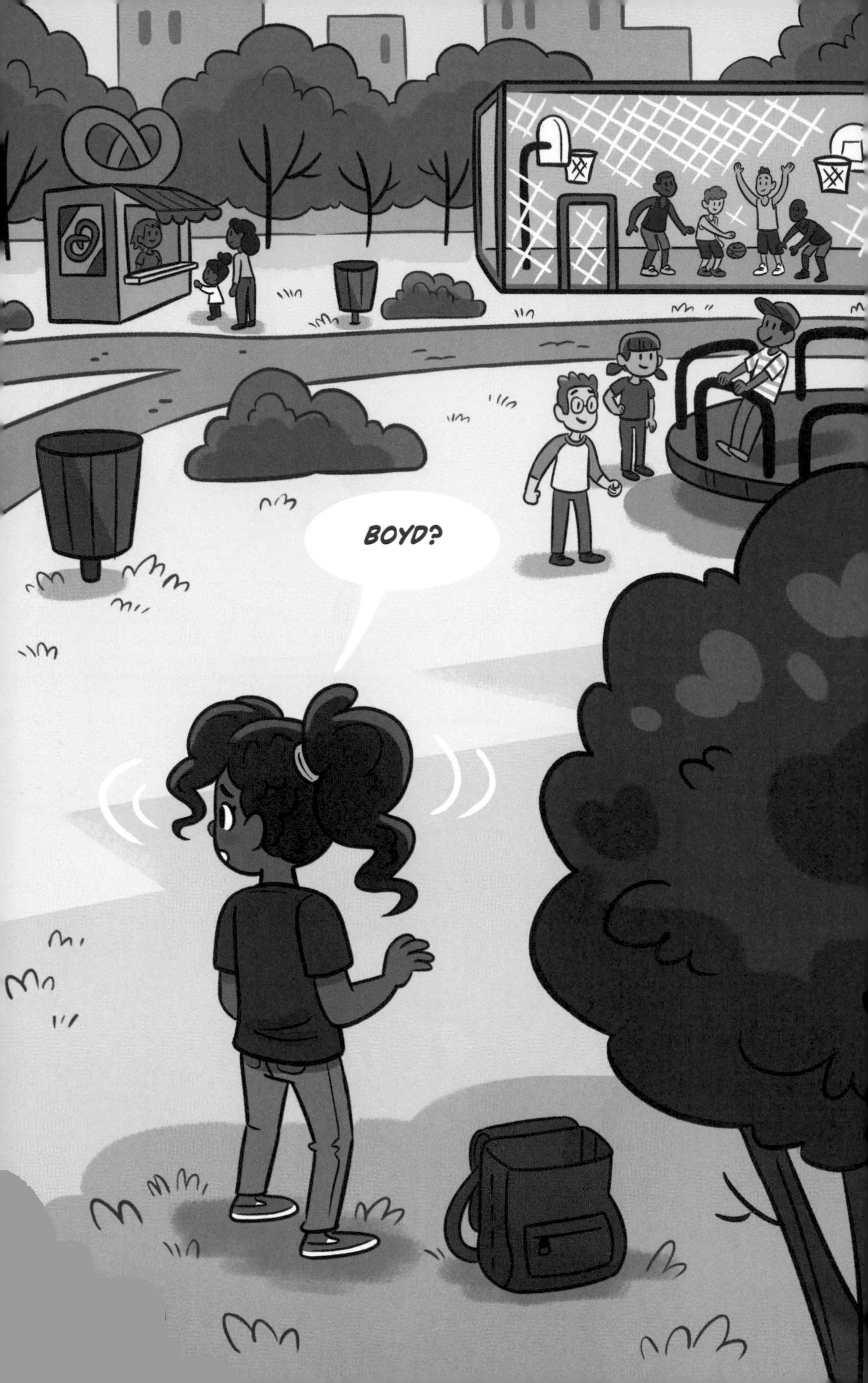
BOYD?

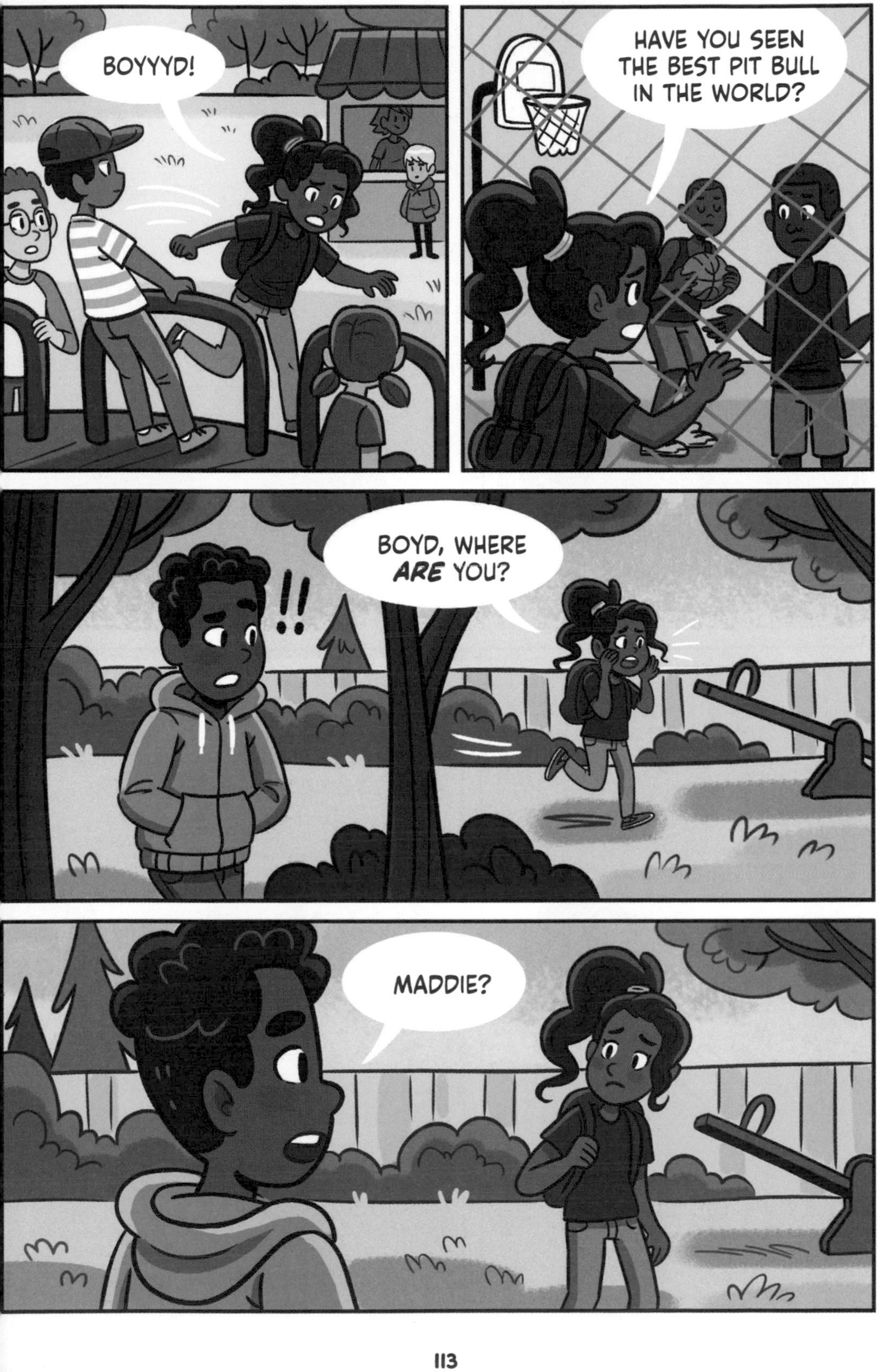

BOYYYD!
HAVE YOU SEEN THE BEST PIT BULL IN THE WORLD?
BOYD, WHERE *ARE* YOU?
!!
MADDIE?

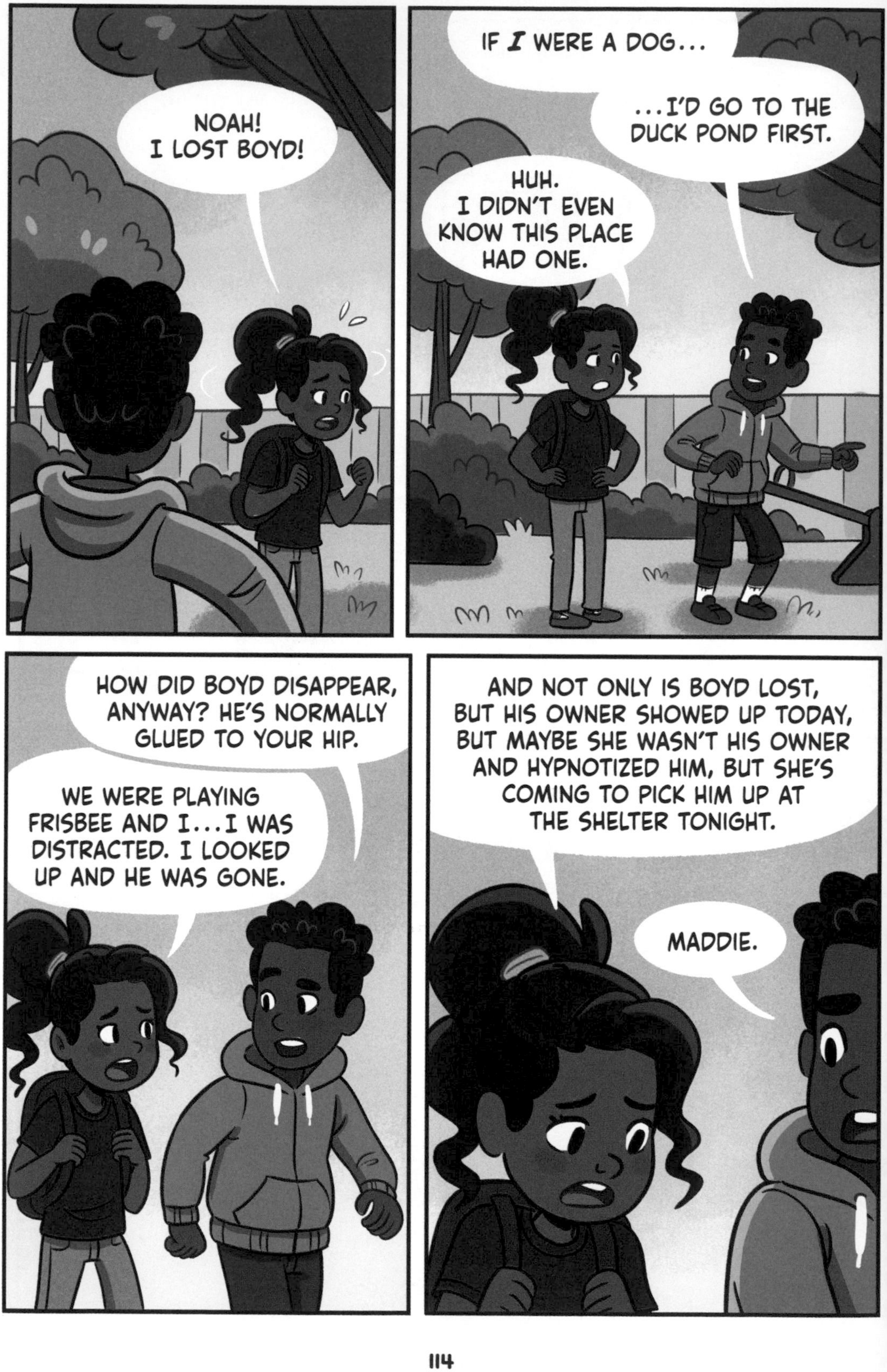
NOAH! I LOST BOYD!
IF I WERE A DOG...
...I'D GO TO THE DUCK POND FIRST.
HUH. I DIDN'T EVEN KNOW THIS PLACE HAD ONE.
HOW DID BOYD DISAPPEAR, ANYWAY? HE'S NORMALLY GLUED TO YOUR HIP.
WE WERE PLAYING FRISBEE AND I...I WAS DISTRACTED. I LOOKED UP AND HE WAS GONE.
AND NOT ONLY IS BOYD LOST, BUT HIS OWNER SHOWED UP TODAY, BUT MAYBE SHE WASN'T HIS OWNER AND HYPNOTIZED HIM, BUT SHE'S COMING TO PICK HIM UP AT THE SHELTER TONIGHT.
MADDIE.

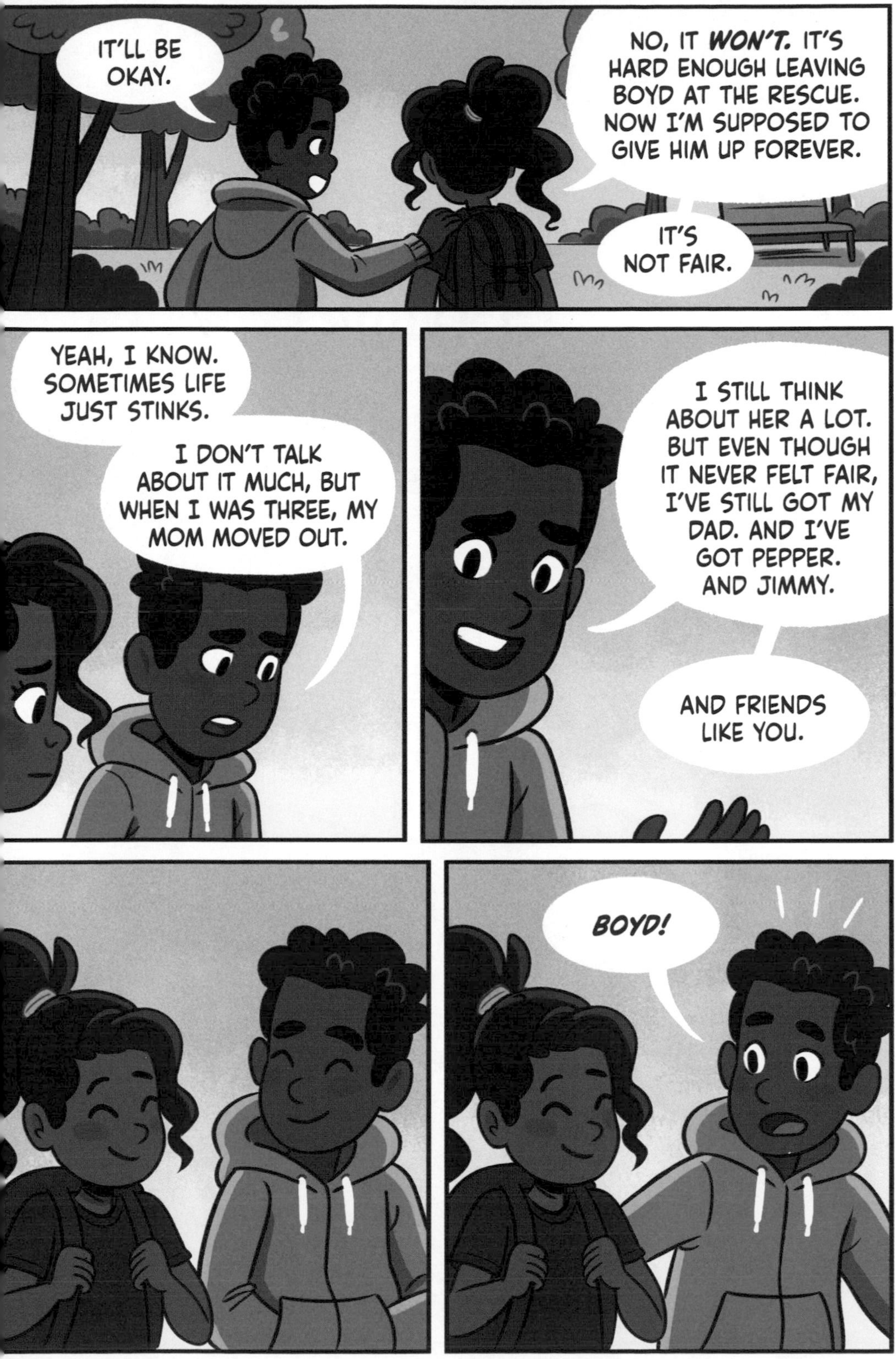
IT'LL BE OKAY.
NO, IT *WON'T.* IT'S HARD ENOUGH LEAVING BOYD AT THE RESCUE. NOW I'M SUPPOSED TO GIVE HIM UP FOREVER.
IT'S NOT FAIR.
YEAH, I KNOW. SOMETIMES LIFE JUST STINKS.
I DON'T TALK ABOUT IT MUCH, BUT WHEN I WAS THREE, MY MOM MOVED OUT.
I STILL THINK ABOUT HER A LOT. BUT EVEN THOUGH IT NEVER FELT FAIR, I'VE STILL GOT MY DAD. AND I'VE GOT PEPPER. AND JIMMY.
AND FRIENDS LIKE YOU.
BOYD!

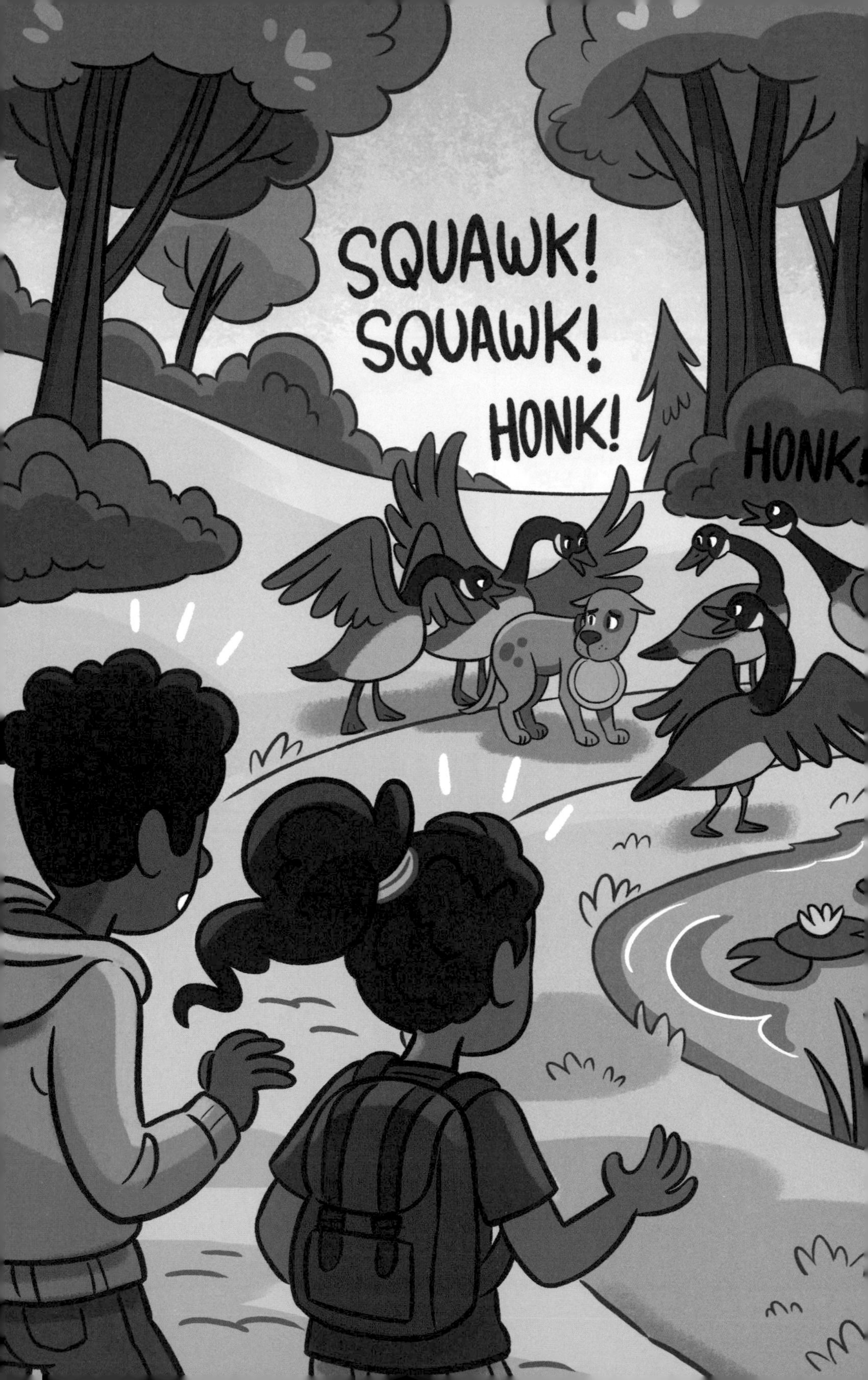
SQUAWK!
SQUAWK!
HONK!
HONK!

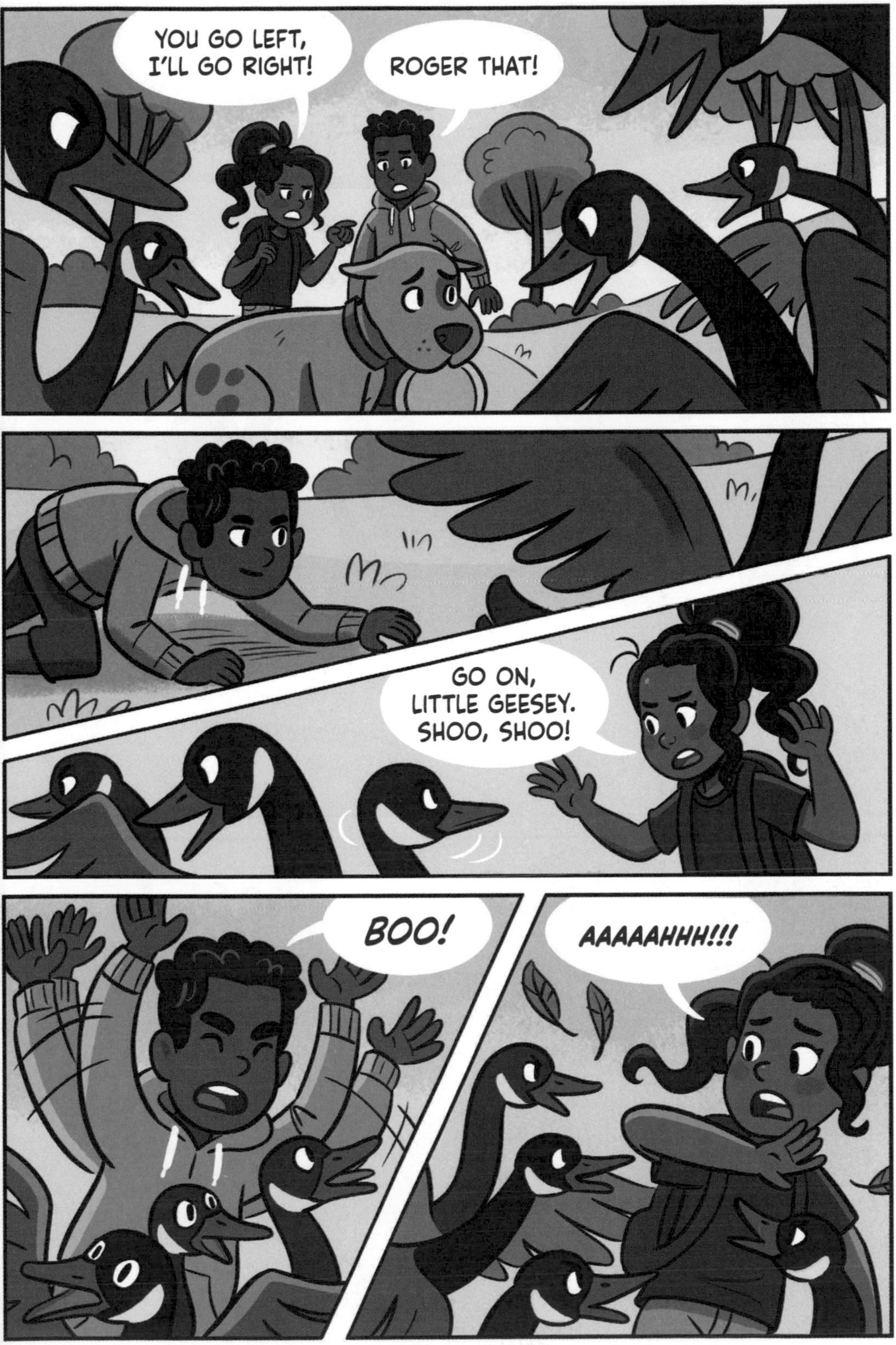
YOU GO LEFT, I'LL GO RIGHT!
ROGER THAT!
GO ON, LITTLE GEESEY. SHOO, SHOO!
BOO!
AAAAAHHH!!!

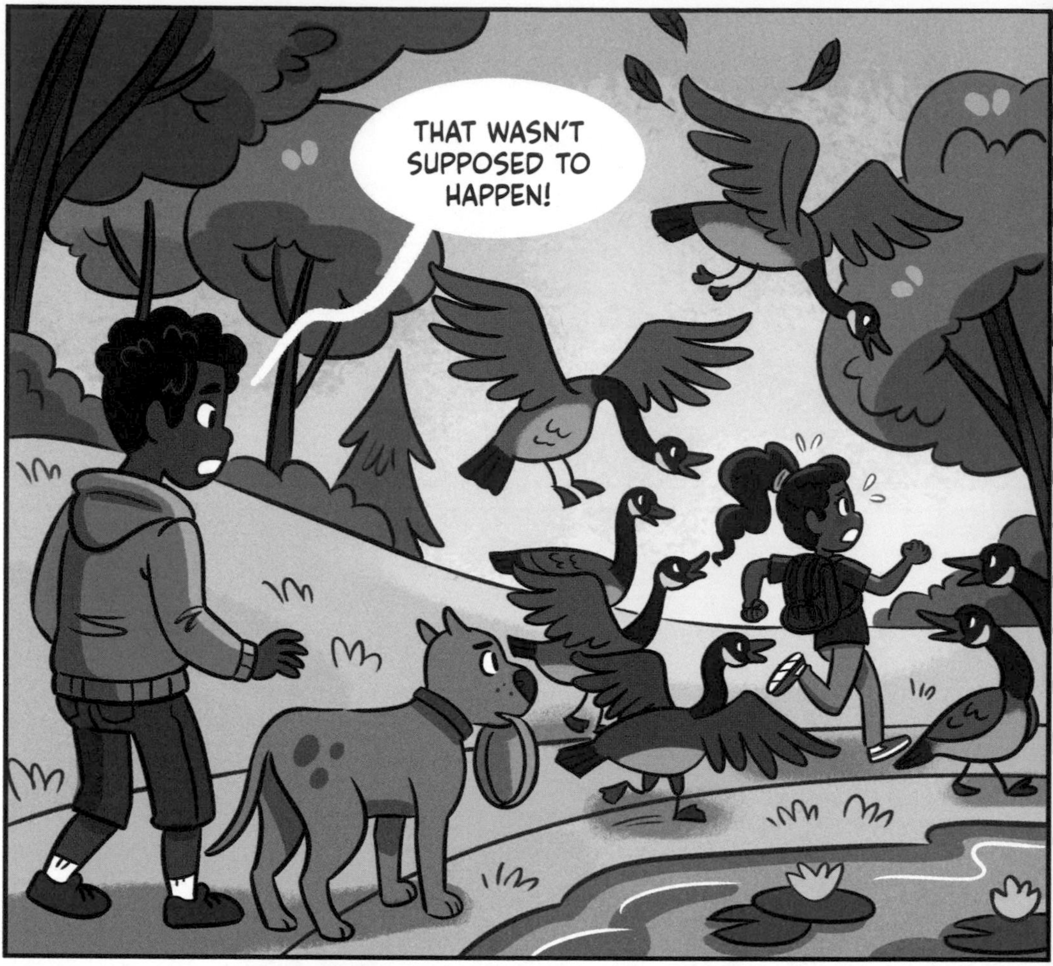
THAT WASN'T SUPPOSED TO HAPPEN!

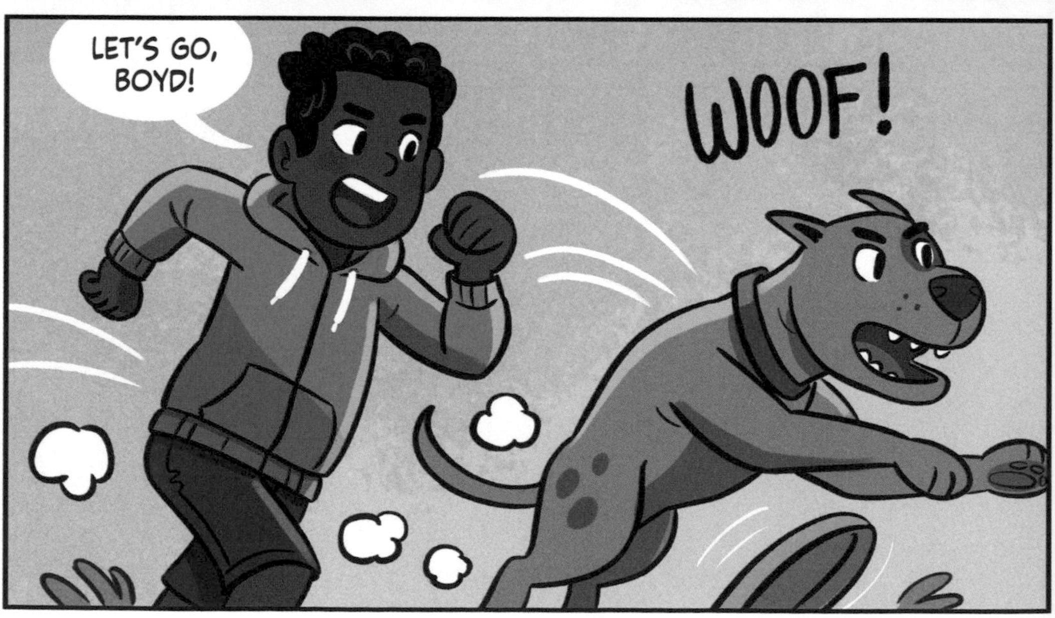
LET'S GO, BOYD!
WOOF!

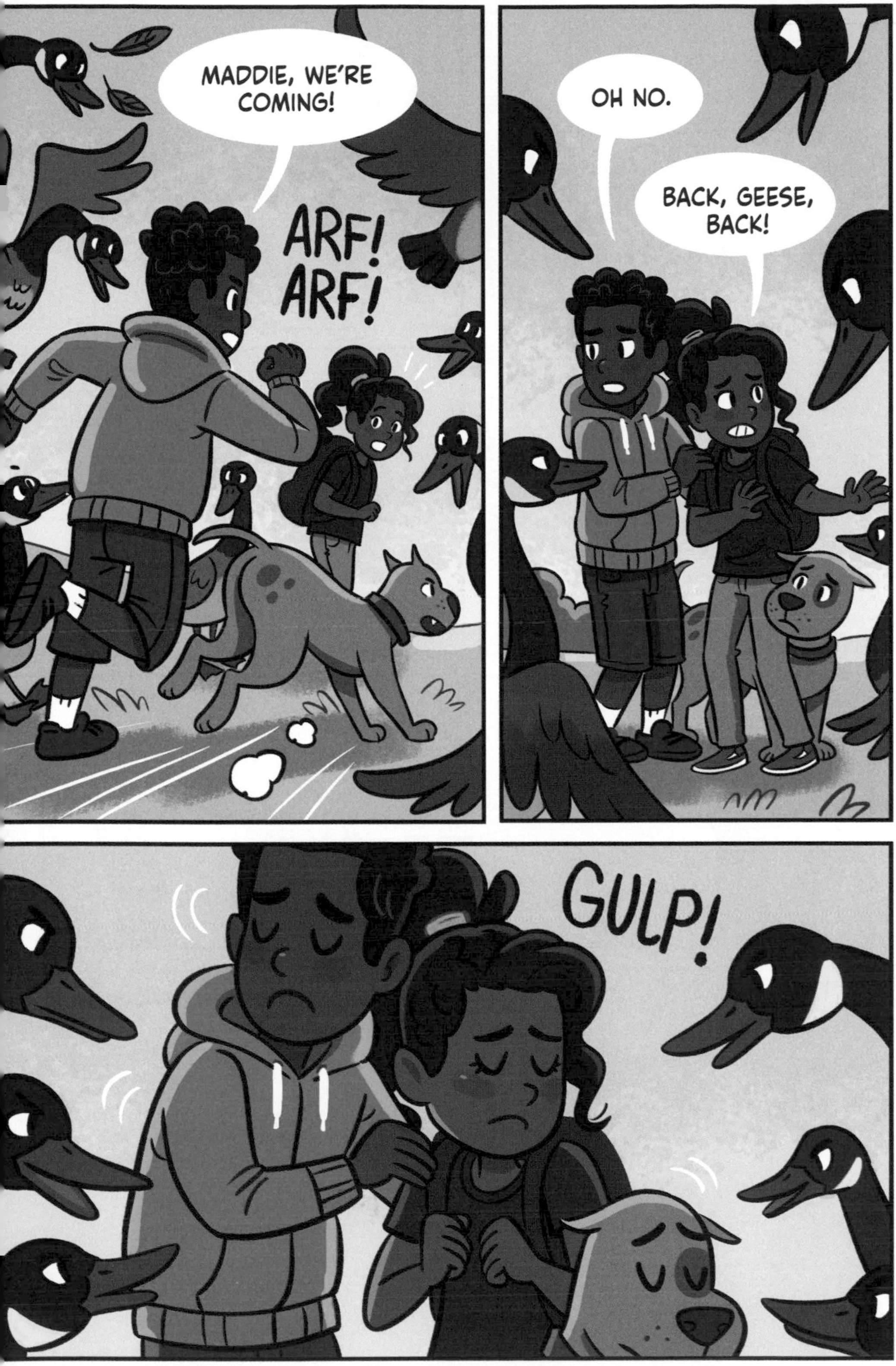
MADDIE, WE'RE COMING!
ARF! ARF!
OH NO.
BACK, GEESE, BACK!
GULP!

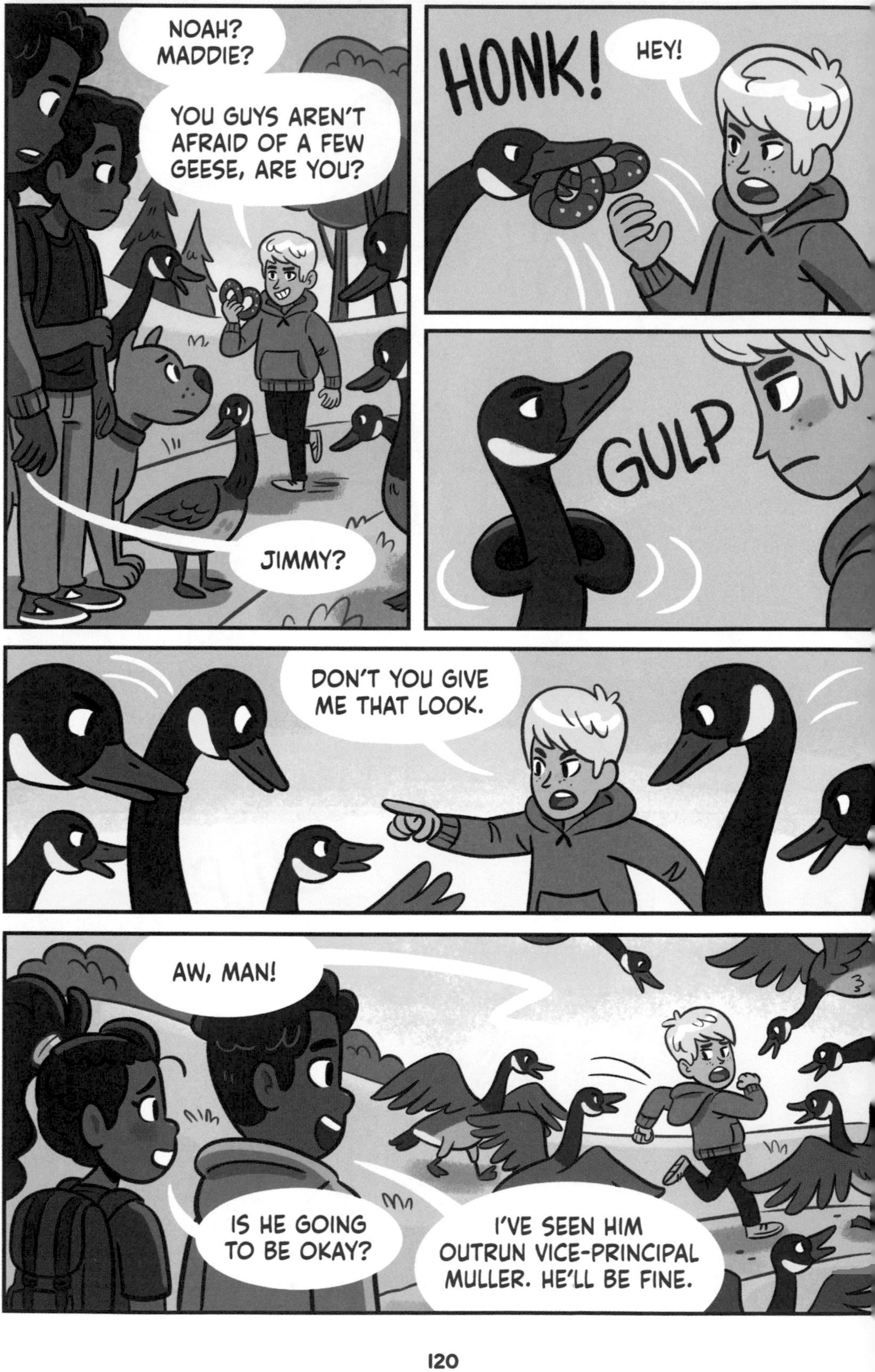
NOAH? MADDIE?
YOU GUYS AREN'T AFRAID OF A FEW GEESE, ARE YOU?
JIMMY?
HONK!
HEY!
GULP
DON'T YOU GIVE ME THAT LOOK.
AW, MAN!
IS HE GOING TO BE OKAY?
I'VE SEEN HIM OUTRUN VICE-PRINCIPAL MULLER. HE'LL BE FINE.

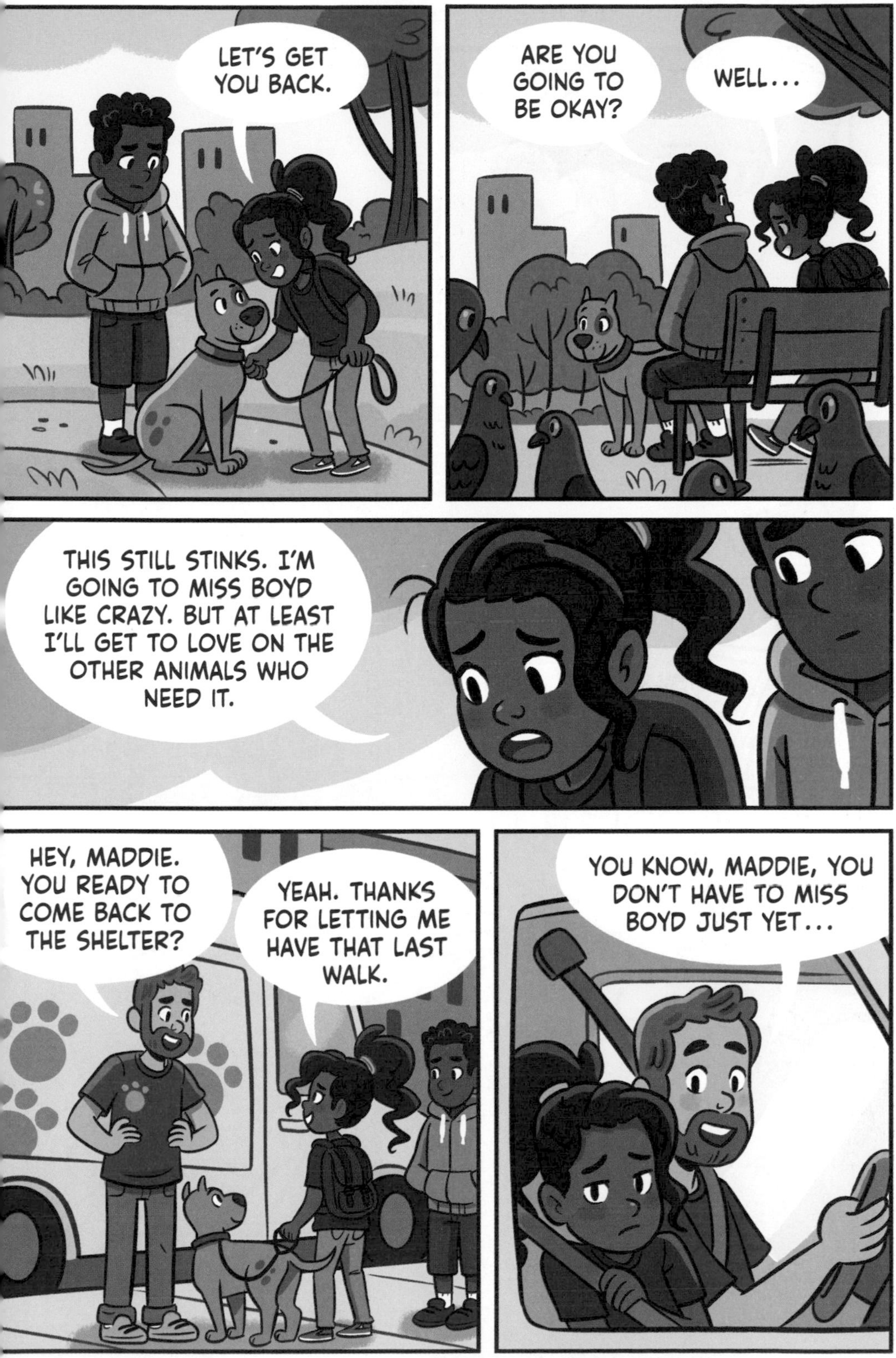
LET'S GET YOU BACK.
ARE YOU GOING TO BE OKAY?
WELL...
THIS STILL STINKS. I'M GOING TO MISS BOYD LIKE CRAZY. BUT AT LEAST I'LL GET TO LOVE ON THE OTHER ANIMALS WHO NEED IT.
HEY, MADDIE. YOU READY TO COME BACK TO THE SHELTER?
YEAH. THANKS FOR LETTING ME HAVE THAT LAST WALK.
YOU KNOW, MADDIE, YOU DON'T HAVE TO MISS BOYD JUST YET...

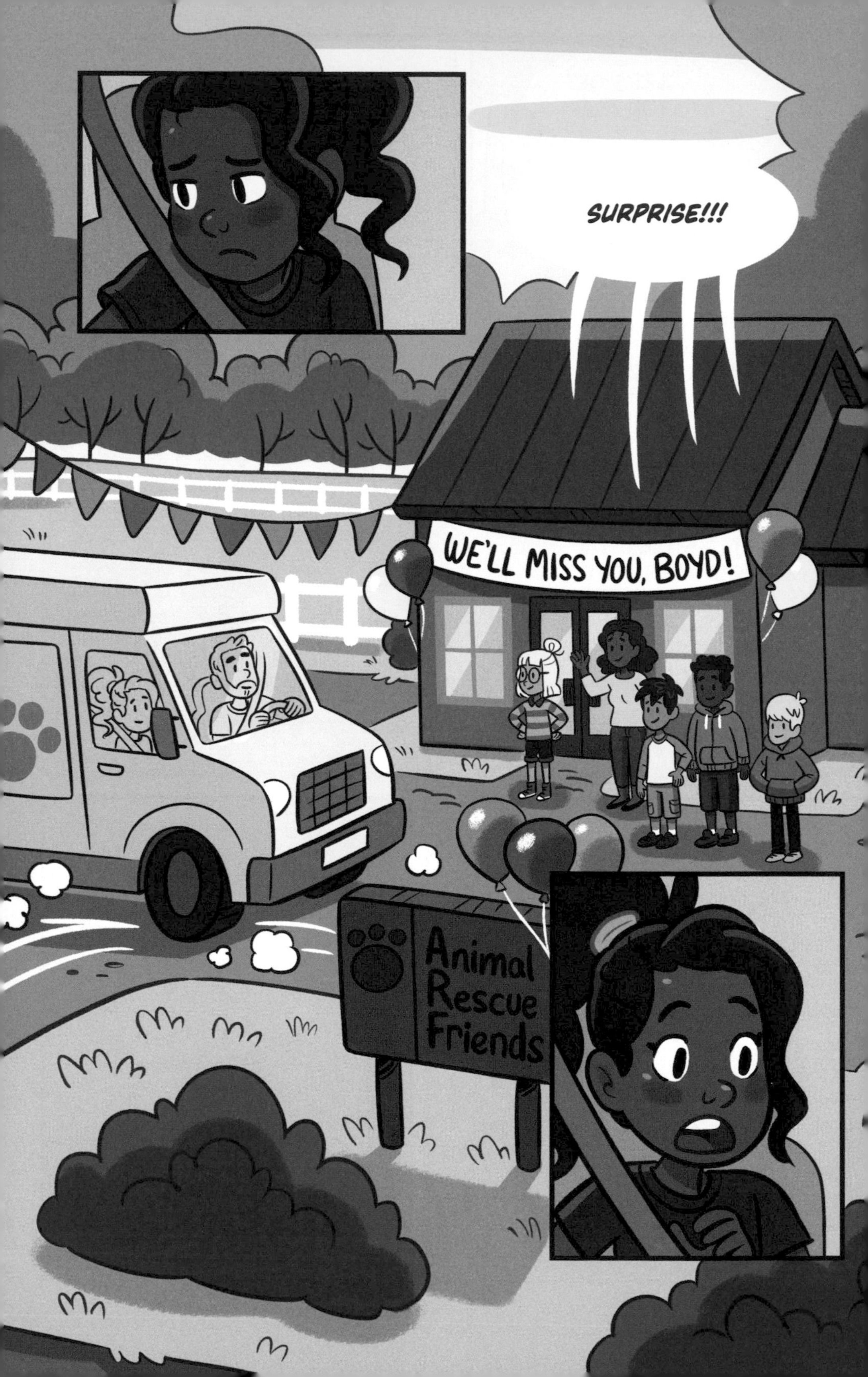
SURPRISE!!!
WE'LL MISS YOU, BOYD!
Animal Rescue Friends

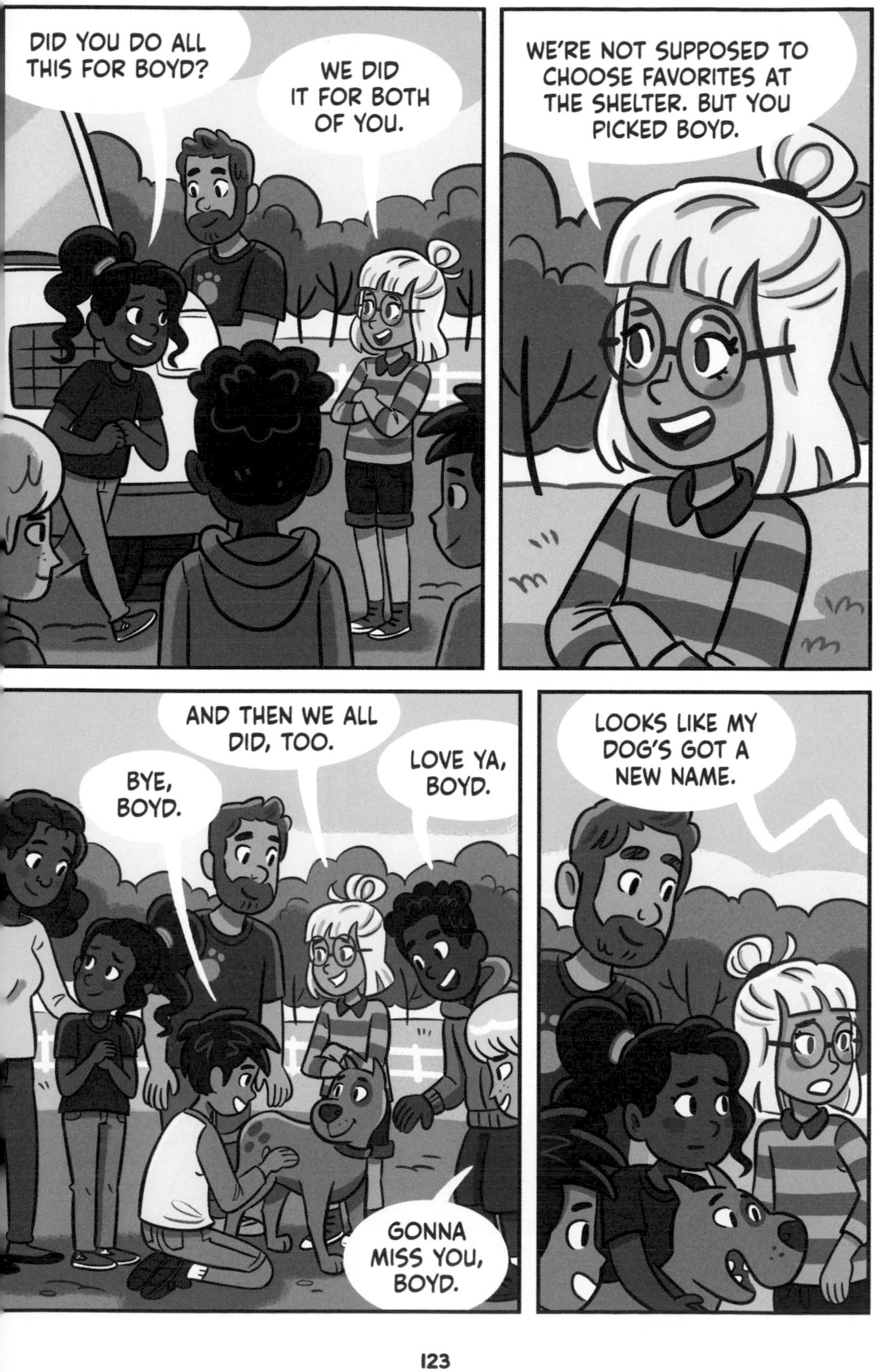
DID YOU DO ALL THIS FOR BOYD?
WE DID IT FOR BOTH OF YOU.
WE'RE NOT SUPPOSED TO CHOOSE FAVORITES AT THE SHELTER. BUT YOU PICKED BOYD.
AND THEN WE ALL DID, TOO.
BYE, BOYD.
LOVE YA, BOYD.
GONNA MISS YOU, BOYD.
LOOKS LIKE MY DOG'S GOT A NEW NAME.

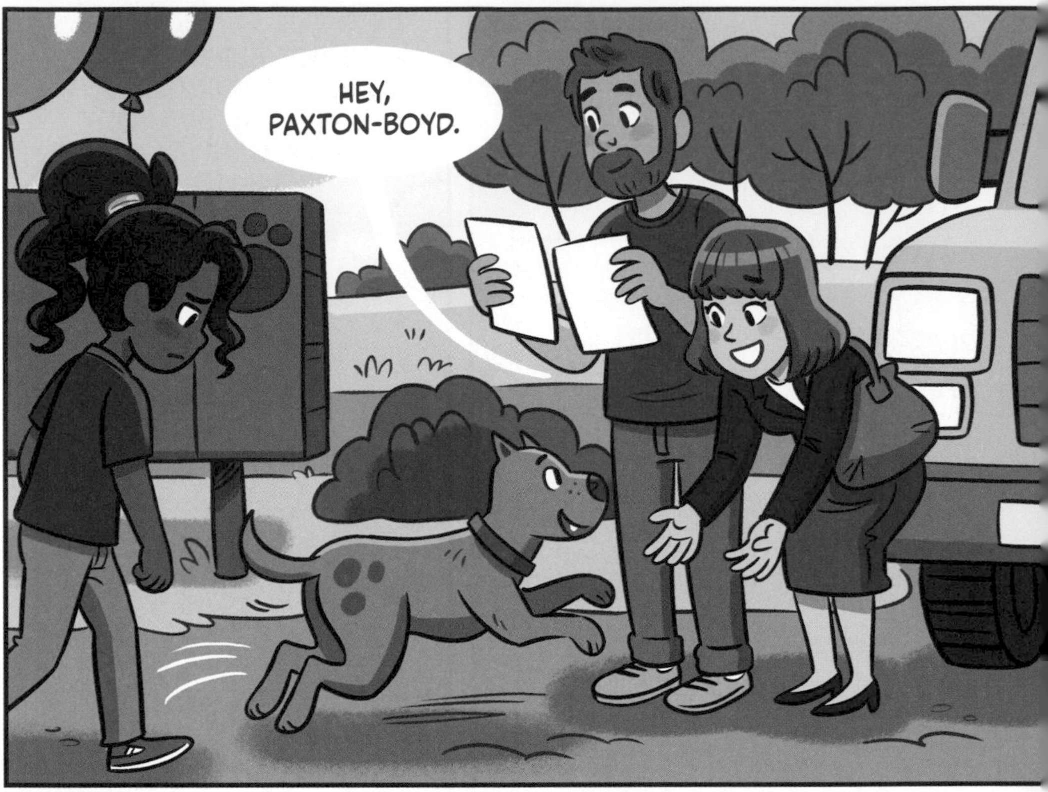
HEY, PAXTON-BOYD.

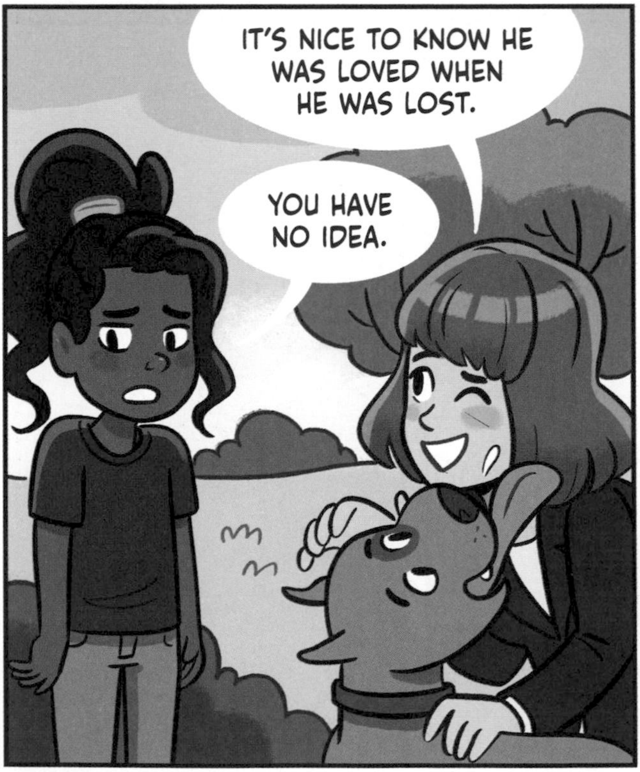
IT'S NICE TO KNOW HE WAS LOVED WHEN HE WAS LOST.
YOU HAVE NO IDEA.

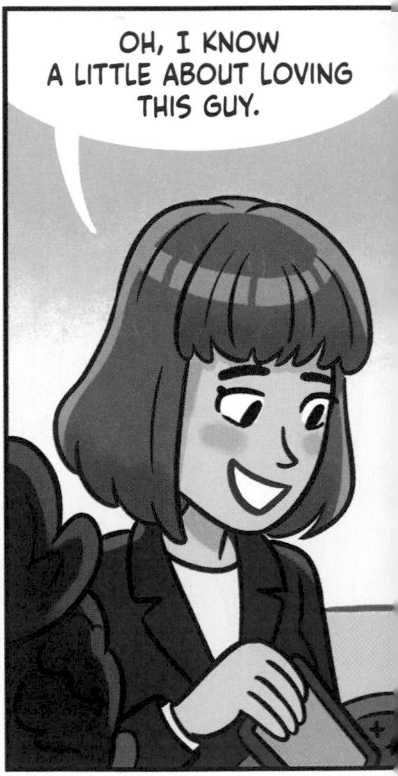
OH, I KNOW A LITTLE ABOUT LOVING THIS GUY.

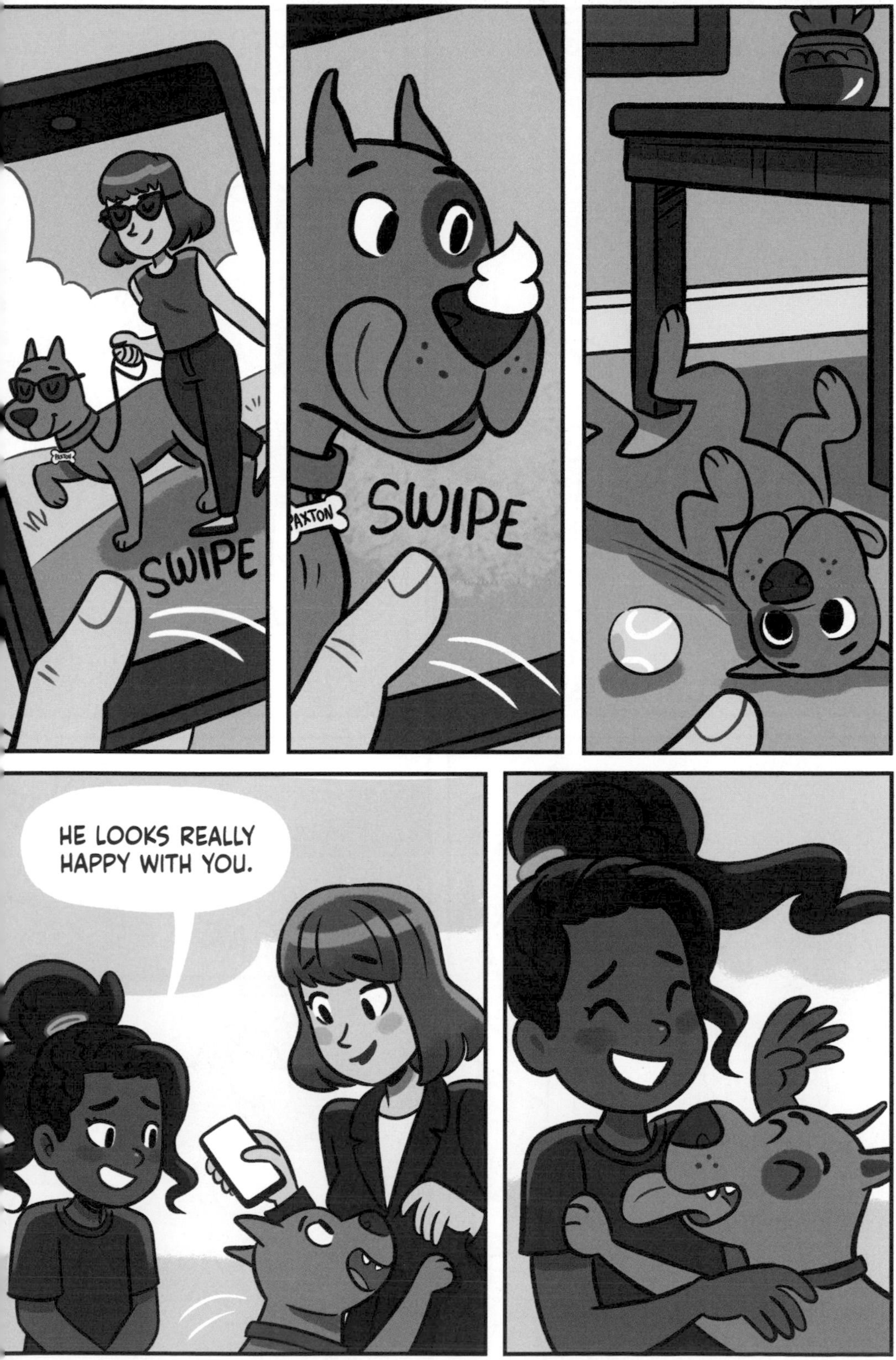
PAXTON
SWIPE
PAXTON
SWIPE
HE LOOKS REALLY HAPPY WITH YOU.

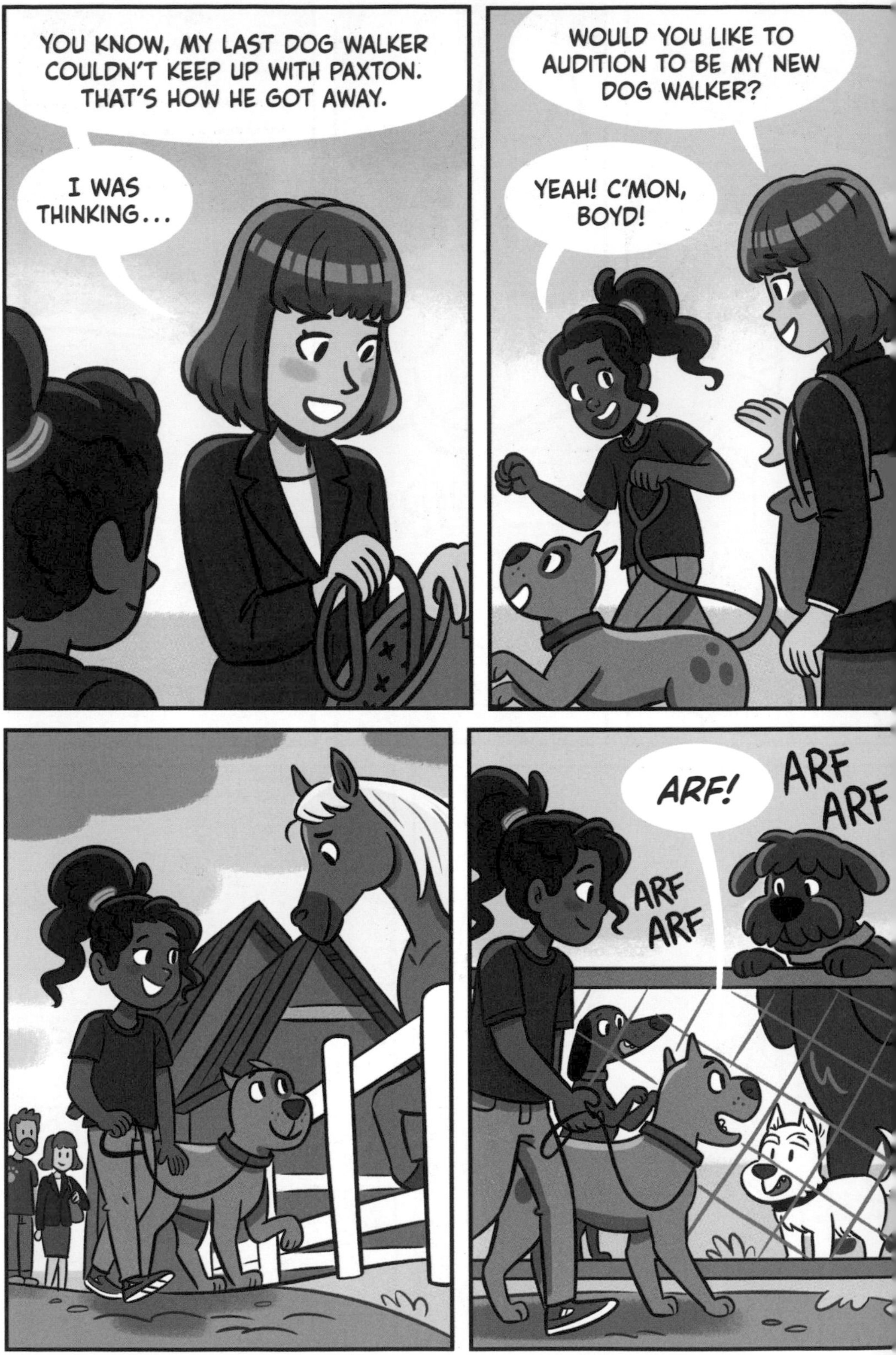
YOU KNOW, MY LAST DOG WALKER COULDN'T KEEP UP WITH PAXTON. THAT'S HOW HE GOT AWAY.
I WAS THINKING...
WOULD YOU LIKE TO AUDITION TO BE MY NEW DOG WALKER?
YEAH! C'MON, BOYD!
ARF!
ARF ARF
ARF ARF

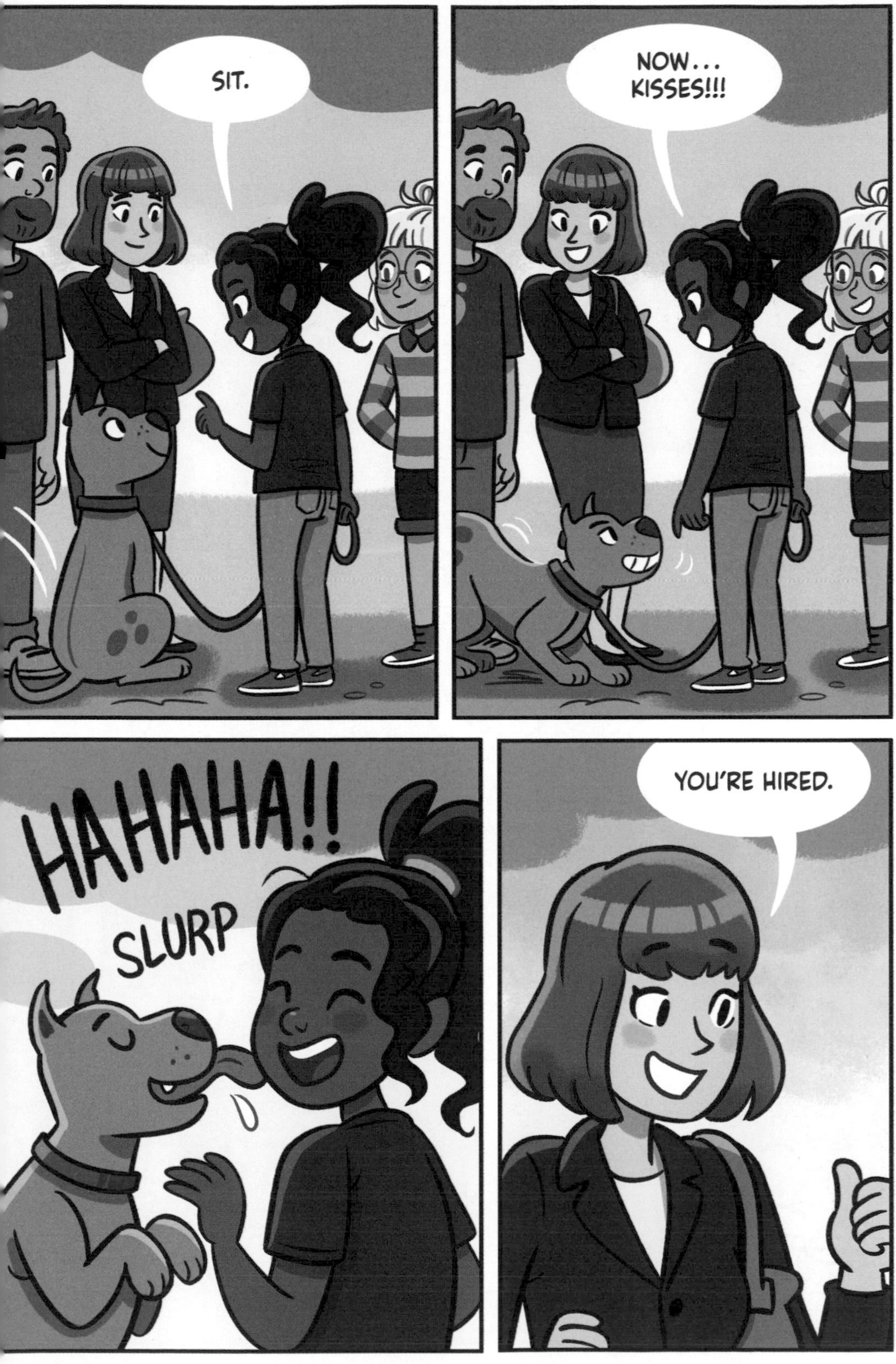
SIT.
NOW... KISSES!!!
HAHAHA!!
SLURP
YOU'RE HIRED.

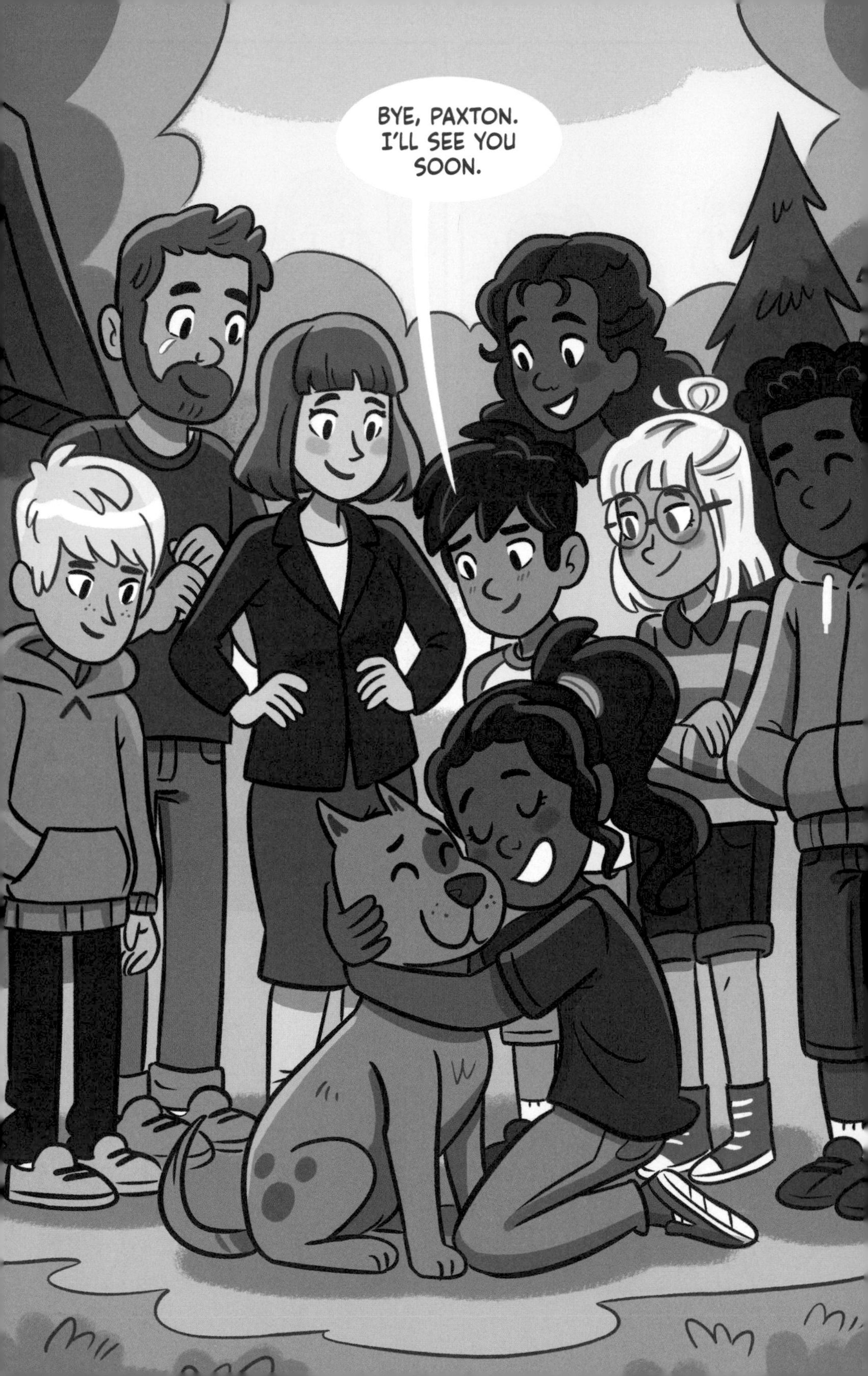
BYE, PAXTON. I'LL SEE YOU SOON.

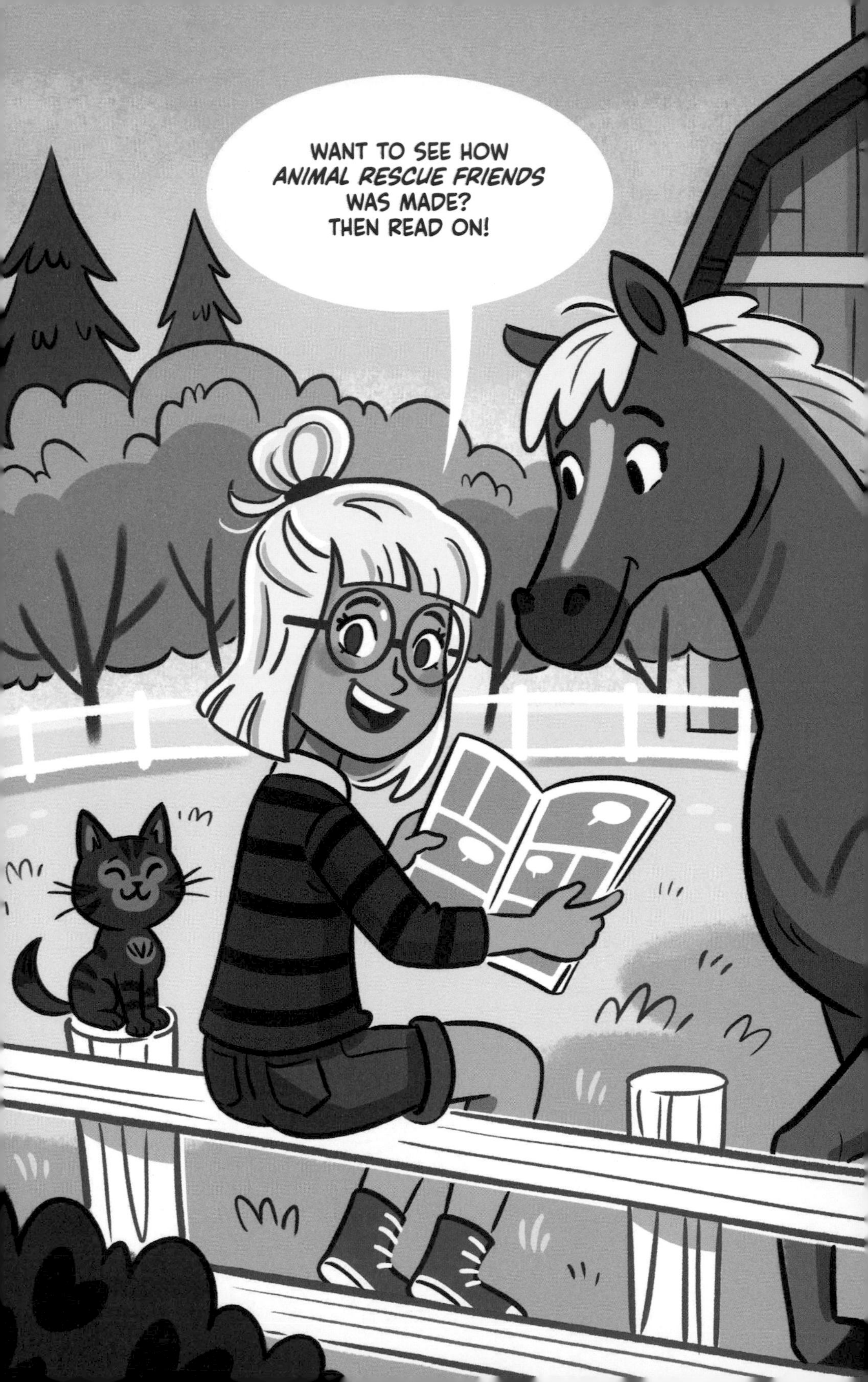
WANT TO SEE HOW *ANIMAL RESCUE FRIENDS* WAS MADE? THEN READ ON!

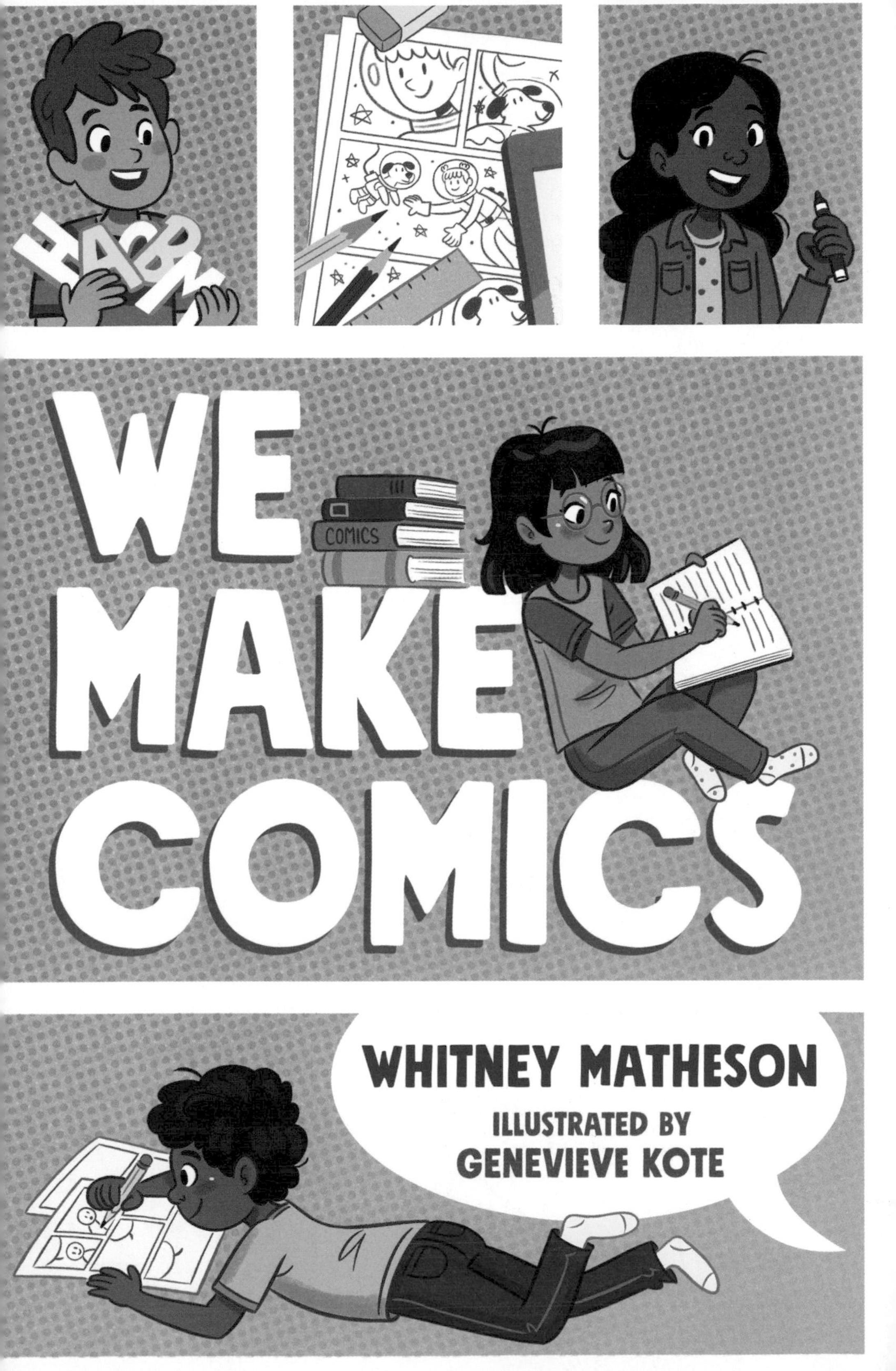
COMICS
WE MAKE COMICS
WHITNEY MATHESON
ILLUSTRATED BY
GENEVIEVE KOTE

ALL ABOUT COMICS!

Today, we can read comics almost anywhere: in books, on phones and tablets, and in newspapers and magazines. Here are just a few types of comics enjoyed all over the world.

Which ones do you read?

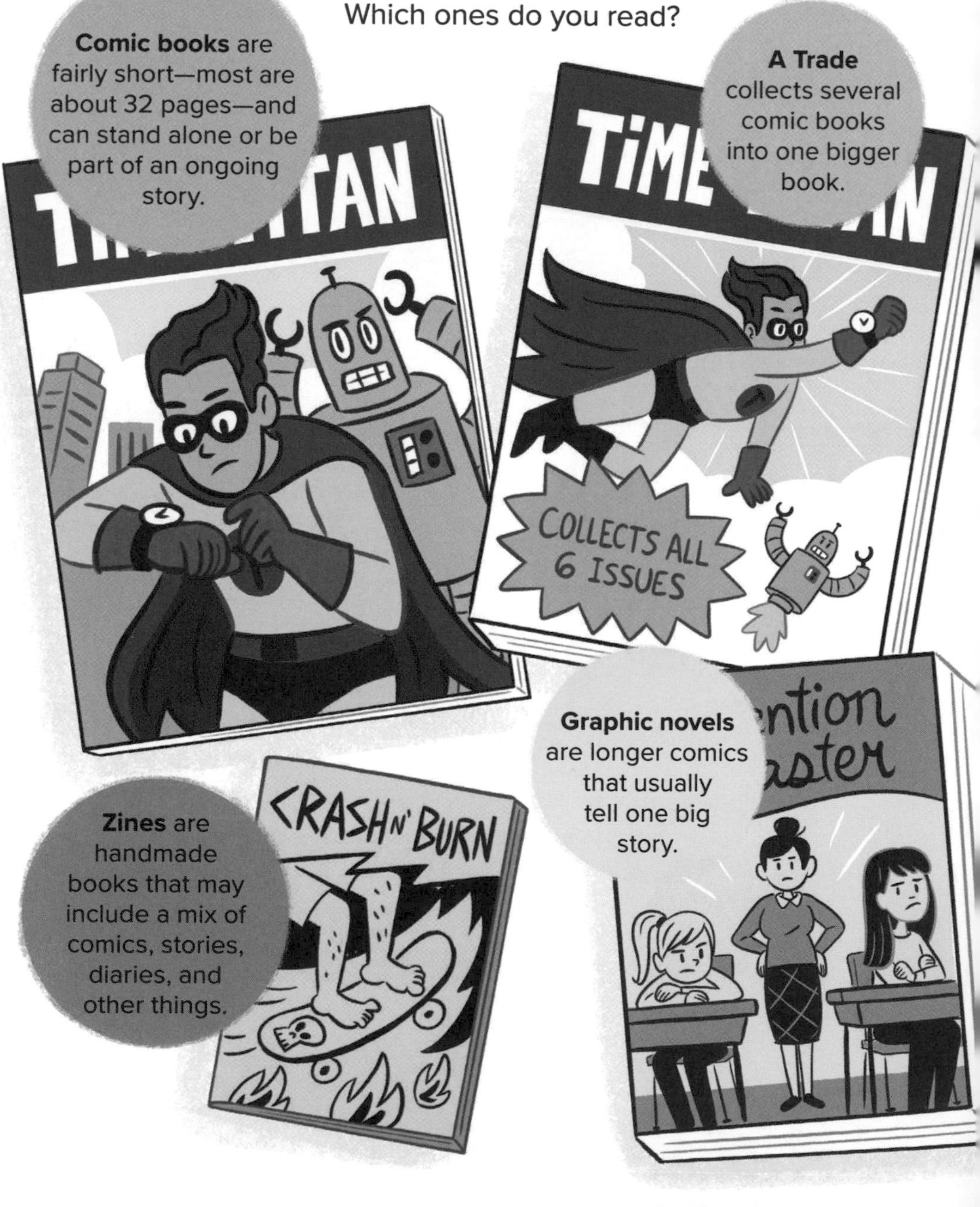
Comic books are fairly short—most are about 32 pages—and can stand alone or be part of an ongoing story.
A Trade collects several comic books into one bigger book.
COLLECTS ALL 6 ISSUES
Graphic novels are longer comics that usually tell one big story.
Zines are handmade books that may include a mix of comics, stories, diaries, and other things.
CRASH N' BURN

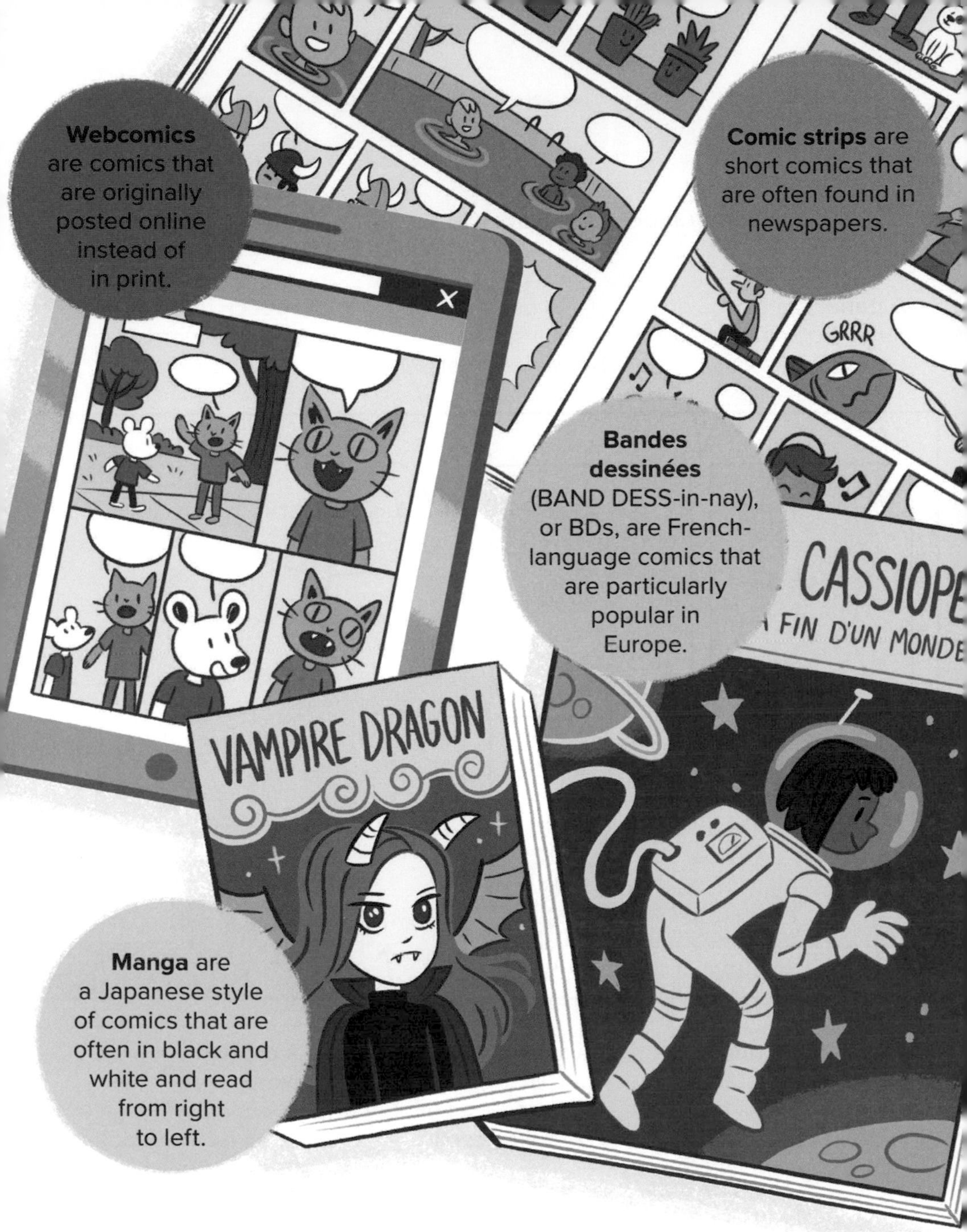
Webcomics are comics that are originally posted online instead of in print.
Comic strips are short comics that are often found in newspapers.
GRRR
Bandes dessinées (BAND DESS-in-nay), or BDs, are French-language comics that are particularly popular in Europe.
VAMPIRE DRAGON
Manga are a Japanese style of comics that are often in black and white and read from right to left.

Today, most single-issue comic books cost between $3 and $4. Back in 1938, a comic book cost just 10 cents.

If you keep comics long enough (and in great condition!), they might even become valuable one day. In 2014, a copy of *Action Comics #1*—the first Superman comic—sold for more than $3 million!

COMICS ANATOMY

How well do you know the parts of a comic book?

A **panel** is a box on a comic-book page that shows action.

A **gutter** is a space between panels.

A **speech bubble** contains the words a character is saying.

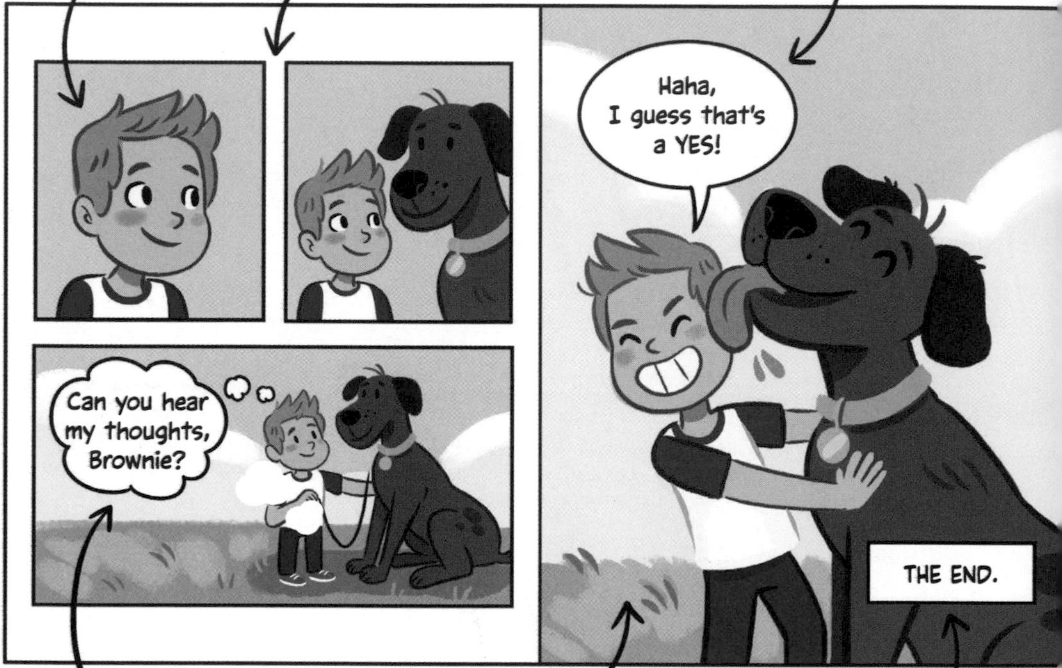

Can you hear my thoughts, Brownie?
Haha, I guess that's a YES!
THE END.

A **thought bubble** contains a character's thoughts. (It has bumps instead of being round like a speech bubble.)

A **splash page** is a big illustration that introduces or ends a comic.

A **caption** contains words that explain the action and aren't spoken by a character.

A **spread** is a picture that covers two facing pages.

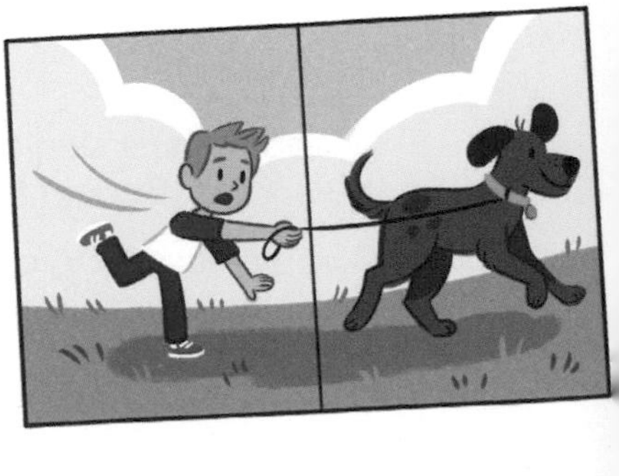

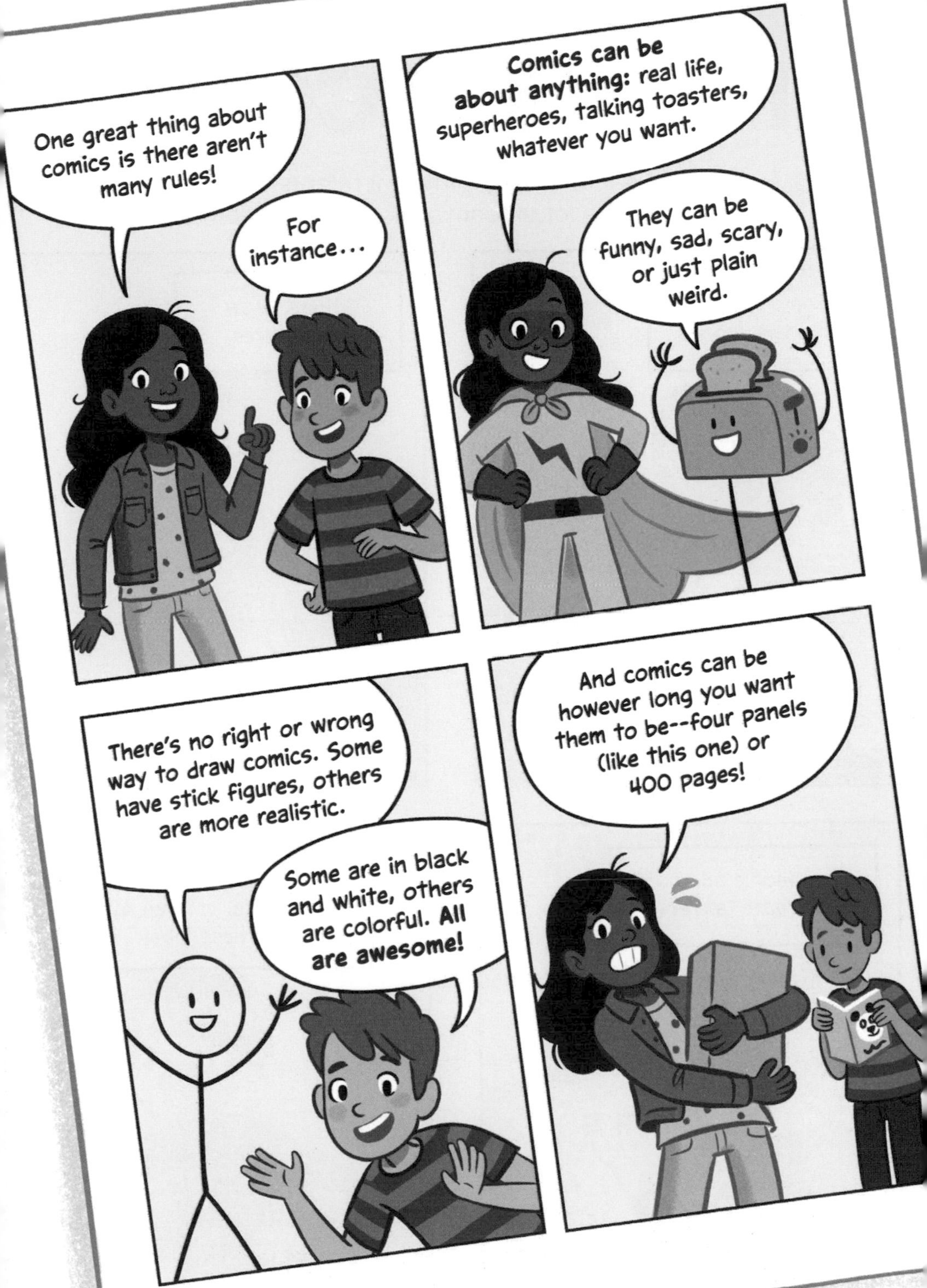

One great thing about comics is there aren't many rules!
For instance...
Comics can be about anything: real life, superheroes, talking toasters, whatever you want.
They can be funny, sad, scary, or just plain weird.
There's no right or wrong way to draw comics. Some have stick figures, others are more realistic.
Some are in black and white, others are colorful. All are awesome!
And comics can be however long you want them to be--four panels (like this one) or 400 pages!

WHO MAKES COMICS?

It takes many different talents—
and a whole lot of teamwork—to make comics.

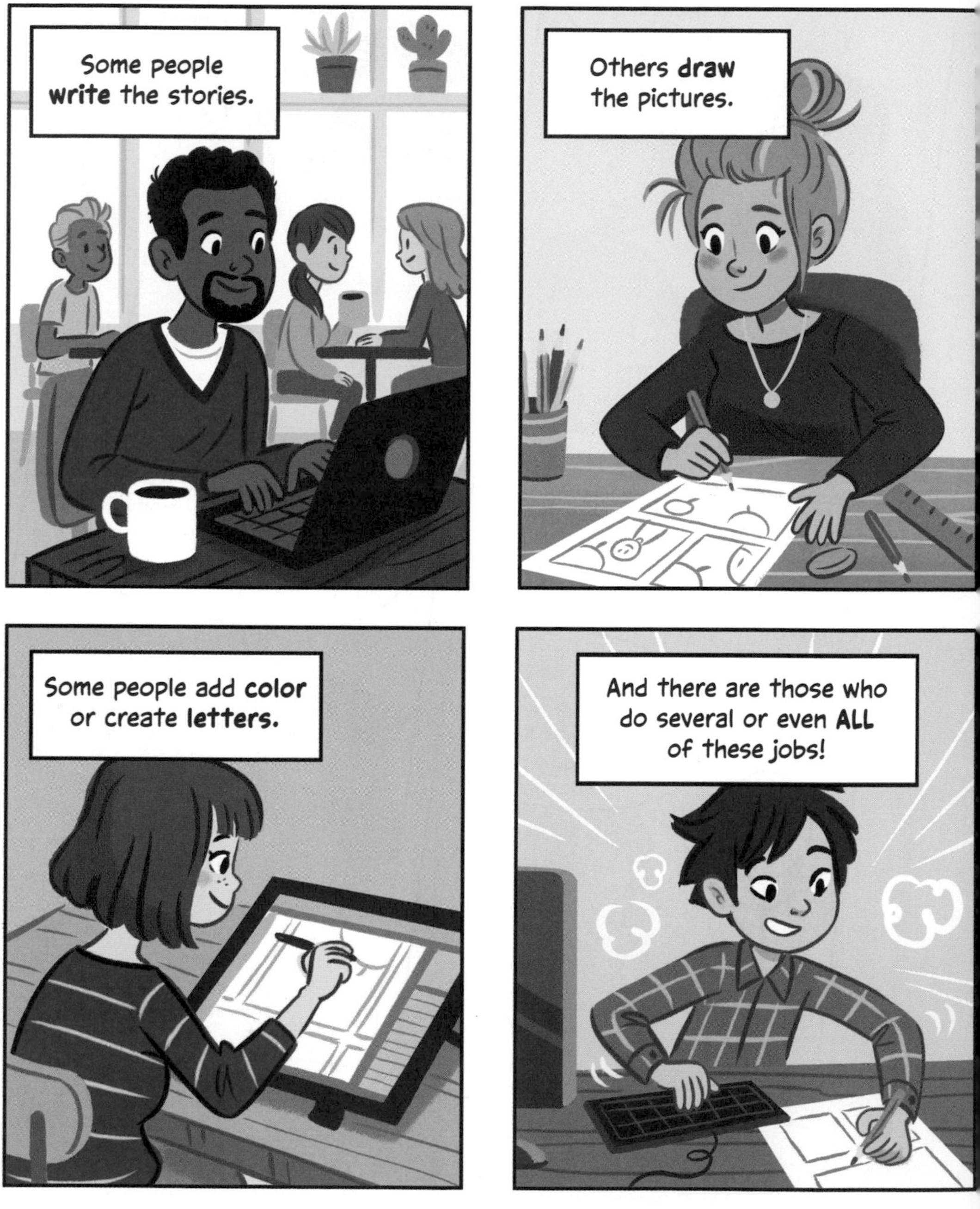
Some people **write** the stories.
Others **draw** the pictures.
Some people add **color** or create **letters.**
And there are those who do several or even **ALL** of these jobs!

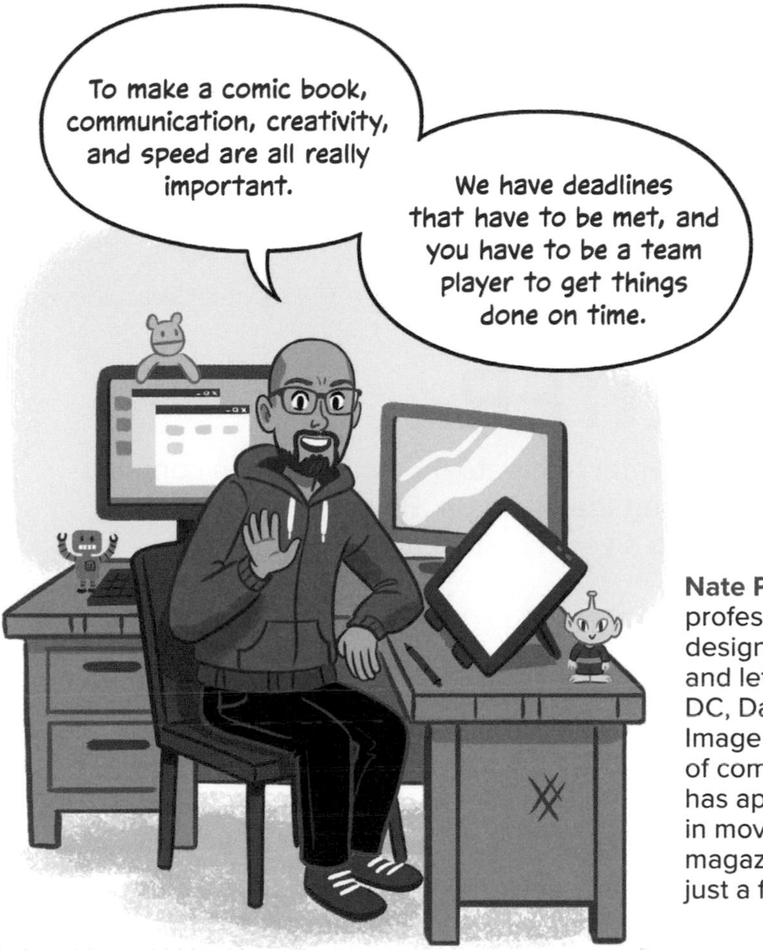
To make a comic book, communication, creativity, and speed are all really important.
We have deadlines that have to be met, and you have to be a team player to get things done on time.

Nate Piekos is a professional graphic designer, typographer, and letterer for Marvel, DC, Dark Horse, and Image Comics. Outside of comics, his work has appeared on TV, in movies, and in magazines, to name just a few places.

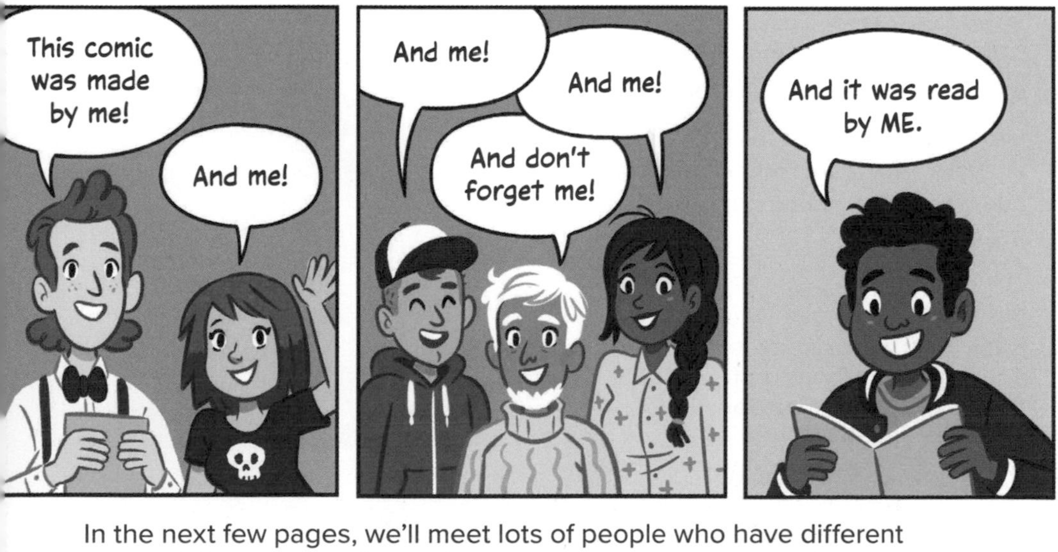
This comic was made by me!
And me!
And me!
And me!
And don't forget me!
And it was read by ME.

In the next few pages, we'll meet lots of people who have different skills but who all love the same thing: making comics!

THE WRITER

Every comic needs a writer to create the **script,** which contains the story, the action, and the dialogue. Being a writer takes a lot of work, but it's also a very creative and fun job!

Meet **KATE LETH,** comic-book writer!

Kate: When I'm working as a writer, there's a whole art and production team to work with. I'll plan the story and write what's going to happen on each page of a comic, as well as what each character says.

For writing, I just use my laptop (or my iPad with a keyboard, if I'm on the go). I write comic scripts in a basic text program like Microsoft Word or Pages or Google Docs.

Comics can be everything from short, funny memes to huge, groundbreaking graphic novels. There are no limits except the borders of the page, and even those can be played with.

Sometimes I collaborate on story ideas with the art team, sometimes not—it all depends on the project. It's more fun when we work together.

I love sending a script to an artist and getting art back. Some incredibly talented person takes my words and turns them into comics! It's amazing!

Kate Leth writes comics and animated series. She has written for Marvel, Hasbro, Crunchyroll, and Cartoon Network.

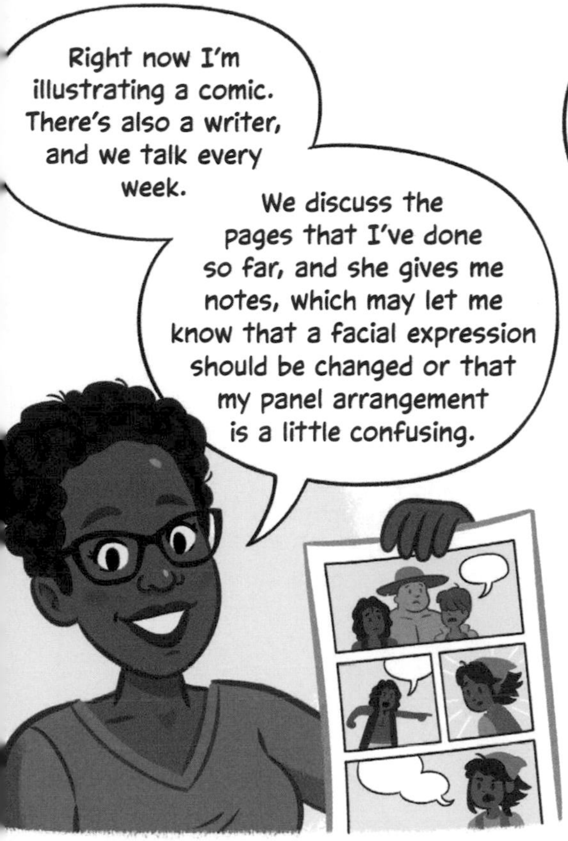
Right now I'm illustrating a comic. There's also a writer, and we talk every week.
We discuss the pages that I've done so far, and she gives me notes, which may let me know that a facial expression should be changed or that my panel arrangement is a little confusing.

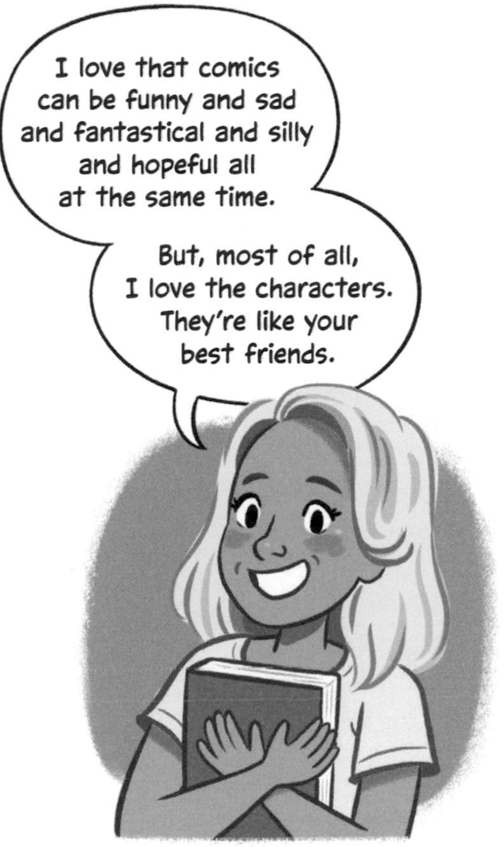
I love that comics can be funny and sad and fantastical and silly and hopeful all at the same time.
But, most of all, I love the characters. They're like your best friends.

Nilah Magruder is the author of *HOW TO FIND A FOX*, *M.F.K.*, and other books for kids. She has written for Marvel and illustrated for Disney and Scholastic, and she is currently illustrating an upcoming graphic novel for Kokila Books. Nilah lives in Los Angeles, California.

Jennifer Holm and her brother, Matthew Holm, are the creators of award-winning and best-selling graphic novel series including *BABYMOUSE*, *SQUISH*, and the *SUNNY* series.

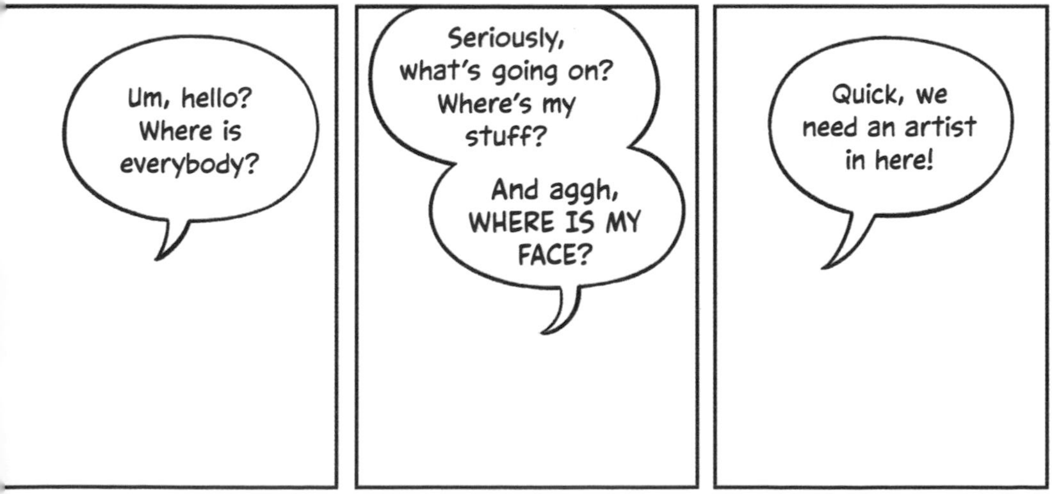
Um, hello? Where is everybody?
Seriously, what's going on? Where's my stuff?
And aggh, WHERE IS MY FACE?
Quick, we need an artist in here!

THE PENCILLER

A penciller is an artist who sketches early versions of the comic. Some pencillers work digitally by drawing on special computer tablets. Others work the old-fashioned way, with pencil and paper!

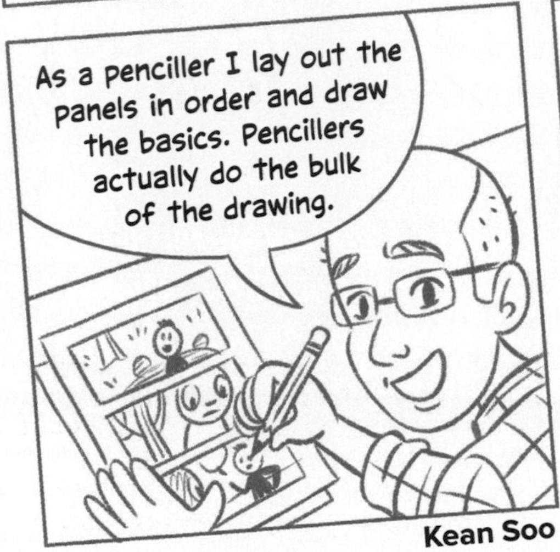
As a penciller I lay out the panels in order and draw the basics. Pencillers actually do the bulk of the drawing.

Kean Soo

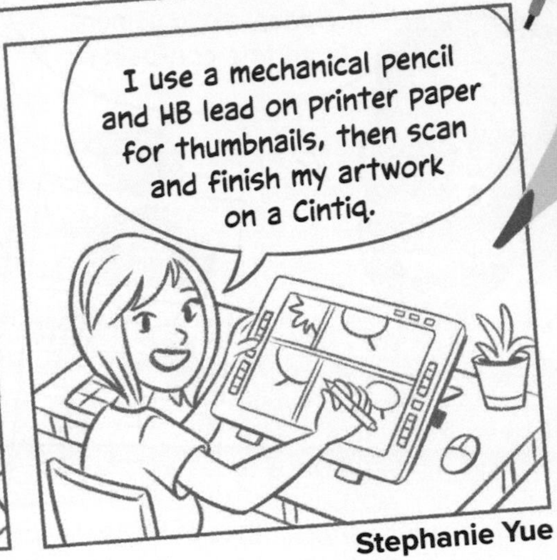
I use a mechanical pencil and HB lead on printer paper for thumbnails, then scan and finish my artwork on a Cintiq.

Stephanie Yue

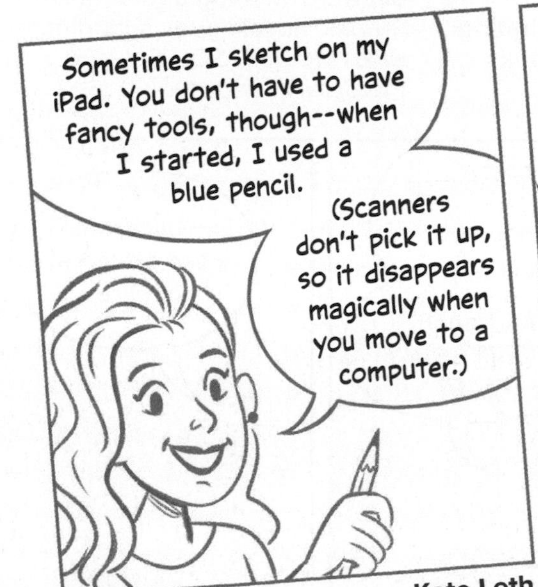
Sometimes I sketch on my iPad. You don't have to have fancy tools, though--when I started, I used a blue pencil.
(Scanners don't pick it up, so it disappears magically when you move to a computer.)

Kate Leth

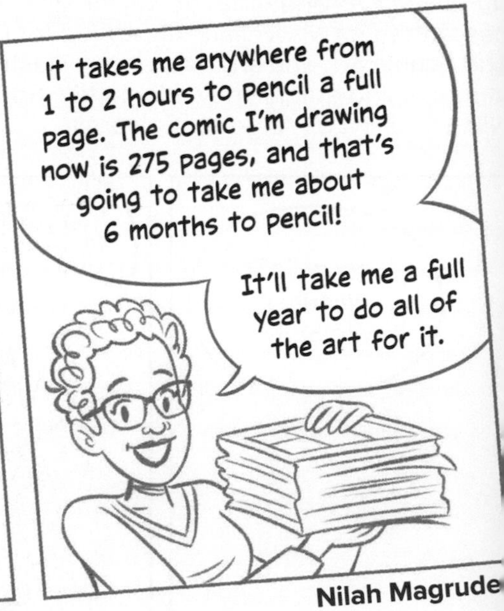
It takes me anywhere from 1 to 2 hours to pencil a full page. The comic I'm drawing now is 275 pages, and that's going to take me about 6 months to pencil!
It'll take me a full year to do all of the art for it.

Nilah Magrude

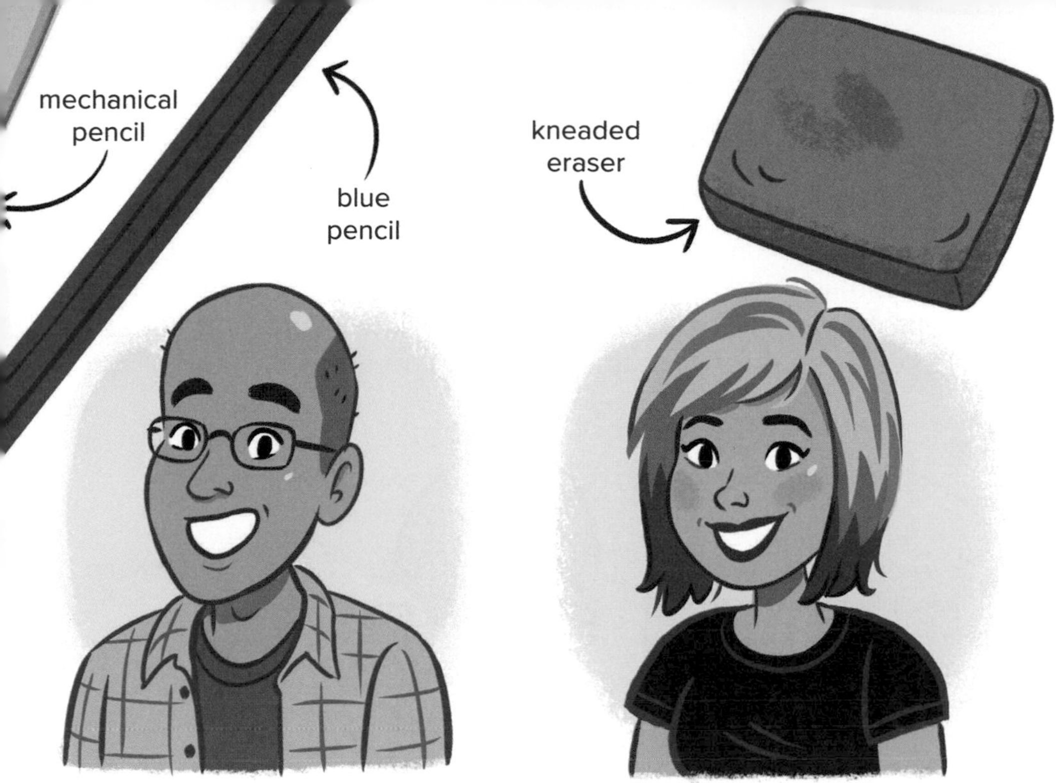
mechanical pencil
blue pencil
kneaded eraser

Kean Soo is the author and illustrator of the award-winning graphic novel series *JELLABY* and *MARCH GRAND PRIX* and was also an assistant editor and contributor to the *FLIGHT* comic anthologies. He lives in Toronto, Canada.

Stephanie Yue has illustrated comics, picture books, and graphic novels for Lerner, Scholastic, Random House, and more. In her other life, she practices martial arts, climbs things, and takes Vespas and motorcycles on extended journeys.

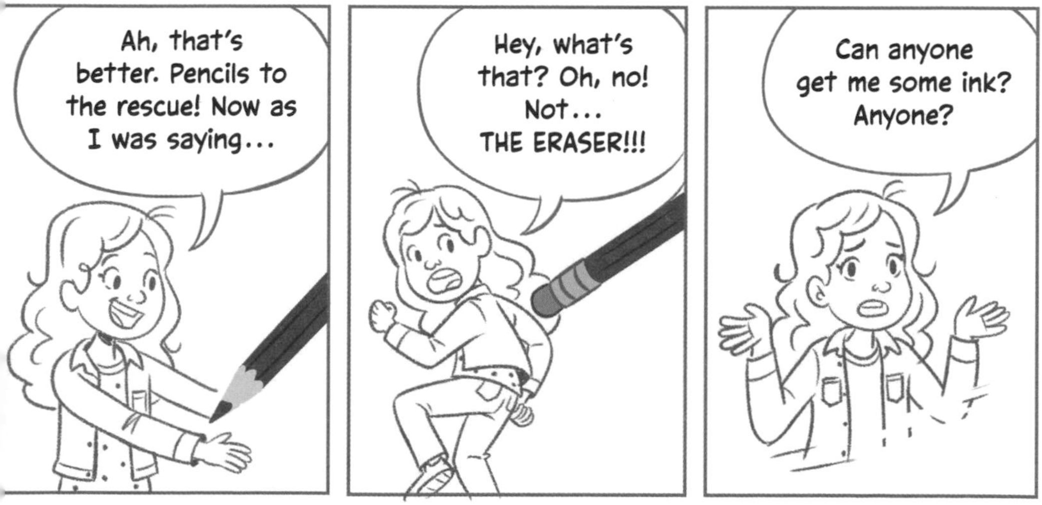
Ah, that's better. Pencils to the rescue! Now as I was saying...
Hey, what's that? Oh, no! Not... THE ERASER!!!
Can anyone get me some ink? Anyone?

COMICS FACT: Because so many artists work on computers, not all comics have a penciller. For some, pencilling is combined with the next job we'll talk about.

THE INKER

Once a comic has been pencilled, the inker goes over each panel with ink and adds more detail. Like pencillers, some inkers work on a computer. Others prefer to use pens with bigger tips to create thicker lines and fine-point pens for small details.

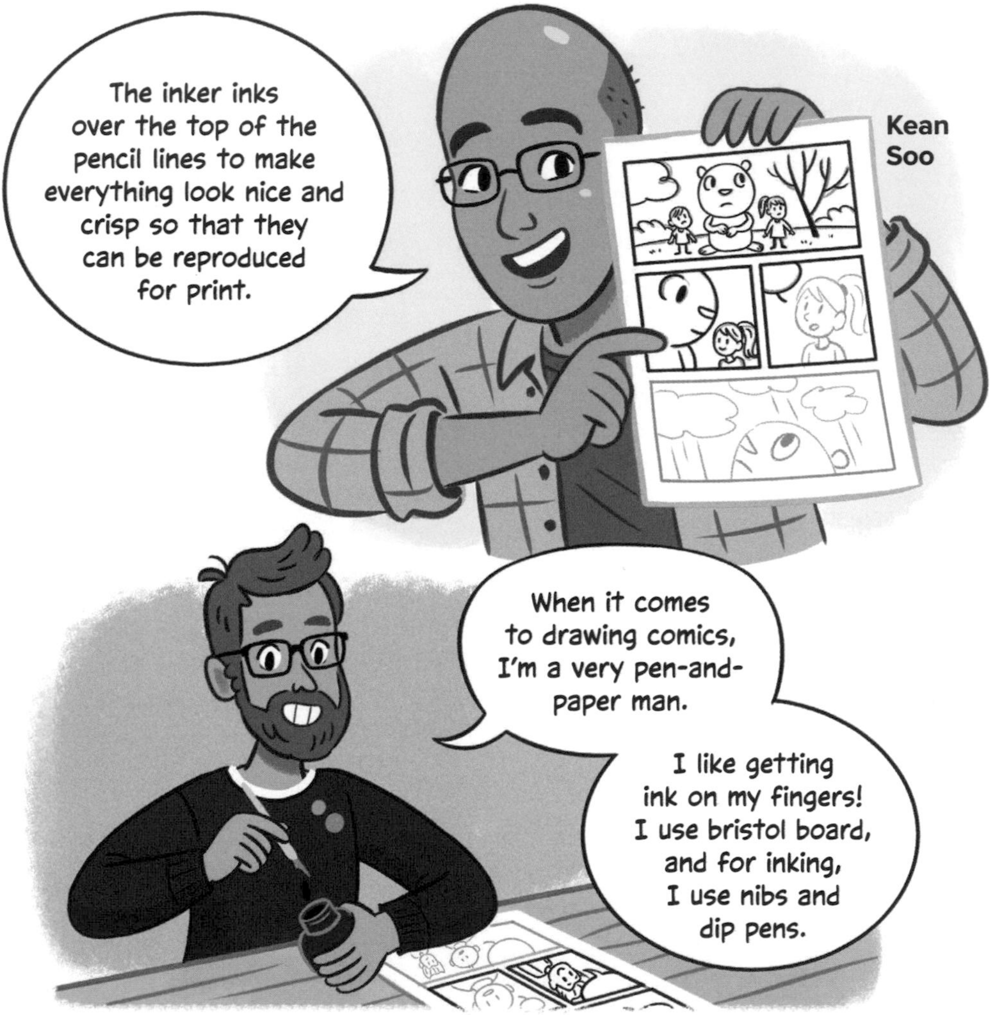
The inker inks over the top of the pencil lines to make everything look nice and crisp so that they can be reproduced for print.
Kean Soo
When it comes to drawing comics, I'm a very pen-and-paper man.
I like getting ink on my fingers! I use bristol board, and for inking, I use nibs and dip pens.

Pranas T. Naujokaitis is an Ignatz Award–nominated Chicago-based cartoonist whose comics include all-age, licensed, autobio, and handcrafted minicomics. Recent work includes writing for the *RUGRATS* comic series by Boom! Studios and *DINOSAURS IN SPACE: OUT OF THIS WORLD,* by Blue Apple Books.

Many art supply stores sell drawing paper with guide lines printed on them, which can help when making comics. (You can also find some comic templates online to print at home.)

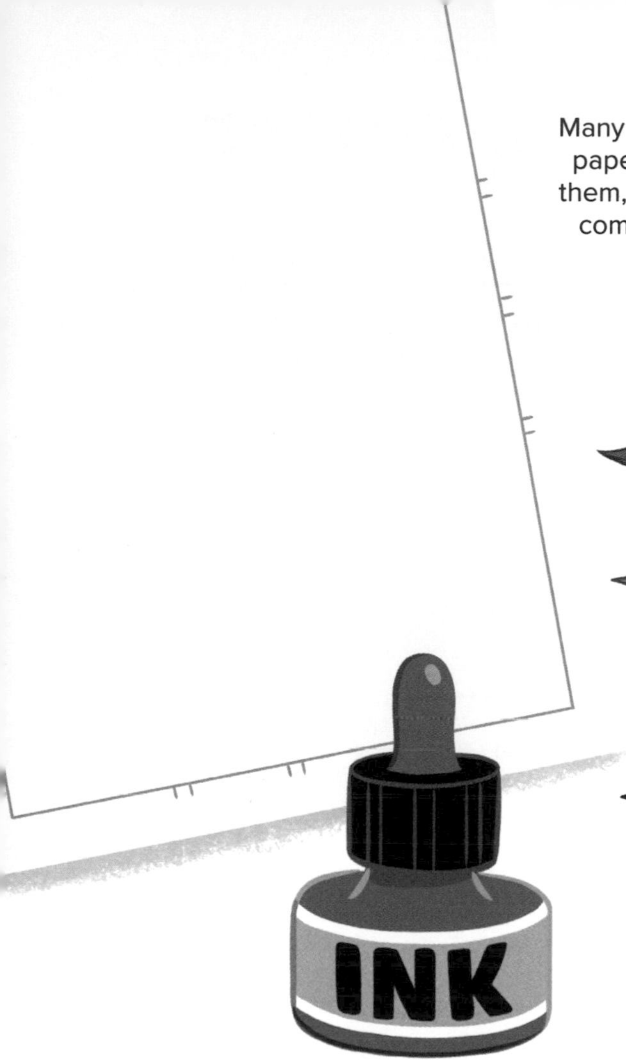
INK

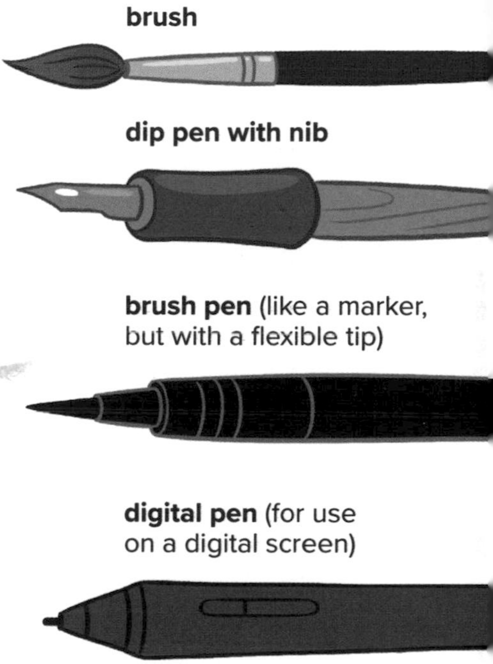
brush
dip pen with nib
brush pen (like a marker, but with a flexible tip)
digital pen (for use on a digital screen)

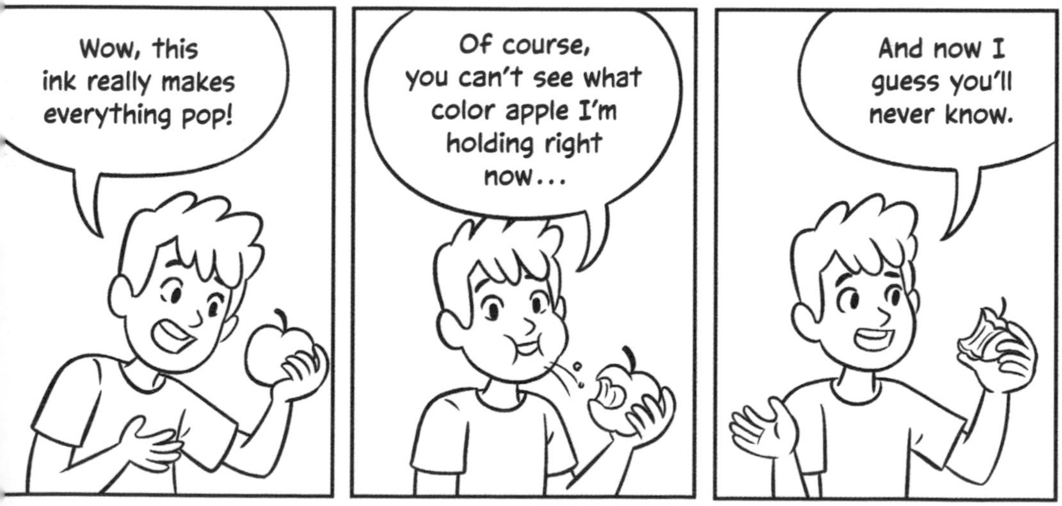
Wow, this ink really makes everything pop!
Of course, you can't see what color apple I'm holding right now...
And now I guess you'll never know.

THE COLORIST

Can you guess what a colorist does? Yep, you got it: After pages are inked, the colorist brings them to life with beautiful, dazzling color! Like inkers, some colorists use computers, while others color with ink on paper.

A colorist's job is very important, and it takes a lot of time. And, of course, if a comic is in black and white, it doesn't need a colorist!

Meet **STEVE HAMAKER,** comic-book colorist!

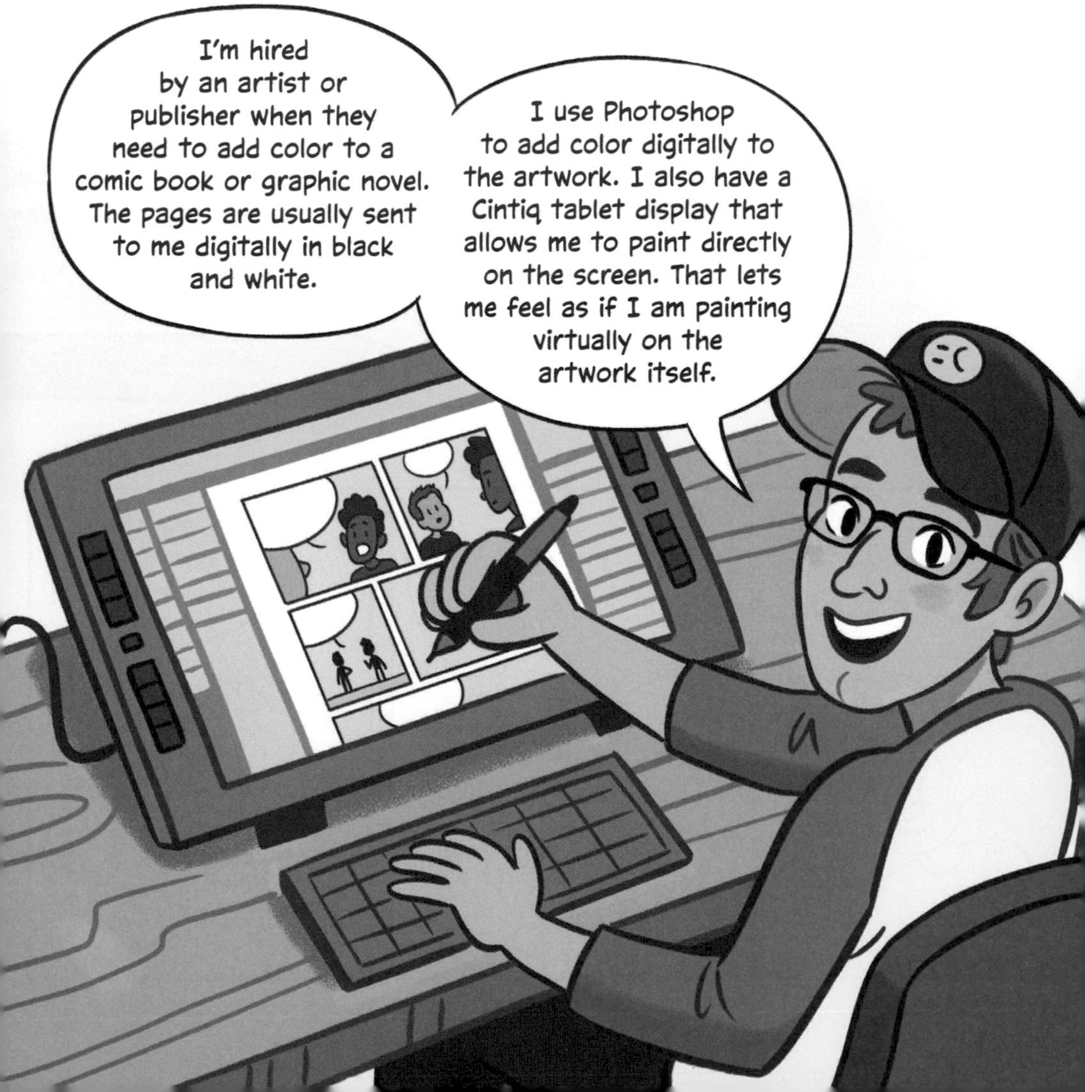

I'm hired by an artist or publisher when they need to add color to a comic book or graphic novel. The pages are usually sent to me digitally in black and white.
I use Photoshop to add color digitally to the artwork. I also have a Cintiq tablet display that allows me to paint directly on the screen. That lets me feel as if I am painting virtually on the artwork itself.

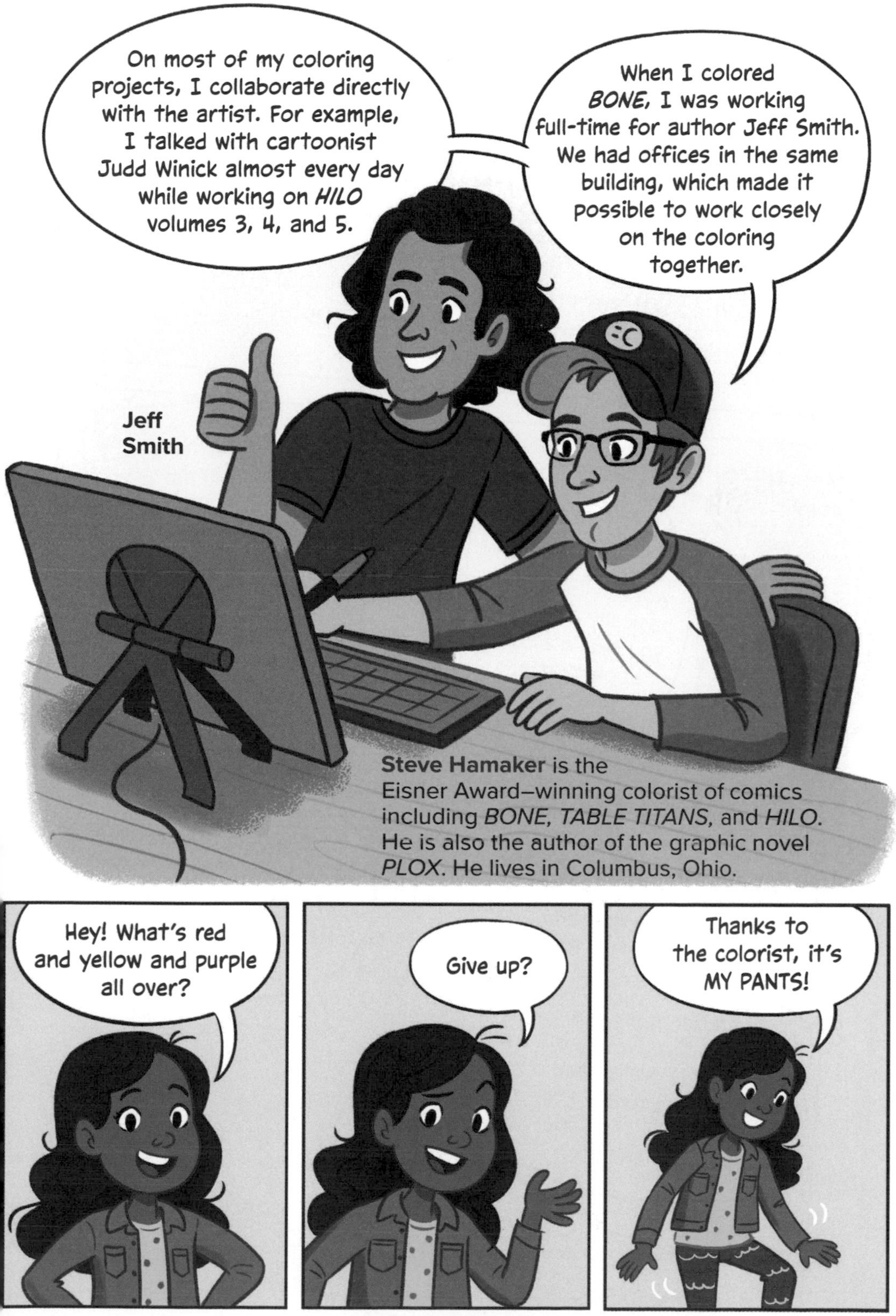
On most of my coloring projects, I collaborate directly with the artist. For example, I talked with cartoonist Judd Winick almost every day while working on *HILO* volumes 3, 4, and 5.
When I colored *BONE,* I was working full-time for author Jeff Smith. We had offices in the same building, which made it possible to work closely on the coloring together.
Jeff Smith
Steve Hamaker is the Eisner Award–winning colorist of comics including *BONE, TABLE TITANS,* and *HILO.* He is also the author of the graphic novel *PLOX*. He lives in Columbus, Ohio.
Hey! What's red and yellow and purple all over?
Give up?
Thanks to the colorist, it's MY PANTS!

THE LETTERER

Often called the "unsung heroes of comics," letterers deal with text, or letters, on the comic-book page. While letterers used to do everything by hand, today many of them use computers.

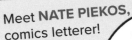 Meet **NATE PIEKOS**, comics letterer!

 Letterers create all the sound effects, word balloons, and basically everything you see in a comic book that has to do with text.

We take the writer's script and the artist's pages of art, and we marry them together.

Sometimes, we also get the book ready for print. Some of us design logos and the fonts we use, too.

Lettering is almost all digital these days, but certain jobs really need a hand-drawn touch. For those, I still use good old paper and ink.

 A couple of years ago, I worked on *GREEN ARROW* for 32 issues, and all the titles and sound effects were painted with brushes!

 SPLAT!

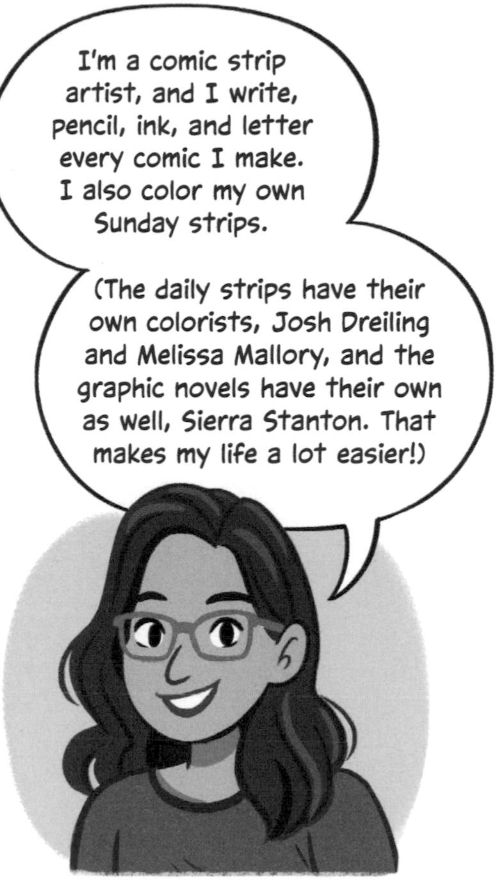
I'm a comic strip artist, and I write, pencil, ink, and letter every comic I make. I also color my own Sunday strips.
(The daily strips have their own colorists, Josh Dreiling and Melissa Mallory, and the graphic novels have their own as well, Sierra Stanton. That makes my life a lot easier!)

Dana Simpson is the best-selling author of the *PHOEBE AND HER UNICORN* comic strip and book collections. She lives with her husband and her cat in Santa Barbara, California.

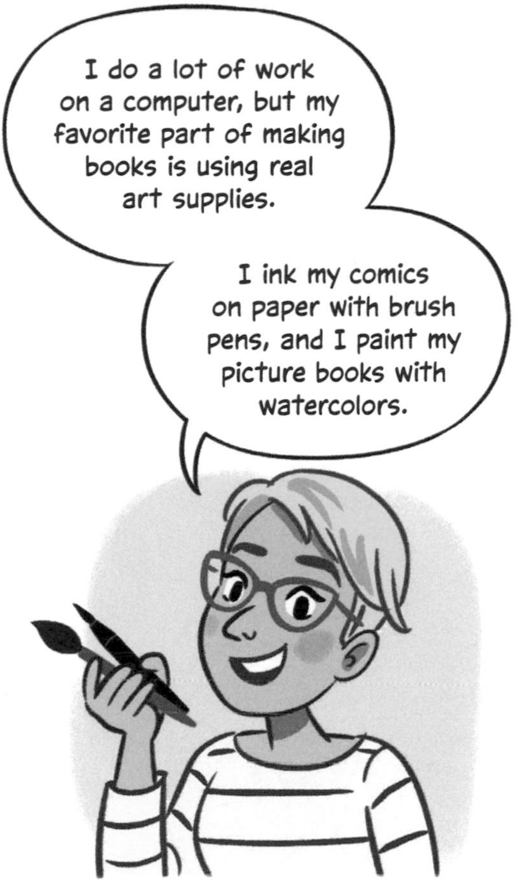
I do a lot of work on a computer, but my favorite part of making books is using real art supplies.
I ink my comics on paper with brush pens, and I paint my picture books with watercolors.

Vera Brosgol is an Eisner Award–winning cartoonist whose books include *ANYA'S GHOST* and *BE PREPARED*. She lives in Portland, Oregon.

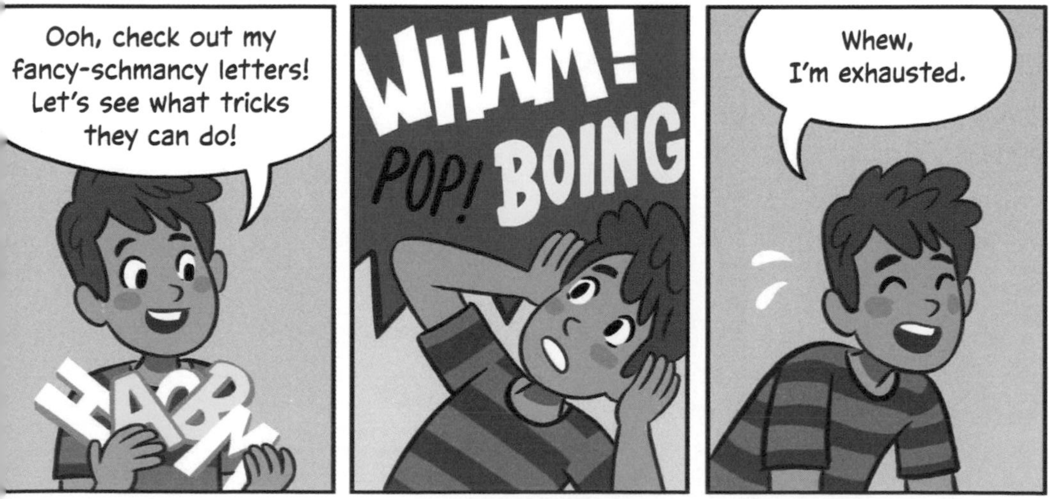
Ooh, check out my fancy-schmancy letters! Let's see what tricks they can do!
WHAM!
POP!
BOING
Whew, I'm exhausted.

THE EDITOR

Editors are the amazing, invisible forces behind every great comic. Editors work with writers and artists to make sure their comics are the best they can be—and are finished on time!

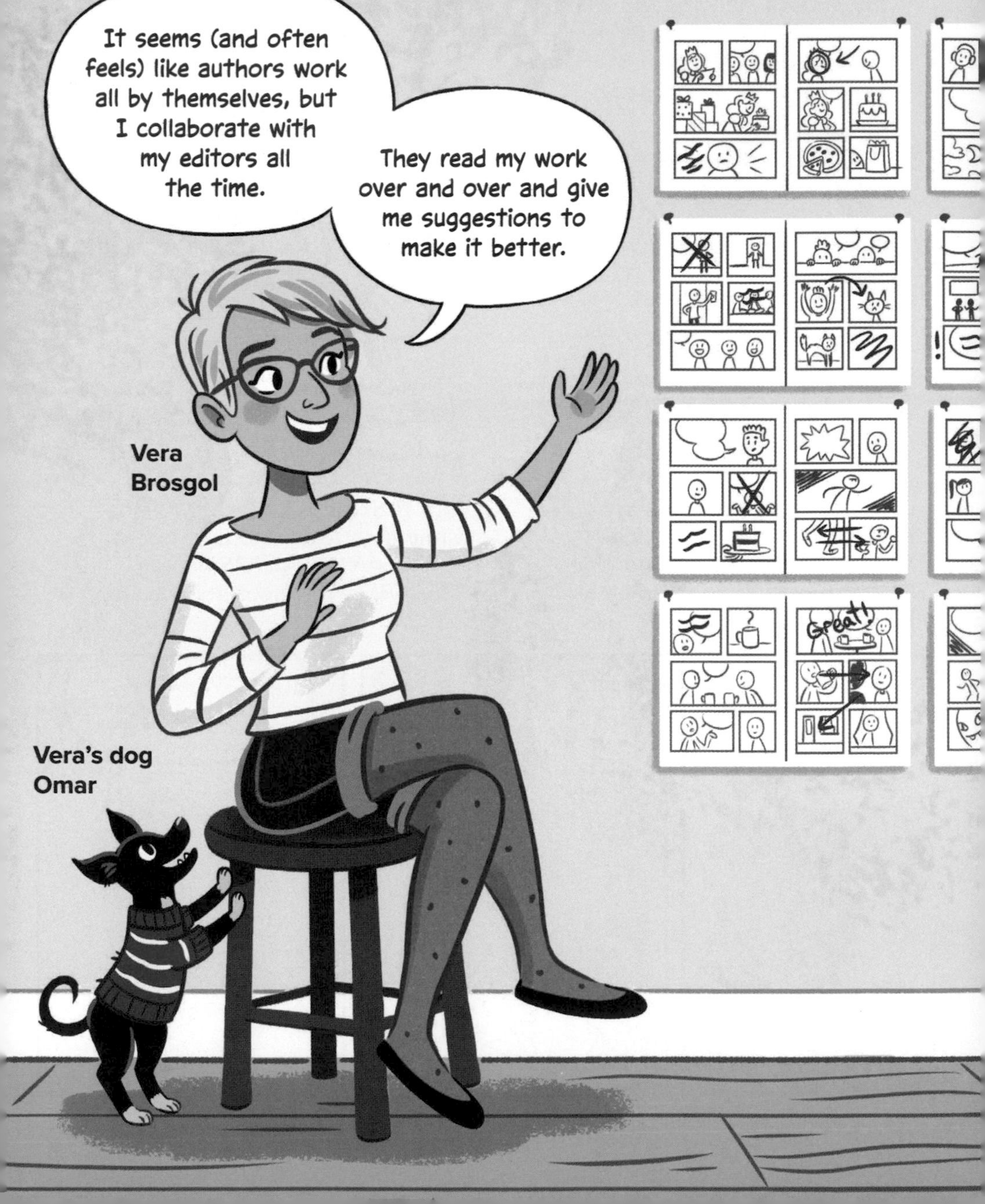
It seems (and often feels) like authors work all by themselves, but I collaborate with my editors all the time.
They read my work over and over and give me suggestions to make it better.
Great!
Vera Brosgol
Vera's dog Omar

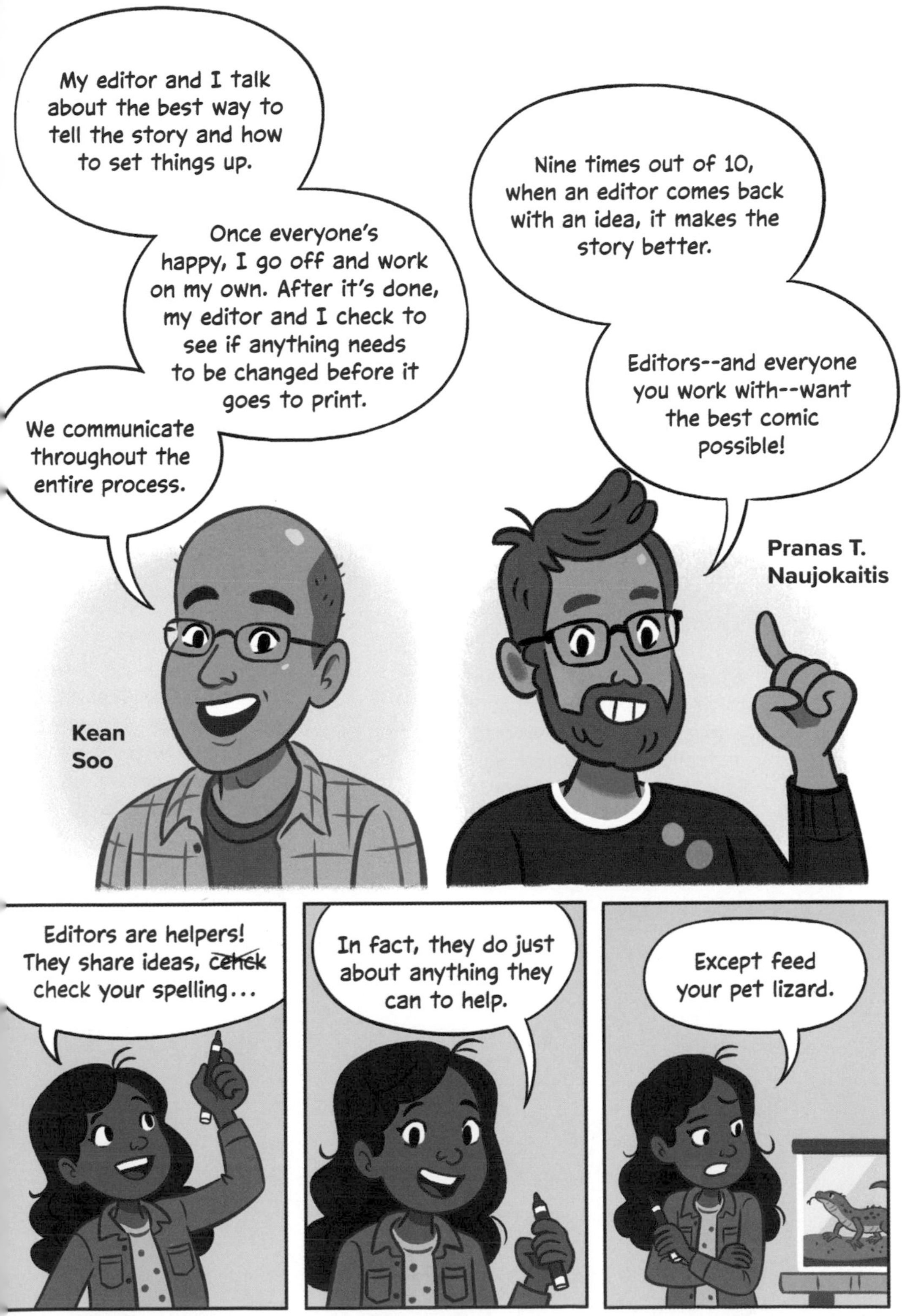
My editor and I talk about the best way to tell the story and how to set things up.
Once everyone's happy, I go off and work on my own. After it's done, my editor and I check to see if anything needs to be changed before it goes to print.
We communicate throughout the entire process.
Kean Soo
Nine times out of 10, when an editor comes back with an idea, it makes the story better.
Editors--and everyone you work with--want the best comic possible!
Pranas T. Naujokaitis
Editors are helpers! They share ideas, ~~cehck~~ check your spelling...
In fact, they do just about anything they can to help.
Except feed your pet lizard.

NOW YOU MAKE COMICS!

Are you inspired to make your own comics? We hope so! Your fellow comic-makers have a few tips to help you get started.

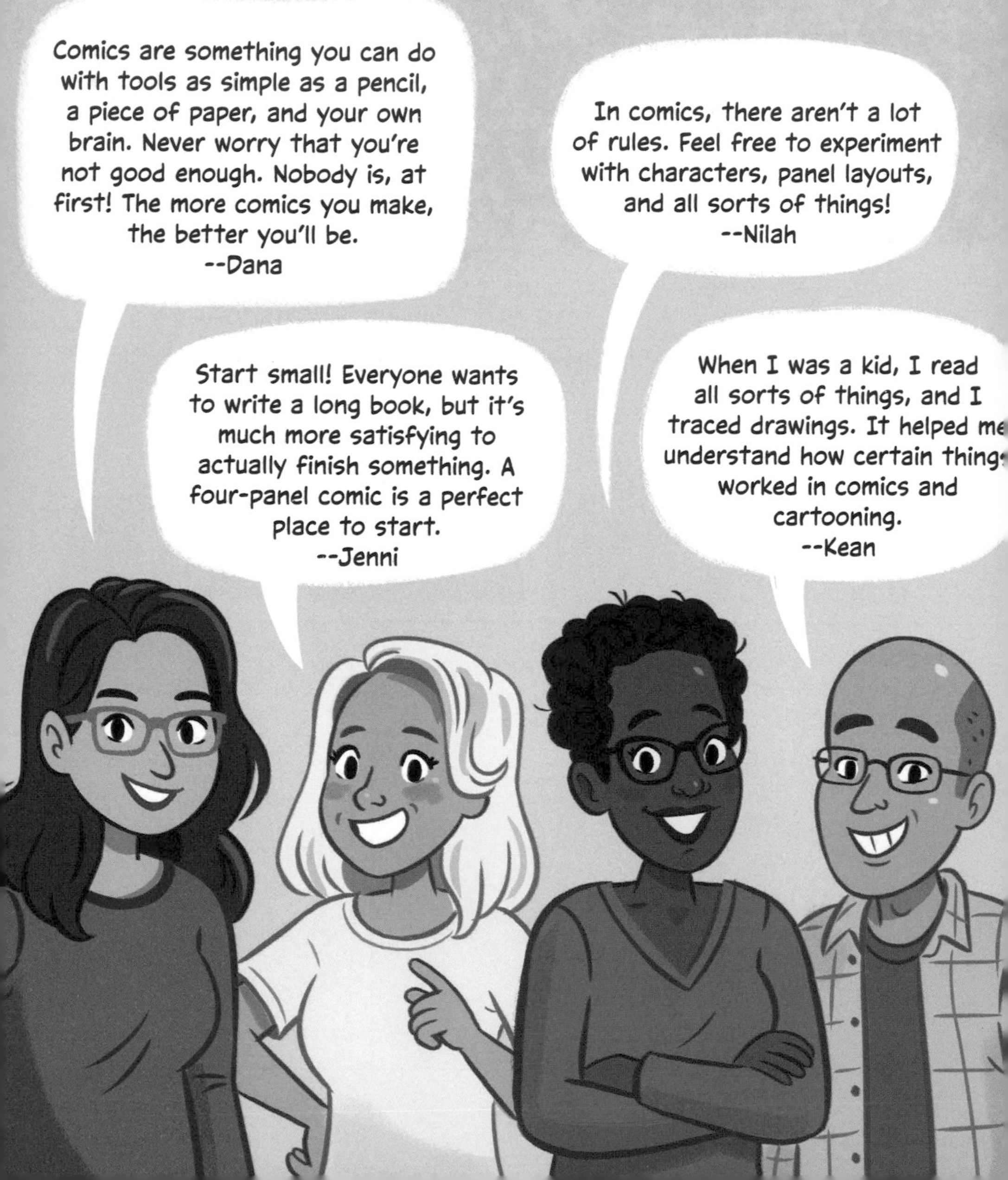
Comics are something you can do with tools as simple as a pencil, a piece of paper, and your own brain. Never worry that you're not good enough. Nobody is, at first! The more comics you make, the better you'll be. --Dana
In comics, there aren't a lot of rules. Feel free to experiment with characters, panel layouts, and all sorts of things! --Nilah
Start small! Everyone wants to write a long book, but it's much more satisfying to actually finish something. A four-panel comic is a perfect place to start. --Jenni
When I was a kid, I read all sorts of things, and I traced drawings. It helped m understand how certain thing worked in comics and cartooning. --Kean

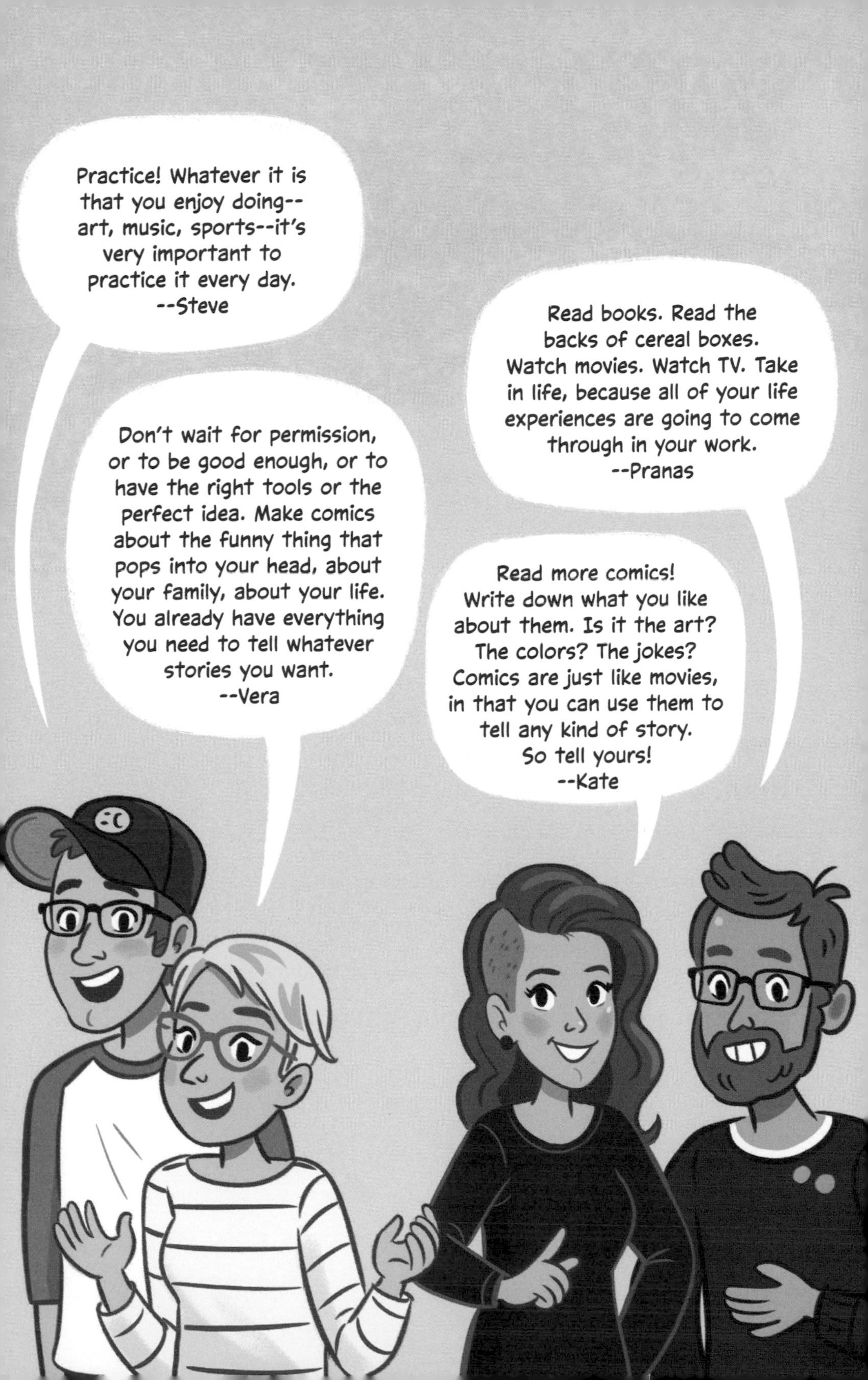

Practice! Whatever it is that you enjoy doing--art, music, sports--it's very important to practice it every day. --Steve
Read books. Read the backs of cereal boxes. Watch movies. Watch TV. Take in life, because all of your life experiences are going to come through in your work. --Pranas
Don't wait for permission, or to be good enough, or to have the right tools or the perfect idea. Make comics about the funny thing that pops into your head, about your family, about your life. You already have everything you need to tell whatever stories you want. --Vera
Read more comics! Write down what you like about them. Is it the art? The colors? The jokes? Comics are just like movies, in that you can use them to tell any kind of story. So tell yours! --Kate

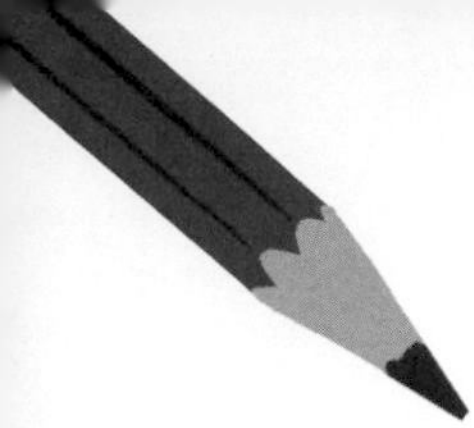

GLOSSARY

Want to talk like a cartoonist? Here are a few words used by artists, writers, and other people who make comics.

bristol board - a type of paper that's good for drawing (you can find it in an art supply store)

Cintiq - a special computer screen artists can draw on

deadline - the date or time something must be finished

dip pen and nib - a type of pen dating back to the 19th century and still preferred by some cartoonists. Called dip pens because the nibs, or tips, are dipped into pots of ink, these pens let artists draw flowing fine and wide lines.

font - the specific look of a set of characters

gutter - the space between panels in a comic

HB lead -"H" stands for hardness, "B" stands for blackness. On the light to dark scale of pencil tones, HB is in the middle, which is the closest to a no. 2 pencil.

layout - the arrangement of text and pictures on a page

manga - a Japanese style of comics, often read right to left

panel - a box on a comic page that shows action

Photoshop - a brand of image-editing software

script - the written text of a comic that contains its story, action, and dialogue

thumbnail - a basic miniature sketch artists use to plan their work

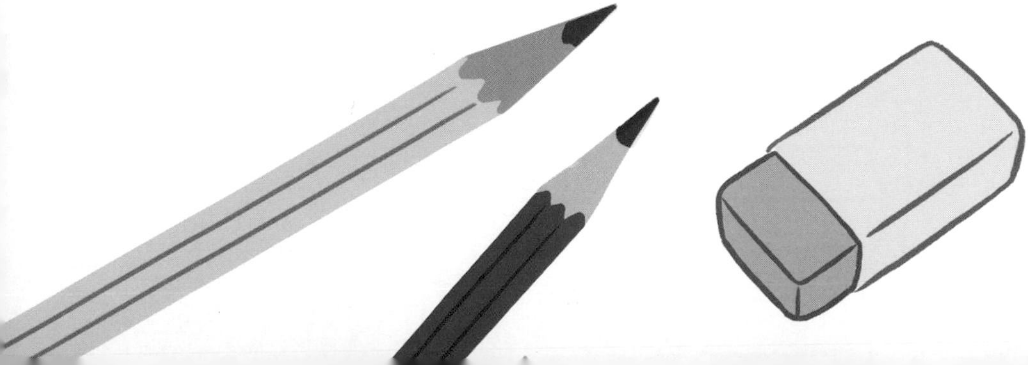

ABOUT THE AUTHORS AND ILLUSTRATOR

Meika Hashimoto grew up on a shiitake mushroom farm in Maine. She is a children's book editor and lives deep in the woods with her husband, two rescue mutts, and a calico cat. She is the author of *Scaredy Monster, Kitty and Dragon, The Magic Cake Shop,* and *The Trail.*

Gina Loveless fell in love with kids' books when she was eight and fell back in love with them when she was twenty-eight. She earned her MFA in creative writing from California Institute of the Arts and resides in eastern Pennsylvania.

Whitney Matheson is a writer and a huge fan of comics! She lives in Brooklyn, New York, with her husband and daughter. Learn more about her at whitneymatheson.com.

Genevieve Kote is an illustrator living in Montreal, Canada. She loves reading manga and graphic novels. View more of her work at genevievekote.com.

HAVE YOU HEARD ABOUT epic! YET?

We're the largest digital library for kids, used by millions in homes and schools around the world. We love stories so much that we're now creating our own!

With the help of some of the best writers and illustrators in the world, we create the wildest adventures we can think of. Like a mermaid and a narwhal who solve mysteries. Or a pet made out of slime.

We hope you have as much fun reading our books as we had making them!

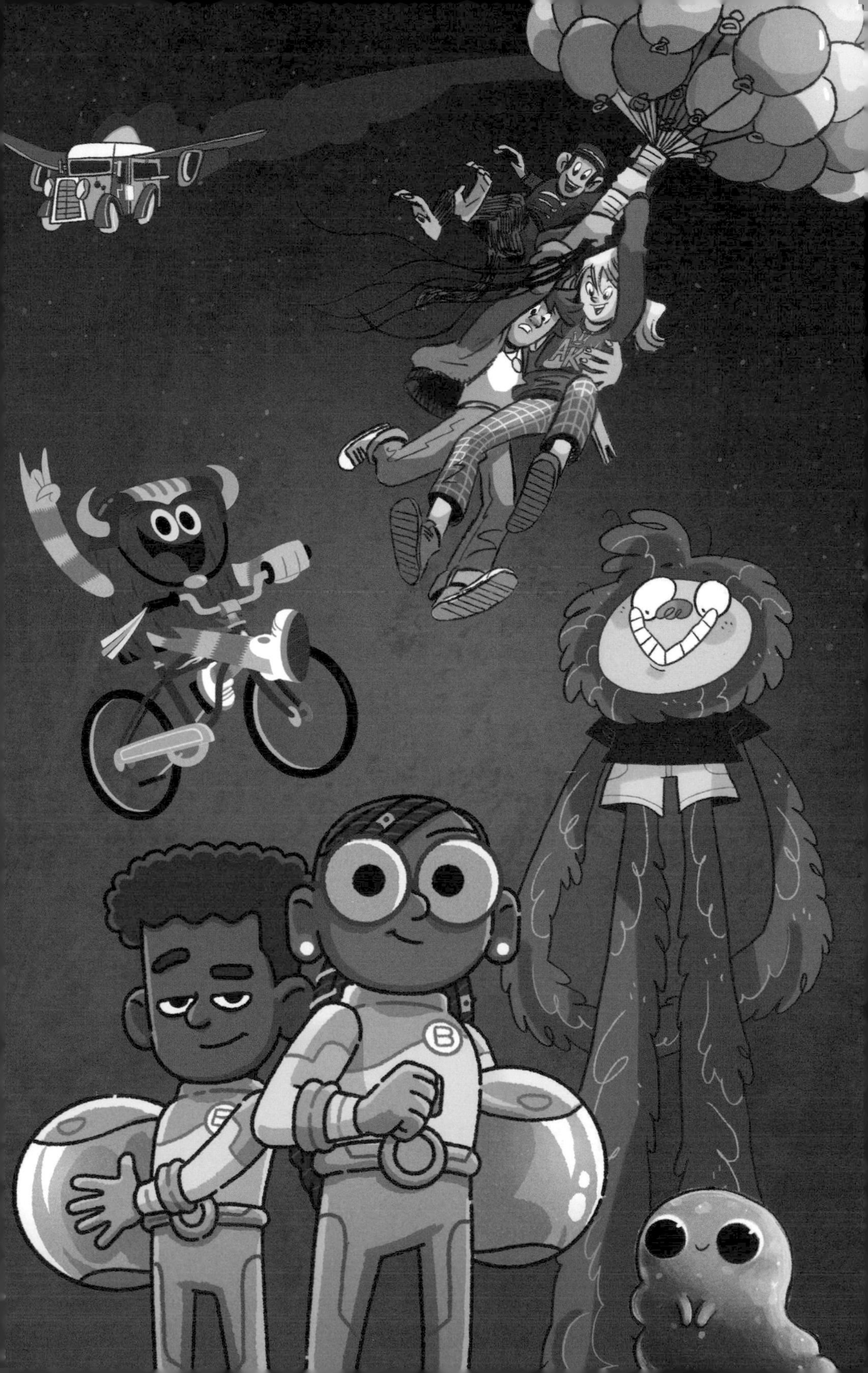